THE WORLD IS MY MISTRESS

BY THE SAME AUTHOR

Felicitavia
When the Time Comes
The Ashram
Anandamurti: The Jamalpur Years
Devi
Song of the Taino
The Jazz Master
In the Land of the Saints

THE WORLD IS MY MISTRESS

DEVASHISH

InnerWorld Publications

San Germán, Puerto Rico

www.innerworldpublications.com

"If I hadn't been born in India, I would have been born in Brazil."

— Likely apocryphal but reputed to have been said by Anandamurti when he gave the newly acquired fazenda in Minas Gerais the name Ananda Kirtana.

PART ONE

SIDDHARTHA

1

*I*T DIDN'T FEEL LIKE a dream. It felt like a wave, a surging, fecund mass lifting her out of the vacancy of sleep and into an odd medley of images from her past that seemed to be pointing toward her future. Standing on the black-and-white cobblestone sidewalk of Copacabana, listening to the nearby murmur of the ocean and staring at the ruby slippers on her feet, the only flash of color in an otherwise noir tableau. Could it be? Was she finally going home? She closed her eyes, clicked her heels three times, and repeated the magic incantation. Within moments the wind started picking up and the lapping of the water thickened into a low roar. Sure that her long exile was about to end, she felt a warm caress on her forehead and her eyes blinked open. But instead of the smiling face of Auntie Em, or some other ancient matriarch, she found herself staring at a thin sliver of sunlight in a dimly lit room. Disconcerted, she lifted her head from the pillow and peered into a shaft of morning sun that had slipped under the slatted vinyl blind near the foot of the bed. Only then did she remember where she was: the beach house at Cabo Frio, lying next to Fernando on his parents' king-size bed.

Strange dream, she mused, as she sat up and massaged her temples. How long had it been since she had thought of that film? Probably not since she had returned to Brazil after her year at Berkeley, where she had first seen the movie and thought it a perfect example of that peculiarly American love for idealist fantasy. She could still feel a lingering sense of anticipation, a vague premonition that something portentous was about to happen, but the image itself seemed downright comical. Standing on that famous sidewalk in Dorothy's Technicolor slippers, clicking her heels three times and intoning "there's no place like home, there's no place like home." From Rio to Cabo Frio in a blink of the imagination. Except that Rio was home, not Cabo Frio, but maybe she shouldn't try to read too much into it. It was, after all, just a dream.

A quick glance assured her that Fernando was still dead to the world, his face pressed into the pillow, his bare shoulders and curly brown hair glistening with a thin sheen of sweat. Taking care not to wake him, she padded softly to the bathroom, where she had left her bikini hanging from the towel rack the previous night after a starlit dip in the ocean. Strange to think that she hadn't even owned a bikini until she'd moved to Rio. She had been too self-conscious for far too long, especially about her body. Thank God that was in the past, though it had certainly taken her long enough. This was her favorite: bright-orange bikini briefs and a sky-blue halter top with a flaming orange sun over the left breast that Fernando had picked out for her in a swim shop in Copa. They set off her eyes, he'd said, which she'd never quite understood since her eyes were hazel, but he liked it and that was all that really mattered. That and the fact that he liked her when she was inside it, which was more to the point.

She scribbled a note for him, grabbed her tote bag, and got a banana and an apple from the kitchen on her way out, emerging from the back patio directly into the anodyne glare of the Cabo Frio sun. She shielded her eyes and picked her way past the scraggly brush pine that ringed the property and continued down through the natural corridor between two dunes that led to the beach, where she laid out her *canga* some ten meters from the tide line and pulled off her T-shirt, taking a couple of minutes to enjoy the raw warmth of the sun on her skin before she applied a generous coat of sunscreen. The air was tangy with that salt-water-seaweed smell, and the scudding of the waves all but drowned out the distant sound of some popular tune she didn't recognize. Fernando was right when he'd called Cabo Frio the sanctuary of the gods: the blue-green shimmer of the bay, the smoky hills rising up from Parrot Island, the perennial freshness of the ocean breezes—if it wasn't for the crowd of tourists that would soon be descending, she could almost imagine Aphrodite or Calypso walking along the shore, picking shells and stones from the sand and skipping them across the surface of the water for the pure joy of watching them bounce.

Smiling at the thought, she plunged into the ocean, the refreshing coolness finally banishing the last vestiges of sleep. She felt a little like a goddess herself, cavorting in the cool waters that sent delightful shivers through her body until it adjusted to the symbiosis of sun and ocean on a warm summer morning. Twenty minutes later she was back on her *canga*, nibbling on her apple and trying to decide which book she should settle into first: the one she had planned on reading, Nélida Piñon's classic *The Republic of Dreams*, a hefty multigenerational saga she had first read when her mother gave it to her for her sixteenth birthday, a dense, hallucinatory portrait of a Brazil that she had mostly taken for granted until Piñon's fractured prose helped her to begin perceiving the hidden fractures of the society she had been born into; or the one she had plucked on a whim from Fernando's parents' bookshelf the previous night, Hermann Hesse's *Siddhartha*, her attention drawn by the cover illustration of a bright-gold Buddha set against a sky-blue background, very nearly the same colors as her halter top. After a moment's deliberation, she decided on Hesse's slim volume, whose colors set off her eyes, if her boyfriend was to be believed, hoping for some light reading with which to begin the day, until Fernando and his friends joined her on the beach.

She wasn't disappointed. The opening page sped by in the space between one wave and another, transporting her as if by a conjurer's trick to an Indian village where she watched a handsome young man and his friend practice exotic Brahmin rites—expiatory ablutions in the river at dawn, reciting the sacred *om* in silent meditation, performing Hindu sacrifices in the mango grove—the familiar magic act of closing her eyes to one world and opening them to another. When she learned of his discontent and his doubts on page three, of the disquiet in his soul that wafted from the smoke of those sacrifices, she felt her excitement mount, the growing recognition that she had entered one of those rare stories that held up a mirror to her life. What good were these ablutions, these sacrifices, these invocations of the gods, Siddhartha asked, if they did not bring happiness? Of what good was this life of daily observances in the bosom of his family if it did not bring him lasting fulfillment? Of what good was his religion if the teachings of his father and the other Brahmin priests amounted to nothing more than blind belief? They could have been her words, if allowances were made for the twenty-six centuries and fifteen thousand kilometers that separated them, and when Siddhartha left his family to join the ascetics in the forest, standing motionless all night in his father's room until his father relented and gave his permission, she saw herself in his image, leaving her parents' home in Campinas to attend the Federal University of Rio, the culmination of a crisis in faith that had begun in early adolescence.

She had loved her Roman Catholic faith during her childhood: the rich scents of incense and candles in the dim interiors of their local cathedral; the low hypnotic rumble of the liturgy, all the more attractive for its mystifying unintelligibility; the strange and captivating stories she would hear during her weekly catechism classes; above all, the sense of an all-powerful being watching over her, giving meaning to a life that would otherwise have been all but inexplicable. Her parents were devout adherents to the faith, and her maternal uncles were both priests — one Jesuit, one Benedictine. During their infrequent visits they would populate her childhood fantasies with guardian angels hovering over her at night and patron saints parsing her prayers to see if she would one day be worthy of heaven. But as time went on, the stories grew odder to her ears, and a day came when their strange allure gave way to incredulity. She remembered that day as if it were yesterday: listening to Brother Ivan in his black frock reading from a book of Bible stories during catechism class in the lead-up to her confirmation, her sudden realization that the stories she was listening to were fundamentally no different than any of the teen novels she was reading — pleasant, well-meaning fantasies. And if Brother Ivan truly believed in these stories whose truth he had no way of knowing, then he was a well-meaning hypocrite, though the word probably hadn't been part of her vocabulary back then (the image she'd had was that of a black-robed parrot blithely repeating words it couldn't understand). From there the whole doctrinal edifice came crumbling down — the virgin birth; the death and resurrection of the historical Jesus (according to her uncles, the minimum required belief to call oneself a Christian); the twin pillars of heaven and hell (an incorruptible body rising from a worm-infested grave on the day of judgment for those who were fortunate enough to enter paradise; and eternal suffering in a lake of fire for the rest, i.e., the greater part of mankind); a benevolent God demanding the sacrifice of his only begotten son to forgive humankind its sins, a sacrifice that would have been unspeakably cruel had any human being demanded the same — the once-fertile mysteries of her childhood turning into fictions in her adolescent mind, filling her with doubts that went far beyond the teachings of the Church.

Paula continued attending Sunday mass with her parents, but the rich pageantry of the dominical services soon became an empty ritual she sat through as an exercise in patience; and though she never completely stopped believing in God, the ever-widening scope of her voracious reading continued to erode what remnants of her Roman Catholic faith remained, leaving her with no real belief in anything other than the fidelity of her doubts. When it came time for her to attend university, her primary criterion was that it be as far away from her family as reasonably possible. She didn't have to stand motionless for an entire night like Siddhartha to secure her father's permission, but she did have to stand firm for an entire year while he tried to convince her to remain at home and attend the University of Campinas, where he was the head librarian. Her mother was only slightly less insistent in her own understated way, and it took all her determination to hold to her resolution until her parents finally gave her their blessing to set out for the jungles of Rio to live life on her own terms.

Freedom had its price, however, as Siddhartha soon discovered when he joined the ascetics and found himself laboring under many of the same limitations he had faced under his father's roof, but without the comfort of his former beliefs or the warmth of his family. In her case as well, the discontent and disquiet did not go away, even as she gradually left behind the torturous awkwardness of her adolescent years in an almost ascetic quest for self-actualization that eventually won her the unexpected boon of a boyfriend from the upper crust of Rio society, a handsome, athletic plastic-surgeon-in-waiting whose barely tempered braggadocio seemed like the perfect cure for her chronically wavering self-esteem. When Siddhartha left the Samanas, drawn by tales of the Buddha, Paula was right beside him, and when he heard the Buddha preach, her heart swelled as it had as a child when she'd listened to the reading of Jesus's sermon from the Mount of Beatitudes, her impressionable young mind filled with intimations of the Savior's love and mercy. She had wondered then what it would have been like to sit at his feet as Mary Magdalene had, and she felt a similar thrill now when Siddhartha met the Buddha on the road and saw the perfect equanimity in his eyes. When the young Brahmin declined to accept the Venerable One's shelter after telling the Buddha that only through leaving behind all teachings could he reach the truth, Paula had to blink back her tears, shaken by that courageous but terrible decision, foreseeing the grim solitude that awaited him, the kind she had known all too well during her first few semesters in college when loneliness had seemed a pitiless and constant adversary.

It was at this moment, just as Siddhartha was leaving the grove of the Perfect One, that her Indian enchantment was broken by the sound of footsteps tramping in the sand and a cascading rush of raucous laughter that sounded the notes of her name like the keys of an out-of-tune piano. Startled by the sudden discord, she turned her head to see Fernando leading his friends single file through the dunes. He had a cooler in one hand, a boom box in the other, and a towel draped over his bare shoulders. His friends Ronaldo and Guilherme, landed members of the same Rio elite, were close on his heels, followed by their girlfriends, Rosário and Petra, stepping gingerly with their flip-flops in their hands and their eyes on the sand, on the lookout no doubt for any shiny bauble or bit of driftwood that might mar their otherwise perfect feet. The girls were wearing brightly colored bikinis that Paula instinctively compared to her own, although it was what the bikinis barely covered that elicited a momentary spike of envy. She knew she would never be able to compete with those slim, tanned, well-toned bodies that seemed to breed like flies on the beaches of Copacabana, Ipanema, and Leblon—which, as she remembered, is exactly where Ronaldo and Guilherme had met them, the latest contestants in a rapidly revolving door of entrances and exits—but what irked her most was this persistent wish that she somehow could, as if they were denizens of a world that made her own seem drab by comparison.

"Typical Paula," Fernando said, as he knelt down and fiddled with the boom box dial. "A beautiful day at the beach in Cabo Frio and she has her head buried in a book."

"What are you talking about? I was in the water while you were sleeping it off. You already missed the best part of the day."

"Well, there is that. We might have overdone it just a bit on the beers last night."

Fernando's jocular smile brought forth a few sheepish giggles from the two girls as they laid out their *cangas* next to Paula's and began smearing each other's backs with sunscreen. Ronaldo and Guilherme unfolded a trio of beach loungers, and moments later the boys were racing toward the water, taking three or four huge strides into the sea before they flung themselves headlong into an oncoming wave.

Petra and Rosário hung back for a few minutes while they finished applying their sunscreen. They exchanged a few pleasantries with Paula—what a great beach this was, how much they liked the house, how cute the boys looked in their swimming trunks—and after a half-hearted effort to get her to come in with them, the two girls joined their boyfriends in the water.

Paula was tempted. It had gotten noticeably warmer, with the sun approaching its zenith, but Siddhartha's story was too compelling. Fernando liked to tease her for spending too much of her life glued to the pages of a book, and though there were times when she was inclined to agree with him, she had found the perfect defense for indulging her passion for literature in the pages of a Javier Cercas novel: "the experience of reading is both an affirmation and a negation of the world and of one's own identity that transforms the reader into an immobile traveler who flees from reality and from himself in order to better understand both." The quote had elicited a raised eyebrow from Fernando, as she remembered, but there were times like these when it was absolutely true.

She picked up the boom box and set it down near the foot of the *cangas*, angling it toward the water and placing the cooler behind it to shield herself from the pulsing beat of Brazilian popular music, determined not to let the music gain a foothold in a land where it did not belong. Then she lay back down to follow Siddhartha as he took an abrupt and unexpected detour, forsaking the forest for the city and the life of worldly enjoyments and mundane cares that he had hitherto forsworn as an ascetic in search of the ever-elusive peace of the Great Beyond, the life of those he now took to calling the "child people," for he saw them as children dedicating themselves to their childish games with a passionate earnestness that such transitory pastimes did not deserve. With a confidence that his penniless condition did not seem to merit, he plunged into the pleasures of the art of love with the beautiful Kamala, the peerless courtesan, seeking out the most fleeting and most fascinating of those transitory desires; and yet he remained a spectator, watching his own life as if it were a show from which he remained aloof, while all the while secretly envying the ability of the child people to fully lose themselves in the drama of their existence, in the all-entrancing world of *samsara*—the wheel of birth and death, as Hesse defined that unfamiliar word in his glossary.

Paula knew what it meant to be an outsider. She had grown up with a sense of being an outsider in the land of her birth, as if life were something she watched from the pages of a book or the windows of a bus or a seat in a movie theater. It was one more reason why she had yearned to break free of Campinas, feeling instinctively that if she was going to know herself then she had to know the great wide world, and she had approached its gates from the forest of her youth with the same determination as Siddhartha and a barely bridled passion that was all her own. It had not been easy, but she had eventually found her Kamala in Fernando, the grail of the heart that had been forever out of reach until this sloe-eyed youth turned his eyes on her and miraculously failed to look away. And like Siddhartha the happiness she found would prove insubstantial, a transitory mirage that fled her grasp the moment she tried to close her hand.

One morning Siddhartha woke from a disturbing dream to find that he had become old and weary and nearly dead inside. In his dream the songbird that Kamala kept in a gilded cage was dead, and with the silencing of its voice came the certainty that he had thrown away all that was meaningful in his life. He was rich and respected among the child people, but all his worldly accomplishments had only served to separate him from his soul. And then something in him did die, and in that selfsame moment he left his palatial mansion and his beautiful pleasure garden and disappeared into the forest, knowing that he would never return.

As Paula closed the book and looked out across the water, she couldn't help but think of her own life in the same terms: her enduring longing for the right job, the right boyfriend, the right life. She had it all now, everything the world had assured her would confer lasting happiness, but the malaise had not gone away. If anything, it was only getting deeper, and suddenly she was afraid that if she did not do something soon she would wake to find that the songbird inside her had died. She was not as world-weary and empty as Siddhartha, but if she let the years go by as he had, yoked to the same senselessly spinning wheel, would that not also be her fate?

The sun was at its zenith now, just beginning its slow descent toward the western horizon, and the beach was filled with bathers, with bobbing heads and peals of laughter, with pockets of music and the enticing scents of Brazilian food wafting from picnic baskets and portable stoves. The beauty she had noticed earlier was still there, like a faintly glowing aura, but there was something else as well: the underlying anxiety of life slipping through her fingers, like water through the cupped hands of one of those bathers, defying all efforts to give it any permanence. She could feel it penetrating her skin like the sun seeping through her pores, and she was still trying to shake that uneasy feeling a few minutes later when Fernando came splashing onto the beach and threw himself beside her without bothering to towel off, beads of seawater glistening on his skin as he cocked his head and flashed a self-satisfied smile. His friends were right behind him, and the swirl of conversation they brought with them put a temporary halt to her Indian odyssey.

An hour later, the three young couples were seated at a round wooden table in Fernando's favorite pizzeria, a sprawling, consciously rustic establishment three blocks from Forte Beach, with a generous view of the water and a pair of wood-burning stoves that filled the spacious room with the aromas of an earlier century. The menu listed forty different pizzas, along with calzones, spaghetti, ravioli, linguine, tagliatelle, and a long list of antipasti and Italian salads. The owners were first-generation Italians but they catered to the tastes of their adopted country with a variety of sweet pizzas, including Paula's favorite—chocolate banana, with Brazilian bananas and semisweet chocolate imported from the old country.

But as much as Paula enjoyed the excellent food and the convivial atmosphere, she couldn't banish the specter of Siddhartha's long fall from grace. His ambivalent description of the child people kept coming back to her, his amused dismissal of their follies and his hidden desire to be able to lose himself in the world as they could, and it seemed to Paula that she and her companions were the child people of his story, drifting aimlessly in the banalities of trivial conversation while they gorged themselves on pizza and joked with their waitress. There was an earnestness to their lighthearted banter that she hadn't noticed before, as if they were trying to fill empty words with a meaning those words could not accommodate, as if by merely keeping the conversation afloat the emptiness could be held at bay for one more day. Paula had never been very good at the kind of superficial banter Fernando and his friends seemed so accomplished at, and she wondered now if it was precisely this earnestness she lacked, this willingness to invest the words she heard and the words she spoke with a significance they did not deserve. Especially her own words, which were often little more than the clothes she wore to hide her doubts. And if her words were dressed in such dubious colors, then didn't it stand to reason that everyone else's might be as well? Perhaps that was why she read as much as she did. In the hope of a chance encounter with something closer to the truth than the ragged costumes of everyday life. In the hope of finding what she had found in *Siddhartha,* whose words had for a precious couple of hours held up a mirror to the trivialities of her existence, a mirror whose reflections continued to haunt her as she prattled on, doing her best to uphold her end of a vapid conversation.

They were sipping expressos when Fernando reminded everyone that if they were going to see any dolphins that afternoon they had best be going. He picked up the tab and they piled into his brand-new SUV, a gift from his parents, and barreled down RJ102 to Arraial do Cabo, the next town over, where he had booked a tour boat, the colorful *Pirates of the Caribbean*, with an image from the film blazoned across the face of the upper deck and a skull and crossbones on the prow. *Pirates* was a Disney movie and the boat was positively Disneyesque. Gaudy in that unapologetically commercial, pop-culture sort of way, and thoroughly incongruous when set against the pristine waters of the bay and the picturesque hills rising from Cape Island. The owner of the launch was just as incongruous. He had long auburn hair held in place by a red pirate's bandanna, a gold hoop hanging from his right ear, a loose-fitting cotton shirt with half the buttons undone, exposing an aptly tawny chest, baggy pants tied at the ankles, and a sash around his waist—a costume taken straight from the wardrobe of Johnny Depp, as one glance at the mural on the upper deck was enough to confirm.

"You picked a good time to go dolphin watching," he said, as he untied the last mooring rope and pushed the boat free of the dock with what looked to be an authentic harpoon. "We have a southerly wind today and that makes the water much clearer than your dastardly northeasterly wind. Right time of year also. There are lots of sardines and cuttlefish at the moment—they like the warm water—and that means lots of dolphins. I spotted two different schools yesterday out near Pig Island, and with the water this clear you'll be able to see right through to the bottom. They're curious animals. They like to follow the boat, check out the passengers, I imagine, so you should get a pretty good look once we find out where they're hanging today."

The captain brought the boat up the shoreline and angled past Pig Island, where some unusual rock formations jutted out of the shallow waters, slabs of sandstone and granite that had been shaped by the water and the wind into freeform sculptures, including one that formed a nearly perfect arc that a small boat could pass through, prompting Paula to take her phone from her purse to snap some photos. They had just skirted the island when the captain spotted a school of dolphins to the starboard side and turned the boat in a wide circle to come up behind them. He slowed to a crawl as they neared the animals, and just as he had predicted, they started swimming alongside the launch at a distance of no more than a few meters, whipping past the prow and then doubling back to satisfy their curiosity. The water was deeper here but clear enough that they could see the animals dive for the bottom and come up again, weaving among their cohorts as they divided their time between their dinner and the open-air theater that awaited them at the surface.

Paula counted as many as twenty of the creatures, several of them mothers with their young, staying close to their offspring. "You see, Paula?" Fernando said, wrapping a muscled arm around her shoulder as they leaned over the side of the boat. "I told you this was going to be a weekend to remember. I don't know that I've ever seen so many dolphins in one place. But that's Cabo Frio for you. Orcas, penguins, dolphins—you name it, it's got them. Dolphins by day and parties by night. Makes you wish we could get out of Rio more often, doesn't it?"

"Sure does. Especially when your parents have a house on the beach."

"You better believe it, baby. You travel with Fernando, you travel first class all the way."

It was no exaggeration. Paula had grown up in a middle-class family and she had always considered her family reasonably well off, especially once the stratification of Brazilian society had started to round itself into the pastel tones of the familiar. But she hadn't truly known what well-off was until Fernando turned his cerulean-blue eyes on her during her final month in graduate school and proceeded to sweep her off her feet—a fairytale-like ending to what had felt like six years of being the ugly stepdaughter in the dull corridors of her university. She had had a smattering of off-again, on-again relationships, none lasting longer than a couple of months, and never with someone who had anywhere near the panache, the good looks, and the self-assurance of her Fernandinho. They had all been nerds like herself. Not the kooky, quirkily brilliant kind of nerds that had become fixtures in American movies, but the plodding, self-conscious, persistently awkward kind who tried to buoy their low self-esteem by excelling at their studies—in short, mirror reflections of herself. But Fernando had made her see another Paula that had, up until then, steadfastly failed to appear in her mirror. Not the ungainly, overly tall, painfully shy wallflower with the decidedly unremarkable features who had struggled to make friends throughout her adolescence, but an attractive, mature female with an overabundance of talent and an uncommon intellect who was destined to set herself off from the pack. Which was the only kind of girl that Fernando could see himself with, he confided to her at the end of their third date, a

Djavan concert at the Canecão after dinner and conversation at one of Copacabana's most stylish restaurants. He had had enough of these cookie-cutter Rio girls with their made-to-order tans, their frivolous conversation, and their barely concealed aspirations of snagging a rich husband with a spacious apartment in Ipanema, Leblon, or Barra da Tijuca, preferably within a two-minute walk of the beach. At his age he wanted substance in his life (he was all of twenty-five at the time, barely older than she was), and he was wise enough to know that he had hit the jackpot in Paula. All this after three dates and a handful of conversations in the university dining hall.

It didn't matter that she was a full five inches taller than him, that she still hadn't learned how to use makeup to highlight her best features (whatever those were), that no matter how long and hard she looked in the mirror (something she had started doing a whole lot more of after she began going out with Fernando), she still had trouble locating the fascinating femme fatale that he talked up with an unrestrained aplomb that set off involuntary tremors in random parts of her body. Either he was telling the truth and this was him at his unselfconscious best, or else he had had a lot of practice. Whichever it was, he had set his sights on her and she was a willing target. He became her teacher in the arts of love, as Kamala had been Siddhartha's, and for a while the elixir of his presence in her life had been everything her schoolgirl fantasies had made it out to be, abundantly fed by an endless stream of novels, movies, and television serials celebrating the elusive, life-restoring properties of the ideal romantic relationship. But the euphoria had eventually given way to routine, even if that routine included expensive restaurants, front-row concert and theater tickets, elegant dinners in the family penthouse in Lagoa, and a ready-made circle of "in" friends who would never have given her a second glance had Fernando not been standing beside her. Perhaps it was this more than anything—the knowledge that all her accomplishments, including winning the affections of the man standing next to her in the boat, grinning in delight as his eyes followed the flashing shapes cutting through the water, had been nothing more than a palliative, temporarily masking the pain but offering no hope of a lasting cure—that made Siddhartha's despair ring so true in her ears. *Samsara.* Yoked to the wheel of birth and death, going round and round in circles but never arriving anywhere, a game for children, to be played enthusiastically once or twice, or even ten times, but not again and again and again with no hope of ever getting off that wheel.

It was dusk when they made it back to the beach house. They sat around the kitchen table for a while sipping Chianti and reliving their afternoon adventures before heading off one by one to take a shower and change for the evening. The sounds of music and the murmur of a myriad distant voices could be heard coming from the beach, announcing the onset of another summer evening at Cabo Frio, when the beachfront turned into an amorphous, constantly eddying party scene comprised of little groups of revelers, a theater dedicated solely to the pleasure principle that wouldn't drop its curtains until dawn.

As Paula headed out the door and into the Cabo Frio night, something of the old excitement caught hold of her, and she decided it was high time she shook off the aftereffects of her literary musings. After all, the night was young and so were they and she had her beau by her side. Some of her very best hours had been spent on the beach with Fernando, and there was no reason why tonight should be any different. There were portable stereos wherever they walked and an occasional guitar banging out the chords of a familiar tune, prompting everyone in earshot to sing along. There was even a makeshift band at the north end of Forte Beach — two acoustic guitarists, two percussionists, and a singer perched on the steps of the Praça das Águas, with their guitar cases open for passers-by to fill with change. There were pockets of dancing, and at one point they joined a sizable crowd for close to an hour, dancing samba on the sand in front of a huge boom box with detachable speakers playing Cartola, Gonzaguinha, Paulinho da Viola, and Marisa Monte. They had brought a trio of six-packs with them and a small supply of the finest marijuana, whose sweet fragrance wafted like incense up and down the beach, and soon Paula had no idea what had gotten into her after reading that book. Fernando was a marvelous dancer by anybody's reckoning — there were times when she would rather sit and watch the rhythm flow out of him so as to be able to absorb every gleam and glint of his marvelous body, rather than have to reserve a part of her consciousness for her own pedestrian steps as she did her best to keep up. There was a half moon above and a soft glow from the distant streetlights, and together they combined to cast an aura about her boyfriend that made him seem like a Brazilian Tom Jones: lusty but kindhearted, flawed but amenable to the transforming goodness of the virtuous Sophia, a well-meaning satyr with a roguish smile and a rugged but handsome face, his bare torso glowing like a bronze centerpiece under the spreading mantle of the night sky. His falling in love with her had been the high-water mark of her life, and dancing samba beside him on the beach made her aware once again of just how lucky she was.

But as the night deepened she couldn't escape the feeling that even this was one more turn on an endless wheel. In another life, at another time, she couldn't have wished for more, but despite her best efforts to lose herself in the revelry, the glow eventually wore off, along with the buzz from the three long drags she had taken of Amazonian White Widow when the evening was just getting going; and when it did, the uncertainties that had plagued her all day were waiting for her, as if refusing any longer to be held down by the wayward antics of the young. Shortly before twelve Guilherme suggested they head over to an alehouse a few blocks from the beach for some snacks and a restorative libation, a suggestion that was quickly seconded, and when they reached its doors Paula pulled Fernando aside and told him she wasn't feeling well—the onset of menstrual cramps, it seemed. He flashed a quick look of annoyance but recovered quickly, gallantly offering to walk her back and catch up with the others later. "No way, babe," she said, the virtuous Sophia firmly lodged in the back of her mind. "You're having too good a time. You stay with your friends. I'll take an Uber." Fernando put up a short-lived protest and then handed her the house keys and reached for his phone to call for her ride. Paula kissed him with a tear in her eye and went in to say a quick goodbye to the others, who had managed to snag a just-vacated table, but her mind was already in the forest with Siddhartha, anxious to find out what would happen to them both, teetering as they were on the edge of uncertainty.

Ten minutes later she was back at the beach house, reaching for the book that she had left on the night table and pausing before she opened it, as if a sacred ritual were about to begin and she needed a moment to genuflect, knowing that their destinies were intertwined. She felt this as surely as she felt the book in her hands, and at that moment she had a premonition that she had come to a crossroads in her life, that the direction she took from here on out would depend on the century-old map that she was about to consult.

Leaning back on her pillow, Paula followed Siddhartha through the forest until he came to the same river he had crossed after leaving the Buddha's presence, in what now seemed like another lifetime. He was weary and hungry, but above all he was tired of his life, tired of the terrible emptiness he felt inside. Thinking to throw himself into the rushing waters and put an end to this form he so despised, he grasped the trunk of a coconut palm that grew on its banks and prepared himself to welcome the waters of oblivion. But at that moment, from the distant reaches of his soul, came a long forgotten sound—the sacred syllable *om*, the sonic footprint of the Divine—and instead of releasing his body into the waters, he laid his head on the roots of a tree and sank into a rejuvenating sleep. When he awoke, it was as if to another life. Sitting beside him was a saffron-robed monk, a disciple of the Buddha whom he recognized as his childhood friend Govinda, who had seen him sleeping in that dangerous spot and broken his journey to guard the sleeping man. They talked for a short while, each glad to see the other after so many years, and then they parted ways—Govinda to rejoin his master and Siddhartha to the unknown path that he now looked forward to with eagerness, knowing that the old Siddhartha had indeed died so that a new Siddhartha could be born.

Paula followed him with an eagerness of her own as he met the same ferryman who had once ferried him across that river and asked him if he could stay and be his apprentice. Followed him as he learned from the saintly Vasudeva how to listen to the river until he could hear the voices of all creatures in its waters, separately at first and then conjoined, until they were the voice of life itself, the voice of endless becoming, while the days melted into months and the months into years, bringing with them the peace that is born from profound contemplation. Followed him as one day, years later, the beautiful Kamala, accompanied by her young son—their son—came to the ferry on a pilgrimage to see the dying Buddha make his final voyage into nirvana, only for a serpent's bite to put an end to her journey, her final breath coming as she lay on Siddhartha's straw bed, looking up into his peaceful eyes and thinking that it was just as well that her pilgrimage ended here. Followed him as Siddhartha became seized by one final great attachment, blinded by an all-too human love for his pampered, grief-stricken son, until one morning he discovered that the boy had fled, and despite all his searching he could not be found, opening one final wound in Siddhartha's heart that would not heal until the river granted him the final vision of Oneness, opening his ears to the great song of being that flowed for all eternity through every living and nonliving form, the voice of the one Self that had eluded him through a thousand lifetimes—until now. Followed him as Vasudeva departed for the forest, to merge into the Oneness, and as

Govinda reappeared to close the circle, returning to this man with the eyes of the Buddha who sat with him on the riverbank and gave him the vision of nirvana that the now-aged monk had longed for his entire life and had despaired of ever achieving.

When Paula turned the final page and watched Govinda bow with reverence before this motionless old man whose smile was the embodiment of all that was holy in the world, she closed the book and held it in her hands, bowing her head in conscious imitation of the grateful Buddhist monk. Then she closed her eyes and gazed as if for the first time into her murky interior. This was what her life had been propelling her toward all along, she realized, as she groped her way through the darkness within. Enlightenment, nirvana. Words that had held no meaning for her until now. And yet now they seemed like the only words that did, words so huge the world itself could not contain them.

She had no idea how long her reverie lasted, but the book was still cradled in her hands when she was startled by the sound of voices and the opening of a door. Quickly, almost frantically, she shut off the light and dove under the covers. She was not ready to return to the world she had left behind. Not yet. For now all she wanted was to remain in the forest with the motionless Siddhartha, until the dawning of another day opened the curtain on her future.

2

Paula's passion for books went back nearly as far as she could remember. She had gotten her first library card at seven, and she still remembered that day as one of the happiest of her childhood. Alice, Pooh, Fudge, João Sem Medo, Mônica, Miss Prudence, Peter Pan, Bilbo — and of course, Hermione. She was ten when the Portuguese translation of *Harry Potter and the Philosopher's Stone* was released in Brazil, on the first day of the new millennium, and until she arrived in Rio eight years later, if anybody had asked her who her best friend was, she would have told them it was Hermione. Not that anybody ever asked, which was perhaps as clear a testament as any to how difficult a time she'd had making friends while she was growing up. By her own reckoning she had read *The Philosopher's Stone* fourteen times by the time her parents dropped her off in Rio, and another half-dozen times before she completed her graduate studies six years later, part of her by-then-yearly ritual of reading the entire series once through — though by this time it wasn't for the thrill of the story or the muted pleasure of her nostalgia for those bygone days; rather it was to see how a master translator went about her work, performing the seemingly impossible alchemical task of transforming J. K. Rowland's plethora of puns, peculiar names, and idiosyncratic wordplay into an eminently readable and thoroughly enjoyable Portuguese, without sacrificing the charm of the English original.

Rowland's translator was Lia Wyler, Brazil's best and most sought-after English translator and the one person Paula most looked up to as she was working her way toward an undergraduate degree in English literature and translation studies. When she was ready to begin her graduate work, Lia Wyler was teaching graduate seminars in English-to-Portuguese translation in the Pontifical Catholic University of Rio, and that was the deciding factor in shifting her studies to the PUC campus in

Gávea—in truth, the only factor. Her parents were pleased that she had decided to continue her studies in a Catholic school, but religion had nothing to do with it. Lia Wyler had become a real-life hero, and from the moment she set foot in her classroom the energetic septuagenarian became her mentor. Paula's dream was to become Brazil's second-best English-language translator; and the best way to do that, as far as she was concerned, was to learn at the feet of the master.

She had kept in touch with Lia since her graduation from PUC two years earlier—the older woman (now a sprightly octogenarian) periodically recommended her for translation jobs, seemingly determined to see her protégée firmly established in the field before she retired, though the greater part of Paula's income still came from the English classes she taught, primarily in the corporate world for businesses whose employees needed to upgrade their English skills, and from occasional gigs as a simultaneous interpreter. But deciding where to go after *Siddhartha* was not the kind of thing she could email her former professor about. Had it been a question of literature, Lia would have been the first person she turned to and likely the only one—she had that much faith in her judgment on all matters pertaining to the world of language. But spirituality was another world altogether. Paula considered calling one of her uncles (Raimundo, the Benedictine, was in Angola on a two-year mission, but Alfredo had recently returned to Brazil after nearly a decade in Italy, where he was posted at the Jesuit's Cultural Center of Brasilia), but no matter how open-minded she knew them to be, the kind of enlightenment that Siddhartha had experienced fell outside the accepted purview of the Roman Catholic faith, and she felt sure that they would try to steer her toward a more mystical-leaning branch of the Church, or perhaps recommend a few mystic-minded Catholic authors. She was still pondering her choices while rereading *Siddhartha* in her apartment in Jardim Botânico when she turned the final page and noticed the stamped imprint on the flyleaf at the back of the book: *The Bodhi Tree: Rio's friendliest and most enlightened bookstore* (she had taken the book with her, sure that Fernando's parents wouldn't mind). As soon as she saw the imprint she knew what she should do next. She had spent a good part of her life tracing a path through the world of books, and considering that it was, fittingly, a book that had set her on her quest, she couldn't think of a more appropriate next step than a visit to an enlightened bookstore.

That Saturday morning, after teaching her one class of the day, English Conversation for Business Travelers, in a downtown office building, she headed for the address on the flyleaf: Rua Santa Marta in Copacabana, a five-minute walk from one of her favorite haunts, the hugely popular Saraiva bookstore with its enormous show windows and tastefully arranged displays of the latest releases. The Bodhi Tree was far more modest. Instead of a wide, open-air entrance with the name of the bookstore blazoned above it in glowing neon, it had a simple mauve door, a hand-carved wooden sign with The Bodhi Tree written in calligraphy above an engraving of a rotund Buddha with an open book in his hands, and a single small vitrine with a handful of books on display, a storefront so nondescript she had probably walked past it more than once without noticing it was there.

A soft tintinnabulation of glass chimes sounded as she opened the door and stepped into what would have otherwise been a conventional bookstore were it not for the portrait gallery on the upper walls and the sweet scent of incense wafting from the checkout counter just beside the entrance. As she took stock of the shelves, her eyes kept straying to the pictures hanging above them, and after a while she abandoned her perusal of the book titles and focused her attention entirely on the portraits. There was a Jesus, a Buddha, and Hindu depictions of Shiva and Krishna, but the vast majority were photos, both black-and-white and color—spiritual teachers of one magnitude or another, judging by the power of their gaze or the quality of their smile (and in some cases, the artificial halo around them). She began walking slowly around the store, studying each of the portraits as she passed, as if she were in an art gallery soaking up the otherworldly magic of the masters. None of them were labeled, and apart from the Dalai Lama and an aged Mother Teresa peering down at her from her blue-and-white wimple, Paula didn't recognize a single face, which made her realize how limited her spiritual education was. Indeed, some of the photos had such a powerful effect, she felt as if she were caught within a force field, rooted to the spot as she studied every line in that particular saint's face, as if she could somehow discern their level of spiritual attainment by the quality of their eyes or the curve of their smile, each of them reflecting in their own unique way the peace and wisdom she had imagined in the Buddha's eyes when Siddhartha stopped him on the road.

It took her the better part of an hour to complete her circuit of the store and the nearly one hundred portraits that adorned its upper walls, and that lengthy communion with a gallery of unknown saints made her realize, if she hadn't known it already, that this was no ordinary bookstore. It was nearing lunchtime now. There were very few customers and only two employees that she could see: the young woman at the checkout counter and an older woman in outlandish hippie attire who was unpacking a box of books in front of the section labeled "Modern Yogic Masters." She wore a flaring quilted skirt uniting every color of the rainbow in no perceivable pattern, a long-sleeved tie-dye blouse, a trio of diaphanous shawls of wildly contrasting colors, and a cluster of bead necklaces that clattered when she moved, topped off by a long, unruly shock of salt-and-pepper hair that cascaded over her shoulders and around her face like a riotous mane on an untamed mare, yet another reminder that this was a bookstore unlike any she had ever entered.

The first thing Paula noticed when she started browsing the stacks in earnest was that there were nearly half as many English books as Portuguese, and strangely enough, they weren't separated by language. Each section had books in both languages, often side by side, with an occasional Spanish volume tucked in between. It was hard to imagine that the store could have so many bilingual customers, but then it occurred to her that it was probably simple economics, the price of doing business in a niche market in Brazil. It was unlikely that many esoteric books generated enough revenue to warrant their translation, not in a world where Portuguese accounted for only 3% of the book titles published each year and less than 1% of the world's magazines and newspapers. Still, it might be an interesting avenue to pursue, she thought, a specialized niche where she wouldn't be in competition with her mentor. She picked out a book on Buddhist philosophy and turned to the copyright page to see where the publisher was located, but she was diverted from her musings by the sound of a warm, gravelly voice in the vicinity of her left shoulder.

"Can I help you find something?"

Paula turned to find that the hippie lady had somehow materialized behind her without the clacking of her beads giving her away. Ordinarily she would have said no. She knew her way around a bookstore better than most employees, and she preferred to let her instincts guide her. But this was unfamiliar territory, and there was a trustworthy note in the older woman's voice, as if her gravelly contralto was weighted with decades of felicitous advice.

"Sure, why not," she said. "I was looking for something on Buddhism, something about nirvana, maybe?"

She paused for a moment but the older woman just smiled and nodded, waiting for Paula to continue. There was a calmness to her, as if she had all day and all night for Paula to make it to her next thought.

"Well, the reason I came is I was reading *Siddhartha* this past weekend, by Hermann Hesse? Do you know it?"

Once again the woman smiled and nodded.

"Well, that got me thinking about nirvana, and then I saw your address on the flyleaf. I guess what I was wondering ... I'm not quite sure how to put it ..."

"Where to go from here?"

"Exactly! That's exactly what I was thinking. Does that make sense?"

"Of course. That's why Hesse wrote the book. So he could help you take that next step. Now let's see ... I don't think this section is the place for you right now." She scrunched up her nose and shook her head. "Nah. Let's leave philosophy for later. Here, come with me."

Paula followed her to the back of the shop where they passed through a doorway hung with a curtain of beads and emerged into a space half again as large as the one they had left. It was crammed with bookshelves and had the same plethora of earthly saints in simply framed photos peering down from the walls, but there was a cozy sense of disorder here that made Paula feel right at home, the feeling accentuated by a scattering of worn armchairs and old sofas, most of which, to her surprise, were occupied by people reading or chatting softly with their neighbors. There was even a small counter at the back with snacks and drinks for sale.

"This is the used bookstore. I think you'll find it more to your liking. I'm Maya, by the way. This is my place. And you are?"

"Paula."

"Very nice to meet you, Paula. Now let's see if we can't find the books your destiny has picked out for you today."

Paula followed Maya as she plunged into the stacks and stopped in front of an unlabeled shelf so crammed with used books that a goodly number were lying on top of the upright volumes. After a quick scan, she plucked a book and handed it to Paula. Then she was off down the aisle at the same brisk pace, Paula trailing behind her like a ward in attendance on her patron. Another pause, another lightning scan, and another book that settled into Paula's waiting hands. Maya then turned a corner and doubled back, selected another book without needing to scan the stack, and handed it to her, stopping twice more in the same aisle to repeat the ritual while Paula started to grow alarmed at the quantity of books she was carrying. Finally, her cicerone lifted a finger in affirmation and turned to the facing shelves with a pleased smile, as if she were turning to greet an old friend.

"Ah yes, we mustn't forget Richard Bach. Let's see now, *Illusions?* Um ... no, not quite yet. Ah here, just what the shaman ordered. Have you read *Fernão Capelo Gaivota?*"

"No."

"Perfect then. Oh, no! I don't seem to have a Portuguese copy at the moment, only English. We may have to get that from the new books. How is your English?"

"Not bad. It's what I do for a living, actually. I'm an English teacher."

"Of course you are. It's like I always say: there are no accidents in this world. If I had my way, the Academy of Letters would banish that word from the dictionary. Or least print a disclaimer acknowledging that there is no such thing: open parenthesis, a primitive belief, semicolon, such as the belief that the world was flat, close parenthesis. As if one look at the horizon wasn't enough to know that the world was curved."

Maya shook her head in mock dismay and added *Jonathan Livingston Seagull* to the stack of books in Paula's arms, with its silhouette of a gull in flight against a dark-blue background. "I actually teach an English class myself," she said. "Thursday evenings, English for Spiritual Seekers. Maybe we can have you in one day as a guest lecturer. Now why don't you make yourself at home in one of these comfy armchairs. There's an empty one right over there. You just sit and read for as long as you want and see if any of these books call to you. If *Siddhartha* brought you here, it was for a reason, and most likely it was to hand you off to your next book. That's the way it usually works. A book is just a person you can't see. They teach you something and then point you in the direction of your next teacher. Whatever lesson you're meant to learn next, I suspect you'll find it in one of those books you have in your hands. Or if not in one of these, then in one of those." She pointed toward the stacks. "It's a room full of spiritual guides, the ones in the pictures and the ones in the books. They're all here to guide you on your way. Now you sit and enjoy the journey. If you need me, just call. I'll be around. That's what *I'm* here for."

Maya patted her on the cheek like a doting grandmother and sashayed off in a rustle of garments and a clacking of beads. Paula watched her until she vanished through the bead curtain, both charmed and bemused by this unexpected woman, and then settled into the vacant armchair. She set her books on the small table beside the chair and picked up the last of Maya's selections: *Jonathan Livingston Seagull.*

It was a slim, elegant volume, punctuated by beautiful black-and-white stills of seagulls in flight, and Paula soon found herself racing through its pages. Nearly a third of the way through, Jonathan had his break-through, reaching terminal velocity at 214 miles per hour, a dizzying achievement and the first time that a gull in his flock had ever flown so fast. But instead of being celebrated for his accomplishment, he was made an outcast for violating tradition, banished to a solitary life on the Far Cliffs. "Life is the unknown and the unknowable," the elders told him, "except that we are put into this world to eat, to stay alive as long as we possibly can." A vexatious outcome that was no less vexatious for the fact that Paula saw it coming. What she didn't see coming was the two radiant gulls who pulled up alongside Jonathan one evening at the end of a long and fruitful though solitary life, lived alone in skies that his fellow gulls would not travel, a fate Paula could easily identify with. But it was not heaven they came to escort him to, but a higher life on this same earth, lived among similar beings who had left behind their squabbling over food to embark upon the journey to perfection.

At twenty-six, Paula was still skimming the surface of her life, still squabbling over food among her fellow human beings, but she was eager to spread her wings and start practicing flight as Jonathan had done at the beginning of his journey. And thanks to Richard Bach, she now considered herself forewarned: not everyone in her life would understand or sympathize with her quest; and if so, then their lack of comprehension was something she was going to have to learn to bear. She hoped her spiritual journey would not prove as solitary as Jonathan's, but she knew she had to be ready for whatever trials awaited, until her own pair of radiant gulls pulled up alongside her to escort her to her next incarnation.

"Heaven is not a place, and it is not a time," Jonathan's instructor told him as he began a new life among his spiritual peers. "Heaven is being perfect." Four simple words that rang like a church bell in her imagination. How long would it be before she would be among friends who felt the same? And how lonely would she get before she was? The thought gave her pause, especially when she took a quick mental inven-tory of her friends and colleagues, but one look around the bookstore was enough to give her hope, for there was hardly a free seat in the house, and none of her fellow travelers were reading fantasy novels or crime fiction or the latest political memoir. Like her, they were reading guidebooks on the path to perfection, trusting in the wisdom of those invisible mentors who were speaking to them from the pages of their books or the silence of their photos.

Just as Vasudeva had helped Siddhartha hear the voice of Endless Being in the river that flowed past their forest hut, Jonathan's mentor helped him to overcome the limitations that bound him. He showed his winged pupil that truly there are no limitations—once we learn to see beyond the cage of our bodies to our true nature, the infinite Self that is present everywhere at once, throughout all time and all space, "as perfect as an unwritten number." And then the teaching came full circle. Jonathan returned to his original flock—not as a prophet, or as the Son of the Great Gull, as the gullible or incredulous in the flock tried to make him out to be; nor as the devil incarnate, as he appeared to those whose fears outstripped their understanding; but as one who had learned the truth of his being and had come to share his wisdom, to help others find the fulfillment and meaning that would otherwise be barred to them. Jonathan had learned the greatest of all lessons, that of love and compassion, and he had returned to brave their ire, their incomprehension, and the terrible inertia of their superstitions, so that he could help those who were willing to be helped—the ultimate hallmark of a great soul.

This is it, Paula told herself, blinking back a tear as she turned the final page and closed the book, remembering Siddhartha's vision of Oneness and the conviction that had filled her in its aftermath. This is why she had been put on this earth. Perfection, the undiscovered land within whose unseen shore she had set out to find. She looked at her watch. An hour had passed since she had sat down. An hour that felt like a lifetime, as if she had been transported to a place in the space-time continuum where time sped up and then returned to her own planet, stunned to find that a mere sixty minutes had passed after what had felt like sixty years. And yet she was still in another world, the world of The Bodhi Tree, as far from the Rio she had known up until then as to be in another galaxy, enveloped in a protective cocoon and surrounded by a gallery of watchful guides who were there to make sure that when the butterfly emerged, it would know how to spread its wings.

Cradling the book in her hands with a fondness that had been growing steadily since she first picked it up, she felt a momentary pang of guilt—she had read the entire book without paying for it, something she couldn't imagine happening in any other bookstore. But that was easily remedied, she decided. It belonged on her bookshelf at home, where she could pull it out whenever she wished, cognizant of the importance that a certain seagull, enamored with the prospect of flight, had assumed in her life.

Paula didn't leave The Bodhi Tree for another two hours, staving off her hunger with an açai and a couple of large *pão de queijos*. By the time she left she had read half of another book and added three more to her sizable pile, including a copy of *Siddhartha* to replace the one she had borrowed, making sure that it had the identical stamp on the flyleaf at the back: *The Bodhi Tree: Rio's friendliest and most enlightened bookstore.*

Maya was behind the counter when she went to pay for her books, working at a computer. As Paula was handing her credit card to the cashier, Maya looked up from the monitor. "You have the glow of destiny on your brow, my dear," she said. "And a rather large pile of books. Did you find what you were looking for?"

"I'll say. And more."

"I thought you would. Come back anytime now. And don't feel like you need to buy anything. Some of my best customers just come here to read."

When Paula closed the door behind her to the tinkling of the glass chimes, the sudden assault of street noise and the traffic on Barata Ribeiro made her feel for a moment as if she had just been flung backward by an oncoming wave into the turbulent confusion of her old life. But then she felt the weight of her book bag, like a hefty mace slung over her shoulder as she strode forth into battle, an image drawn straight from Tolkien, and her feet regained their steadiness. She had her work cut out for her, she knew that. This was no fantasy with its predictable tropes and easily foreseen outcome. It wasn't a role-playing game with each of the participants scripting their part before joining their companions at the table. This was real life, as messy and as unpredictable as it got, but if a pair of invisible mentors from the previous century could get her this far, she felt confident that the ones in her book bag would see her safely through to the next stage in her journey.

3

AULA EASED THE BREAD pan out of the oven and set it on the counter to cool. Then she started grating the cheese for the fondue—a large block of Gruyère and a slightly smaller one of Emmentaler. She had already dissolved the cornstarch in a quarter cup of kirsch and set it aside. The shrimp was thawed out and succulent, the sauces were on the dining-room table—mustard, rose, Catupiry, and tartar, all homemade—and a chocolate-passion-fruit *pavê* was cooling in the fridge along with a green salad. Only the fondue was left and she wanted it to be perfect. And that, as she understood it, was the crux of the problem. The desire that just wouldn't go away, no matter how much she tried to keep her mind in the present, looking for the gap behind her thoughts where all was guaranteed to be peace and light, the ever-elusive eternal present that did its eternal disappearing act whenever she looked its way. Stay present, she reminded herself. Chop wood, carry water, grate cheese. Don't feed those thoughts with your attention, don't add fuel to the fire and they'll burn out for lack of kindling. And for a few minutes she was back in the moment. She watched the Gruyère slide from her grater in long curling strips, trying to catch every nuance of the Now as she slid her hand back and forth in smooth, even strokes: the creamy yellow of the cheese, darkening toward its edges; the slight cramping in her fingers as the strokes mounted up; the sweet, malty aroma of the bread a few feet away—rosemary, olive oil, sesame, and three kinds of organic flour; the hum of the air conditioning unit, holding at bay the stifling heat of another Rio summer. The few thoughts she noticed seemed to float through the kitchen like dust motes in the AC's backwash, barely ruffling the surface of her consciousness. But then it came back again, just as strong and just as persistent—she wanted it to be perfect—and again she was caught in the current of her desire, carried off into the past by this mind that she was slowly coming to recognize as the source of all her troubles.

Images from the previous weekend filled the canvas of her attention, starting with the row she had with Fernando after seeing a movie at the Laura Alvim cinema club, an Argentinian film that she had been wanting to see for some time. Walking up Viera Souto afterward, heading for that bar he so liked, the one where Jobim and Vinicius had famously seen an eighteen-year-old neighborhood girl, Helô, walking by each day on her way to the beach and were so taken by her tall, tanned beauty and the poetry of her gait that one day they unfolded some napkins and penned "The Girl From Ipanema" (or so they tell it)—well, she wouldn't call it a row, exactly, but then again, he could have made an effort to be supportive, grunting like that when she told him she was considering becoming a vegetarian, like she was an impetuous six-year-old trying to see what she could get away with: "Why would you do something like that?" "Because it's healthier, for one." "Excuse me, but I'm the doctor here, and that's debatable. Highly debatable. I don't want to get into it with you, you've obviously made up your mind. Without consulting me, I might add. Your boyfriend. And a physician. Anyhow, you could stand to lose a few pounds. At least that's one thing a vegetarian diet's good for, as long as you don't get anemic, and from what I can see there's no danger of that. As you may remember, I did tell you to take it easy on the chocolate. I mean, I know it's Christmas and all, but you're a big-boned girl. You have to be careful with the weight." *Cara de pau!* The nerve of that guy! Does he have any idea how full of himself he can get sometimes? Then again, she hadn't exactly been very friendly that night, caviling and carping the way she did, and ever since there had been this undercurrent of tension on the phone—nothing overt, but she could sense it—in fact, she could almost hear his unspoken thoughts on the other end of the line, the ones where he was telling himself that this girl is starting to get on my nerves, and she was just as much to blame for that as he was, that's why she needed this dinner to be perfect, because once they made it to the beach at Copa for the New Year's bash and got caught up in the madness, TV Globo said they were expecting well over two million people this year—

Just then she caught herself. She took a deep breath, wresting her attention back from the all-consuming vortex of the past and future. Somehow the cheese was down to its last nub and she hadn't been there to see it grated. The mind, she thought, shaking her head. It's like being strapped into a roller coaster sometimes — nothing you can do but hold on for dear life and hope you don't have a heart attack on the way down. But of course, there is something you can do. You just have to do it.

She took a few deep breaths and concentrated on the feel of the air entering her nostrils, following it down into her lungs and out again, a centering exercise she had come across in the Hermógenes book that was lying on her night table, an advance scout from the rapidly growing battalion of books beside her bed that marked her as The Bodhi Tree's latest and most loyal customer. She took the bottle of Sauvignon Blanc from the fridge and measured out an even cup, hoping that the familiar movements would help her ward off the next onslaught. She poured the wine into a rounded soapstone pot, part of a prized set she had bought from a small workshop in Ouro Preto, added another splash, and turned on the burner. She sprinkled in the grated cheese and kept stirring while it melted, then the kirsch, and when the fondue was smooth and bubbly she turned off the stove and transferred the pot to the fondue stand in the middle of the dining-room table, lighting the butane flame and turning it down as low as it would go. So far so good. She was feeling more settled now, calmer, more attentive. She still wanted the dinner to be perfect, but the desire wasn't pressing on her chest like it had earlier in the day, when her anxiety had begun creeping up with the thermometer. She was still here, still in the Now, or as close as she could reasonably be. Eckhart Tolle would be proud. She surveyed the table — the brand-new linen tablecloth with a design copied from the Copacabana sidewalks, black and white waves rippling gracefully from one end of the table to the other; the twin table settings with her best china, the wine goblets he had given her on her birthday, and Tramontina silverware, complete with fondue forks; and now the steaming cheese fondue like a golden aromatic centerpiece. Perfect.

She went back into the kitchen, cut up the bread into cubes, careful that each piece had a side with crust, and put them in a bowl. Then she brought the bread, the shrimp, and the salad to the table, and lastly the Sauvignon Blanc in a bowl of crushed ice. Fernando had texted her just before leaving the house, and as she surveyed her handiwork, pleased with what she saw, the buzzer sounded from downstairs. Only ten minutes late. That just might be a record, she thought. And it was certainly a good sign. She hoped. Although … and then she smiled as she buzzed him in, amazed at how her mind just wouldn't stop.

"Remember that plastic surgeon I was telling you about a couple of weeks ago, Dr. Peteca?" Fernando said, dipping a piece of bread into the fondue pot.

"The one who's a friend of your father?"

"That's the one. Mentor, more like it. He was a big inspiration to my dad back when he was getting started."

Fernando was in high spirits and had been from the moment he entered. Fondue was one of his favorite dinners—both cheese and shrimp—but she knew the food had little to do with it. Whatever tension she had felt these past few days on the phone had apparently dissipated on his way over from Lagoa. Or else it had been her own fears she had heard on the phone. An underlying tension that she had not perceived but invented. Conjured up by the pain-body she had been reading about in Eckhart Tolle's book, that residue of leftover hurts that insisted on seeing the worst in every approaching situation, thereby ensuring that the worst came to pass and thus perpetuating its own existence.

"I spent yesterday morning in his clinic in Botafogo. He took me around, showed me the facilities, and get this—he told me to come to him first once I completed my residency. Said he's always on the lookout for bright young physicians for his clinic."

"So you are still set on going into plastic surgery?"

"Hell yes. Are you kidding? That's where the money is. I'll keep working with my dad until March—after all, he paid for medical school. But after that it's the residency training program in plastic surgery, baby, right here in Rio. Do you have any idea how much these guys charge? Try eight thousand dollars for a facelift—US dollars—three thousand for liposuction or breast enlargements. As many as five or six procedures per day. You do the math. Peteca has a mansion in Gávea, a fifteen-hectare estate in Angra dos Reis, and a helicopter—with a pilot—to fly him back and forth. Not to mention a private plane and an apartment in Los Angeles. Oh, and he only works eight or nine months a year. The rest of the time he's off jet setting. Now that's the kind of life I was born for. Tell me if it's not. None of this slaving around for a few hundred thousand reals a year. Oh yeah, I almost forgot—he also told me that he heard how well I did in medical school. Can you believe that? This guy's been keeping an eye on me. Knows a good thing when he sees one."

When Paula mentioned an article she had read about a Rio lawyer who had spent six months in the hospital from an infection after having her buttocks reshaped and couldn't sue because she couldn't find the woman who had performed the procedure, Fernando went into a ten-minute rant about the rash of unlicensed, untrained practitioners who were giving the industry in Rio a bad name. "Some aren't even doctors at all!" he groused. "The huckster who shot up Vania's back-side didn't even have a medical degree. Did they mention that in the article? We have the best plastic surgeons in the world. It's New York, Los Angeles, Rio, and São Paulo—and not necessarily in that order. That's the problem with this goddamn government. I don't mind them lining their pockets a little as long as they do their job, but that's just the problem—they're not doing their job. They need to crack down on these fly-by-night operations. There are regulations, for Chrissake, but does the government bother to enforce them? Hell no. It burns me up. Well, until they get around to doing their job, people are just going to have to be careful, that's all. Check their accreditation, see how much experience they have. You go into Peteca's clinic and it's all right there on the wall. Medical degrees, government certification, newspaper arti-cles, even photos of Peteca with some of his famous clients—models, movie stars, the whole nine yards. There are always going to be some charlatans around, trying to make an easy buck, but they're not hard to sniff out if you use a little common sense."

Paula smiled and asked Fernando if he was ready for the *pavê*. It was one of his favorite rants—the government not doing its job—and he was good at it, which was why she had brought up the article.

He stretched his interlaced hands above his head, cracked his knuckles, and then patted his stomach with both palms. "I think I have a little room in there. Especially for passion-fruit-chocolate *pavê*. By the way, you outdid yourself this time, Paula. It was perfect. Although maybe I should withhold judgment until I taste the *pavê*."

Perfect. There was that word, and now that she'd heard it she wasn't about to deny herself the momentary thrill. Eckhart Tolle might not approve, but could there really be that much harm in a little emotional payoff? She savored the glow as she cleared the table and went to get the *pavê* out of the refrigerator, saving a sliver of her attention for her breath. When she returned with the dessert and a couple of small plates, she served Fernando a sizable portion and a much smaller one for herself. *The rest will be in the fridge,* she thought, feeling a rebellious twinge as she thought back to his remarks about her weight.

"Some coffee, *meu amor*, or more wine?" she asked when they were done with their dessert.

"Coffee."

Paula suggested they move to the sofa, where she had strategically placed a copy of *The Power of Now* on the coffee table. When she returned from the kitchen with a pair of steaming cups of a Bahamian vanilla-nut blend that she had picked up in Zona Sul, Fernando was turning over the book to have a look at the back cover, with its highlighted Oprah quote and its promise to change the reader's life for the better. From time to time Fernando would ask her about whatever book she was reading at the moment, and as she had hoped, this turned out to be one of those times. She had made cautious mention in the past weeks of some of the novel ideas she had encountered during her recent excursions into the world of spiritual literature, but none of those discussions had lasted more than a few minutes before veering off to a topic more to his liking. This time the conditions were more propitious. They had some time to kill before leaving, and after a particularly satisfying meal he liked to sink into the sofa and let some light entertainment facilitate his digestion—usually with the help of a movie or a television serial, but at times a good conversation would do, and at such moments he was often happy to let Paula do most of the talking.

The Power of Now had become her favorite book, for exactly the reason Oprah had mentioned on the back cover—its practical ability to transform her thinking. It had been a month since she had opened *Siddhartha* on the beach at Cabo Frio, and in those four short weeks her spiritual quest had given new meaning to her life, the kind of meaning that she had sought in vain ever since her youthful disillusionment with the Catholic faith. She couldn't claim that her troubles were behind her—it was too soon for that—but there were moments of clarity, moments of pure joy even, slipping through the cloud cover like a dazzling peek at a hidden sun, and the one book that had done the most to part those clouds had been *The Power of Now*. And so, though she was careful not to seem overeager, it was hard for her to hide her enthusiasm for Eckhart Tolle's teachings. When Paula told Fernando the story of how Eckhart had awakened one morning in a state of extreme depression, overwhelmed by the feeling that he couldn't live with himself anymore, only to realize that if he couldn't live with himself, then there must be two of him, the one he couldn't live with and the one that was aware of that troubled ego-self, she actually got up and started pacing up and down in front of the sofa, unable to contain herself as she began describing the key insight that had led to his spontaneous enlightenment. It was the single most important thing she had discovered in her few short weeks on the spiritual path — that the essence of Being was consciousness, and consciousness was beyond suffering, beyond all the transitory afflictions of her life — and no one she had come across until now had expressed that singular truth in a language as clear and as precise as that of the self-styled secular spiritual teacher from Germany whose book Fernando held in his hands while he listened to Paula give vent to her inspiration. It amazed her, she told him, what a profound difference the simple act of attention to the here and now could make, how almost all our suffering could be traced to the mind's obsession with the past and future, and from the relaxed smile on Fernando's face she could see that her impromptu monologue had drawn him into the present moment as well. His smile was even more evident in his eyes, and it was just in that instant that Paula ran into one of those gaps in the stream of thoughts that Eckhart Tolle had described, one of those luminous fragments between the end of one thought and the onslaught of another, when the mind's automatic switch fails to kick in, leaving one's consciousness free to breathe in the full awareness of eternity — before the thinking mind drops its opaque veil once again, as if in backlash against this unwarranted abdication of its customary throne. It was his eyes that did it, her momentary awareness of how beautiful they were, how the blue of his irises seemed the perfect counterpoint to the sandy brown waves of his hair, a small slice of eternity that she would have never experienced had she been a prisoner of her thoughts. The glow must have been obvious, because Fernando smiled appreciatively and toggled her switch to the on position with a few well-chosen words.

"Bravo, Paula. Very well said. If I didn't know better, I would have sworn you'd majored in philosophy. In fact, you might have missed your calling. You know, you might want to think about becoming a guru one day. Those guys make a lot of money. Take that guy in the Universal Church. What's his name?"

"You mean Edir Macedo?" she said, her mind involuntarily plummeting back to earth.

"That's the guy. Macedo. I remember reading this article about him in *Veja*. I mean, this guy, he not only has a private plane, he has a whole fleet of private planes. Do you know he owns Brazil's second largest TV network and has half ownership in a bank? And get this, he is not only a billionaire in US dollars, a bunch of his pastors are multimillionaires in their own right. And it all started with his sweet tongue."

"You're not seriously comparing Eckhart Tolle to Edir Macedo?"

"And why not?"

"Because Edir Macedo's a crook, for one. And so are his pastors."

"You mean the money laundering? He's just following the example of our illustrious politicians."

"Are you kidding? That's just the tip of the iceberg. You know how they got all that money? By exploiting the poor and the gullible. And this I know for a fact. These close friends of my parents, the Sepúlvedas, have a maid who belongs to the Universal Church. Her pastor convinced her to give her entire life savings to the Church — twenty-eight thousand reals. It took her fifteen years to save up that money and he manipulated her with promises of heaven until she gave him every last penny. A week later she came crying to the Sepúlvedas for an advance because she couldn't pay her bills. She's a single mom and didn't even have the money to buy school books for her kid. They got the story out of her and marched her right down to the church to talk to the pastor and try to get her money back, at least part of it. Do you know how much they got back? Nada. Zip. Zero. Not a single penny. He went off on the merits of charity and service to the poor and how no sacrifice goes in vain in the eyes of God. Well what about *her* poverty? What about buying books for *her* kid and putting food on *her* table? A woman in his own parish. Stonewalled them completely. No pity. Not a single drop. She was depressed for months after that. They had to give her a loan just to see her through."

Fernando started to laugh but one look from her put an end to it.

"Okay, maybe Macedo and his cronies aren't the best example. But seriously, there are a lot of well-intentioned evangelical preachers who aren't crooks. Their people swear by them, and they seem to do pretty well." Fernando rubbed his thumb and fingers together in the international symbol for moola to show what he meant. "Not as well as Macedo, of course, but they do okay. A whole lot better than English teachers, that's for sure. And they help people. That's more what I meant when I said you might want to think about becoming a guru. You know, the good kind."

"You can't compare an evangelical preacher to a spiritual teacher like Eckhart Tolle or the Dalai Lama."

"Are you so sure about that?"

"Absolutely."

"Well I wouldn't be if I were you. They're in the same business, after all."

"And what business would that be?"

"The business of selling happiness, of course. They may have a different spiel—your ET may be more psychological, more New Age, more hip, and that's cool. Evangelical preachers are more old school—put your troubles in the hands of the Lord and the Good Lord will wash you clean, that sort of thing. But it's the same business. They're selling happiness. Listen to my words, follow my teachings, buy my book, buy a ticket to my talk, put some money in the collection plate, and your life will be better. Whether any of that actually works or not is debatable, but whose to say their methods don't work just as well as Eckhart Tolle's?"

"Because they don't, that's why. One's religion and the other's spirituality. Evangelical preachers are teaching blind belief. They're peddling superstition, Nando. Eckhart Tolle is teaching people how to overcome suffering and achieve real lasting happiness through a scientific psychological process."

"That's easy to say, Paula, but not so easy to back up. I mean, it sounds nice in a book, it sounds especially nice when you say it, but I've heard evangelical preachers who sound just as convincing, and the people who follow them can tell some equally inspiring stories about how their lives were transformed by their teachings. So who's to say, really? You got to keep an open mind and take it all with a grain of salt. Whether it's politics, religion—hell, even medicine. If it helps, it helps—even if you just think it helps. As long as you don't become a fanatic and think you've cornered the market on the truth. That's when things get out of hand. That's how most wars get started."

"You can rest easy on that account," Paula said, trying to keep her capricious emotions from knocking her off her mark. "Eckhart Tolle is about as nonfanatic as you can get."

"Well hallelujah for that. I don't want to have to visit you in the loony bin someday, find out that you're telling people you're the reincarnation of Joan of Arc, sent to Brazil by the next ET to lead the benighted masses out of the darkness of ignorance."

Fernando broke into a loud guffaw, roundly pleased with his bon mot.

"Oh my God," he said, glancing at his watch, "I totally lost track of the time. I told the guys we would meet them around ten. We'd better get started." Fernando crinkled his eyes and smiled, the most sensuous of his many nuanced smiles that she had filed away in her data bank for instant recognition. "But I'll tell you what. If you want a mystical experience, I can promise you one in the bedroom when we get back.

If you're up for it. It will do you good. You've been kind of distracted lately, if you don't mind me saying so. Off your game, so to speak."

"I know," she said, doing her best to conjure up a coquettish smile, not quite sure if she pulled it off with a little war of her own threatening to break out inside."But don't worry, I won't be distracted when we get back. I promise you, I'll be all there. I'll use the Power of Now."

Fernando smiled and gave her a thumbs up. "Now you're talking. Okay then, time to party. Let's go welcome in the New Year. Copacabana is going to be rocking tonight."

Paula went into the bathroom to get ready, a few final moments of relative calm before they faced the storm of the annual New Year's celebration—a couple of million partygoers on the beach at Copacabana and a midnight fireworks display that had no rival anywhere in the world. She took a couple of deep breaths as she peered into the mirror, directing her attention to the brisk, invigorating splash of cold water on her face, the oily feel of the soap on her hands, the slight scratchiness of the towel as it warmed her neck and sopped the drops from her face; and with that brief visitation of the Now a little space opened up, enough of a crack to allow in the comic sense of the theater of her life. Stay in the present, she intoned under her breath. Keep your focus on the Now, no matter how loud and crazy it gets tonight. The rest is just a fiction invented by the ego, so be careful—you know how you love your fiction. She noticed then that her eyebrows could use a little accenting. She picked up her eyeliner and started shading the curve of her eyes, just enough to set them off. She stepped back and took a second to admire her handiwork, hoping that Fernando would approve, that she would make a good impression among his friends. Then she shook her head and laughed, struck by the absurdity of her desire, the way it had hijacked her thoughts and taken them for a spin, out of the present and into an imaginary future. It never stops, she thought. Well, nobody said this was going to be easy. Not even Eckhart Tolle, no matter how easy he makes it seem.

4

T**HE** B**ODHI** T**REE** **HAD** an open area at the back of the used bookstore that Maya used for classes and events, and it was there that Paula found herself a few weeks later for a talk on Spiritism, going directly to Copacabana after her six p.m. class. The guest speaker was a protégé of Chico Xavier who had been personally trained by the legendary medium. He was in his late fifties, short and squat, unlike his mentor, and without the thick glasses and rocking head movements that had made Xavier seem like a blind seer from some pre-Christian civilization. Paula had seen video clips of the celebrated medium — nearly everyone in Brazil had, at one time or another (a few years earlier a popular television show had named him the greatest Brazilian of all time, based on a survey of their viewers) — but most of what she knew about Chico Xavier was colored by the prejudices of her parents, who considered him a hoaxer and a corrupter of Catholic dogma, albeit a gentle, well-meaning hoaxer. Spiritism was reported to be the fastest-growing religion in Brazil, with over four million adherents and millions more who dabbled when the spirit moved them, but despite its firm Christian underpinnings her staunchly orthodox parents considered it a threat to the true faith, a heretical cult that would have been shown no quarter during the heyday of the inquisition, its followers burned at the stake if they did not recant their heretical beliefs (and perhaps even if they did). Psychic healing, automatic writing, reincarnation, mediums who conversed with spirits as readily as with live human beings, spirit worlds that closely mimicked our own — these were just some of the practices and beliefs that had long since been branded as heresy by the Church (due in part, no doubt, to their stubborn persistence among the Christian faithful). Paula's parents had often expressed their dismay at this anachronistic affront to modern Catholic doctrine. "Can people really be so gullible?" they would say, shaking their heads in tandem. "They claim to be Christians but they behave as if they wouldn't recognize the Bible if someone hit them over the head with it." Paula had heard these kinds of comments all her life, and as a result she had grown up thinking of Spiritists as misguided crackpots who inhabited a kind of religious netherworld populated by the phantoms of their overactive imaginations. But as Dr. Ayala wove anecdotes about his mentor into a variegated tapestry of Spiritist teachings, Paula soon realized that Spiritism was as much a philosophy as it was a cult. He talked at length about the law of karma and how reincarnation was the only logical explanation for the terrible injustices so rampant in the world, how the gradual purification of the soul through successive incarnations was an incontrovertible fact that had been substantiated by numerous studies of very young children who remembered their previous lives and furnished evidence that had been corroborated by investigators. Much of what he said would have fit comfortably in the esoteric texts she was reading, but what set him apart was his talk of spirit entities and the worlds they inhabited. She couldn't help but think that the stories he told would be more at home in the pages of a novel, a thought that was reinforced several days later when she read the popular Spiritist classic *Nosso Lar*, a novelistic depiction of a Rio doctor's entrance into Astral City, one of the lesser spirit worlds (a Portuguese-speaking spirit world, no less, populated principally by Brazilians), dictated to Chico Xavier in 1943 during a series of mediumistic trances by the spirit André Luiz, one of 450 books that Chico would transcribe over a period of sixty years through a process known as psychography.

Dr. Ayala had made the acquaintance of André Luiz during his own trances, and he assured his audience that the disembodied doctor was coming to the end of his stay in the spirit world and would soon transit back to Earth—presumably to Brazil where he would take the lessons he had learned during his fruitful sojourn as a disincarnate spirit and apply them to his next incarnation, accepting the necessary penance of forgetfulness in order to work his way up the ladder to enlightenment. Ayala hinted that André Luiz's karma would lead him to be a psychic healer in this coming life, combining his long-held desire to minister to the bodies of suffering human beings with the lessons in psychic energies that he had learned in the spirit world while working as a spirit doctor in the Ministry of Regeneration. If Dr. Ayala was to be believed, the world would soon have a second John of God, the famous Spiritist healer in Goiás who had been treating up to three thousand people a day for the past fifty years, conducting psychic surgeries with nothing more than an unsterilized kitchen knife and reputedly curing people of everything from terminal cancer to schizophrenia, though he attributed all his cures to the spirit entities he incorporated.

Though at times Dr. Ayala seemed to be more interested in the spirit world than the one he actually inhabited (after an initial internal shake of the head, Paula decided to withhold judgment), the principal thread that ran through his talk was the subtle intricacies of the law of karma, and during the question-and-answer period at the end, which included some amusing anecdotes about the karmic implications of romantic relationships, he told a story that seemed as if he had singled her out for a parting lesson. The heroine of the story was a devout and goodhearted young woman from a small town in the heart of Minas Gerais, a seemingly ordinary girl who had gotten engaged to a boy who was generally acknowledged by her peers to be "out of her league" but who in spiritual terms was actually well behind her, something she only became aware of when the veil of romantic attraction began to fall away. The boy was an inveterate skeptic who clearly didn't think much of her Spiritist leanings, and she was faced with the difficult choice between showing her fiancée the door or going through with the marriage in the hope that she could reform his seemingly intractable nature. She opted for the latter, with a little nudge from the good doctor. Her karmic challenge, as communicated to her by Dr. Ayala through the power of his mediumship, was to learn the lesson of compassion; and the outwardly impressive but inwardly benighted boyfriend was the vehicle God had chosen for her to learn that all-important lesson, the corresponding party in a karmic contract she had entered into before birth. Despite the perils of tying her fortunes to a materialistic beau, she accepted the challenge of bringing his soul to the spiritual path, something she accomplished with the aid of a little well-timed subterfuge, and the reward for her sacrifice was a leap in evolution and the satisfaction of knowing that she had been instrumental in opening the eyes of a fellow human being to the world's one enduring truth. And in the kind of fairy-tale ending that Paula had always loved, she had been rewarded for her sacrifice with the best of both worlds—a handsome husband from an affluent family who ended up following her down her chosen path.

Despite her Catholic upbringing, Paula had never thought of herself as a particularly spiritual person, but if the Spiritist teachings on reincarnation were true, then she had arrived in Cabo Frio with a spiritual consciousness acquired in other lives that was only now beginning to blossom. Of course the same might conceivably be true of Fernando, but given what he seemed to think of her New Age "infatuation," that seemed rather unlikely. She had no way of knowing if the medium had sensed her predicament from the podium and chosen that particular story because it was precisely what she needed to hear, but from what she had understood of karma it made little difference. She was in that bookstore because she was meant to be there. Wasn't that the whole teaching of karma in a nutshell, condensed to its irreducible essence? That everything that happens, happens for a reason? That the lessons we need to learn are being imparted to us in each succeeding moment as part of a specific curriculum designed to lead us to enlightenment? That the challenges we face along the way are the homework God assigns us? She didn't know much about spirit guides, other than that we were all supposed to have one, or much about God, for that matter, but she was starting to get a grasp on karma. Unbeknownst to her, she and Fernando had signed a karmic contract—otherwise they wouldn't be together—and she suspected that if she had a chance to read it she would find it written somewhere in the fine print that she had agreed to practice compassion by doing her utmost to bring him to the spiritual path. And if that were true, then she could live with that. After all, like the girl's fiancée, Fernando was handsome and charismatic, in his own worldly way, and would never want for money.

Paula was just beginning to think about Fernando's part of the contract when a healthy round of applause brought her attention back to the here and now. Dr. Ayala had finished his lecture and a crowd began to form around the medium while Maya set up a table for the customary book signing. Paula was headed for the thermoses of complimentary herbal tea at the snack counter when she heard someone call her name. She turned to see a wiry, olive-skinned man coming toward her, wearing jeans and a loose-fitting T-shirt with the blue and white stripes of the Argentina national football team.

"Paco! Well this is a surprise. I didn't know you were here. Are you a Spiritist?"

"No, I'm not a Spiritist, just a patron of the bookstore," he said, with a somewhat dismissive air. "I'm a Zen Buddhist."

"Really?"

She was surprised at this revelation from her student. Paco had been attending her English-conversation class at a language school in Copa for close to a year now, a taciturn Argentinian in his midforties who invariably sat in the back row and let his classmates do the talking.

"For many years now," he said. "And you? Are you a Spiritist?"

Paula shook her head. "No, I'm nothing, really. Just a seeker, for the time being."

They started comparing notes on the lecture—or rather, Paula shared what she thought while Paco nodded and added an occasional monosyllable. A few minutes into the conversation Maya came up to them with a cup of herbal tea in one hand and a copy of Dr. Ayala's latest book in the other, a gift from the psychographic doctor.

"Do you two know each other?" she asked.

"We do," said Paco. "Paula is my English teacher, and in my experience as good an English teacher as you'll find."

"And you know Paco?" Paula asked Maya, trying to deflect the complement.

"Who doesn't know Paco in these circles? He's the spiritual Gauguin of Rio painters. Destined to be unappreciated by the wider public until after he's gone. But those of us who are in the know, know. Has he given you any of his cards yet?"

"His cards?" Paula shook her head.

"Paco, I'm surprised." Maya frowned, only half in jest, as if she were remonstrating with an adored younger brother. "That's not like you."

"I was waiting for the right moment."

"And what is this, if not the right moment?"

"I was getting around to it."

Paco fished out an index-size card from the cloth bag hanging from his shoulder and handed it to Paula with a ceremonial bow. On the front was a reproduction of an impressionist painting, an autumnal mountain scene with a monk in orange robes meditating by a pond in the shade of a large ficus.

"Wait a second," Paula said, after studying the card for a few moments. "Isn't this the painting hanging behind the cash register at the entrance to the store?"

"It most certainly is," Maya said, with a hint of pride in her voice. "I think it's one of Paco's finest. Which is why I wanted it to be the last thing anyone sees when they are leaving the store. So they don't forget why they're here."

"You painted this?"

"You sound surprised."

"That's one word for it. Wow. I absolutely love this painting. In fact, I'm always glad when there's a line at the register so I can spend a few more minutes with it. It's a landmark in this place. You never mentioned you were a painter. Of course, you never mentioned much of anything, despite the fact that my class is supposed to be a *conversation* class."

Paco shrugged, looking not at all displeased.

"Paco is an advocate of silence over substance," Maya said with a momentary chuckle. "I think he likes to let his cards do his talking for him. Go ahead, turn it over."

Paula turned the card over. On the back was a quote from Rumi: *You are not a drop in the ocean; you are the ocean in a drop.*

"That's beautiful. Who is Rumi?"

"He was a thirteenth-century Persian poet and a great Sufi master," Paco said. "You'll find his books right over there."

"Aisle three, with the other Sufi poets," Maya added, pointing toward the stacks.

"Do you always carry these cards around with you?"

"He hands them out pretty much everywhere he goes," Maya said. "Which is why I'm surprised you hadn't seen them. I have the whole collection. I can't afford the paintings, other than the one, but I've got all the cards. I'm convinced they'll be collector's items one day."

"You're also convinced that I'll be famous one day and there's no sign of that happening."

"After you're dead, my friend, as I've made clear on more than one occasion. It's in your chart and it's in your hand. More importantly it's in the paintings. The Western world just isn't ready yet for spiritual painters, but it will be. And when it is ... look out. People will be falling over themselves to own one of your paintings. You'll see. Mark my word."

"And how exactly am I going to do that if I'm not going to be here?"

"We'll come back in our spirit bodies and have a look. And if not, there's always the next incarnation. Who knows, maybe in your next life you'll be able to buy one of your own paintings. You certainly can't afford them in this one."

Maya beamed in amusement and laid an affectionate hand on Paco's shoulder, then excused herself to rejoin her guest of honor. After she sashayed off in a familiar rustle of garments, Paula availed of the opportunity to satisfy her curiosity about her Argentinian student. She learned that Paco had lived in Brazil for more than two decades, almost all of it in Rio, living a hermit's life in an old loft a few blocks from the bookstore with a futon for a bed and a room full of paintings in various states of composition. He had a job as a night janitor in a middling Copacabana restaurant where he had started off as a dishwasher, and his total lack of monetary ambition dovetailed perfectly with his vows of artistic purity. He rarely sold a painting and had never made the least effort to exhibit his work. Those he did sell were purely by referral from people like Maya who told their friends about this monk-like Zen artist who was a century or two ahead of his time. Either that, or he was a throwback to medieval Japan when painting was a passion, not a profession, a meditative pursuit for cultivated souls and a Zen practice as revered as the tea ceremony. Had he been born in Japan in medieval times he might well have been a wandering monk, sleeping in caves or under trees in some remote mountain region and painting his mystical landscapes on village walls and roadside boulders to remind his fellow travelers that all paths lead to the same destination. In modern-day Rio, however, he was a janitor working two or three hours a night, six nights a week, and earning just enough to pay his rent and food and keep him in art supplies, supplementing his income with the occasional sale of a painting that he neither solicited nor took pride in. What he cared about was his art, his privacy, and his Zen practice, to which he dedicated the same unalloyed singlemindedness that sustained his art. When Paula asked him if he gave out his cards as a way to advertise his work, she met with a scowl that could have brought her lukewarm cup of herbal tea to a boil. "I am not a prostitute," he said, the words landing like a lash across her face. "My paintings have a spiritual purpose, the same purpose as the quote on the back. They are vehicles of awakening. If someone wants to buy one of my paintings so that they can be reminded of the path whenever they look at it, then well and good. I *may* sell it to them—for a price that makes them conscious of its spiritual value. But if they don't have a spiritual purpose for wanting one of my paintings, then I won't sell it to them at any price. My cards serve the same purpose. They are vehicles of awakening. I hand them out to those people who are ready to receive them."

The words obviously cost him some effort, and Paula wondered if it was because he was out of practice or if he were simply pained that she had dared impugn his character, attributing commercial motivation to a man who had long since left behind such egotistical concerns. She mumbled an apology and made a note to herself to tread lightly the next time around—assuming there was a next time. Nevertheless she admired his passion. There was something brutally honest about it and fearlessly unapologetic, as if the niceties of polite conversation were a welcome sacrifice at the altar of truth. It wasn't something she was used to, but the jarring quality of his words didn't feel like a reproach but rather like a kind of intimate revelation, a raw depth of feeling she wasn't accustomed to from any but the closest of friends.

After a short silence, the conversation shifted to meditation and the roots of Zen practice. Paula wasn't quite sure whether he had nudged her in that direction or she him, but she was eager to hear how he had gotten into Zen and just how necessary he thought it was to follow a particular tradition or a particular teacher.

"In my opinion, if you are really serious about spiritual practice you have to have a teacher. No one can become a disciple without a teacher, and no one can reach enlightenment without first being a disciple. The ego has to be surrendered and that's the essence of what it means to be a disciple. If all you want to do is dabble then it doesn't matter, but personally I'm not interested in dabbling."

"I guess that makes sense. I've been trying to meditate on my own for a couple of months now but I haven't had much success. Maybe it's time I started looking for a teacher."

Paco gave a noncommittal shrug. "It's up to you, but I would certainly recommend it. If you're interested, my teacher is going to be in town this weekend for a retreat. The retreat is closed to the public but we are having an open meditation and satsang with her Friday night. You're welcome to accompany me."

"Your teacher is a her?"

"Coen Sensei. The first Brazilian woman to receive the dharma transmission. She spent twelve years in a monastery in Japan with Yogo Suigan Roshi before he sent her back to Brazil to open up a Soto Zen temple in São Paulo. That was more than twenty years ago. Since then she's become the most famous Zen teacher in the country."

The first Brazilian woman to receive the dharma transmission? Paula didn't know what that was, but it sounded significant. And she was a woman! A Brazilian woman who was also a famous Buddhist teacher. This was an opportunity she couldn't miss.

"Can I bring my boyfriend?" she asked, remembering Dr. Ayala's story.

"Of course. Is he interested in spirituality?"

"Not as such. Not yet, I should say. In fact, he seems to think it's all a big con game. But that's precisely why I want to invite him. He needs it more than anyone. He just doesn't know it yet. Maybe this will be just the spark that gets him going."

"Okay then, bring him along. If you think he's ready. But a word to the wise: don't throw your pearls before swine."

Paula had heard that phrase so many times while growing up she automatically completed it in her head: if you do, they may trample them under their feet, and then turn and tear you to pieces. She felt a quick flash of vexation—after all, he didn't know Fernando—but she decided not to take offense, strange as it sounded to hear one of her parents' favorite Biblical quotations coming from the mouth of a Zen Buddhist. She was sure he meant well. He might even like Fernando once they met, though on second thought she wasn't quite so sure.

They made arrangements to meet up in front of the bookstore on Friday, and a few minutes later Paula excused herself and headed for her car. Instead of going straight home, however, she took out her phone and googled Coen Sensei, knowing that the real challenge was going to be convincing Fernando to come. They didn't have anything fixed for Friday night, but that wasn't going to make it any easier. What she needed was an angle, something to catch her boyfriend's interest without him suspecting that she might be trying to convert him.

She read a short bio of the Brazilian nun, which included some of the awards she had won and a list of the prestigious venues where she had been invited to lecture, all of which looked promising for her purposes, and then she discovered something even better. Not only was Monja Coen from a prominent São Paulo family that dated back to the settlement of the country, three of her cousins had founded the seminal rock band The Mutants in the 1960s, along with Rita Lee, Brazil's foremost female rock star, who at the time was married to one of the cousins. The Mutants had been Paula's favorite rock band during a critical phase in her adolescence, which in her eyes was enough to make Monja Coen royalty once removed, but more importantly Fernando was even more of a fan than she was. In fact, he still had posters of The Mutants on his bedroom wall. They were heroes to him in the same way Pelé was, magical figures from the legendary generation that had changed the world forever, and though it was a bit of a tenuous connection it might be enough. As a first cousin of the Baptista brothers and a true child of the sixties who had married at fourteen and divorced at seventeen with a daughter in tow, she had dived headlong into the hippie celebration of sex, drugs, and rock and roll under the wild and creative mentorship of her famous cousins (during which she had already begun to meditate), and she had emerged as a successful journalist and a published author. And oh yes, years later, the first Brazilian woman to receive the dharma transmission in the Zen tradition, which, as Paula now googled, was a custom in which a person was chosen as a successor in an unbroken lineage of masters and disciples that supposedly traced itself back to the Buddha himself. In short, Monja Coen was a certified exotic, colorful enough that she just might pique Fernando's interest, especially if Paula didn't mention that the program included meditation. It would just be a talk by an intriguing personality that one of her students had invited them to, an interesting prelude to dinner and a night on the town. The girl in the story had essentially tricked her beau into becoming a Spiritist, and Paula wasn't above a few tricks of her own.

Satisfied with her strategy, she drove home and went straight to her laptop to watch some videos of the Brazilian Zen master whose precocious life had led her to the spiritual path, a real-life Siddhartha whom Paula couldn't wait to meet.

5

S OMETIMES THINGS JUST FALL apart. The sky collapses and before you know it you are huddled in an alley, trying to avoid being scorched by falling stars and other assorted cosmic debris — no warning, no rhyme or reason, and just when things were going so well. It happens. Life is the ultimate enigma machine. Hence the enduring aura of mystery. The kind of mystery you could do without when you're knee deep in the muck and the mire through no obvious fault of your own. But that wasn't the case this time. This time it was her own damn fault. She had been undone by her own worst enemy, rising from its slumber at the worst possible moment.

She had invited him over for lunch, knowing that like herself he was more pliable after a good meal, and she had assigned a watchful guard to her tongue, which had grown a touch unruly lately. No alluding to his love affair with materialism. No quotes from the Buddha, no extolling her latest literary discovery from The Bodhi Tree. Fernando was many things, but a fool he wasn't. And for a while everything went exactly as planned. She had made a green salad and his favorite feijoada, a black-bean stew with chunks of smoked provolone, seasoned with parsley, coriander, and chili, served over rice and topped with roasted cassava flour, with stir-fried kale and orange slices on the side. When they were done eating, she put on a Mutants CD — their pioneering first album, which had achieved legendary status over the years — and steered the conversation toward the glory days of the sixties, a period in Western civilization they both idolized, conscious of how tame and uninspired their own era was by comparison. It was a meandering, placid, lazy conversation, a perfect compliment to a satiated stomach that lasted the duration of the record. Fernando was drumming his fingers on the table to the opening piano figures of the concluding track, "Ave Genghis Khan," when Paula told him about the invitation to a talk by a first cousin of the Baptista brothers who had followed them into the heart of the psychedelic movement before becoming a seminal figure in an equally mind-altering world as a Zen master and one of the country's wisest and most recognizable faces.

"And she's a woman," she added, "which might not mean much to you, *meu amor*, but this country needs more women like her breaking down barriers."

Fernando listened with apparent interest to her account of Coen's colorful past and nodded in appreciation when she mentioned Coen's invitation to lecture in the offices of the President of the Republic, the interview on *Provocation* she had watched on Youtube, and her many friendships with other cultural leaders in Brazil. But when she brought the conversation back to her upcoming talk, he inhaled sharply and shook his head. "Too bad it's Friday," he said. "I wouldn't mind going, but I've already got other plans."

That's when her unwanted visitor took over, the pain-body's indignant grimace shattering an invisible mirror and sprinkling cut glass into her voice.

"And what exactly has come up that's so important you can't spend Friday night with your girlfriend?"

"I'm going over to Guilherme's," he said, his voice stiffening. "He asked me to partner up with him for a World of Warcraft tournament this weekend, and the opening round's Friday night. I couldn't get out of it. You know how he depends on me."

"You're telling me you're going to play video games the entire weekend!"

How many times had she heard the cliché "spitting venom" and silently criticized the author for lazy writing? But in this case the expression couldn't have been more apt. She could feel her words burning his skin, turning his freckled face an unbecoming shade of red. Her hackles had started rising the moment he said "Too bad it's Friday," and they were still on their way up when she chose to invest her words with the full force of her disdain. In the time it took him to tell her why he couldn't come, she had already dredged up all the real and imagined slights he had subjected her to since the beginning of their courtship and decided that this was the coup de grâce, worthy of whatever invective she could muster.

She didn't quite remember what she said after that, so identified was she with the rough beast that had taken control of her. What she did remember was Fernando's face slowly growing redder, his chin receding into his neck, his glacial silence doing its best to repel her unwarranted anger with an equally potent force field of interstellar cold. The worse of it was that she could literally see herself falling off the precipice, sabotaging weeks of spiritual endeavor with each succeeding word, and yet she was powerless to stop. It was as if a harridan from another life had gleefully borrowed her vocal cords while she looked on in horri-fied silence — well, the horror came later, when she finally admitted to herself how badly she had messed up. She had been too carried away in the moment to do anything but react.

When she did finally get down off her high horse (how long had her tirade lasted, three, four minutes?), she couldn't resist a final unnecessary barb. "And when exactly were you going to tell me? Friday afternoon? A last-minute text message? That would be your style. And don't think I haven't seen you looking at your watch."

That was followed by a full minute of silence before Fernando asked her if she were done. Paula barely acknowledged his question, still in the full flower of her indignation, though somewhere in the deep dark recesses of her psyche she was aware of how unfair she had been.

"First of all," he said, the words advancing slowly out of the silence like a locomotive struggling against the weight of a long string of car-riages before easing its way out of the station, "I was actually about to tell you. I didn't know I had a deadline. Secondly, I don't need to apologize for spending a weekend with my friends. We hadn't made any plans, so there were none to break. A man has to have some space to breathe in a relationship; otherwise he'll suffocate. Some women don't seem to understand that. I didn't think you were one of them but maybe I was mistaken. And lastly, I know what this is about, and it's not about me having made other plans for the weekend. This is about you wanting me to follow you on your New Age kick and get-ting angry because I don't see things the way you do and I have the temerity to tell you so. Which just so happens to be my right, by the way. You don't have a monopoly on the truth. Neither do I, but I don't go around trying to convert you to my way of seeing things. You want to sit around in your underwear and contemplate your navel, okay, I'm cool with that. I haven't complained, I haven't preached. You want to believe in some mystical explanation for the universe? No problem. Everybody's entitled to a fantasy life. I could say a thing or two, but I haven't. Live and let live. And now I'm the bad guy because I want to spend a couple of days with my friend playing video games? Something I haven't done for quite a long time, I might add. I play video games. I admit it. But that's no different than your talk about reincarnation and yogis in the Himalayas living for a thousand years and traveling from peak to peak by closing their eyes and thinking themselves there. It's just a video game you're playing in your head. The only difference is that mine requires a computer. Like I said, you're entitled. But when you start criticizing me for wasting my time, when you start implying how materialistic I am, as if I were living in the dark ages, when you start telling people where they're going wrong and what they need to do to get their lives together — well that, my darling, is where you've lost the plot. From where I'm sitting you don't have your life any more together than the next guy. And if you think you do, that just makes it worse. Now I was looking at my watch because I have to be back in the clinic in thirty-five minutes and the traffic happens to be murder out there. Much as I *don't* want to continue this conversation, I will add one more thing before I do actually have to leave: I think that under the circumstances it's just as well we don't spend this weekend together. After what just went down, I think we could do with a little time off, give us a chance to clear our heads. Why don't you text me during the week and we'll see where we're at."

Fernando made no move to leave. His voice had flattened out and his eyes had grown more impassive the more he talked, as if he had managed to access a level of control over his emotions that she was light years from achieving. There was something infuriating about that. What she wouldn't have given in that moment for a New Age mirror that could reveal the hidden prejudices behind that face! Even without it, she was sure she knew what he was thinking: that her spiritual convictions were just a means of climbing a pedestal that her middle-class upbringing and remedial social skills had denied her, a chance at long last to feel that she was better than the rest. Did he see the irony in that, or was it totally lost on him? If ever there was anyone who rode the entitlements of privilege to the top of his own private mountain, it was Fernando. To his credit, he treated it as a game, but he had been bred to believe that he was better than the greater mass of humanity, an unconscious outlook on the world that hid itself behind a mask of self-confidence and composure.

"Anything you want to add before I leave?" he said, forcing his way into her reverie.

"Sorry, I was just thinking about the high horse you've been riding your entire life. It must be so hard to see anything clearly from way up there."

Fernando shook his head with a look of disgust and glanced at his watch. "Look, Paula, I really have to go. I have to be back in just under thirty minutes now and I can't be late. We can talk about this next week. Maybe by then you'll have that burr out of your saddle, to continue with the cowboy metaphor. Give my regards to your Zen master, but now I have to run."

And just like that he was up and out the door.

Paula watched him go without so much as saying goodbye, still puffed up with resentment, but within moments of hearing the door click shut, the air went out of the balloon, reducing it to a flaccid piece of rubber. For a long while she sat there slumped in her chair, staring at the wall, trying to find some justification for her anger. She could hear the monotonous tick of the clock on the wall behind her, the seconds passing at an agonizing pace, and as they receded into the background, she found it more and more difficult to attribute any reason or rationale to anything she had said. A familiar sense of panic started grabbing at her from the edges of her consciousness, its tendrils reaching out as they had so often when she was younger. Without thinking she reached for her phone, as if it were a life jacket, and started typing a message: *sorry, don't know what I was thinking (PMS maybe?); won't happen again, I promise, have a great weekend.* She hit "send" without a moment's reflection and then spent an anxious, overwrought minute while the clock's secondhand struck over and over again like the lashing of a whip — until she heard the ping of her iPhone and felt a flood of relief when she saw its screen light up and the word "Ok" beneath Fernando's name. Less than she had hoped for, but more, perhaps, than she deserved. A single monosyllable that spoke volumes about the mental state of the man at the other end. He was irritated, obviously, but not so irritated that he wouldn't answer. "Ok" meant that there was something to repair. "Ok" meant that she had time to set things right. "Ok" meant that this was just a setback, an ugly misstep but no more than every couple had to go through on their way to higher ground. She sent back a string of emojis that started with chagrin, morphed into hope, and ended with love. A few simple images to stand in for the thousands of words that she wasn't capable of saying and which probably would have only made things worse. Thank God for text messages and emojis, she thought. Had they been back in the sixties she might have gone running after him, which would have been the last thing he would have wanted.

Despite wanting nothing more than to curl up on the couch with a pillow over her head, she roused herself from her chair and started getting ready for her afternoon and evening classes at G2 Ocean, the maritime shipping company that paid her a healthy fee to refine the English-speaking skills of its employees, who were frequently on the phone with clients from around the world. She would have liked to take refuge in the moment but she gave that up as temporarily impossible. Her mind was too distraught to focus its attention on what her body was doing. It needed time to think, time to open a window into the past in an effort to come to grips with the darkness that had made such an unwanted intrusion, to understand how two months of spiritual exercises could lead her to the kind of vile eruption that had sent her boyfriend running out the door. And so she gave it free rein as she cleared the table and made her way to the bathroom for a long hot shower.

She had never been an angry person, not even during the worst of her adolescence or the blackest of her moods. She had long prided herself on being "low-maintenance," ever since she had first watched *When Harry Met Sally* during her college years and fell in love with the phrase—not only when it came to her boyfriend but in all her relationships. Accommodating, supportive, easy to get along with, decidedly un-picky and thankfully bereft of the nagging gene that had undone many an otherwise promising relationship—that was how she saw herself, a nurturing Cancerian who knew the value of being laid-back. She had never gotten on Fernando's case like this before, and the worst of it was that there was every sign it wasn't just a one-off thing. There was something seething inside her, some accumulated gumbo of resentments that she was only just becoming aware of. And if it was coming out now, it meant that it had been there all along, steeping in a covered pot. Eckhart Tolle's name for it couldn't have been more apt: the pain-body, giving it a shape and substance, the ego's dark shadow that fed off the mind's unconscious fears and accumulated heartache, but she could just as well call it karma, the heavy baggage she had been dragging around since God knows how long. She had read in one of those books by her bedside that the spiritual purpose of relationships was to bring to the surface the unacknowledged and unfaced karma that ordinary life could not, providing the intensity, the vulnerability, the emotional fire needed to force those buried imperfections into the light. As uncomfortable as it might feel—and there was no denying how uncomfortable she felt—there was no way around it, no other recourse but to face those hidden demons. Which meant, of course—turning it over in her mind with a rueful sliver of a smile—that in one way her regrettable meltdown was a good thing (though she doubted Fernando would see it that way).

The girl in Dr. Ayala's story had been a model of compassion, but Paula suspected that she had had her share of emotional setbacks before she could become a positive, enlightening influence in her fiancée's life, something the doctor had probably glossed over for the sake of compression (knowing that stories are a condensed simulacrum of real life). That reminded her of one of her parents' favorite Biblical stories, the parable of the sower and the seed. Their focus was always on where the seeds fell, never on the seeds themselves. But how could you know if the soil was barren if the seeds weren't fertile to begin with? If her spiritual life was going to flower, she was going to have to own up to her own failings and not make Fernando an easy target. Who knows, maybe that was all he needed. Let him enjoy his World of Warcraft tournament. She would apologize properly after they had their little break and use the lash of her conscience to spur her to greater awareness, the kind of solvent that would one day dissolve the pain-body for good. In the meantime, meeting an authentic Zen master could only hasten the process. When it did come time for Fernando to accompany her on the spiritual path, she wanted to be ready, a wise and compassionate influence like the girl from Minas. After all, there was a reason they were together, and the name of that reason was *karma*.

6

THE ZEN SATSANG WAS held in a second-floor yoga hall on Ipanema's busiest street, Ataulfo de Paiva, and by the time they found parking and walked the intervening blocks, it was nearly time for the program to begin. The place was crowded, nearly two hundred people by Paula's estimation, but they managed to find some free space at the back, just in front of the double row of chairs that had been set out for people who had trouble sitting on the floor. Monja Coen arrived a few minutes later, making her way to a simple black meditation cushion at the front of the hall, flanked by two large flower vases. She was sixty-eight years old, with the shaven head and dark robes of the Zen renunciate, but she seemed much younger than her age, despite the wrinkles on her face and hands, as if her Zen practice had preserved the spirit of her youth, even as time had laid siege to her body.

Coen gave the microphone a tap and asked in that distinct Paulista accent that Paula knew so well from her videos, "Is everybody happy to be here in this moment, in this hall, on this Earth?" To which her audience answered yes in what was very nearly a single voice.

"*Beleza.* Then let's take advantage of all this good company and do some meditation together."

She began with a short introduction to zazen, instructing the gathering in the intricacies of Zen posture and then requested everyone to join their palms in the traditional greeting called *gassho.*

"*Gassho* has many different meanings," she said, as her mirthful gaze swept slowly across the hall. "It symbolizes the relationship between the absolute and the relative, between heaven and earth, negative and positive, God and the human being; and it is with the hands in this position that we greet the place where we are going to meditate, the place where Buddha manifests himself, where wisdom manifests itself. Then we turn in each direction to greet everyone in the hall, because all of us share the same nature. In this way I recognize the Divine in every living being, in each and every one of my neighbors, and I am thankful for their presence, because it is much easier to meditate in a group than to meditate alone."

When she was done with the greeting, she dropped her hands into her lap, palms up with the left hand on top of the right and the tips of the thumbs touching.

"We call this the cosmic mudra. We are in the hands of the cosmos and the cosmos is in our hands. You can close your eyes if you wish, but we recommend keeping the eyes half open, because in truth the internal and the external are not separate. There is a unity between what is happening outside me and what is happening inside me, and our half-open eyes facilitate our awareness of that unity. Finally, we remember that Buddha sat down alone beneath a tree and thus we do the same. We are in a group, but it is as if each of us were alone, as if each of us were Shakyamuni, the historical Buddha, sitting beneath the tree of enlightenment. Thus we begin zazen, the encounter between our individual witnessing consciousness and the essence of our being."

Coen guided the first few minutes of the meditation in a fluid, lilting contralto, directing everyone to observe their breath, the various sensations of their body, and above all their thoughts, allowing the flow of images, emotions, and internal dialogue to continue unimpeded until they became aware of the space between and behind their thoughts, the essence of pure being that lay like an unbroken fabric behind the mind's impermanence.

When the gong sounded to signal the end of the meditation, its metallic resonance ebbing and flowing like a tidal wash in the labyrinth of her thoughts, Paula glanced at her watch: forty minutes, longer than she had ever sat before. It hadn't been the prettiest of sights, this excursion into her inner theater. More than half of those forty minutes had been spent obsessing about how she had left things with Fernando, "obsessing" being a word she would not have used had she not been so starkly aware of how her mind returned over and over again to the same images and emotions: her unwarranted invective; her boyfriend heading for the door, his face buried behind a mask of glacial silence; the anger, insecurity, and panic that had waylaid her like a rabid dog—a constantly recurring theme that she was forced to endure against her volition like Alex in *A Clockwork Orange*. The feelings were so visceral, so immediate, that it was almost impossible to step back and see them for what they really were:

mere thoughts, ephemeral wisps of passing cloud sullying the bright clear space that contained them. Even when her mind gained some relief toward the end of the meditation, she still felt as if she were being led along on a leash, following her thoughts and desires like an obedient puppy: things she needed to take care of for work, fantasies about the future, even making a note to herself not to let Paco's invitation complicate their student-teacher relationship, a note she mechanically jotted down in her mind at least half a dozen times. But despite the internal clamor, there were moments when she caught glimpses of a luminosity behind the clouds, enough to give her hope that freedom was not beyond her reach, no matter how far away it seemed.

Paco was still meditating when Monja Coen began her talk with an invocation to the three jewels of the Buddhist path, and he continued meditating until the talk was over, a strangely disconcerting and yet fortifying reminder of just how much of a neophyte she was. Coen chanted the invocation in Japanese, then in Pali, and finally in Portuguese. As Paula recited the chant in Portuguese along with the crowd—I return and take refuge in the Buddha; I return and take refuge in the dharma; I return and take refuge in the sangha—it struck her how similar her name sounded to *koan*, the Zen practice of concentrating on a word or phrase that defied intellectual explanation, such as "What is the sound of one hand clapping?" and she wondered if the jovial Zen nun was herself a kind of *koan*, as indeed the world itself. But then the talk began and the thought vanished, another passing cloud in the play of impermanence.

Monja Coen was an accomplished speaker, as Paula already knew from her limited exposure to the Zen nun on Youtube, and yet the videos hadn't done her justice. Her manner seemed so natural, so everyday human, that Paula felt as if she were sitting in a room with a warmhearted, garrulous grandmother who had the charming habit of chatting about whatever came to mind, the soul of spontaneity. Stories would pop into her head, seemingly at random, punctuated by short bursts of laughter, anything from her most recent trip to the doctor to sitting in the airport in Sapporo with her master, and invariably each story or anecdote would evoke some common-sense wisdom elicited by her predicament that would never have occurred to Paula on her own but which suddenly illumined scores of similar incidents from her own life. Only at the end of the narrative would she discover that this unexpected insight was in fact the flowering bud of a traditional Zen teaching—life as seen through the lens of a mind trained in the Buddhist mode of perception. The same life Paula was leading, the same quotidian incidents and preoccupations, transformed and transfigured into an entirely new vision of reality.

One such story, the last of the evening, forced a wedge into Paula's consciousness that continued opening up space in the days and weeks to come. Whenever Coen's master in Japan came to the women's monastery to teach, he would always drink from the same cup, the only glass cup in the entire monastery. One day a novitiate inadvertently broke it when she let it drop during the washing up. When she told the master, sure that she would get some sort of reprimand for her lack of mindful attention, he broke into a broad smile and said, "How wonderful! I'm going to have a new cup."

"I'm not going to lament what I don't have," Coen said, opening up her hands in a graceful gesture. "I'm going to see what reality presents me with and smile, because everything is an expression of Buddha nature. I'm not going to lament the past. Something new is always arriving, and I am going to receive it with equanimity and joy. That's what I felt the master was saying, and it has stayed with me ever since. In time I realized that this comes from a deep encounter with our true self. This is what zazen does for us. It allows us to access the essence of our being. And the essence of our being is free from blemishes, it is free from suffering, it is free from everything. It is simply free. If sickness comes and pays me a visit, let me see how I can receive this welcome guest, what kind of arrangements I can make. Take vitamin C, take an antibiotic—if that's what my consciousness or the doctor tells me. Make the necessary arrangements, whether it is a common cold or a disease that has no cure. In either case, my true nature is free. We all know that health isn't permanent. Nothing is permanent. If we don't get sick and die young, we get old and die old. That realization is what set Shakyamuni Buddha on his quest for enlightenment. Here is this prince, living in a royal palace. He has everything that is good in life. But even so, he is going to get sick, he is going to get old, he is going to die, as will every one of us. And so he sets out on a quest to find the way beyond suffering—or rather, to find that true self that is untouched by suffering, that is beyond impermanence.

"This is a very interesting understanding in Buddhism. There is a part of us that dies, but there is also a part of us that doesn't die. Aha … now that should give us pause. We have our five senses and we have a consciousness that deals with everything we see and feel and think, that interacts with the world, both internal and external. And that consciousness stores those experiences inside us. It's an extraordinary apparatus that records everything that happens, even when we're asleep. It is all stored inside, even though we may not have access to it. And if we go deeper into that storehouse, we discover that not only are our individual experiences stored there, but also all the experiences of our past lives. This is something that can be directly experienced, though it is very difficult to do. But not only are our individual past lives stored in our consciousness. If we go even deeper, we find a consciousness of all past lives, of all the people around us. Not only those we can remember, three or four generations back, but all the lives ever lived. The human DNA. That memory is also inside us. These are different levels of consciousness, and each has a name in Buddhism. But behind them all is our true self, which we call our Buddha nature. And this Buddha nature, this true self, doesn't die. It is not the soul exactly, as we tend to think of it. It is not something fixed or permanent that leaves one body and enters another. When we access our Buddha nature we access the essence of pure being, which is the essence of all life, not just my own. Of all beings, all objects, even the planet on which we are sitting. And when we come in contact with this—not just on a mental level, as a concept, but when we experience it with our entire mind and body—we recognize the sacred that is in all of us. It is not just in some special persons, in this saint or that god—it is in all of us and in everything. We are all a reflection of that sacred self. In India there is a greeting, *namaste*. What does *namaste* mean? It means, I recognize the sacred in me and I greet the sacred in you. When we perceive this, when we actually experience it, then life becomes light, it becomes joyous, because everything that happens is an opportunity for growth, a step on the path to enlightenment. The person who comes and bothers us is another face of the master, because she is showing us our weaknesses. That part of me that I need to strengthen. We start to realize that everything is an aspect of our being, different facets of the same diamond, and thus we are co-responsible for everything we experience. And if we are co-responsible—and we are—then let us do better. Let us become examples of the spiritual path. If our outlook is fixed we are in prison. But if we can expand our vision then we can become free. This is what Buddhism proposes. Let us transform ourselves, let us escape this cycle of lamentation and change the way we perceive reality so that life becomes better and better—not just for us, but for all living beings."

Monja Coen scanned the crowd in silence while her smile expanded to its limits. Then she brought her folded palms to her chest. "I want to thank each and every one of you for your presence here this evening. May the merits of our practice extend to all beings, and may we all become the enlightened path."

Her parting words were met with a reflective silence. Paula felt the urge to stand up and clap as hard as she could, but she restrained herself when she saw that she would have been the only one to do so. A minute or two later people started to get up and move toward the exits, except for the small circle that formed around the Buddhist teacher, who seemed happy to remain there and chat. Paula glanced over at Paco and was glad to see that he had finally broken his meditation.

"Would you like to meet Sensei?" he said, turning a pair of glittering eyes on her.

"Really?"

"I think we can manage a quick hello before she leaves."

She followed Paco to the front, where they slipped through the small gathering, most of whom seemed to smile at him in recognition. When Monja Coen saw him standing there she laughed.

"Ah, Paco, how nice to see you. And you've brought a friend."

"Sensei, this is Paula, my English teacher. She's new but she's quite serious about learning to meditate."

Coen grabbed Paula's hands and gave them an affectionate squeeze, her infectious smile and warm, tranquil eyes quickly overcoming whatever nervousness Paula felt.

"I am so glad to hear that. The world needs more meditators. Will you be attending our retreat this weekend?"

"I … ah … I didn't know about it until a couple of days ago," Paula said, stumbling over her words. "I'm afraid I have to work."

"Next time then. And if you are ever in São Paulo, come and meditate with us in the temple. We have a nice community there and you are more than welcome."

As they were headed for the door, Paco seemed impressed. "Sensei was very taken with you. I was surprised she invited you to the retreat—it's not a public program—but maybe I shouldn't have been. You obviously have some very good karma."

Paula wasn't so sure about her good karma, but she did set her alarm that night for six a.m., one hour before she usually got up on Saturday mornings to get ready for her nine-o'clock class. She was still groggy when she made it to the bathroom, but a cold shower brought her to her senses. Then she settled onto the edge of a cushion at the foot of her bed and crossed her legs, one in front of the other, as Monja Coen had instructed. "Spirituality is a discipline," Paco had said on the ride back, and the words had stuck with her. According to him (no doubt learned from his teacher), Zen could be boiled down to one fundamental practice: sitting in meditation, day after day, month after month, no excuses, no letup. She had read about the importance of regular practice but it hadn't really registered, perhaps because she had no fixed practice of her own, just suggestions from the many books she had read that she would try out for a few days or a week or two before moving on to the next technique that caught her fancy. Monja Coen had recommended half an hour minimum for zazen, preferably at the same time every day, and so she sat for half an hour, determined not to give in to the temptation to abandon her cushion in an attempt to flee from the specters of her inner struggles that assailed her the moment she sat down, as if they had been lying in ambush, waiting for this propitious opportunity to launch their attack.

Wherever her anger came from—and to that she could add her insecurities, her angst, her illusions and disillusions—they were just thoughts. They weren't her. The real her was sitting somewhere behind those thoughts, looking out on the universe within. She couldn't see the real her yet, the pure essence of her being. It wasn't as easy as looking in a mirror. But she knew it was there. Nor did she know if Monja Coen was the teacher she was now sure she needed if she were going to have any chance of achieving what Siddhartha had achieved, both the real one and the one in Hesse's novel. But she trusted her. Her words clearly didn't come from books, of that she was sure. They came from direct experience and the experience of a long line of teachers that stretched back to the Buddha. Her words had sounded within Paula like the gong of truth—she wasn't her anger, she wasn't her wounded sense of pride or her faltering self esteem; she was something far deeper and infinitely more real, looking out from the far shore of the ocean of consciousness, waiting to be discovered.

Paula decided to wait till the end of the week before she texted Fernando. Not much time for what she intended, but enough for what Coen Sensei had advised: to make the best use possible of the time she had. For herself, for Fernando, for all living beings. And that began on her meditation cushion, her true place of power. When she finished her zazen she did *gassho* once again to an empty room, knowing that the entire cosmos fit inside that room as it fit inside her hands.

7

PAULA TEXTED FERNANDO AFTER her Friday-morning zazen session, and she was disappointed when he texted back that he had plans that weekend. He suggested they meet up the following Friday and she had to make an effort to curb her impatience, taking solace in the thought that when they finally did hook up it would be an evening to remember. There was so much she wanted to tell him, from her remorse over her bad behavior to the excitement she felt over the wakeup call life had given her, the chance to drink from a brand-new cup, but the extra week would give her more time to prepare and she thought she could sense a willingness in him to come at things fresh after giving themselves space for due process—if that wasn't too much to read into the smiling emoji with sunglasses that ended his message. She had been meditating twice a day, everyday, since Monja Coen's talk, and the thirty-minute sessions were already having a noticeable effect on her mood. She felt more centered, more cognizant of her weaknesses and more confident that she was on her way to overcoming them. Nothing extraordinary but enough, she hoped, that he would not only notice but approve.

They agreed to meet up for an early dinner that Friday. He left it to her to pick the venue and she texted him the address of a fashionable vegan restaurant in Leblon that Paco had recommended as among the city's best, vegetarian or otherwise. Coen Sensei didn't come right out and say that her disciples should be vegetarian. She raised questions, challenging questions that made her students think, which was one of the things Paula most liked about her—there was no dogma involved. She was like zazen itself: no backing down from reality as you tried to see beyond the appearances to the truth hidden by the veil of the mind. But after watching a Youtube clip of the Buddhist nun talking about the ethical basis of vegetarianism, Paula decided that there was no reason for her to put it off any longer, despite Fernando's contentious remarks on the subject (which she was sure had more to do with her not asking his advice). She hoped he didn't see any ulterior motive in her choice of restaurant, but if he did, she would make sure he knew that she had no intentions of cramping his culinary style. She would go on cooking whatever he liked, whenever he liked, and they would continue to frequent his favorite restaurants, where there were always vegetarian options to choose from.

It was an awkward reunion at first. Fernando seemed a little out of sorts as they got a table and began looking over the menu. His usual air of self-confidence was absent and he seemed a little fidgety, which wasn't like him, but his discomfort was understandable, considering how they had left things two weeks earlier. She was a little on edge herself and it probably showed in equal measure. She would have liked to talk it out right from the get go, while they were waiting for their meal—she was sure that what she had to say would soon set them both at ease—but a crowded restaurant wasn't the place for a heartfelt confession. That would have to wait. In the meantime the conversation was pleasant enough after a hesitant start—her work, his patients, what their friends were up to. Nothing of any real consequence, no mention of Monja Coen or World of Warcraft, but it felt good just to be talking and her nervousness soon began to dissipate.

After the meal, which was every bit as exquisite as Paco had promised (the fact that it was vegan never came up), she suggested they go for a walk along the beach before they made a final decision on whether to take in a movie or see if they could get tickets for Fernanda Torres's one-woman adaptation of *The House of the Happy Buddhas* in Oi Casa Grande (from the review she had read, she was all in favor of *The Happy Buddhas*, the comedic sexual adventures of a sexagenarian from Bahia distilled into a ninety-minute monologue by the award-winning actress and scriptwriter, thinking that it might be a good way to rekindle their dormant eros).

It was still light out as they headed down Afrânio de Mello Franco to the water. It had been a particularly hot day, but the worst of it was over and a cooling breeze made the ocean walk particularly pleasant. They stopped for a cold coconut water at one of the kiosks that fronted the beach, and she took advantage of the idyllic setting to ease into the apology she had been rehearsing for the better part of two weeks, having distilled it down to the pure essence of what she had learned about herself in the interregnum, the good, the bad, and the ugly: her unresolved anger (which clearly had little to do with him); her penchant for being overly critical when she would have been better served by taking a good long look at herself; but also her willingness to change, her desire to make it up to him, her determination to use this latest setback as an opportunity to face her character flaws and become a better companion. The first step was recognizing what she had to work on, and thankfully she was already seeing progress. More importantly, she had the best of all possible incentives: she loved him and wanted nothing more than to be the best partner possible, the kind of partner he deserved. She would have liked to mention the role meditation had played in clearing her mind and enabling her to become more conscious of her "stuff," but that could come later, after he had come to appreciate the new and better Paula. No sense complicating things unnecessarily while they were still on slippery ground, especially when her apology went on longer than intended, not quite the distilled essence she had imagined but every word straight from the heart.

Fernando listened without interruption while he nursed his coconut water, but there was something vague and disquieting in his eyes that only became fully apparent to her when she finished her disquisition. Rather than being set at ease by her fervent confession and salutary assurances, he seemed even more tense than before. While she waited for some response, he confined his gaze almost entirely to the white plastic table, seemingly locked in a mortal struggle to organize his thoughts, and when he finally spoke there was a heaviness in his manner that was completely out of character.

"Thanks for sharing that, Paula. I always knew you had a good heart."

"It's how I feel, Nando. The god's honest truth. You deserve better from me and you're going to get it. You can rest easy on that account."

Only Fernando didn't look at all at ease.

"Are you okay?" she asked. "You're not coming down with something, are you?"

"No, it's not that. I guess I just wish this had come sooner."

"So do I. But I'm done beating myself up about it. You've got to learn from your mistakes and move on. What else can you do? What I do know for sure is that things are going to be better from here on out."

Once again Fernando lowered his gaze, as if the words he was searching for might be inscribed somewhere on the worn surface of their table.

"Does a couple of weeks really make that much difference?" she asked, after the silence had begun to make her uncomfortable.

"In this case, it makes every difference."

Paula felt a sudden clenching in the pit of her stomach, the first stirring of an old terror, coming at her from out of the darkness with its aura of unseen menace.

"I don't understand," she said, suddenly afraid that she did.

"I don't know how to say this, Paula, so I might as well just come right out and say it. I just want you to know, I didn't mean for it to happen. I know it sounds cliché but it's true. It just happened."

"What are you saying, Fernando?"

"I ah … I met somebody else."

Paula didn't register any conscious shock at first, perhaps because the deeper part of her was already in shock.

"Did you sleep with her?" she asked, barely aware of the tears welling in her eyes.

"Those aren't the words I would have chosen, but yes."

"You bastard," she said, her voice dropping to a whisper.

"I guess I deserve that."

"Really, Fernando? One fight and you go out and sleep with another woman? After all we've been through? How could you? I would have never cheated on you, no matter what."

"That's probably true. I don't deny it."

By now the sense of betrayal was so overpowering, Paula's tongue seemed to have swollen in her mouth as the anger and the pain came at her in waves.

There was a long pause before he broke the silence. "Are you going to say something?"

"Who is she?" she asked—not because she wanted to hear the answer but because it was the only thing she could think of to say.

"Janine. You've met her."

Paula drew a blank at first but that was followed by a sudden shock of recognition. "Do you mean Guilherme's cousin, the psychologist?"

Fernando nodded and the image that rose up in her mind confirmed her worst nightmare—sandy blond hair framing an attractive face dappled with freckles, the tanned, silky body of an Ipanema girl who had grown up on the beach, a paragliding enthusiast with a Ph.D. and a successful practice—in short, exactly the kind of girl that she had feared Fernando might one day leave her for, the deluxe model of the Girl from Ipanema, the one with brains.

"Wait a second. Isn't she in that dance class you've been taking Monday evenings. That's right, I remember seeing her that time I picked you up. I never understood why you wanted to take a dance class, you're such a wonderful dancer already. Now I get it. You were taking it together. So this has been going on for some time, hasn't it? Right behind my back."

"No, it hasn't. It's only been a week and a half. Okay, there was some chemistry there, I admit it, but I never let it go anywhere. And I never would have if things had been okay between us."

"So what are you saying? That it's my fault?"

"No, I'm not saying it's anybody's fault."

"That's funny, seeing as you're the one who was unfaithful."

"Look, I just meant that things haven't been right between us for a while now. We've been moving in different directions. You know that as well as I do. And that's nobody's fault."

"So that's it then? You hook up with Janine in your dance class and it's sayonara?"

"Look, I hate the way it happened. I feel like a shit, I really do. I wish I could have a do-over, but I can't. What's done is done. But if we are honest about it, this isn't really about Janine. Well it is … but it isn't, if you know what I mean. Hell, I don't know what I'm saying. I don't feel any better about this than you do, you know."

"I doubt that."

"Well it's true. I'm not proud of myself. I should have worked things out between us, one way or the other, before I even thought about looking at another woman. Although in this case she came after me. Anyhow, that's neither here nor there. What I mean is that I should have handled things better and I'm sorry about that. I know how much it hurts and that's on me. I've got to live with that. But at the same time we have to be realistic. We want different things out of life. And there's nothing wrong with that, I'm not saying there is. There just comes a point where it doesn't make much sense anymore to be together."

No, it didn't make much sense, but not in the way he meant. What didn't make sense was this sudden rupture tearing the ground from beneath her feet, the mind-numbing unfairness of it. This wasn't how it was supposed to be. This wasn't how it was supposed to end—if it had to end at all. Not when life was finally starting to make sense. They were supposed to be at the beginning of something, not the end, the beginning of something they had both been waiting for, a chance to finally make it to higher ground.

She mumbled something as Fernando voiced a few hoary platitudes—how much she meant to him, the memories he cherished, the hope that they would always be friends, not wanting to throw that away—but she had little notion of what she said, other than that her voice sounded to her as if it were coming from a tomb. Eventually he ran out of words and they sat in silence for a while, barely looking at each other. Dusk had settled in and a few stars had begun to glimmer in an unclouded sky, but the atmosphere felt oppressive, as if a summer storm hung over their heads.

"Are you okay, Paulinha?" he asked, breaking the silence.

What kind of a question was that? Worst of all was hearing him call her his "little Paula." That was the tipping point. The authentic and unwarranted intimacy that she just couldn't bear at that moment. "I'm sorry, Nando," she said, lifting her pocketbook to her shoulder. "I'm not feeling too well at the moment, as you might imagine. If you don't mind, I think I'm gonna go."

Fernando nodded. "So I guess there's no point in getting those theater tickets now."

Paula stared at him in disbelief, appalled by his lack of sensitivity. She shook her head and for a moment she actually felt a flash of pity, like a brief speck of blue amid a mass of low-hanging clouds. "Thank God we came in separate cars," she said. "Oh … no wonder you suggested it. You were already planning your ambush."

"C'mon. I wasn't thinking anything of the sort. There were things that had to be said, that's all. There still are, you know."

"I don't know what to say to that, Fernando."

"You don't have to say anything. We can leave it for some other time."

In truth, there were a thousand things she wanted to say, but none that were worth prolonging the agony. She got up without a parting hug, or even a parting glance, and started walking down the sidewalk, her legs so heavy she felt as if she were wading through fresh-poured concrete, the tears still wet on her cheeks. When she made it to the parking garage she sat in the car with her hands gripping the steering wheel for what must have been ten full minutes before she started the engine. Then another five before she put the car in gear and pulled out. Fifteen minutes in suspended animation while she watched her mind explode, hurtling through galaxies of rage and despair like a runaway comet.

She had never known this kind of betrayal before, just as she had never known the kind of closeness she and Fernando had enjoyed—which is precisely what made it so painful. The pain and the glory had stepped hand in hand into her life clothed in male flesh, each doing its best to convince her of its immortality and incorruptibility, and now there was nothing left but the shards of her shattered illusions.

Afterward she couldn't conjure up a single image from the drive home, only a blank reel of a mind cut loose from its moorings, which made her wonder how she made it back in one piece. Somehow she managed to sit on her cushion and feign meditation in the vain hope that it might help (it only made it worse), followed by an hour wrestling unsuccessfully with a book and another two trying to self-medicate with the soporific offerings of late-night television, only to finally achieve the dubious solace of a jumbled skein of ragged dreams, a dreamtime documentary spliced together from a series of disconnected disappointments. When she woke up for the last time with the clock inching toward noon (she had called in earlier to cancel her morning class), that sad tapestry seemed to be the final summation of her life.

8

IT DIDN'T TAKE LONG before the loneliness began to set in, taking up residence alongside the anger and the pain. Paula had been in Rio for eight years now, but other than Fernando she didn't have anyone she could pour her heart out to, no one whose door she could show up at unannounced for a good cry. She had made friends during college, fellow students with whom she had played role-playing games or piled into a car with to go to the movies or a concert or a party, but by and large she had lost touch with them in the two years she and Fernando had been together (a loss that at the time hadn't registered as anything more than a blip on the radar), and it only added to her depression to realize that the people she was closest to were Fernando's friends first and hers only by way of association. There was a time when she had shared nearly everything with her mother, but though they still talked on the phone, those days had receded to the edge of obsolescence, and her sister was too wrapped up in her own world, not that they had ever been that close. Her best and only truly close friend was her Fernandinho — had been her Fernandinho — and he was the one person she couldn't call. Not that she wasn't tempted. Despite the ongoing skirmishes in the battleground of her mind, there were occasional lulls when she fantasized about agreeing to a no-fly zone where they could put aside their feelings and be there for each other. Like some of the exes she had seen on-screen that had remained sounding boards for one another even in the midst of a difficult breakup, faithful barometers of the inclement weather that neither could understand without the other. She had even resorted to hiding her phone once in a kitchen cabinet to keep her from reaching for it during a late-night video session that she spent curled up in an empty bed watching *On a Clear Day You Can See Forever*, a 1970 Barbara Streisand movie about two star-crossed soulmates whom the wayward winds of destiny would blow apart, forcing them to wait until a future life before they could be together. She kept waiting for his text, waiting for him to call, rehearsing what she would say when he told her that Janine had been a mistake, that his flesh was weak but his spirit was growing stronger, that he would be a different man if she found it in her heart to take him back. An ever-expanding dialogue that reached its culmination on the two-week anniversary of his admission of infidelity, when she sat down at her laptop and wrote a three-page email that she had the prudence to trash before her mouse could reach the send button. And that was as close to perdition as she got until she received his text exactly twenty days into their mutual exile.

It was a Thursday evening and Paula was practicing meditation in her bedroom, another typical zazen session that consisted mostly of combative interchanges with her presumptive ex-boyfriend while simultaneously trying to distance herself from those imaginary dialogues. The phone was lying beside her meditation cushion and she was startled to see Fernando's name awash in a soft turquoise luminescence. Whatever thoughts were in her mind fled instantly but she resisted the impulse to reach for the phone. Instead she struggled on as best she could, her heart racing while her mind was dragged back and forth between excitement and dread, as if it were tied to two competing teams of horses, until the timer on her meditation app sounded, the ironically named "bliss timer." With a trepidatious sigh, as if she were in a courtroom and her sentence was about to be handed down, she did *gassho* and had Siri read out her most recent message.

"Just checking in. Hope u r ok. Don't forget, u will always have a special place in my heart."

Paula's breast swelled as hope came rushing in, but it receded just as quickly, as she recognized the unmistakable undercurrent of solicitous detachment in that faceless, toneless message. The words of an ex-lover who wants you to know that he is still your friend—forgetting that friends don't crush their friend's heart and then make out as if nothing had happened. No hard feelings, he seemed to be saying, almost as if he were standing next to her, mouthing the words while he patted her on the shoulder—eventually we'll laugh about this and be glad we're still friends. Maybe so, but she still had hard feelings, and painful ones as well, knowing that she had given the best two years of her life to a man who had thrown her over for a buffed and blond airhead who wouldn't threaten any of his comfortable, air-conditioned notions (admittedly, Janine was anything but an airhead, but the image gave her comfort).

It was at that moment that she was finally willing to accept that it was truly over, steeling herself for one last tidal wave of pain that never came. She was sure now that Janine hadn't been a dalliance. Or if she was, it had led him in a direction from which there was no return. They were ex-lovers now. It was time to turn the page.

She waited twenty-four hours to answer his text, doing her best to adopt the same I've-moved-on-but-still-care-about-you tone: "It's all cool. What's past is past. Wish u all the best." She still would have liked to talk to him—an exchange of text messages seemed like the cowardly way out—but she couldn't bring herself to dial his number. She was on her own now, and she couldn't help but feel as if all the gains she had made during the time they had been together had been summarily undone.

Paula had made two trips to The Bodhi Tree during those three weeks—the only times she had ventured beyond the confines of her apartment other than to go to work—and she spent the aftermath of Fernando's text message searching the newest additions to the stacks of books beside her bed for clues of where she might go next. She had bought several Hermann Hesse novels during her last visit, hoping for a reprise of *Siddhartha*, but the book she picked up that Friday evening and could not put down for the rest of the weekend, much of which she spent scrunched up on her couch with old bossa nova records playing in the background, was a stark and depressing departure from *Siddhartha*—and, as it turned out, exactly what she needed.

Harry Haller, the hero (or antihero) of *Steppenwolf*, was a man after her own heart   lonely, overly attached to his books, profoundly uncomfortable with the conformist, consumerist, bourgeois society in which he was seemingly trapped, and yet quietly dependent on its comforts, a man who had been cast aside by his wife, but who, despite his subsequent depression and his peculiar fascination with the idea of suicide as a viable means of escape, felt the call of a spiritual reality beyond time, beyond sorrow, beyond the petty setbacks of an unrealized life, and who heeded that call throughout the unfolding of the book with the help of Hermine and Pablo, a pair of unlikely mentors. Yes, he was a man and old enough to be her father, and the society he railed against had disappeared nearly a century earlier—what she knew of it came from novels, silent films and grade-school history books—but many of his thoughts seemed to be her very own, captured in print as in a mirror, and the lessons he learned in his journey appeared to be the very same that she would need if she was going to successfully make it out of the magic theater that she had unwittingly found herself in.

Laughter was the first of those lessons, the ability to see one's life as a piece of theater, to enjoy it for what it really was: a show, nothing more, nothing less, for which the price of admission was your so-called sanity. *For Madmen Only!* read the sign above the entrance to Hesse's magic theater, and Paula suspected that the long-dead Austrian with his straw hat and round, wire-rimmed glasses was cautioning her not to take herself so seriously, to remember that she was just an actress in a play, an actress who would play many different parts before her career was over — a thousand different souls in one body was how he put it — and that none of those different selves was her actual self. Harry Haller opened the story caught in a struggle between the wolf in him and the man, but by the time he left the magic theater at the end of the final act, he had realized that he was so many selves they could not be counted, an infinite number of Harrys appearing and disappearing in the theater's gigantic mirror, like so many pieces on a chessboard for him to position as he willed — and that behind them all was the mirror without which they could not exist, the Eternal Self in which all of life was reflected.

Twilight was encroaching at her window that Sunday when she finished the book. In that same instant she jumped off the sofa and started pacing the living room, rereading out loud the final lines with the book held out in front of her and her free hand motioning in the air like an old-time actor declaiming before a spellbound audience:

"I understood it all. I understood Pablo. I understood Mozart, and somewhere behind me I heard his ghastly laughter. I knew that all the hundred thousand pieces of life's game were in my pocket ... I would traverse not once more, but often, the hell of my inner being. One day I would be a better hand at the game. One day I would learn how to laugh. Pablo was waiting for me, and Mozart too."

That's it! she told herself. Her long-dead mentor's message driven home. Life not only didn't end with Fernando, it didn't end with death. It was a game she would keep on playing until she got it right, until the final veil fell away, revealing the Eternal. In the meantime, it was time to stop taking herself so seriously. She had recently been admitted to one region of her inner hell, and no doubt there were others in there somewhere, but it was time to move on, time to get ready for the next act. She was on a journey, and until she made it to nirvana the only way out was through. And just like that, she decided that her period of mourning was over. She put down the book, picked up her phone, and scrolled through her contacts until she found Paco's number. On the way back from Monja Coen's talk, he had invited her to the collective zazen program he attended Wednesday evenings in a yoga studio in Botafogo, organized by an eclectic coalition of Rio's Zen practitioners. The next act might as well begin by getting out of the apartment, and collective zazen seemed like the perfect opening scene.

Paco was waiting in the street in front of his loft when Paula pulled up. When he got into the car he handed her a card with a painting of a rotund Buddha sitting at the edge of a forest lake, his mirthful eyes looking up at the horizon while his equally mirthful reflection in the water seemed to be gazing back at him. The quote on the back read: *When you realize how perfect everything is, you will tilt your head back and laugh at the sky — Buddha.*" The synchronicity was startling. It had been weeks since Paula had laughed, and only days since she had decided that this was the first lesson she needed to put into practice. Harry Haller had Hermine to teach him how to dance and how to laugh. Paula didn't have anyone, now that Fernando was out of her life, and Paco didn't strike her as someone who laughed all that much, if at all, but maybe he could stand in for Hermine for the time being, at least for this first dance. Paco and whomever else her destiny chose to be her unlikely mentors.

The collective zazen was well attended, some forty participants of all ages, shapes, and sizes, sitting like miniature mountains on their cushions for two forty-minute sessions sandwiched around ten minutes of walking meditation during which they traced solemn circles around the hall with their eyes lowered, mindful of every step. Afterward Paco introduced her to some of his friends, co-disciples of Monja Coen, and the spiritual conversation that ensued with actual live human beings was like a revelation of what life could and should be. There was even a bit of humor and some light, rippling laughter that somehow got inside her and forced out a giggle or two, surprising her at how easy it was. And perhaps that was all she needed, just a crack to let some light in, because on the ride back, when Paco asked about her boyfriend and she told him what had happened, his reaction elicited her first full-bodied laugh in a very long time.

"The bastard," he said, his throaty baritone striking just the right chord. "Oh, sorry, it just slipped out."

That's when the laughter started rolling up inside her chest, erupting moments later like a dam bursting its gates. "That's okay," she said, when the floodwaters settled enough to return to her the use of her vocal chords. "If you only knew how many times I've thought the exact same thing these past few weeks. But without the laughter. Anyhow, I'm done with that."

"Good for you. And if you don't mind my saying so, I think you're better off. If he couldn't appreciate you, then it's his loss, not yours."

Paula laughed again, surprised at how good it felt after being so long out of practice.

That Saturday morning she made her now-habitual trip to The Bodhi Tree. The bookstore opened at ten and Paula arrived half an hour later, straight from her only class of the day. After asking the girl behind the register if Maya was in, she went to the small room at the back of the used bookstore that doubled as an office and consultation room. The door was open and through the curtain of beads that hung from the lintel she could see Maya sitting at her desk with her back to the door, sifting through some papers.

"Maya, *bom dia.*"

Maya swiveled in her chair and broke into a cheerful grin. "Paula, how nice to see you. Can I help you with anything?"

"I was wondering when you might have time for a consultation. I was able to get my time of birth from my birth certificate."

"Ah, so you want that reading we talked about? How does right now sound? I don't have anyone scheduled until twelve."

It was exactly what Paula had been hoping for. The closest she had gotten to an astrology reading was walking by a palmist's and stopping to look in the window, but ever since she'd learned that Maya offered astrological readings and spiritual counseling for a quite-reasonable 115 reals a session, it was more a question of when than if, and with her life having veered so far off course, now seemed like the perfect time.

Paula sat down on the love seat and looked around the small room while Maya printed out her birth chart. The decor was what she had come to expect of Maya: exotic but homely, with just the right amount of clutter. An easy chair opposite the love-seat, a bookshelf, her desk, some filing cabinets hand-painted with psychedelic flowers, and every inch of wall space covered with esoteric hangings, pictures, and paraphernalia.

With her chart in hand, Maya plunked herself down on the armchair and set her phone down to record the consultation so that Paula could listen to it later if the spirit moved her. Paula knew that Cancerians were known for having a nurturing nature; placed a lot of importance on the home, family life, and friendships; and could sometimes be moody — all of which were more or less apropos in her case — but her exploration of astrology hadn't progressed past a single turbulent summer in her early teens when she had religiously read her daily horoscope, hoping to find some sign that the storm clouds that were darkening her horizon would soon be lifting. When they finally did lift, there was no indication of it in her horoscope, and she soon dismissed her obsession as a juvenile grasping at imaginary straws. But Maya's reading had nothing in common with the overly general prognostications and seemingly random commonplaces that populated the truncated texts in the astrology section of *Correio Popular*. She began by explaining each of the exotic glyphs sprinkled across her natal chart — a confusing latticework of planets, quadrants, angles, points, and aspects that taken in their entirety were reputed to comprise a detailed map to the human psyche. A few months earlier Paula might have scoffed at such a claim, but as Maya interpreted each of the glyphs in her chart and their varied interrelationships, Paula began to feel as if she were present at a ceremonial unmasking of her inner landscape — every foible, every insecurity, every lacuna in her sense of self, every lesson that had planted itself in her path and demanded her attention, each of them rising from the map in lockstep and each a facet in a diamond that was tending toward perfection in what seemed to be a painfully circuitous manner. A map so clearly and meticulously traced that Paula felt as if she were privy to the shaping of her psyche. She was startled by the preternatural lucidity, by the unexpected appearance of character traits she had never paused to notice but which she recognized instantly the moment Maya pointed them out, their glyphs and position in her chart adding meaning that she might never have discovered on her own, without the symbolic language of the astrological arts. She had already begun to think of Maya as a surrogate shaman figure, mostly for the books she recommended, which for some uncanny reason always turned out to be exactly the books she needed, but also for the cryptic observations and suggestions that never failed to strike a chord inside her. But by the time the reading of her chart was nearing completion, Paula was looking at her with something more akin to awe. It was the art, she realized, that made the reading possible (by itself, a monumental realization), but the fact that it could be so skillfully interpreted by this apparently outlandish woman was a revelation that made her question her own powers of judgment.

"Your birth chart gives us the overall picture, but now let's have a look at what's going on in your life at this particular junction in time. I think I have a pretty good idea already but we'll see what the colors say."

"The colors?"

Maya smiled and pointed to the top shelves of the bookcase in which a hundred or more small bottles of different colored liquid were arrayed in a tasteful display.

"They belong to the Aura-Soma color system. What I'm going to have you do is select four of those bottles in order. Whichever colors attract you most, then the next most, and so on. That combination of colors will tell us a lot about the lessons you are working on right now; although from your chart and your aura, I would guess that in this particular phase in your life you are under the guidance of the bottle called 'Star Child,' which has a lot to do with working with your inner child. On the spiritual level, it symbolizes a new beginning, disillusionment followed by an integration of deeper aspects of the self. On the mental and emotional level it symbolizes the healing of destructive emotional patterns, especially those carried over since childhood. And on the physical level it heals burns and open wounds." Maya reached out and squeezed Paula's hand. "Correct me if I'm wrong, but I think you have one particular wound that is very much open right now."

Paula felt herself redden. She lowered her eyes to the carpet, with its circular representation of the zodiac, and nodded. "Can you read that in my chart?"

"No, not in your chart, my dear. In your face. I've been around too long not to recognize the signs."

"Is it that obvious?"

"It's not easy to hide these things. Not that there's any reason why you should."

Paula gave her a quick rundown of what she'd been going through, and Maya gave her hand another squeeze.

"I know how it is, my dear. I've been there. More than once. It does hurt."

"It does, but I'm getting over it. Trying to make a new beginning, like you said. That's why I thought it would be a good time to get a reading. I was hoping you could help me figure some things out. I know we're not done yet, but you've already given me a lot to think about."

"Well, if I might give you one more thing to think about before you choose your colors, there is an old Chinese proverb that marriage is debt. In other words, relationships are all about karma. How long were you and your boyfriend together?"

"About two years, give or take."

"I think that's long enough to qualify. The idea is that the reason we get into relationships, especially longterm relationships, is that we have some karma to serve with this particular person, or else we have some specific karmic to burn and they're the perfect person to provide us with that opportunity. But once that karma is finished then usually so is the relationship. Some last a year, some last a lifetime, some have to be carried over to a future life. If it really is over with Fernando, then it means you served the karma you had to serve and now you are free to move on to the next lesson. I don't know if this will make sense to you right now, but I actually find that comforting. We tend to place so much importance on how one particular person makes us feel—I know I do, though thankfully not nearly as much as I used to—but if it's true that life is a spiritual journey—and we both know it is—then each of these relationships, no matter how long they last or how they end, is just a stage on the journey. You can't stay in the same place forever; otherwise you'd never make it to your destination. And we can't have that, now can we? Of course, a good relationship can be really wonderful, and if it lasts a lifetime, then that's great. But really, what is a good relationship? In spiritual terms wouldn't it be that relationship that most helps you to grow?"

"Sure."

"Okay then. So let's celebrate our failures just as much as our successes. Or more—because they usually have more to teach us. There is a nice quote by Confucius that I really like: 'Our greatest glory is not in never failing, but in rising every time we fail.' It's that effort to rise up again that makes us grow. Now why don't we choose those colors. It's an especially useful way of gaining insight into the main theme of your life at this moment in time, and how your past *and* future relate to it. So don't be surprised if what you choose has something to do with romantic relationships."

Amazingly, the first bottle she picked out, a beautiful blue over pink, turned out to be B-20, Star Child. Paula looked at Maya in disbelief, but the older woman merely smiled and motioned for her to pick a second bottle, followed by a third and then a fourth, each of the two-toned bottles calling to her nearly as strongly as the first. After Maya explained the significance of each bottle and interpreted the meaning of the order in which she chose them, adding further revelations to what had already been an immensely insightful session, she took out a beamer light pen and applied colored beams of light, the same colors she had chosen, to specific acupuncture points so that the meridians could then transmit their healing energy to those bodily systems and organs that were out of balance. She taught Paula how to shake the bottle of Star Child and apply the herbal oil mixture in a band around her fourth and fifth chakras and gave her a detailed set of instructions on how to use those colors in her daily life, from the clothes she wore to the decor of her apartment. By the time Paula left Maya's consultation room — armed not only with her birth chart and a bottle of Star Child for daily applications, but also with an assortment of pomanders, quintessences, color essences, and archangeloi to help accelerate the transformation process, firm up her aura, and energize her personal space, all tucked into a cloth tote bag with the store's name and a golden Buddha on it — she was dizzy with information and mildly euphoric. Too giddy to drive home, she decided. Instead, she headed for the stacks to grab a book on astrology that Maya had recommended, a late-seventies classic called *Astrology, Karma & Transformation*. She then got herself a cup of herbal tea and plopped down on one of the easy chairs to begin processing her experience.

The tea helped. Her entire body was tingling, as if she had imbibed a potent effervescent elixir, but the combination of rose hips and chamomile helped to steady her senses and ground her in the moment. She could feel the Star-Child ointment glowing on her skin, between her breasts and around her neck, almost as if those two particular chakras were acting as cosmic transmitters, sending her individual energy out into the atmosphere to commingle with the energies of all the other living beings on this planet and beyond; and gradually, as she focused on that glow, she felt a sense of calm descend like a light mist from the sky. A new beginning. A soon-to-be flower breaking from the bud. Painful and glorious at the same time. She had come to the store that morning hoping for a renewed sense of direction, for some light to break through the dense, heavy mass of clouds that had obstructed her vision. An hour and a half later she was above those clouds, looking at the world from a vantage point she had never experienced before. A world that suddenly seemed very different than the one she had inhabited these past twenty-six years — for her previous lack of altitude, no doubt. She knew it was only temporary, as all things were, that she would come back to earth soon enough, but for now she was content to sit there and enjoy the feeling.

Karma & Transformation. She wasn't ready to open the book yet, but the title spoke volumes. She had reached the end of one stage in her journey, putting paid to whatever karma she and Fernando had been fated to work out together, and that implied transformation, getting ready to emerge from her chrysalis into yet another form. She still had no more idea of where she was going than when she'd walked in, but perhaps that was part of the lesson — to surrender to the process and let the divine hand guide her, as it had always been guiding her, despite her stubborn efforts to hold on to the wheel. To rise up from failure and be whatever she was supposed to be, whether butterfly or moth. Until she failed again so that she could undergo yet another transformation.

Satisfied with that thought, she closed her eyes and settled back into the easy chair, the unopened book face up on her lap with its beautiful pastel drawing of a multicolored butterfly spreading its wings.

9

ARLY FALL WAS PAULA'S favorite weather. Pleasantly warm during the day, pleasantly cool at night, and not too humid, unlike the spring. The most comfortable days of the year. She would have wished that her inner climate were as pleasant, but inner peace wasn't a matter of waiting on the weather. It took work, painstakingly hard work, but after Maya's consultation she was convinced that better days were ahead, even if the weather within was still uncomfortably choppy.

The following Saturday she saw a poster in the bookstore announcing the visit of a Sufi teacher, Sri Harimayi Devi. "You know, you were the first person I thought of when they asked me if they could put up the poster," Maya said, when she asked her about it. "I haven't met her but she teaches Sufi dancing, and I was thinking that might be exactly what you needed, something to put some color in your aura. Rumi says that whosoever knows the power of the dance dwells in God. He also says that dancing is when you tear your heart out of your chest and rise out of your body to hang between worlds. I always remember those lines when I think of Sufi dancing."

Paula still carried in her purse the first card Paco had given her with that gorgeous Rumi quote about being the ocean in a drop, though she had yet to explore his poems. But Maya had become an oracle for her and the oracle had spoken. As soon as their chat was over, she headed straight to aisle three where the Sufi poets were housed, and minutes later she settled into her favorite recliner with a cup of herbal tea and a pair of Rumi anthologies, *The Dance of the Soul* and *The Flute and the Moon*. It didn't take her long to recognize the Delphic prescience of Maya's words. The poetry was stunning, both lyrical and deeply mystical. Above all it was imbued with the language of love — divine love — and as she read she became aware of how thirsty she had become for the music of the heart. She admired the Zen tradition and owed much to her new-fledged practice, but there was something missing in her soul that Zen had left untouched and unrequited, and Rumi's words seemed to speak directly to those empty spaces. "This is love: to fly toward a secret sky, to cause a hundred veils to fall each moment. First, to let go of life. Finally, to take a step without feet." It seemed the essence of what she hungered after, the missing element in her inner alchemy, as if she had been waiting all her life for the poet to give it words. "Only from the heart can you touch the sky," Rumi had written, and she believed him because his words alone were enough for her heart to take flight. Fernando had lifted her up at times, higher than she had ever been before, but she knew now that her feet had barely left the ground. A few pages further on, she read that a thousand half-loves must be forsaken to take one whole heart home, and she recognized immediately the half-love that Fernando had been—through no fault of his own. She had been looking for the wrong love in the wrong places, and for that reason all her joys and sorrows had danced to the tune of half-loves, leaving her heart adrift with home no better than a distant shadow on the horizon.

Five days later she was standing outside the Aqualung Ecological Institute, looking up at Nossa Senhora da Glória do Outeiro, an eighteenth-century Catholic church set on a tree-shrouded hill that was widely considered one of the jewels of the city, part of a mulling crowd that was being held at bay by a white-robed usher. Eventually he opened the entrance doors and she followed the streaming crowd through the foyer and into a spacious hall. The lights in the hall had been dimmed and a ring of thick white candles with bright flames marked out the dance floor, where a circle of men and women in long white robes and conical hats sat facing the center of the candlelit orb with their eyes closed and their hands crossed over their hearts. At the center of the circle sat a woman in identical robes and headdress whom Paula could not take her eyes off of as she was funneled with the rest of the spectators to the open areas outside the circle. There had been a picture of Sri Harimayi Devi on the poster, wearing those same white robes and a loosely tied turban, a sturdy, smiling woman in her midforties with almond-shaped eyes and long wavy black hair who seemed to be staring into the camera from a secluded Middle Eastern hideaway, and Paula felt her excitement mount as she studied the Sufi teacher, who like her fellow dervishes appeared to be lost in an inward trance.

For several minutes the only sound was the murmuring of the spectators. By then Paula had become aware of a group of musicians seated

on a small stage at one end of the hall, silently fingering their instruments—harmonium, tambourine, tabla, and a long, end-blown bamboo
flute that she would later learn was called a *ney*. Suddenly, without any
signal or introduction, the tambourine player raised his instrument
and played a sustained shake roll. Moments later the flautist intoned
a deep, drawn-out note that stilled the remaining murmurs of the
crowd. The tabla and harmonium joined in next, and then the two
female singers, as the group, which the poster had listed as the Mevlana
Folkloric Orchestra, launched into a hymn written by Rumi in honor
of the prophet Mohammed. This was followed by the first in a series
of devotional chants during which the Sufi teacher, whom Paula had
not ceased to watch for a single moment, rose solemnly to her feet with
her hands still crossed over her heart and her robes brushing the floor.
The circle of dancers rose with her and started circling around her
counterclockwise with slow, measured steps, placing one invisible foot
forward after another in time to the music and pausing between each
step. A few minutes later, Harimayi Devi bowed deeply from the waist.
When she straightened she began turning slow circles with her right
foot as a pivot and the left stepping gracefully around it. Gradually she
unfolded her arms, opening them to either side as her pace quickened
and her skirt began to flare, revealing a pair of tight-fitting white pants
that reached to her bare feet. Then she raised her right hand and lowered
her left as her revolutions increased in speed, her head drooping to the
side with her eyes still closed, as if her gyrations had carried her out of
her body and into a nameless realm of divine forgetfulness. Moments
later the dervishes who encircled her came to a halt and began spinning
in place in identical fashion, one hand raised toward the heavens, the
other pointing toward the earth, spinning faster and faster until the
entire candlelit circle was filled with their gyrations, like a constellation
of celestial bodies spinning round a central sun.

Paula was mesmerized by the spectacle. As one song flowed into the
next, she found herself living vicariously through the dancers, felt herself
spin and soar, even as her body remained rooted in place, identifying so
deeply with the dervishes that their ritually induced inebriation became
her own. Never had she been in a theater or cinema hall that had evoked
such feelings, a sense of the cosmic mysteries being enacted before her
and through her, filling her with such a profound sense of connection
that the walls of the institute seemed to melt away, opening her up to
the universe beyond—and all of it, from the tiniest atom to the great

celestial bodies, spinning in tandem, drunk on the wine of motion and the music of love.

Nearly twenty minutes passed before the dancers slowly spun to a halt. After a short pause, Harimayi Devi placed her hands once again on her chest and bowed. Then she joined her palms together and lifted them to the sky, her neck arched, her eyes gazing upward. After a motionless pause, during which she seemed to be touching the heavens, she brought her folded palms to her chest and then lowered them to touch the earth before bringing them once again to her heart chakra, while Paula and the rest of the audience followed the other dervishes' example and returned her greeting.

Two more dances followed: one in which the dervishes formed two lines while Harimayi passed up and down, between them and around them; and the other, in which the dancers spun across the dance floor in seemingly random fashion with their eyes closed but without ever once colliding, an aleatory play of electrons, as it seemed to Paula, repelling and attracting each other according to some unknown law, a perfectly choreographed enactment of the subatomic universe at its most chaotic, though Paula was sure no choreography was involved. For what she could see, they had abandoned themselves to the vagaries of the dance, and the dance carried them safely home.

The hour-long performance ended with the same reaching toward the heavens and bowing toward the earth, after which the dervishes fanned out and picked up the candles, reprising the same solemn steps with which they had begun the evening. They brought the candles to the stage where they placed them in a glowing semicircle in front of Harimayi Devi's cushion. When everyone was settled, the Sufi teacher greeted the audience and began explaining the history and significance of the dervish dances they had just witnessed, a ritual known as *sama*. It had its origins, she explained, in a mystic trance that Rumi had experienced while listening to a goldsmith's hammer. Feeling as if he were a planet whirling around a divine sun, he began to spin; and ever since, the dervishes have whirled, paralleling with their movements the motions of the cosmos.

"The prophet Mohammed tells us that God said, 'I am a hidden treasure but I love to be known. For this reason I gave birth to the creation.' From this love and this need came the verb *kun*, 'be,' and also *irji*, 'return.' This is the origin of the longing of the creation for the Creator, the causal force that makes the planets and atoms and indeed the entire universe spin. This spinning is the ultimate expression of the love that penetrates and permeates the creation in its quest to return to the Beloved, who is its origin and its destiny.

"When a Sufi crosses her arms across her chest, she symbolizes the number one, for God, and when she spins she lets go of her ego and surrenders to the Divine. Her arms open, the right hand reaching for the sky to receive God's blessings, the left hand for Mother Earth, connecting her with the cradle of her birth. As her body sways, she forgets herself and becomes united with the Divine Lover. Her heart fills with passion and the dance becomes a dance of ecstasy. She becomes a vehicle for the Lord's love affair with the creation — for love is the only way to truly experience the beauty of this universe. By becoming free of herself, she is purified by love and sees only the Beloved wherever she turns. Therefore, say the Sufis, dance and know the freedom that only divine love can bring. Dive into the infinite ocean of God in search of himself. 'Wherever and whatever you are,' says Rumi, 'whether you are an infidel, an idolater, or a fire worshiper, even if you have broken your vows of repentance a hundred times, come. This is not the gate of despair, this is the gate of hope, the gate of love. Come, again and again, come. That is the only lesson: come.'"

Paula had never been much for dancing, but she liked to think that it was more for lack of opportunity than for lack of vocation. She had been to one high school dance, her sophomore year, a mortifying experience that began by waiting around for a boy to ask her to dance, an invitation that never came, and ended with her on the dance floor with some of her fellow wallflowers, only to discover that she apparently had no aptitude for the complicated steps of her native land. Even the nerdiest of her classmates could samba, but try as she might she could not. She had to wait eight years for her next real opportunity (other than dancing in the aisles at concerts and some self-conscious shimmying to techno-beats and rock numbers at the occasional college party), when she fell in love with Fernando and decided that having a real boyfriend for the first time in her life was worth the effort of taking a few lessons, enough for her to keep up with him at parties but not enough to elicit any enduring passion for the pastime. But when one of the singers stepped to the microphone at the end of the evening to announce a two-day workshop in Sufi dancing that weekend in the same venue, Paula was one of the first to sign up, and it didn't take her long to discover that dancing was as much a part of her as the yearning for God. By the time the weekend was over, Paula had learned a half-dozen ritual dances and spun enough to fly her like a top halfway across Brazil.

The overriding sensation she was left with when the workshop ended, apart from the vertigo that filled her senses like an exquisite champagne, was that she had spent her entire life trapped in a box — a box fashioned from other people's expectations, a box in which the love she had been looking for was not the love she had been taught to believe in. And yet somehow, over the course of those two days, she had spun herself out of the box — or if not all the way out, then at least far enough to realize that freedom lay on the other side. Sri Harimayi Devi — who had received her name from an Indian master and surprisingly turned out to be a Sephardic Jew by birth, born and raised in São Paulo — talked of love whenever the dancers paused to catch their breath. Love was the lifeblood of the dance, she bade them remember, but not any finite, niggardly love that wrapped its tentacles around your ankles, but an infinite divine love, deeper and wider than the ocean. The love that set the planets spinning in their orbits and made flowers bloom in their reaching for the sun. She talked of a life without limits, and the dancing made Paula feel as if that life were within reach — if she could only forget herself and surrender to the whirl of free spirits around a sun that neither rose nor set. Not only the dance of the dervishes, but the dance of the universe, the dance that was going on all around her in all its faultless glory, the eternal, lovestruck dance of the creation enamored of the Creator, drunk on the wine of the Beloved's boundless beauty. Paula had been practicing mindfulness almost since the day she first stepped into Maya's bookstore, but she had never felt more present than she did now, inside her spinning body. Never had she felt more aware of her place in the cosmos, a speck of living dust orbiting joyously around its Creator.

"A true Sufi is never idle," Harimayi said on one of those breaks, as they sat on the floor, breathing heavily and letting her words ease their tiredness like a soothing breeze. "She knows that love is service and service is love, and thus she serves the creation wherever and whenever she can, knowing that the one she serves is her Beloved in one or another of his myriad disguises." It was a refrain she kept coming back to throughout the weekend, the message sinking in a little deeper each time until Paula realized that it was a truth so obvious she couldn't understand how it could have passed her by. Two sides of the same coin, which was perhaps why her pockets had always been empty. Love had always been a feeling, too tenuous to hold on to for long, too exhilarating to do anything but run after it when it was gone. She had never thought of love as a verb, as a call to action that by its very nature took one beyond the purview of the ego, the kind of action whose fragrance was the feeling she found so enticing but whose roots were an unshakable commitment to the welfare of others. She had longed for love and looked for it in a thousand futile places, instead of the one place she should have been looking all along: in the wellsprings of her very own actions.

During the closing ceremony, Sri Harimayi gave a short talk and concluded by saying, "Every day the Beloved appears before us in a thousand different forms, waiting for our embrace. So let us embrace him by serving each of those forms in whatever way we can. It may be something as simple as a smile for a person you pass on the street, or something as huge as what our sister Sara is doing"—she reached out and squeezed the hand of one of her assistants—"running a Sufi hospice for the terminally ill in North Rio. Either way, it is the same dance, hand in hand with the Beloved. Until we lose ourselves and the two become one."

The program ended with the students lining up for a parting hug from the Sufi teacher. Paula was near the end of the line, and as it snaked forward she felt her words stirring something deep inside her that had long been left unattended, an empty space that was too large to be filled by meditation alone. The feeling became even more pronounced when her turn came and she was swallowed up by Harimayi Devi in a motherly bear hug. It was an embrace she could have prolonged for ages, and when the smiling Sufi finally let her go and gave her her blessing, Paula was filled with the conviction that she had to give something in return, that the glow in that marvelous woman's eyes as she held Paula's gaze before turning to the next person in line was itself a call to action. Moments later she sought out Sara and asked her if she could visit her at the hospice, that perhaps there was some small way she could help. "I'd be delighted," Sara said as she handed Paula her card, and the warmth in her voice was all the confirmation Paula needed that this was the next step in her journey.

10

"ᴅᴇᴀᴛʜ ɪꜱ ᴏᴜʀ ᴡᴇᴅᴅɪɴɢ with eternity."

Paula was taken aback when she saw those words blazoned above the entrance doors to Sacred Heart Hospice, a sprawling two-story house in the Vila Isabela neighborhood of North Rio. As words of spiritual wisdom, she could appreciate their beauty, but to be the first thing she saw upon entering the hospice was disconcerting, and she could only imagine how a patient or their family members might feel. Death was coming for her, as it was coming for everyone, but acknowledging that inescapable fact and welcoming it were two entirely different matters.

Her visit began with a volunteer leading her to Sara's second-floor office where a silk banner on the back wall carried another Rumi quote: "I died as a mineral and became a plant, I died as a plant and rose to animal, I died as an animal and I was man. Why should I fear? When was I less by dying?" Below the banner, Sara was typing away in front of a computer monitor, but when she saw Paula she sprang to her feet and gave her guest a kiss on each cheek and a welcoming hug.

Sara was a tall, attractive brunette in her early forties who seemed equally at home and nearly as exotic in slacks and a blouse as she had in her Sufi robes and conical hat. "I was so glad you said you wanted to visit," she said. "It's always special when our residents get to see a new face, especially someone as young and as full of life as you. It helps them appreciate the beauty of the world they'll soon be leaving. Here, let's have a cup of tea, and afterward I'll take you around to meet them. You'll see what I mean."

The world they'll soon be leaving? Like the banner on the wall, Sara's words seemed almost unfeeling, considering the circumstances, and in no way indicative of the warmth she felt from the woman sitting across the desk from her, sipping a cup of cinnamon mint tea. Did she talk to her patients in that same way, she wondered, reminding them of their impending death as the sign above her head and the one above the entrance doors did? Of course, Sufis believed that death was not a finality but a gateway in a journey to a higher life, but Paula doubted that many, if any, of Sara's patients were Sufi, and even if they were, death was still a terrible thing to face, no matter how profound or beautiful her words.

Paula shifted uneasily in her chair as Sara began telling the story of how she got into palliative care, nearly two decades earlier, when she went to England to continue her medical studies and ended up working at St. Christopher's alongside Dame Cicely Saunders, the woman credited with popularizing the hospice movement throughout much of the world, including Brazil, which had been embarrassingly late to recognize the need for it (though that was rapidly changing). What had drawn Sara to the field as a young woman was the emotional and spiritual focus of hospice care, in which compassion was the principal methodology, and she credited her hospice work with eventually leading her to the Sufi path. It was then that Paula gave voice to her discomfort.

"If you don't mind me asking, I'm a little puzzled by that sign when you come in, death is our wedding with eternity. To be honest, it kind of threw me for a moment. If I were dying, I don't think I'd like to be reminded of it. Isn't that just a little morbid?"

"Would you have us pretend?" Sara said, looking surprised, but her words were quickly followed by a smile. "My dear, they know perfectly well they're dying. It's not something they can forget. Nor should they. There's nothing morbid in that. It can be frightening, of course, but while fear is natural, it's not healthy. *Especially* when a person is approaching their death. For the terminally ill, fear is the great enemy. In fact, the only enemy. Granted, the pain can be terrible at times—most of our residents have one form of cancer or another—but pain can be managed. That's something you learn when you study palliative care: how to manage the pain, how to make them as comfortable as you can in their last days—without clouding their consciousness, as far as humanly possible. But how they deal with their fear is what makes all the difference. If you can't overcome your fear, or at least learn to live with it, comfortably and authentically, then it will poison your last days on earth. We don't want that. No one does. And you don't overcome fear by closing your eyes to it. Quite the contrary. That's the one sure way to keep it alive. And we're not in the business of doing that. We're here to help them through what will be the most important, most transformative period of their life—and make no mistake about it, there is nothing that helps a human being grow faster, or become more truly and honestly human, than being faced with the prospect of their own death—and fear will only get in the way. Life is and should be a celebration, and at no point more so than when you reach the end of that life. They have a whole life to celebrate, a whole life to be grateful for. Think of it: a lifetime of unique memories, unique encounters, unique challenges, a lifetime of beauty that they've had the privilege to experience in a way that no other human being has ever experienced. That's worth celebrating. It's worth saying goodbye to properly, from the heart, and you can't do that if your consciousness is clouded by fear.

"At the same time, they need to prepare themselves for what's coming next. Death is not the final curtain; it's a transition to a new beginning, and like any journey it's best to be prepared. Sure, it can be frightening, we all know that, but that's just one face of the unknown, one among many. Death has many faces, and the more you open your heart to God the more you realize that most of them are beautiful beyond measure. Rumi says that we should die happily and look forward to taking up a new and better form. The sun must set in the west before it can rise in the east. I want them to die happy. I want them to open their hearts and embrace their death. It's a great challenge—absolutely—but only by accepting that challenge can they succeed. And the same goes for us. For me, for my staff, for all the volunteers who work with us. We're helping to prepare them for their passage, but we are also helping ourselves, because really, the only difference between them and us is chronology. And believe me, no one knows this better than our residents. They know that tomorrow or the next day we are going to be occupying their beds. That's why I always tell my staff—they are helping us just as much or more than we are helping them.

"But doing is so much better than talking. What do you say we go around and I introduce you to some of our residents? The proof is in the pudding, as they like to say in England."

It was a lot to process, but whatever trepidations Paula felt about making death a welcome guest, they fell away in the course of an afternoon with Sara and her staff. She met all twenty-four of the current residents—Sara avoided the word "patients"; they were residents and this was their home. She and her staff, along with the volunteers and relatives, were part of an extended family whose main work was not just to make the residents comfortable but to share with them the love and support and admiration that was the bedrock of any healthy family. And along the way to allow wisdom to enter on its own, whenever it chose to make an appearance.

Paula sat by their bedside and joined in the conversations and the games, and even sang a few songs with the same voice Fernando had derided as being out of tune but which everyone in the hospice seemed to find perfectly tuneful, and afterward, when she reflected on her experience, she was hard pressed to remember an afternoon filled with such a perfect mix of laughter and of tears. She felt uncomfortable at the beginning whenever the conversation turned to death — or to their "passage," as they termed it — but by the time the afternoon was drawing to a close, she noticed, quite surprisingly, that the specter of death no longer had the same sting it had when she first passed through the hospice doors.

Her visit ended with a short seminar for relatives and friends in a small conference room on the ground floor, one in a series of ongoing classes that Sara encouraged all the residents' visitors to attend whenever they could find the time. It lasted forty-five minutes and for Paula it could as well have been entitled "A Seminar in Practical Spirituality." During her talk Sara emphasized that the best gift anyone could give their loved ones in this last phase of their life was the gift of a tranquil and loving heart, and she thus encouraged them to help the staff and volunteers make the atmosphere of Sacred Heart a peaceful and joyous one in which to celebrate their loved ones' lives and wish them well on their continued journey. To that end, she talked about how to deal with their own emotions more than anything else, how to find peace and meaning in a transition that was as natural as childbirth and just as sacred. The seminar ended with a guided meditation in which they visualized themselves radiating peace, love, and faith in the unerring hand of the Divine to those who would soon be leaving them.

When Paula said goodbye to Sara a short while later and headed for her car, she felt as if she were spinning, as if she had been spinning all afternoon, surrendering her ego to the Beloved with her eyes closed and her body whirling through space. Somewhere along the way she had stopped thinking and had started simply being, letting the current carry her along as she followed Sara from one encounter to another. "Love is service and service is love," Harimayi Devi had said, and those were exactly the right words for what she experienced that afternoon. The missing part of her heart, waiting patiently for her in the most unlikely of places, in a home for the terminally ill, under the guidance of a woman who had begun their acquaintance by teaching her how to dance.

11

The hospice looked out on Troubadour Park, and Paula was taking a long walk through the park after her shift, something she had made a habit of doing after she started volunteering. It was a chance to let the experience of working with the terminally ill penetrate a little deeper before the distractions of ordinary life returned to claim her attention, a buffer zone between a world that looked out on the unknown with courage and dignity and one that barely looked anywhere at all, so preoccupied did it seem with the trivialities of daily life. She had had many important moments in this park over these past two months: thunderclaps of inspiration that stopped her in her tracks, flashes of insight that lit up her interior landscape with a clarity that seemed otherworldly, even short stretches of calm that surpassed anything she had achieved in meditation. On this particular day in early June she found herself humming the tune to Gonzaguinha's "O Que É, O Que É?", which for some reason had been spinning around and around in her head all afternoon. She stopped under an ornamental palm by the edge of the cement pond, mildly surprised at how good she felt, and quietly sang the opening verse:

> I stand by the purity of the children's answer:
> That it's life, and life is beautiful, so beautiful.
> To live and not be ashamed to be happy
> To sing and sing and sing
> Of the beauty of being an eternal apprentice
> I know that life can be better and it will,
> But that doesn't stop me from repeating:
> It's beautiful, it's beautiful, it's beautiful.

It was overcast and chilly but the park was full of laughing children as they played on the swings and slides and performed acrobatics on the skateboard ramp, and it might well have been a scene very much like this one that had inspired Gonzaguinha to write his famous anthem. A leaden sky that some would call dreary, a winter chill creeping in under the denim jacket that rarely made it out of her closet. But the children didn't seemed to notice. They were too absorbed in their merriment, too intent on their escapades to impose the kind of demands on nature that adults were wont to make: a clear, sunny sky in winter and a canopy of clouds in summer, when the Rio sun was officially downgraded from pleasant to brutal. As if the beauty of nature was somehow dependent on the comfort of human beings. Paula shook her head and laughed before taking a seat on a park bench — as much at herself as at the rest of the human race, for she had done her share of railing at the weather, and not that long ago. In her case, she had been so up and down these past few years that she would have happily blamed it on the weather, if that wasn't so patently absurd. But something was changing. The inclemency was passing, and the calm sense of well-being that had snuck up on her unnoticed at the close of this chilly June afternoon was proof of that. Part of it, she knew, could be directly traced to her experiences at Sacred Heart. It was getting increasingly difficult to feel sorry for herself in face of the reality check that confronted her every time she passed under Rumi's words and entered the facility to spend a few precious hours supporting those brave souls who were consciously getting ready to say goodbye to the only life they knew. Precious, because so few hours were left to them and so they did everything in their power to make those hours count. And while she was with them, she had no choice but to do the same. For a few hours each Wednesday and Saturday afternoon her own life slipped into the background, so far into the background as to practically disappear from sight, and when the day drew to a close and she stepped back into the life she had temporarily left behind, those few hours of absence felt like welcome breathing room in an oppressively congested world.

Life was still confusing and complicated. It was still an emotional roller coaster that sometimes left her dizzy, but maybe the clouds didn't need to pass just yet for the beauty to start shining through. Maybe it was enough to spend a few hours helping others to know that love and beauty could be found in the most unexpected places — as for instance, on a park bench where a nondescript girl was content to watch the children at their games, despite the random drops from a darkening sky that had begun to wet her eyelashes. She zipped up her jacket a little tighter and let her mind skip along with the music, feeling like a star child herself, playing in the incipient rain:

> Some say that life is worth nothing in this world,
> That it is a mere drop, a moment, a passing second,
> While others say that it is a profound divine mystery,
> The love-filled breath of the Creator.
> The questions keep spinning in our heads
> Until we become dizzy,
> But I stand by the purity of the child's answer:
> It's life, and life is beautiful, it's beautiful, it's beautiful.

An image popped into her mind and she laughed, blinking back what was either a tear or a drop of rain: the last time she had accompanied Paco to the Zen satsang, two weeks earlier, going straight from the hospice to Copacabana to pick him up outside his apartment. They had argued on the way to Botafogo, and it seemed to her as if they had been characters in a medieval morality play, she playing the part of the heart and he the head. She had begun devouring biographies of yogic gurus and Sufi saints—*Miracle of Love, The Message in Our Time, Death Must Die, Living with the Himalayan Masters*—becoming enamored of the lives of these spiritual teachers, and she found herself wondering aloud in the car why the Zen tradition never spoke of devotion to God or service to the creation as royal paths to supreme realization.

"There's a night and day difference between emotion and devotion, my dear," Paco said, with a knowing glance. "It's the difference between ignorance and knowledge. Real devotion isn't emotional. It's being devoted to the path, to the teachings, to the teacher. To the sangha, the dharma, the Buddha. Anything else is a distraction. Whatever waves arise in the mind, no matter how enticing, let them go. Let it all settle until the pure Buddha mind shines in its own light. In the end, it all comes down to meditation."

But it didn't all come down to meditation. At least that's what she argued. The heart was just as important as the head. If the heart was like a desert, what was the point? Life was too precious not to embrace it in all its dizzying glory. And back and forth they went, right up until the moment they entered the zendo doors. She could laugh about it now, but at the time she had spent the first zazen session pitying Paco's girlfriend, should he ever find one, and the second berating herself for being so unkind, considering that he had introduced her to Coen Sensei and Zen practice in the first place.

But she hadn't changed her mind. Meditation was an exercise. It wasn't a replacement for life but a tool to help her face it. And for once this wasn't something she had read in a book. It was something she had discovered on her own. She enjoyed her zazen practice, difficult as it was—she certainly wasn't about to give it up—and she loved the Zen teachings and the Monja Coen videos she sat through at least once a week. But her one weekend of Sufi dancing and her hours at the hospice had made her realize that as valuable as the Zen experience had been, it wasn't her chosen path. She wanted to dance, she wanted to sing, and she wanted to serve, and it was becoming increasingly clear that this growing predilection was pointing her down a different road.

For a while she entertained the possibility that Sufism might be the path that destiny had chosen for her. She loved the celebratory acknowledgment of life in all its diversity. She loved the music and the dance, and several times a week she would put on a Sufi CD and a white skirt and blouse and spin in the solitude of her apartment, doing her best to recapture the magic of that one weekend with Sri Harimayi Devi; and whenever she heard similar music in the hospice, she could feel herself spinning unnoticed as she sat with the residents and journeyed through their world. She loved Sufi poetry and the Sufi stories—so different from the Zen stories she so enjoyed but just as fascinating and just as profound. But she had grown used to the hard work of taming the mind through meditation, that diamond-edged inner exploration that sought to lay bare the innermost secrets of the human self through mental discipline and deep introspection and which seemed to be almost entirely absent from the Sufi tradition. As was the intricate philosophical framework that she was still groping to decipher but which had begun to ignite a smoldering passion in her for esoteric knowledge.

If she had her way, she would have liked to fuse the two—the cool, nonverbal introspection of Zen with the flamboyant dance of the dervishes and their emphasis on serving the creation—and then add one further ingredient: the strong spice of social activism. The world was going to hell in a hand basket, as her mother used to say during her teenage years in those warm moments when they switched to English as a special feature of their mother-daughter bond (her mother was also an

English teacher who had preceded her to the States by twenty-five years for her own exchange year abroad). Like most college students, Paula became politicized when she arrived in Rio, a preoccupation that only grew more acute during her year at Berkeley, as she became increasingly aware of the multitudinous threats that menaced her future, from the destruction of the Amazon and the inevitable ecological disaster that was forming in its wake to the rampant corruption among Brazil's politicians that had recently led to the impeachment of its president, a political furor championed by powerful right-wing politicians who were themselves under fire for graft and corruption. She had been a leftist, a fan of the worker's party and of Lula, but once she started meditating she became convinced that neither the left nor the right were fit to govern her country—or any other country, for that matter. Buddha had preached the middle path, and it seemed to her that until the world was governed by serious meditators who walked that middle path in a conscious effort to go beyond the ego, people would continue to suffer at the hands of vested interests. Social activism wasn't a part of any spiritual tradition she had come across—perhaps because politics was a drug that few could handle without it swelling their ego, and the gurus were prudent enough not to complicate things for their disciples—but Paula was confident she could add it on her own without it going to her head. First, however, she had to find her path and that wasn't proving easy. Maya was an eclectic and she admired Maya no end, but eclecticism wasn't for her. She needed one road, not many; one teacher who could see her past the pitfalls that were sure to be looming up ahead. The question was how to find one. And how to know it when she did.

The books she had been reading lately were filled with stories, both miraculous and mundane, of disciples who had found their guru, and what they all had in common was the sense of coming home, the feeling of having waited all their lives for this one moment, the moment when the master appeared and everything finally fell into place. The moment when all doubts were removed and the journey began in earnest. Each tradition was the same in that respect, whether Buddhist, Sufi, or Hindu, but lately she felt drawn to the yogic path—swayed, no doubt, by the astonishing powers and magnetic personalities of the gurus that populated the pages of her books. It seemed the closest thing to the blending she was looking for: advanced meditation techniques, a profound philosophy, an emphasis on service, a tradition of devotional singing, even a bit of dancing. They didn't spin but they did sway, and that seemed good enough for her.

One month earlier, Maya had caught her skimming through the section on Hindu gurus and told her about a popular Brazilian teacher, Prem Baba, who taught the Hindu path with a Brazilian flair. Paula had felt an immediate tremor of anticipation. Could he be the one, she thought? An authentic Hindu guru born and raised in Brazil? She practically ran home, where she fired up the computer and went straight to his website, marveling at the story it told of how an unknown guru had spoken to him in a vision, calling him to India at the age of thirty-three. That was the evening of Prem Baba videos. It began with Prem welcoming her to his Youtube channel with a São Paulo accent—a curious departure from the thick Indian accent of the Hindu teachers she had hitherto found on Youtube. But he certainly looked the part. A face that could have easily been Indian. The long white beard and flowing locks. A captivating smile and calm voice that seemed to spring from a tranquil inner fount. But when she lay down on her bed after three hours of listening to the now-familiar teachings, she knew he wasn't the one. She didn't know how she knew, but she knew, and the surety she felt was accompanied by a profound sense of disappointment. She wanted so badly to find a teacher, her teacher, the one all her books had promised. "When the disciple is ready the guru will come," went the famous refrain, and all she could think about that night, as sleep eluded her, was how long it would be before she was ready.

She was feeling better about herself now, but the sensation that she was cooling her heels outside the entrance doors, waiting to gain admission to the main event, hadn't gone away. If anything, it had become stronger and more persistent. It was there behind the ups and downs, the enduring conviction that the reason she was alive would not become clear until she found her teacher.

The scattered drops had turned to a steady drizzle and Paula looked up from her reverie to see that the park was almost deserted. A few parents were gathering up their children and twilight had appeared out of nowhere to dapple the world with shadow. She couldn't ignore the cold now, penetrating under her jacket, and her face and hair were slick with moisture. She bounced up and started walking briskly toward her car, realizing with a sliver of apprehension that a deserted park after the sun went down was no place for an unaccompanied woman in Rio, even in a relatively safe neighborhood like Vila Isabel.

Two weeks later, Paula decided that a strenuous trek might be a good way to discharge some of her mounting frustration. She still had no clear sense of what she was meant to do with this life, other than remain patient until the universe saw fit to show her the path, but she did know what she wanted to do with her Sunday morning. She looked out the window of her apartment and then at the forecast on her phone: sunny and clear, with an expected high of 25°C—after several chilly, sunless days when the noontime temperatures hadn't broken twenty. The perfect day for what she had in mind. She slipped a letter pad into her backpack along with a windbreaker, some light climbing gear, and an umbrella, just in case the meteorologist was not in fact omniscient, and then she was out the door in her new hiking boots, headed for Sugarloaf and the two-hour trek up the face of the mountain.

She left the car at Red Beach and walked for a couple of kilometers along a shaded footpath until she found the narrow trail that Fernando had shown her a few weeks after they first met. It had been a while since she had made that hike, either up or down the mountain—not since Fernando had left her—and for a moment the mere sight of the trail brought back a flood of unsettling memories. Strange, after all this time, that those emotions could still get the better of her, despite her firm belief that he was safely in the rearview mirror. She shrugged it off as best she could and started clambering up the rocks, and the exertion was enough to bring her scudding back into the present. There was one twenty-meter section where she had to use her climbing gear, but she managed it now as she had managed it then, this time without Fernando's help, and thereafter the trail turned into a normal hiking path, a little steep at times but nothing out of the ordinary for a woman two weeks from her twenty-seventh birthday, with good hiking boots and a healthy pair of lungs.

When she got to the top she found an empty table near one of the telescopes that looked out over Guanabara Bay. She hadn't beaten the tourists entirely but they were few at this hour, and she took some time to catch her breath and nibble on the fruit and cheese she had brought for breakfast. Afterward she spent some minutes admiring the view through the lens of the telescope before she sat back down, drew out her pad, and began writing the letter she had come to write, glancing up now and then to draw inspiration from the sparkling blue waters and receding horizon that never ceased to enthrall her whenever she made it to Sugarloaf.

Dear God,

I know you are out there somewhere, hidden behind or within all this astonishing beauty that I am sometimes fortunate enough or quiet enough to be able to appreciate. I know you are hidden inside me as well, as I look out over the bay and write this letter. Or rather, I have faith that this is true, since I have yet to hear your voice or feel your unmistakable presence in my heart. If it is true that you reside within me, as all your saints and spiritual masters have confirmed, then you know why I am here and what I have to say. But I will say it nonetheless: I want to find you, to see you, to feel your presence within and around me. I want to know that you are mine and I am yours, that you are my own true self, the one I have been searching for since before I came into this world. I know it will take time, that it is not a question of a day or a month or a year. I know it will take all my effort and perhaps all my tears. I am ready for that. But how can I find you if you don't show me the path — my path, the one I am destined to walk? How can I find you if I cannot see the road up ahead? Please, enough of these veiled signs that I am too illiterate or too blind to read. No more signs at all, I beg of you. Please send me a teacher who can point out the way. I will do the rest, I promise. No matter how much effort it takes, no matter how many tears I cry, I will do what you ask of me, I give you my word. So I beg you once again, Lord, with all my heart: please show me the path that you have chosen for me in this life. It is all I want: a fighting chance to make the journey back to you.

Your devoted and loving daughter,
Paula

All that was left now was to complete the ritual that had come to her during meditation two days earlier. She took the letter and folded it with meticulous care into a paper airplane, as she had done so many times as a child when she had taken pride in how aerodynamic her paper airplanes were, almost like miniature kites. The sun was arcing toward its zenith in a nearly cloudless sky and an intermittent breeze was blowing out toward the bay. She closed her eyes and said a prayer of her own devising. Then she drew back her arm and let her prayer fly in the form of an airborne letter. It glided out toward the water and then a gust of wind lifted it in the direction of the sun. Paula watched its flight until it seemed to disappear in the sun's radiance. She closed her eyes then and imagined the Lord of Light gathering her heart's desire into his waiting arms. When she opened her eyes a minute or two later the airborne letter was nowhere to be seen. Her head told her that it had likely fluttered down to the ragged mountainside, caught somewhere in the tangled brush, but her heart told her that it had reached its destination. And she was going with her heart.

PART TWO

THE WORLD IS MY MISTRESS

1

HE NEXT MORNING PAULA drove into Botafogo, where twice a week she taught a pair of morning classes in a small private college. Afterward she stopped by the student union for a glass of fresh-squeezed orange juice, and as she was leaving she noticed a poster on the bulletin board with a picture of a monk in a bright orange turban and tunic. Above his head in bold print it read: *Change Yourself; Change the World*. She stopped for a closer look, drawn not only by the caption but by the look on the monk's face. Rather than staring into the camera, he was looking off into the distance with an air of tranquil absorption, the look of a young Western yogi (he couldn't have been more than forty) who is sure of his path and confident that he will soon reach his fabled destination. The mystical bent of his gaze contrasted with the title of the talk he was due to give that night in the college, and that intrigued her. The two things she wanted most in life given equal weight, as in the motto at the bottom of the poster: *Tantra Yoga — Self-Realization and Service to Humanity*. She couldn't help but remember her letter and its ritual flight over Guanabara Bay, but she had no illusions on that account. She had been through too many struggles during her short time on the spiritual path to think that finding her teacher would be as simple as posting a letter on the cosmic airways. It's just a lecture, she told herself, yet another among the many she had attended during these months of spiritual searching. But at the same time she had been feeling drawn to the yogic path and it seemed, at the very least, that this would be a step in that direction. If it turned out to be anything more … well, she would find out soon enough.

It was five minutes to seven when she found the hall, a large oval-shaped classroom laid out like a small auditorium, with a dozen ascending rows of cushioned chairs curving in a half moon and a podium at the front with a large projection screen and a lectern flanked on either side by a table and chairs. Behind one of those tables, the monk in the poster was conversing quietly with a young man and woman. Paula found an empty seat in the third row, and shortly after seven the young man went up to the lectern and fiddled with some unseen controls until the screen lit up with a picture of several hundred people meditating in a public square in what looked to be London. He sat back down and the monk stepped up to the lectern and addressed the audience in American English while the girl at the table translated for him with a microphone in her hand.

"My spiritual master once said that we have yet to create a human society worthy of the name. In Sanskrit, the word for society is *samaj*, which means 'to move together toward a common goal.' I think all of us, with a little reflection, can agree that the global society in which we live, a society that wherever we turn is rife with violence, exploitation, and intolerance, has yet to learn how to move together toward a common goal, which for now let us call human happiness or human welfare. My name is Dada Kamaleshvarananda, and I am a tantric yogi and a social activist, and this evening I am going to talk to you about what we need to do to create a true *samaj*, a human society worthy of the name, capable of providing an environment for everyone on this planet in which they can maximize their human potential and achieve true and lasting happiness, and why that change has to start with us. Why, as the popular saying goes, we must be the change we seek."

It took a few minutes for Paula to get past her annoyance at the lacunas in the translation, and she had to restrain herself more than once from blurting out the right word when the translator hesitated or got it wrong. But soon she was so caught up in his talk that she forgot her initial annoyance—so much so that after a while she was actually glad for the translator's lack of fluidity because it gave her time to process his ideas and even take some notes, though by then she had already turned on the voice recorder on her phone. If need be, she could always edit out the translation later.

He started out by talking about social injustice on a global scale in an assertive tone that carried echoes of Arundhati Roy and other well-known activists whose talks she had listened to on Youtube during her college days, but less histrionic, without the overt indignation that always seemed to fuel those speakers and which had fueled her as well, inspired by their example. Unlike them, however, he traced this state of affairs back to a shared ignorance that was and had always been at the root of such attitudes and actions.

"We often rail at the exploiters," he said, "and place the blame for a wide variety of our collective ills at their feet. And this is perfectly understandable, since their actions have doomed untold millions to misery. But have you ever stopped to question why they do what they do? Why do powerful capitalists go to such great lengths to accumulate wealth they could not use in twenty lifetimes while millions of people are literally going hungry? Why do political demagogues become drunk with power and victimize the very people whose welfare they hold in trust?"

He paused and looked around the hall, apparently waiting for an answer that never came.

"For the same reason anyone does anything—to be happy. The same longing that motivates every one of us in this room, except that it is expressed in a profoundly misguided way. On some level, consciously or unconsciously, they think their wealth or their power will bring them the fulfillment they desire. What they fail to understand is that one day they are going to have to pay the price in suffering for the suffering they've caused. It may not be today, it may not be tomorrow, it may not even be this lifetime, but it's coming, because no matter how powerful anyone may think they are, no one can circumvent the laws of nature, and there is one fundamental law in this universe that governs our actions. The philosophers call it the law of action and reaction, but we know it simply as karma. What goes around comes around. The suffering we cause is the suffering we will meet on the road ahead, the account that will one day have to be paid in full. That's the nature of ignorance. We fail to see the consequences of our actions. But it goes deeper than that. Nothing happens in a vacuum. If we look at their ignorance with unclouded eyes we will see that the greater part of it has been imposed by a society that is itself laboring under the heavy clouds of ignorance, confusion, and selfishness, a society that is rife with dogma—and by dogma, I am not only referring to religious dogma but to social, economic, and cultural dogmas as well, wherever that ugly word rears its ugly head. Just as the crusaders were taught by their religion that murdering infidels and robbing them of their patrimony was a virtuous act, thus condemning those same crusaders to incalculable suffering through the inescapable law of karma, the capitalist magnates of our day have been taught by our culture that the accumulation of great wealth leads to great happiness, when in fact the opposite is true, since it is a verifiable truth that simplicity is more conducive to inner peace and well-being, just as it is a verifiable truth that material wealth is limited, and thus if one person or one community or one country accumulates excess wealth, then others are bound to be deprived, which leads to social unrest and collective suffering, as I am sure many of you are well aware of.

"Now we tend to think of such people, unscrupulous capitalists, political demagogues, and so on, as enemies of the human race, enemies of collective welfare, and it is very likely that they think of social activists like myself who want to put a stop to their exploitation as their enemies. But neither is true. We are all fellow travelers on the same path. Some of us are profoundly misguided, no doubt, and because such people harm themselves as well as others, we must make efforts to stop them—not out of rancor or enmity or indignation but for their own good as well as for the good of others. Just as we would help a family member who can't stop drinking by hiding the whiskey. The real enemy is ignorance, and until we remove that ignorance from ourselves as well as from the world around us, we will never be able to eliminate injustice and build a truly benevolent human society."

It was a novel perspective in her experience—compassion for the exploiters instead of indignation. It caught her by surprise at first, but once she got over the cognitive dissonance, it was refreshing to see an activist talking out of love rather than out of anger. She could see it in his face, in the passion with which he spoke and the way his eyes seem to light up the room.

"No amount of social activism, he continued, "can lead to an ideal human society, the one we all long for in our hearts, if the seeds of ignorance remain within us, buried but not burnt. They will certainly sprout one day, given the right conditions, and we will be left facing the same dilemmas we are facing today, in one form or another. And if we are to overcome that ignorance, then there is only one way to do it: one individual mind at a time. One candle in a windowless room makes for a feeble light, but that one candle is capable of lighting others, and when the room is filled with candles they illuminate every nook and cranny of what was once a benighted room.

"Now this may sound odd to you, but in a very real sense we are all responsible for the situation the world finds itself in today, for we are all co-creators of our human destiny. There is a deeper level of reality in which we are all connected, and it is at that level that we must learn to live and act if we are to make this world what it can and will be. And that is not possible without discovering the truth behind our existence and that of the world around us, without answering the first and greatest of all questions: who am I and why am I here?"

The monk leaned forward on the lectern, propped up on his elbows, his eyes shining like one of his metaphorical candles while he waited for his words to sink in. No amount of translation would have been enough for her to understand what he meant by the contention that we were all co-creators of our human destiny and thus responsible for the predicament we found ourselves in, but she was with him on all other counts. How could we hope to create a just world when most of us were laboring in the dark? How could we have an enlightened society unless it were populated with enlightened beings—or at least with human beings who were heading consciously in that direction? It made perfect sense, in a way that seemed to echo many of the same thoughts she had had over these past months. And by the nods and murmurs of the audience, she wasn't the only one who felt that way.

When the dramatic pause ended, he segued into the intuitional science of Tantra yoga, which he called "the oldest and most powerful system of personal transformation known to man," a denouement that by now seemed inevitable. The tantric meditation he described was certainly different than the zazen she practiced. There was no mantra in Zen, no yoga postures or breathing exercises to harmonize the energies of the body, but that seemed beside the point. It was the same endeavor in different robes: the quest for direct experience of the truth underlying our existence. A unity of purpose that became even more evident when he ended with a poetic description of the universe as a cosmic drama whose sole intent was to lead living beings toward the Divine Consciousness from which the universe had sprung, a heroic march toward perfection with each of the challenges that presented themselves along the way, be they internal or external, individual or collective, serving as necessary stepping stones in the pathways of spiritual evolution, the modus operandi that gave meaning to the drama, culminating in the full flowering of consciousness when a human being came face to face with the great ocean of being. The script to her life, summed up in a ninety-minute talk that would have been forty-five at most had he not been limited by his translator. She'd been skirting around the edges of this understanding ever since she'd picked up *Siddhartha*, gathering the pieces of the puzzle and trying to fit them together, but it took an American monk to provide a frame and fill in the gaps, and when his talk was over she couldn't help but feel a dazzling sense of gratitude.

The program ended with five minutes of chanting that Dada accompanied on guitar and a five-minute meditation, followed by a half hour of questions and answers, prompting a lively discussion that would have gone on longer had he not been required to vacate the room by 9:15. Paula caught up with him in the hallway, along with close to half the audience, and the discussion spilled out into the street, where it didn't break up until well after ten. She was the last to leave, and she took advantage of her perseverance to wrangle an invitation for lunch at his yoga center (which surprisingly enough turned out to be a scant five-minute walk from The Bodhi Tree, another of those strange twists of synchronicity). And that seemed to her the perfect ending to what had been quite a night. There was no bolt from the blue, no flash of recognition, no sense of her life finally falling into place, no indication that she had met her teacher, but it hardly mattered. A whole slew of candelabras had burst into flame and she was grateful for the light.

2

TRAVESSA SANTA LEOCADIA WAS a short dead-end street on
a steep incline that jutted up against one of those partially
forested granitoid hills that helped make South Rio so picturesque. Paula
left her car at the bottom of the hill and climbed the terraced sidewalk
until she reached number thirty-nine. For a moment she wasn't sure she
had the right address. There was nothing to indicate that this nondescript
three-story building whose front porch was enclosed by an iron grill was a
yoga center—until she noticed a small placard and a bulletin board with
a list of class hours and various announcements. She was about to reach
through the grill to ring the bell when a couple of young women in spandex
pants and T-shirts exited the front door carrying yoga mats. They smiled as
they opened the grill door and stood aside to let her in, before descending
the trio of steps to the sidewalk and resuming their easy chatter.

Paula passed through the front door into a hallway and found the
reception office immediately to her right. A blond-haired woman in
her forties was working at a computer, but most of the space served as
a shop—incense, yoga mats, Ayurvedic medicines, packaged health
foods, and a variety of yoga-related books and CDs.

"Can I help you?" the woman asked, swiveling around in her chair,
a friendly smile on her face.

"Dada Kamaleshvarananda invited me for lunch. I hope I'm not
too early. I'm Paula."

"Nice to meet you, Paula. I'm Maheshvari. Dada is meditating right
now but he should be down in a few minutes, if you want to grab a
chair. There's some herbal tea in the hallway and you are welcome to
browse the shop while you're waiting. I have some work I need to finish
up before I go, but if you need anything just let me know."

She was wearing an orange T-shirt with a highly stylized line-drawing
of a meditating figure and yogi pants tied at the ankle, and as she turned

back to the computer Paula found herself admiring her supple body and relaxed energy. As first impressions went, this was a particularly good one.

She got a cup of herbal tea from one of the thermoses in the hallway and started browsing through the books. There was a large picture in profile of an Indian man with glasses on the rear wall of the shop and she saw the same photo on the cover of one of the books: *Tales of a Tantric Master*. This must be the guru, she thought, as she picked up the book and turned it over to read the blurb on the back. Her interest began to mount as she read that he was considered a social revolutionary by some and a powerful tantric master with supernatural powers by others, but it was followed by a deflating sense of disappointment when she read that he had died the year after she was born.

She had started on the preface when Dada appeared in the doorway, this time without his turban. After a warm greeting, she followed him through the kitchen and into a rear patio where the same young man and woman from his talk were setting a table for lunch — rice and beans, salad, and an eggplant-and-zucchini stew. Unlike the previous night, the conversation was in English, which Rainjit spoke passably well, as did Pushpa Devi, Dada's translator from the night before.

"How is it your English is so good?" Dada asked. "You have practically no accent."

"I got started young. My mom's an English teacher and I grew up watching American movies, so I had lots of practice. I also spent a year at Berkeley as an exchange student. English literature and translation studies."

"Really? I'm from the Bay Area. The South Bay. Palo Alto. Though I moved to LA when I was twelve. So are you also an English teacher, like your mom?"

"I am. And a translator when I can get work."

"Uh oh," Pushpa Devi said, with her thick Brazilian accent. "I can only imagine what you thought of my translation."

"I was impressed actually. It's not enough to know the words when you translate. You have to understand the ideas to get it right and some of the ideas were new to me. I understood everything Dada said, but even so, your translation helped me understand what he meant."

Pushpa Devi was visibly pleased with the accolade and Paula justified it by telling herself that there was some truth to what she said — if only a little.

As they were serving themselves, Dada asked her if she had any experience with meditation.

"With meditation, yes. Yoga, no. Though I have been reading a lot of books lately about different yogic masters. I've been doing Zen meditation for about … five months now. Soto Zen. I learned from Monja Coen. I don't know if you are familiar with her."

"I am. I actually went to a talk she gave in São Paulo last month. Not that I understood anything. It was in Portuguese and I had just arrived in Brazil a couple of weeks earlier. But I liked her. She had a nice vibe. She also does yoga, I hear."

"She does. I've been thinking about taking some classes myself."

"I recommend it. It will help your meditation. Yoga refines and balances the nervous system and the glandular system, and that has a direct effect on the mind."

"And you teach yoga classes here, obviously."

"Not me personally. Rainjit is one of our teachers, Maheshvari whom you met, there are a few others. They divvy up the hours, Monday through Friday. Each of them teaches a different style or styles—it's all on the bulletin board if you are interested. The first class is free."

There was a goodly dose of geniality in Dada's voice as they talked, and Paula didn't wait long to satisfy her curiosity about the guru.

"I was looking at the back cover of the biography, and it said that many considered him a social revolutionary with secret intentions to overthrow the government?"

Dada laughed. "That's what happens when you tell the truth about exploitation. The exploiters get nervous and they start branding you as this or that. And if they really feel threatened, then they try to get rid of you, which is what happened in Baba's case. But dharma always wins out in the end. Great gurus come with a mission, and in a world of vested interests, that's honor bound to generate opposition. And slander. The more successful the mission, the greater the opposition. You don't have to look any further than Christ. He threatened the Roman *and* the Jewish status quo and he was crucified for it. But Christianity eventually felled the Roman Empire."

"That's true."

"Service has always been an important part of the yogic path, and of spirituality in general. Christianity is a great example. But if the people are suffering due to an unjust social system, then their suffering can't be overcome unless we change that system. Feeding the poor is a noble endeavor, but if you don't eliminate their poverty then they are going to be hungry again tomorrow. There is a reason why people are poor and hungry, and as long as you don't address that reason, then their poverty and their hunger are not going to go away. If we want to put an end to it, then we have to find a way to remove the system that generates massive inequality and injustice and replace it with something that works. Granted, that's a much harder task. Which is why we need spiritual practices, so we can gain the strength we need to take on that task. That's what Baba was teaching, and that's why he was branded as a revolutionary."

"That was something I really liked about your talk. I never thought of meditation and social activism going together like that."

"Oh, but they do. You could even say that no one can be an ideal yogi without taking up some concrete work to make the world a better place. Have you read at all about astanga yoga or raja yoga, the eightfold path?"

"A little."

"Okay. So you probably know that the first two limbs or steps in the eightfold path are *yama* and *niyama*, the yogic code of ethics. Turning a blind eye or a lazy mind to social injustice is to allow suffering by omission, and that is contrary to ahimsa, the first ethical principle — not to cause suffering to any living being by thought, word, or deed. Even if it's by omission and not commission. If you could have done something to lessen someone's suffering and you shied away from it, then you're not following ahimsa, and that puts enlightenment out of reach. So if we want to be good yogis we have to do something to put a halt to the injustice that prevents human beings from realizing their full potential — within the limits of our capacity, of course. It may be a very small something, but when you put together a lot of small somethings you get a great something. That's how the world changes: one small something at a time."

"I like that. It reminds me a little of the Bodhisattva vow."

"Sure. But we have to be practical Bodhisattvas. As long as we live in this physical world we can't neglect it. And that means using the mental force and wisdom we gain from meditation and our other spiritual practices to build a better society, whether it's in the sphere of economics, politics, education, what have you, so that everyone has a smoother path to enlightenment. It may not seem to some people like that's part of yoga, but it is. It's right there in the *yamas* and *niyamas*, which are the basis for all the other practices. But it all hinges on meditation. Without that, we won't have the mental force to resist the temptations of the ego."

It almost felt like she was back in the lecture hall but Paula didn't mind. Dada's enthusiasm and conviction were contagious, and that, she decided, was the secret of his charisma. These were the ideas that filled his soul, and as if by contagion she could feel them starting to fill hers as well. She caught Pushpa Devi and Rainjit trading smiles, as if to say that he was at it again, and when they reminded him that his food was getting cold, Paula almost regretted the interruption. He wasn't what she would call handsome but his face had character, the rugged lines of someone who had thought deeply about the world and left clearly carved impressions of his thoughts in the valleys and hills that appeared there. He had a receding hairline and long, sandy-brown hair tied into a ponytail, and if it weren't for the orange robes and his admission that he had grown up in the vast urban tracts of Northern and Southern California, she might have pegged him as a frontier woodsman, a man more at home in a forest or on a mountain face than in a city, something very close to her imagined image of Thoreau, whose *Walden Pond* had gone with her to Berkeley as a preparatory manual for her encounter with the American psyche.

"The thing about Tantra," he continued, ceremoniously pushing his plate toward the center of the table when he was done eating, "unlike some other systems of spiritual philosophy, is that it fully embraces the creation. The very purpose of our being here on this planet is to engage in the drama—to participate in the artistry of God, if you will—as we wind our way toward enlightenment. And as the highest living being, the living being with the most developed consciousness, we are the de facto caretakers of the creation. We're the gardeners and this planet is our garden. And human society is arguably the most important part of that garden, considering our effect on everything around us. We haven't been doing a particularly good job of beautifying our garden, I admit, but that's the challenge. What can we do to help human society reflect its divine nature? And the more conscious you are, the more responsibility you have—or at least, the more aware you should be of your responsibility. In other words, people who meditate: yogis, Zen Buddhists, Christian mystics, Sufis. Those who are working diligently day by day to expand their consciousness. The four of us sitting at this table. That's why we're here: to expand our consciousness and to put that expanded consciousness to work as caretakers of the creation. *Atma mokshartam jagat hitayaca.* Self-realization and service to the creation. *That's* the human motto."

There was a short hiatus while Rainjit collected the dishes and brought them to the kitchen. He returned a couple of minutes later with a bowl of oranges and a trio of paring knives, and Dada picked up where he had left off amid a growing pile of orange peels.

"In the past, serious spiritualists, for the most part, have made a point of staying on the margins of society. Either that, or they cut themselves off from society altogether—forests, caves, monasteries. They didn't want to be contaminated by an unspiritual environment, which is how most spiritual traditions viewed society: a quagmire that any serious yogi should steer clear of. Now that may be true from a simplistic point of view, but we need to put an end to that kind of thinking. First of all, it's inherently selfish. If you abandon society to its fate so that you can achieve your personal enlightenment, that's ego by default, and ego is the one sure bar to liberation. Secondly, no one can truly live in isolation from society. We depend on other people for our survival. Always have, always will. That's true even in a monastery. Even if you grow your own food behind your monastery walls and never leave the grounds, somebody had to make the shovel or the hoe you use to till the soil, somebody invented the plow, somebody taught human beings how to farm, somebody made the loom for your clothes, and so on. You're never truly isolated, no matter how far out on the margins you live. And if you don't help the rest of society elevate themselves then you are bound to be affected. Let's say there's a cholera outbreak in your village. You are not going to save yourself by hiding behind your doors. If you don't combat it, then sooner or later it's getting in. The right thing to do, the prudent thing to do, is to organize your fellow villagers and clean up the environment so you can eradicate the disease through proper sanitation. That way everyone benefits, including you. You generate good karma by doing service *and* you get to live in a healthy environment. If spiritualists band together to clean up our global village then everyone benefits, spiritualists and non-spiritualists alike. And if we don't, if we hide behind our doors and abdicate our responsibility, then sooner or later we are going to have to pay the piper.

"My master was saying in one discourse that everybody feels like they want to do something worthwhile with their lives. It's true—everyone wants to leave a mark on this world—and there is no better mark than to make the world a better place than we found it, to do something that will be of lasting benefit to future generations—who knows, maybe even for thousands of years. What do you say, Rainjit, do you want to leave a mark on this world?"

"Absolutely, Dada."

"Exactly. You see? It is a desire that God has implanted in every human being. It's what separates us from the animals. And you can't accomplish that only by pursuing your individual enlightenment. We have to make this world a better place *while* we are working to achieve enlightenment. That's the magic recipe. And there was no better example of that than my master. He dedicated every moment of his life to the welfare of others. He didn't waste even a single second. Now that's the ideal way to live."

"I have to admit," Paula said, "I felt disappointed when I read that he had passed on. I would have liked to have had the chance to meet him."

"Me too. I never got to see Baba physically. I was a teenager when he left his body. But my dada was a direct disciple who spent a lot of time with him, and one of the first things he taught me was that it didn't actually matter—not on the spiritual plane, or even on the psychic plane. Later I realized it for myself, through my own experience. If he is your guru, he's your guru. It doesn't matter when he left his body or when you entered yours. When he was in his body, he was sitting in India but disciples all over the world felt his presence, guiding them and inspiring them. Now that he's not in his body, his disciples still feel his presence just as strongly. Some say even more strongly. He was there guiding me when I was a boy in California; I just didn't know it. Now I do. I can feel his presence inside me, and it is just as real as when he was in his physical body. That's something a yogi realizes when they're ready. Your guru is your guru is your guru. Not even time and space can get in the way of that."

Dada's passion and conviction were contagious. She found herself wishing that she could feel what he so obviously felt. From there the conversation returned to Tantra yoga, sparked by several of her questions, and they got into a lengthy discussion about the scientific merits of yogic practice: how the various techniques purified the chakras and balanced the glandular system, opening up the way for the ascent of the kundalini; the power of mantra and the science of acoustic roots; the secrets of visualization; diet and yoga postures; the hidden discoveries of yoga psychology and how it far eclipsed the rudimentary understanding of its Western cousin, whose eleven decades of existence could hardly compare to the thousands of years that yogis had been exploring the inner recesses of the human mind through the powerful lens of profound introspection. It was a long and stimulating conversation, and when it ended, Paula felt as if she had just taken an extended ride on a postmodern roller coaster. Yoga was an ancient science, but many of the things Dada talked about were so advanced they seemed to belong to an era far into the future. And as if by some preordained sleight of hand, it was all blended with a social consciousness and revolutionary fervor that pulled at her like a magnet.

Before she left, Dada handed her a flyer for a beginners' retreat two weeks later in Alto da Boa Vista, one of the most scenic spots in Rio, home to Tijuca Park and Christ the Redeemer. The venue was a mansion owned by Jimmy Page's ex-wife that she rented out for events she approved of, yoga retreats being one of them. They were expecting some seventy to eighty participants, primarily young people, and if she was interested in learning tantric meditation, a female teacher was going to be there to give initiation and meditation lessons to the women. That decided it for her. For the moment at least, the universe seemed to be shunting her in the direction of Tantra yoga, and she was eager to see what was coming next.

3

For some reason the address didn't register on her GPS, and instead of a short picturesque ascent to one of the city's most exclusive and secluded neighborhoods, Paula soon found herself on a long odyssey of winding mountain roads without street signs or house numbers, punctuated by periodic stops to ask directions from one of the infrequent locals, who invariably met her with a bewildered look when she told them the name of the street—in short, the story of her life, minus the sea monster or the sirens—until she saw some young people with backpacks entering an unmarked door set in a massive wooden gate and recognized it as a sign from her inner guide.

The house was more or less what she would have expected from the ex-wife of Jimmy Page—a sprawling split-level with a 1970s decor and reproductions of Klee and Kandinsky on the walls. At the rear of the house a spacious American kitchen and a large hall with wooden floors looked out on an elegantly landscaped, downward-sloping backyard, replete with brick pathways, stone fountains, shaded benches, assorted flowerbeds, and an oval swimming pool, all set against the backdrop of the forested hills of Tijuca National Park. But it was the music that caught her attention, and it was the music she would keep coming back to throughout the weekend, like the soundtrack to a movie that kept playing over and over in her head long after she had left the theater. A group of musicians—harmonium, guitar, flute, and assorted hand percussion—were seated in a corner of the hall, chanting the mantra that Paula had heard at Dada's lecture: *Baba Nam Kevalam,* "love is all there is." Their eyes were closed and their bodies were swaying, as if they were both the snake charmer and the snake. Seated around them in a semi-circle were a couple of dozen people, rocking back and forth in identical fashion, oblivious to the hustle and bustle in the rest of the house as the new arrivals deposited their gear and dinner preparations got underway. Their trance-like state reminded her of the festivals at the Isle of Wight and Woodstock that she had seen on video, but whatever ecstasy they were enjoying wasn't marijuana- or LSD-induced. It was the mantra and the music that had them in a state of transport, and once she offloaded her backpack and said a quick hello to Dada, Rainjit, and Pushpa Devi, she joined in and soon started swaying herself, caught up in the infectious vibrations that seemed to spill out of the house, down the mountainside, and all the way to the ocean that lay just out of sight.

Meditation was hard work, Dada would explain early that evening, after the retreat got underway with an hour of gentle, meditative yoga (Paula's first-ever asana class), but chanting was almost effortless. It was like wading into a strong current: all you had to do was let go — the mantra and the music would do the rest. He was introducing the practice of kirtan before the evening meditation, the singing of mantras combined with a simple dance step, side to side with the arms upraised, that turned the preparatory chanting into a wholehearted celebration of existence. "Everything is divine," he went on to say. "Everything is an expression of one infinite universal consciousness — you, me, the stars, the trees, everything we see and everything we can't see. All flowing in one universal rhythm. We think we are separate, we think we are a drop, but in fact we are the ocean. That ocean of divine consciousness is *Baba*, the Beloved, and this universe is nothing but the surging waves of that divine consciousness — *Baba Nam Kevalam*. In kirtan our bodies enter into the rhythm of the dance, our minds into the rhythm of the music, and the ideation of the mantra tunes our spirit to the rhythm of the cosmos. Thus, with the help of the mantra, we surrender ourselves to the divine wave and let it carry us until we cease to be a drop and become the ocean."

Once the kirtan began, it didn't take her long to see its kinship with Sufi dancing. Instead of orbiting around the nucleus of the Divine, in the symbolism of the circular dances of the dervishes, everyone in the jam-packed hall was swaying back and forth in tandem with the universal breath; and from the abandon she saw all around her, most of her fellow retreat-goers were quickly caught up in that universal rhythm in much the same way as Harimayi Devi and her acolytes. Paula was hesitant at first as she raised her arms toward the heavens and tuned her halting steps to the music, held back by a lingering touch of self-consciousness, but it only took a few minutes before the collective energy swept her up in its current. It was more infectious than any concert or festival she had ever been to, and soon she closed her eyes and began to let herself go, trying to imagine herself as a tiny drop surrendering herself to the surging majesty of the sea. She could feel the music coursing through her as the chorus of voices began to shake the bay windows and sliding glass doors, and when some of her companions started jumping in place with their arms upraised, carried away by their exuberance, she started to do the same; and somewhere between then and the time the kirtan ended, her face became wet with tears, the outward expression of an unnamed longing set loose by the power of the mantra.

Paula was no stranger to the power of music to move her to tears — it had happened often enough listening to records in the privacy of her room, and she had once spent the better part of a particularly magical Maria Bethânia concert wiping her eyes with Fernando's handkerchief — but she had no explanation for why it should have happened to her now, dancing kirtan with an abandon that was foreign to her. She was tempted to pass it off as "just one of those things," a convenient euphemism for those unexplained lacunas in the book of self-knowledge, but she was sure there was more to it than that. There always was, even if she were not yet able to decipher the hieroglyphics of her inner alchemy.

When the last notes from the harmonium faded, she wiped her face with her T-shirt and turned her attention to Dada's voice as he guided them through the initial stages of the meditation. Her tears had subsided, but in their wake she felt an unaccustomed lightness, as if she had unloaded a heavy burden that she had been carrying around unnoticed, and when Dada had them expand their inner vision out into the cosmos she could feel her observing eye rising high above Rio, freeing her spirit to soar as it had always longed to do. And then she was out among the stars, singing the mantra in her mind and trying to feel the love of that universal consciousness bathing her in its gentle radiance. It was very different than zazen, and so very beautiful, as if her mind were a planetarium with all the mysteries of existence on display before her inner eye.

When the meditation ended with a soft reprise of the mantra by the kirtan band, she was reluctant to open her eyes, reluctant to leave the theater of her innermost being, but when she did she felt glad to be back, renewed by the practice and eager for what was coming next. Dada stood up and began telling a humorous story about three yogis in the Himalayas, using their extreme and ultimately foolish asceticism as a counterpoint to his far more compelling vision of the modern yogi: spiritually elevated and socially committed, a kind of cross between Che Guevara, Nelson Mandela, and the Buddha that set the tone for the entire weekend. Dinner was spent on the back patio in a whirl of conversation and laughter with kirtan piped in over the outdoor speakers, and that was followed by an evening of cooperative games that had everyone laughing as they learned each other's names and fell blindfolded into their partner's arms and proved that their bodies became harder to lift when they imagined that they were made of stone. It almost seemed a crime to go to bed after that, but Dada warned them with a mischievous smile that they would be getting up early the next morning to greet the dawn with kirtan, meditation, and yoga, following the ancient tradition of the yogis who for millennia could be found in deep contemplation while the rest of the world slept, knowing that the most propitious hour for meditation was the hour before dawn when the world's subtle rhythms reached a state of maximum equilibrium. She doubted there were many in that hall who were used to getting up at such a godly hour, herself included, but soon she was curled up on her sleeping mat like everyone else, finding an agreeable spot outside on the back patio, just beside a flowering rose bush, while the rest of the nearly ninety participants laid out their mats wherever the spirit moved them, something else that reminded her of Woodstock.

The female teacher, who had arrived sometime during the night, gave a talk after the morning practices, an amiable, high-spirited talk that made Paula take an instant liking to her. She was a short, rotund, graying Filipina wrapped in an orange sari who introduced herself as Didi Ananda Jaya, and afterward she called aside the women who wanted initiation or further instruction in meditation for a short chat and then passed around a sign-up list. Paula was fifth on the list, and her turn came during the noon kirtan, when Didi came up to her unnoticed and tapped her on the shoulder. Once again the kirtan had gotten to her, covering her cheeks with a thin viscous sheen, and as soon as they were out the doors and heading down one of the backyard paths, Paula felt the need to apologize.

"Sorry, Didi. I'm not usually this emotional. I don't know what it is. I think maybe I'm not used to being this happy."

Didi laughed, a high-pitched musical chime as bright as the sky above their heads. "It makes me remember when I was starting out. I used to tear up almost every time I did kirtan."

"You did?"

"I did indeed. And I wasn't a crier. It took me a while before I recognized what it was: it was the feeling of coming home. I had a wonderful childhood, great parents, great family, but our real home is the spiritual path. I like to tell people that it's like being on a long ocean voyage, an entire lifetime away from home, and then finally, one day, you see your homeland on the horizon. Who wouldn't tear up? The first time I met Baba I cried a whole river of tears. It was the greatest homecoming a person could ever have. Now come, sit. And don't feel like you need to hold back the tears."

They had reached the back of the property where a woolen blanket was spread out in the dense shade of a Brazilian pepper tree, thick with clusters of red peppercorns. *Ananda Jaya*, she had learned, meant "blissful victory," and Paula could feel Didi's jovial confidence seeping into her as if by osmosis as the diminutive yogic nun explained that it was not she who would be giving the initiation—she was merely a conduit for a greater power, the power of the guru, who would be using her as his representative to conduct the ancient tantric initiation that he had revitalized for the modern age, as all the great tantric masters had done since time immemorial, periodically injecting new life into a tradition that would never fade as long as there were human beings on this planet.

Didi closed her eyes, placed her hands palms upward on her knees, and meditated for several minutes with her head arching back while Paula looked on with the nervous energy of anticipation. When Didi opened her eyes they were shining, and they continued to sparkle for the next twenty minutes while she explained the complicated withdrawal process and gave her her mantra. Afterward they did a short meditation together to make sure that Paula had understood the process—a short but powerful meditation that far eclipsed her experience of the previous evening, the mantra seeming to rise up from deep within her, from the unseen wellsprings of her being—and then finished the initiation with a ritual offering to the guru. By then the tears had reappeared, as Didi had perhaps foreseen, and she made no effort to hold them back. As she was making the offering, her eyes misting over, she thought back to the photo on the altar in the hall, similar to the one she had seen in the yoga center and on the cover of the biography, and she had the uncanny feeling that they were not alone, just as Didi had intimated, that the symbolic offering was not a mere ritual but an act of acknowledgment to a mysterious, invisible presence that her mind was as yet unable to fathom.

Paula spent the rest of the afternoon trying to silently repeat her mantra as Didi had instructed, letting the meaning seep into her subconscious, reminding her that she was one with the infinite ocean of being, a divine spark in a universal blaze. That night they walked on coals culled from a crackling bonfire in the middle of a grassy area close to where she had gotten initiated. She was one of the last persons to enter the line, but despite her initial misgivings she barely hesitated before walking firmly down the scalding path with her eyes fixed forward and the entire group chanting "cool moss, cool moss," as if it were a mantra, voicing their collective determination to show the world that the mind was stronger than the body. Paula chanted the words along with everyone else as she made her brisk walk across the coals in her bare feet, but it was the music of the kirtan band that gave her courage. They were seated next to the bonfire singing the Baba Nam Kevalam mantra with Dada urging them every few minutes to "rock it up," and by the time Paula made her walk she felt as if she were in a kirtan trance. Whether it was that, or the power of their collective will, or simply because the coals weren't really that hot, her feet made it through unscathed and her confidence in the designs of destiny continued to gather force.

The retreat ended the following afternoon at the same spot with one final group activity: the tunnel of love. Dada gave a talk on love as the fulcrum of the cosmic wheel with everyone seated on the grass in a huge circle. Then they split up into two facing lines, forming a tunnel through which pairs of participants passed blindfolded, receiving embraces, caresses, and beautiful words from the living tunnel as they walked, all the while chanting the universal mantra to the accompaniment of the kirtan band. When the last pair had gone through, the tunnel morphed into a circle with everyone holding hands and the kirtan growing in power, and from there into a musical snake led by Dada, weaving in and out of itself in perfectly intuitive, undulating curves. When the kirtan finally ended with a triumphant shout, no one was ready to leave. They continued to circulate for the better part of an hour, exchanging hugs and contact information, and even after it began to thin out, there were pockets of retreat-goers hanging out in the backyard until dusk, talking and laughing in small groups as if they were at a party that was just getting going.

Paula exchanged her fair share of hugs and added more than two dozen numbers to her contacts, but as soon as she saw that Didi had some breathing space, she went up to her to ask a question that had been on her mind for most of the day, ever since she had joined a group of girls by the pool after breakfast and listened with growing envy as they began comparing the spiritual names Didi had given them. Didi gave her a hug — a kind of funny hug from her point of view since Didi barely came up to her chest — and when Paula asked if she might have time to choose a spiritual name for her before she left, Didi grinned and patted her on the cheek.

"I've already chosen one, my dear. Or rather, Baba has. It came to me while we were meditating after your initiation. I was waiting for you to ask."

Paula was both surprised and elated.

"Your name is Priya Devi, she who is dear to God, and because she is dear to God, she is dear to all. Should I write it down for you?"

"Please, Didi."

It was just as the girls had claimed, a name that summed up the essence of what she felt and who she aspired to be, a clear and unmistakable indication that an invisible power was indeed watching over her. She was his beloved, his dear one, his Priya Devi, and always had been, even during those lost, lonely years when she had thought she was alone and forlorn. He had been with her all along, waiting for her to look up and take notice. And now she had.

4

HE FIRST THING PAULA did when she arrived back at the apartment was to introduce her new self to her old self. Dada had mentioned in the retreat that tantric initiation was considered a second birth in the yogic tradition, and after everything that had happened that weekend, she felt as if a door had indeed opened to a new life. And so, when she opened the door to the apartment, she welcomed Priya Devi and gave her a quick tour of her old haunts, pointing out to her new self the trappings of the old. The second thing she did was to gather together every memento that she had kept from Fernando and take them to the trash, deciding that she owed it to her new self to begin life without the encumbrance of the previous tenant's burdens. Despite having assured herself that she had gotten over him, there were still times when she would notice some particularly significant artifact from their time together and stop whatever she was doing to indulge in bittersweet reminiscences, from the lace shawl he had given her that Christmas to the unopened bottle of Chianti Superiore on the shelf above the kitchen stove that they had been planning on opening on her birthday, the one that had just passed ten days earlier without so much as a brief happy birthday message from her ex-boyfriend on her Facebook page. Maybe those dearly purchased indulgences were okay for Paula, but not for Priya Devi. So out they went, along with everything else that tied Paula to her memories of him, enough to fill three large cardboard boxes that she placed alongside the garbage bins so that her neighbors could help themselves before Fernando's leftovers began their journey to a Rio landfill (the bottle of Chianti and the shawl she gave to her landlady on the first floor). She endured a couple of sharp pangs as she took a final look at two years' worth of memories appearing rather forlorn in their abandonment, but the moment she made it back to the apartment the constriction in her chest began to loosen. A new chapter had opened in her life and she hoped that Fernando wouldn't appear in its pages, other than as a warning against future follies.

The next evening she stopped by The Bodhi Tree to tell Maya about her weekend, and she was pleasantly surprised to learn that Maya was familiar with the group, though perhaps she shouldn't have been.

"One of their monks is a friend of mine. They call him Dadinha, on account of how short he is. He lives in São Paulo now but he used to live in the Santa Leocadia center. Did you ever see *Caminho das Índias*? He was the yoga consultant for that soap. He brought me on set once and introduced me to some of the actors. I had a really interesting talk with Juliana Paes about Indian spirituality."

Juliana Paes! Yet another surprise from this surprising woman. Juliana Paes had been her favorite actress during a short but particularly intense period of her life—her second year in college—and *Caminho das Índias*, a weave of intersecting love stories that pitted India against Brazil, had been an important outlet that year, her one sure means of forgetting her troubles—at least for an hour a day, six days a week, during *Índias's* eight-month reign at the top of the Brazilian charts.

"She was one of his students," Maya continued, amused at her reaction. "She meditates and goes on retreats and everything. That's probably why you liked her. You were able to catch the spiritual vibe right through the TV. You know, it's funny, just yesterday I was thinking of Dadinha. The last time I saw him we were talking about a book and it occurred to me that it might be time for you to read it. How's that for synchronicity? Come, let's go get your copy. It will be a present from me to celebrate your initiation. That kind of thing doesn't happen every day. Or even every lifetime."

The book was *Illusions: The Adventures of a Reluctant Messiah*, by Richard Bach. She had seen it on the bookstore shelves and had even made a note to herself to add it to her list, but other books had always intervened. When Maya handed her the slim paperback whose cover featured a blue feather floating against a starlit sky, she had a sudden sense that it was not Maya who was handing her the book but an invisible presence using her as his instrument. It was only a fleeting sensation, but it was enough for her to feel a sense of reverence for what she held in her hands.

It was late when she got home, and with an eight o'clock class the next morning she only had time to read the preface and the opening chapter before turning in for the night, but they were enough to usher her across the threshold of a new world, one that she would be paying regular visits to over the next few days, a world of swaying corn fields, sea-green meadows, and gentle rolling hills that was home to Donald Shimoda, a reluctant spiritual master "born in the holy land of Indiana, raised in the mystical hills east of Fort Wayne."

"Perhaps it is no coincidence that you are holding this book," Richard Bach wrote in the preface (after surprising her by confessing that he didn't like to write and even went to great lengths to avoid it), and she thought to herself that truer words had never been spoken—even if they had been spoken time and again by a multitude of different teachers. She had felt it the moment Maya handed her the book. Some words *were* timeless and inexhaustible, no matter who spoke them, and the growing realization that coincidence did not play a part in her life—or in anyone else's, for that matter—that everything happened for a reason, traced in cosmic ink by a divine hand, including choosing this precise moment in her life for her to read *Illusions*, seemed to anchor her to the earth in a way she had never felt anchored before, even if that reason was beyond her ken.

Tuesday was another long day, with morning, afternoon, and evening classes, as was Wednesday, but she had Thursday afternoon off and she spent it in a shady bower in the botanical gardens after her customary stroll through the orchid pavilion. She finished *Illusions* in one leisurely go (Richard Bach seemed to have a penchant for short books, perhaps because they were so difficult to write), pausing only for a few minutes halfway through its pages to lie down on the grass and try her hand at vaporizing clouds, as the narrator was doing on a similarly quiet afternoon somewhere in the American Midwest.

"If you really want to remove a cloud from your life, you do not make a big production out of it, you just relax and remove it from your thinking. That's all there is to it."

It sounded so simple. So perfectly logical. And yet, being the novice she was, she had no success with the clouds above her head, even the smallest ones, the high-flying cirri, mere wisps of floating condensation that a concentrated mind should have been able to vaporize without breaking a sweat. But perhaps those weren't the clouds Shimoda meant. Perhaps he was referring to the clouds within her mind, not just the high-flying cirri but the low-hanging storm clouds that shut out the sun and threatened the earth with their menacing thunderclaps and a thousand tons of water. Now if she could only learn to vaporize those, it would be a much more useful skill. She thought back to her ceremonial disposal of Fernando's keepsakes, and she grudgingly acknowledged that that particular freedom was not so easily achieved. It was not only Fernando she needed to remove from her mind—it was the desire for the next Fernando, the new and improved version, the spiritual version, the one her mind insisted on conjuring up each time a possible candidate happened on the scene. Illusions. One after another, populating the theater of her mind. Often entertaining and always instructive, like any good movie, but who wants to spend their life in a movie theater? And was that not the point? That the beginning of wisdom is the recognition that all this is nothing but a movie? That our real purpose here is to wake from the illusion and find our way home? No matter how fascinating the drama? In Richard's case, Shimoda had taken him to see *Butch Cassidy and the Sundance Kid* and then interrupted him to ask *why are you here?* at the very instant when Butch and Sundance were surrounded by the Bolivian army. It was a particularly suspenseful moment, and for that reason particularly difficult for Richard to pull his attention out of the illusion and back to the real, but didn't all moments have their own unique brand of drama, which was why we were all still caught up in the movie?

And yet slowly but surely Richard had begun to remember why he was here. When she sat up and rejoined the barnstorming duo, still deep in their mystical conversation, she couldn't help but wonder if she too, unbeknownst to her, might be a messiah-in-training, destined to wake up to a spiritual knowledge of reality she had somehow forgotten. She didn't expect to walk on water or float socket wrenches in a hayfield as a laid-back form of mental exercise like Donald Shimoda, but the mere thought that an enlightened master might be guiding her footsteps was something she wouldn't have dreamed of before she had picked up *Siddhartha* and begun to imagine a world greater than her imaginings. "Imagine the universe beautiful and just and perfect," the *Messiah's Handbook* read, "then be sure of one thing: the Is has imagined it quite a bit better than you have." And she was part of that quite-a-bit-better universe, being guided across the dance floor until she finally opened her eyes to see the Is as it really is.

That Sunday evening she attended the weekly collective meditation at the yoga center, introducing herself as Priya Devi to the devotees she hadn't already met, adding to her sense of having initiated a new life. There was no yoga class, but otherwise the program was much the same as during the retreat: kirtan, meditation, and a spiritual talk, followed by a potluck meal. After his talk Dada announced a one-week intensive in early August that he would be leading in Araruama, another of those beach towns in the Lakes Region that she had visited with Fernando. "Ideological Training," he called it, a chance for interested disciples to immerse themselves in the philosophy and deepen their spiritual practices. The intensive was only three weeks away and Paula knew it would be difficult to arrange the time off on such short notice, but the moment Dada made the announcement she knew she had to be there.

When she approached him about signing up, however, he looked genuinely surprised. "Well, okay, we can talk about it," he said, "but I have to tell you, it's going to be pretty intense—we are going to be doing long practice, the classes aren't going to be for beginners, and there'll be virtually no free time. It's not going to be like the retreat. This is more like boot camp for yogis. You just got initiated a week ago. Don't you think that might be a little much for you just now."

But Priya was not about to be deterred. She told Dada how strongly her initiation had impacted her, and as they made their way to the kitchen and fixed their plates from the wide assortment of dishes that the devotees had brought, she started telling him about her letter and how she had gotten her answer the very next day when she attended his lecture. This gave him pause, and she could see that whatever trepidations he had about her attending were beginning to waver. That's when she brought out her trump card.

"Maybe you can think about it this way: you need a translator and I'm as good as they come. It's my profession. I'm trained in simultaneous translation and I get paid for it. I can go as fast or as slow as you want, and you can be sure that my translation will be totally spot-on, with nothing left out. Plus if I'm translating I won't be able to ask questions, so you'll hardly know I'm there. I'll be no more than a shadow."

Dada leaned over and dropped his voice to a whisper. "Does that mean Pushpa Devi's translation wasn't everything it could have been?"

Priya smiled. "Let's just say I was being polite the other day at lunch and leave it at that."

Dada nodded appreciatively. "You know, a couple of days ago I was actually thinking how nice it would be to have a top-notch translator for these classes, so I wouldn't have to stop and wait after every sentence. I guess you're Baba's answer to my wish. Like I was his answer to your letter. Okay, let's do it."

Priya still had to find someone to cover her classes on what was uncomfortably short notice but she put her faith in the *Messiah's Handbook* and she was duly rewarded. "You are never given a wish without also being given the power to make it true. You may have to work for it, however." And work she did, beginning the following afternoon, picking up her phone and calling everyone she knew who might be able to stand in for her. She had exhausted nearly every possibility she could think of when she remembered Deborah, a college classmate she had lost touch with when Deborah moved back to São Paulo after graduation. It took some telephone tag to get her number—from the friend of a friend of a friend—but when Deborah answered the phone Priya soon recognized the voice of destiny at the other end of the line.

"What a coincidence," Deborah said after Priya told her about her predicament. "I had scheduled those days off months ago so I could take a course at USP and I just heard the course has been canceled. Insufficient enrollment. I've been trying to decide all day what to do that week: go traveling or try to pick up a few classes to make some extra money. Now I can do both. And if you're really happy with me staying at your apartment, then I can't think of a single reason why not. It will give me a chance to meet up with some of the old crowd."

Of course there were no coincidences. Early in *Illusions* Shimoda asked Richard if he believed he were being guided. "Isn't everyone?" Richard answered. "I've always felt something kind of watching over me." This was just another confirmation that Shimoda was right: life was a movie of divine authorship, and the one sure means to wake from the illusion was to follow the promptings of her inner guide. She had never thought to give that guide a name before, but she liked the spontaneity of Dada's reply: "I guess you're Baba's answer to my desire. Like I was his answer to your letter." It was a novel thought but somehow it felt right. And now Deborah was Baba's answer to *her* desire. "And you think you'll be led to a teacher who can help you," Shimoda had said in reply to Richard. Yes, she did, and it seemed now as if she just might have found one.

5

The training took place in a spacious yoga center in one of Araruama's quieter neighborhoods—safely removed from the many beaches that were still impregnated with memories she would just as soon forget. It belonged to a middle-aged disciple who joined in the kirtan and meditation and occasionally peeked in on the classes but was otherwise free to come and go as she pleased. For the rest of them it was just as Dada had promised—boot camp for yogis. For the next seven days Priya rose at 4:20 to a kirtan reveille—Dada walking through the center playing the Baba Nam Kevalam mantra on his guitar—and the routine continued without respite until the night meditation at 10:15. Her knees ached from so much sitting and she was soon wondering about the effects of prolonged sleep deprivation (six hours might have been enough if the girls in her room hadn't stayed up late talking, her included), but despite the sense of being perpetually overextended, Priya loved it. Except for the owner of the center, they were all in their twenties or early thirties, fourteen sisters and six brothers (to use the yoga-speak that she was quickly getting used to), and the sense of camaraderie that sprung up between them as they did time on their meditation cushions and butted heads with the spiritual philosophy was stronger than anything she had ever experienced. Their common passion for the yogic life turned the demanding discipline into a kind of silent celebration that found its expression in a constant undercurrent of good humor. She made friends she was sure would be friends for life, and while she had thought the same thing in college, only to see those bonds dissolve once her studies were finished, there was something about their shared spiritual hunger that bound them together in a way that seemed impervious to the passage of time.

But it was only during an afternoon philosophy class on karma and samskara, the law of action and reaction, that she was able to put that feeling into words—Dada's words. "This is not our first life together," he told them with his habitual self-assurance. "Baba gathered us together in his mission for a reason, and that reason stretches back further than any of us can remember. Let me read you something Baba said when he was giving darshan in Taipai:

"'Say a few years ago, none of you knew that Baba is on this Earth. None of you knew that Baba loves you. But Baba was there, and Baba loved you, though you were not acquainted with Baba … So, when nothing is noncausal, your coming in close contact with me is also not noncausal. There is some cause you do not know. It may be that in the hoary past you were also in close contact with me. It may or may not be on this Earth, on this planet, it may be on some other planet that you were known to me. It may be that on that planet, we sat like this and decided, "Let us go to that small planet known as Earth, and there we may do some work." And, just to fulfill this pledge of ours, we have come here. So nothing is noncausal.'"

Dada took a long pause to look around the room before he put the book down. "And the same is true for all of us sitting here in this room. We aren't companions by chance, because nothing is by chance. We have a shared purpose and a shared history that has brought us together, and it makes no difference if that history is submerged in the shadows of previous lifetimes. That only makes it stronger."

His words were like a bell ringing inside her head. All her life she had felt like a fish out of water, a stranger in a world where everyone seemed to look at her askance. But that was beginning to seem like a distant memory. Ever since *Siddhartha*, and even more so since her initiation, she had felt a growing sense of belonging, a sense of finally coming home, and the intensive reinforced that feeling many times over. "The spiritual family" was the phrase Dada used. "Life lived on the inside." The *Messiah's Handbook* had said the same thing in different words: "Rarely do members of the same family grow up under the same roof." The philosophy he used to back up his assertion clicked inside her mind like the tumblers of a lock falling into place, causing an impenetrable door to swing open. "There are no accidents in this world. Each and everything that happens to us has its origin in the intricate chain of cause and effect, and the sole purpose of this law, as with all the laws that govern the universe, is to lead the living being to spiritual enlightenment." But more than the philosophy, it was the feeling of being in that room with Dada and the rest of her companions that made something click inside her heart. Hers was not a solitary journey any longer. She had companions now and a guide who knew the terrain and would see her safely through the pitfalls that were waiting up ahead. It was the answer to her letter all over again, glowing brighter with every passing hour.

That was day two of the training. By then Priya had already rejected Dada's offer to ease her burden by asking someone else to translate from time to time. It was tiring work but the rewards far outweighed the effort. There was something uncanny and inexplicable that happened to her at times when she translated: she liked to think of it as taking up residence in another person's head. It didn't happen often, but when it did, she often knew what was coming even before the speaker voiced his thoughts, as if she were lodged inside his brain, seeing the thoughts formulate themselves on the canvas of his mind as they raced toward their inevitable conclusion. A temporary partial fusion that seemed to fold time onto itself, so that afterward, when she came out of what she liked to think of as a linguistic trance, she had no awareness of the passage of time, until a glance at a clock or her watch helped to bring her back to the space-time continuum. The same thing happened as the intensive got underway, but with two notable differences: one was the ease with which she was able to remain in that state of heightened linguistic awareness; and the other was the frequency with which Dada's next thought surprised her, even when she could see it coming. So much so that her brain seemed to split in two: while one part of her kept the translation going, as if on automatic pilot, another part was able to stand back and marvel at the ideas that her mouth was formulating in elegant, idiomatic Portuguese.

"There is an old adage in the yogic world: if you want to become an enlightened being you have to start acting like an enlightened being."

They were the opening words to Dada's class the next morning, and as soon as she translated them it was as if the world had flipped, depositing her on the other side of a portal without any awareness of how she had gotten there. It was a simple statement, almost obvious in hindsight, but that didn't negate the power it had to alter her vision of the future. As the translation shifted into automatic pilot, she found herself witnessing flashes from the days and years to come, her habitual behaviors mutating into actions that would make an enlightened being proud. His words became her words, and because he spoke with such deeply felt conviction, she could feel the force of her own words ringing the bells of truth in the bell tower of her conscience.

"Enlightened beings don't react; they act. Their minds don't control them; they control their minds. That is the basis of our interior work, and it begins with one simple premise: life is our friend. Let's say you have a samskara, an inborn tendency, to get angry in certain situations. You can count on life to pair you up with the very people or the very circumstances that are most apt to push your buttons. How wonderful! No, no, don't laugh. This is a divine blessing—a divine decree, in fact—because by doing so the world is acting as a mirror, showing us what we need to work on, and without a mirror it is nigh on impossible to see oneself.

"So I get angry. But I'm a yogi now. My goal is the infinite peace of the enlightened state, and inner peace means freedom from our conditioned mental reactions. As long as we continue to react, our consciousness is in prison. And so I start training myself. The Buddha said, 'Overcome anger with kindness, miserliness with generosity, dishonesty with truth.' While this can also work in the external world, he was really talking about conquering the demons within our minds that keep us from attaining nirvana. So what is the strategy? Raise the opposite wave and the two waves will cancel each other out. Simple physics. Whenever I feel a reaction coming on—in this case, the wave of anger rising in the sea of my mind—rather than try to suppress that emotion, a somewhat dubious and ultimately futile proposition, I try to control my behavior. Instead of giving in to the impulse generated by my mental conditioning and lashing out, I make a concerted effort to say kind things—even if I don't mean it. Eventually, those kind words become a habit, just like lashing out was a habit. And as this new habit grows, your anger automatically subsides. Why? Because you are not feeding it. Anger needs fuel to continue burning, and those hurtful words and actions are the fuel that gives it life. If you continue to say kind things or do kind acts, you deprive it of that fuel, and eventually the samskara becomes so weak it can't provoke you any longer. It is still there but in a weakened state. And in the meantime you're meditating, and the more you meditate, the more your consciousness expands. You begin to think, 'No, no, no, I may be irritated right now, but that's *my* samskara. He is not to blame. That's on me. He is not a bad person. He is a human being, just like me. He is also on the path to liberation. He is just facing down his inner demons right now, just as I am, and one day he is going to overcome them and become the Buddha. He deserves my help.' And then some more time goes by, and one day you find yourself in the same situation and your very first thought is, 'Ah, the Lord has appeared before me in the guise of this man who is under the control of his anger or his pride or his envy so that I may have this opportunity to alleviate his suffering and help him along the path. What a blessing!' Your anger has been replaced by compassion, and lo and behold, you are looking more and more like an enlightened being. And then, when you sit for meditation, it is so much easier because you no longer have those heavy mental waves to deal with. Your progress speeds up. Life becomes more and more blissful. The storm has passed. The Buddha said, 'Sow a thought, reap an action; sow an action, reap a habit; sow a habit, reap a character; sow a character, reap a destiny.' In other words, learn to act like an enlightened being and enlightenment is sure to follow."

The evening program was story hour. They had begun the intensive by taking turns recounting how they had gotten into the spiritual path, extended introductions to the unique story of each person's life that brought her own journey into better focus. That evening Dada took over the spotlight and started telling stories of the guru that ran the gamut from moving to mind-blowing. "Baba stories," he called them, a one-hour carousel that had her spinning round and round in the dreamworld of her imagination.

That first evening of Baba stories was followed by morning and afternoon classes on devotion and the role of the sadguru in the life of a spiritual aspirant, and the timing couldn't have been better orchestrated. As she sat beside Dada and began translating, she found herself once again in that hinterland where time folded back on itself, one part of her translating his words while the other struggled to come to grips with the mind-bending possibility that the Cosmic Consciousness had taken a human shape for the sole purpose of guiding her and everyone else in that room to the ultimate realization. She had felt a similar delirium when she had read *Autobiography of a Yogi* and other storybooks of great yogic masters, but apart from some perfectly understandable daydreaming, she had never realistically entertained the idea that such a thing could ever happen to her. And yet here she was, telling her companions with complete conviction that the guru was living inside them, that he had been there all along, and that it was the strength of their devotion that would bring him out of the shadows and into the light.

"The sadguru is not a philosophical concept," Dada said, paraphrasing Baba, "he is a creation of devotional sentiment. Divine Consciousness is present within you as the atman, the soul, the witness of your thoughts and of your very sense of existence. But without love it is impossible to truly feel its presence, and it is not possible to fall in love with an impersonal entity. For that reason the Divine takes human form, age after age — so that we can fall in love with him. There is no difference between the sadguru and Divine Consciousness, between an enlightened being and the Self. He is one with the Self, and when we fall in love with him, we fall in love with the Self. When that happens, we begin to become aware of his constant presence. We begin to hear his voice pointing out the way, which is the voice of the Self, guiding us infallibly down the spiritual path."

That evening Dada ended the story hour by telling how Dada Dharmadevananda had met the guru, and by the time Priya finished translating she was having trouble controlling her tears. The year was 1959, and Dada Dharma, then known as Asim, was a twenty-year-old student in Ranchi who had been practicing meditation and yoga out of books, an ardent devotee of Krishna who was adamant that he did not need or want a guru. One day in late December, as he was riding his bike home after class, he noticed a sign for a yoga center. He had been thinking about leaving for the Himalayas after classes let out for the winter vacation, to pursue his practices in the legendary haunts of yogis and saints, but he didn't know how to get there or where to go once he did. Who better to ask than a yoga teacher, he thought, and so he locked his bike to a nearby lamppost and entered the center. A couple of men were conversing in the foyer, but when he approached them with his query, they asked him to wait for Dada to finish his meditation. Asim took a seat by the door to the meditation hall, and moments later he heard some loud, guttural sounds coming from inside — "Hum, Baba" — accompanied by thumping noises, as if a body were landing heavily on the floor. When he asked what it was, they said, "Oh, that's Dada. He's meditating. He should be finished any moment now."

Asim raised an incredulous eyebrow but the man was clearly serious. "Meditating? Then why the noise?" he asked, as another "Hum, Baba" and two loud thumps sounded from inside the hall. "Isn't meditation supposed to be silent?"

"Those are occult symptoms. They happen when the kundalini rises."

Ten minutes later the noises ceased and out stepped Acharya Kedar-nath Sharma in an officer's uniform of the Bihar Military Police. He was an imposing figure who exuded an air of supreme confidence and

Asim's own confidence immediately began to waver. When one of the men told Kedarnath why Asim was there, the acharya nodded and pulled up a chair.

"Why do you want to go to the Himalayas?"

"To find God," Asim replied, somewhat hesitantly.

"You don't need to go to the Himalayas to find God. You can do that right here in Ranchi. Do you think God is only in the Himalayas?"

"No, of course not. But it is very difficult to meditate in the city. I live in a student hostel and it is almost impossible to get any peace and quiet there. The Himalayas are said to be the best place in the world to meditate."

"The best place in the world to meditate is wherever you are. When you close your eyes, it doesn't matter what's outside. What matters is what's inside. You won't find God in the Himalayas, young man. You'll find him inside you. Learn meditation from a proper teacher, practice what he teaches with full sincerity, and you will be successful in your search, no matter where you are."

"That may be, I don't doubt it, but I still want to go to the Himalayas."

"Very well then. Give me a piece of paper and I'll write down what trains to take and the names and addresses of some ashrams where you can stay when you get there. But you won't get what you want by running away. Everything you need is right here in Ranchi."

Kedarnath wrote down detailed travel instructions for Asim, along with the addresses he had promised, and then offered to teach him tantric meditation. Asim accepted, and during the coming days he paid several more visits to the yoga center where he received further instruction in meditation from Kedarnath. He was still intent on going to the Himalayas to pursue his dream, but for one reason or another he kept delaying his departure. In the meantime, Kedarnath informed him that the guru would be visiting Ranchi the following week.

"Normally, the rule is that the disciple has to wait six months after initiation before he can see Baba, but I will make an exception in your case."

Asim was not a disciple but he was curious to meet a yogic master. No harm in putting off his departure for another week, he thought.

One week later he found himself sitting in a small crowded hall, listening to a smooth-shaven man in a white dhoti and kurta and thick glasses give a talk that was so abstruse and philosophical he barely understood a word. All around him people were weeping and crying out

"Baba, Baba," and after the conclusion of the talk Asim left the room convinced that the man was nothing more than a clever pundit who was able to befool these gullible people with his high-sounding words.

Shortly afterward, Kedarnath informed Asim that Baba wanted to see him. "Baba said that you came late," Kedarnath told him. "He said that you should have come long before."

These words made Asim even more suspicious. Reluctantly, he accompanied Kedarnath to Baba's room where he found him eating his dinner. Before they went in, Kedarnath told him that he should prostrate in front of the master when he entered, but Asim was not about to do so. He gave Baba his namaskar, folding his hands to his chest, as he would for anyone else that he was meeting for the first time. Baba looked him over and asked, "What is the highest oxide of aluminum?" Asim was too surprised to answer. "Aluminum tetroxide," Baba said. After a couple of similar questions that Asim found equally irrelevant, he was led out of Baba's room, his frustration mounting. Why did I come to these people? he fumed as he got on his bike and headed for home. Why should I have to accept a guru? I don't want a guru. But as soon as he arrived home, he was overpowered by an inexplicable desire to see Baba again. It was a feeling of longing greater than anything he had ever experienced, a sensation that he could only describe as having been forcefully separated from the person dearest to him in his life. By then it was nearing midnight. Knowing that it would be futile to head back at that hour he went to bed, and after a fitful sleep he got up at five, took a bath, and got on his bicycle. It was six o'clock when he arrived, and Acharya Devi Chand Sharma was standing outside the gate.

"Come, Baba is waiting for you," he said as Asim rode up.

"What do you mean, Baba is waiting for me? I didn't tell anybody I was coming."

Devi Chand grabbed his hand and said gruffly, "Come, you will understand everything in due time." He led him into Baba's room where Baba was waiting for him, having informed Devi Chand earlier that morning that Asim would be arriving at six.

This time Asim did full prostration. When he sat up, Baba began recounting details and incidents from his life that no one could have possibly known—one after another, until Asim was convinced that Baba was able to read his mind. Then Baba told him why some of the practices he had learned from books were misguided.

"Do you see now how much energy you have wasted by not having had proper guidance? Do you understand?"

"Yes, Baba."

"You know, if you write something on a piece of paper and put it under your pillow but don't follow it in your life, then it has no value."

I haven't put anything underneath my pillow, he thought. Perhaps Baba's power has reached its limit.

Baba looked him in the eyes and said, "Don't you remember?" Suddenly a forgotten memory flashed in his mind. Some months earlier, he had written some inspirational advice from Aurobindo and the Buddha on a piece of paper and put it under his pillow, thinking to read it each morning when he woke up. But he had forgotten about it and never read it.

"Baba, how did you know that?"

"Your mind told me."

Asim was not satisfied with his answer, since he himself had forgotten the incident. "Who are you?" he asked.

Baba smiled. "I am not your guru. I am your Baba." As the tears began to fall, Baba reached out and touched Asim between the eyebrows. Within moments he became lost in a blissful, effulgent light. When he came out of his trance, Baba asked him to take an oath. The oath was in English, a language Asim didn't understand at the time, but he repeated it as best he could and then asked Baba what it meant. Baba smiled and translated it into Hindi for him. Then he added, "You came very late. I've been waiting for you. You should have come earlier."

For whatever reason, Priya couldn't stop crying that night, though she hid it as best she could, covering her face with the flap of her sleeping bag and feigning sleep. Was it because she recognized herself in Asim's story? Didi wasn't there to tell her that she needn't hold back her tears, but by now it didn't matter. "There is no difference between the sadguru and Divine Consciousness, between an enlightened being and the Self," Dada had said earlier that day, and as she let her tiredness ferry her across the turbulent waters of her emotions, she wondered if the guru would be there to meet her in her dreams, to chide her for having taken so long to get there.

6

$\mathcal{P}$RIYA SAID GOODBYE TO her mom for the third time in the conversation, and this time she was finally able to hang up the phone. She was still used to being called Paula, but it was starting to feel as if Paula were a character she was required to play with her family and students, a mask behind which her real self, the budding yogi, looked out with an ironic smile. Most of the forty-five-minute conversation had been spent listening to the latest gossip about her siblings and miscellaneous relatives, the primary narrative in her mother's life, with the final few minutes reserved for Priya's role in the never-ending story, which would then be added to the next version of the narrative, as heard by whichever member of the family her mother talked to next. As usual her mother asked about Fernando, and as always she ended her inquiry with a wistful air in her voice, as if she were still holding out some sliver of hope that they might get back together, a mother's whimsy that irked Priya more than she cared to admit, laden as it was with the unspoken supposition that her life could not be complete without a man. She wanted to tell her mother that she had found something much better than Fernando, or the next Fernando, but she had learned the wisdom of letting the sleeping Buddha lie. In the past she had tried talking to her parents about the esoteric teachings of Buddhism and Sufism but it had only unsettled them. Why their eldest daughter would want to abandon her Catholic roots was beyond them, and behind their cultured civility she could see them peering down their noses ever so earnestly at the assertions of other faiths that did not accord with the Catholic doctrine they had been raised on. That Tantra yoga was not a religion but a spiritual science was a distinction that didn't fit into their model of the world, and she had found it easier to leave that out of the narrative.

It was nearly two when she put down the phone, which meant she was going to be late for her afternoon session with Dada, but she tarried a few minutes longer to consult the scale and examine her choice of wardrobe in the mirror. Seven pounds slimmer since the ideological training, no mean accomplishment in a single month. She was a strict vegetarian now and was practicing yoga every morning without fail, but it was her increased mental discipline to which she gave most of the credit. The same effort she dedicated to controlling her thoughts was helping to control her calorie intake as well. Another samskara on the run, she thought, smiling confidently into the mirror.

After a few minutes deliberation, she decided to lose the T-shirt and replace it with a pastel purple blouse that she had picked up over the weekend. It had billowing sleeves that cinched at the wrist and a faintly oriental cut that complimented the Kashmiri pants she had picked out of an Indian catalog two weeks earlier. The pants were a little tight in the waist but another week or two and that would no longer be the case.

Twenty minutes later she was opening the grill door to the Santa Leocadia center with the key Dada had given her the previous week, an acknowledgment of how much of a fixture she had become there. He was in the office with his head bent over the computer when she entered, and she paused to savor the moment as she watched him grapple with the most recent changes she had made to his manuscript. He had his back to her but she could almost see the frown on his face as he struggled to come to terms with the Brazilian way of looking at the world.

"So what do you think?" she said. "Does it meet with your approval?"

Dada swiveled around in his chair. "Oh, Priya, you're here. And only twenty minutes late."

"Which makes me ten minutes early by Brazilian time. So, did you have time to go through it all?"

"I'm just finishing up. You did make some fairly substantial changes."

Priya didn't need to ask which changes he was talking about. "It couldn't be helped, Dada. Some things that might work in America won't fly in Brazil. If it sounds too rigid or exclusive, it will turn people off. We have to respect the culture if we want to be successful, and inclusion is the soul of Brazilian culture."

"Don't get me wrong, I'm not complaining, just processing. Like Baba says: we have to adjust with the changes in time, place, and person. Which is why I left your changes pretty much intact. What can I say, you're my culture guru."

His culture guru! She liked that. Especially since it was the God's honest truth. Dada still had a lot to learn about Brazil, and over the past month she had become his de facto tutor. On the way back to Rio from the ideological training, he had asked her if she would have time to help with the translation of a small book he was writing, an introduction to the practices. "Nowadays, if you are teaching anything," he said, "you have to have your book. If you don't, they'll just buy someone else's." She was in perfect agreement. The organization had a couple of introductory books in Portuguese but he wasn't satisfied with them, and he was quite right about the added authority that having his name on a book would confer when he gave public programs. She had agreed to translate it for him, but once she began reading the manuscript, she saw that it needed some serious editing, both for content and presentation. Brazil wasn't the United States, and it was obvious that he had written the book with a North American audience in mind. Fortunately, he was open to suggestions. For the past four weeks they had been revising the manuscript together, with Priya taking advantage of those sessions to give him a crash course in Brazilian culture and psychology, and she had ended up spending nearly all her free hours either at the yoga center with Dada or else holed up in her apartment revising the text or translating the finished chapters. It didn't make for much of a social life, but then Priya's social life had gone into hibernation after breaking up with Fernando, and the way she saw it, she was in the process of redefining what a social life was.

A year ago at this time she would have been looking forward to the weekend, impatient to get through the last of her weekly classes so that she and Fernando could go out and have a good time. Work was work—it paid the rent and afforded a healthy measure of professional satisfaction, a sense that she was making something of her life—but it didn't make her happy in the truest sense of the word. Happiness was something fleeting that she had to run after, and getting there always seemed to hinge on finding something interesting "to do," some pleasurable pursuit that could banish for a time the nagging sense of vacuity that always seemed to be following right behind. But since the intensive she hadn't gone out a single time—other than to the yoga center and The Bodhi Tree—and the absence of the bright lights and the cool crowd, of that once-coveted feeling of being a card-carrying member of the Rio scene, didn't seem like an absence at all. Quite the opposite, in fact. There was a kind of quiet, sedate sense of satisfaction that crept up on her every time she opened her computer to work on Dada's book, and that feeling was compounded several times over whenever she and

Dada were working on it together. "Baba's work," he called it, a phrase she would hear without fail at least once or twice every time she saw him, and the idea was gradually taking root. They were doing their part to change the world, and whenever the thought of going out and having a good time crossed her mind, she knew she would just be impatient to get back to the real social life, the one that revolved around doing her part to create a society worthy of the name.

They went over her changes together until they were both satisfied and then moved on to the next chapter, which contained guidelines for the practice of asanas and illustrative pictures for the different postures. Priya didn't see any problems with the text but she was less than happy with the photos of a young Teutonic male in leotards. They needed a better model in her opinion, and better meant female.

"Isn't that a little sexist?" Dada said, leveling an admonitory eye in her direction.

"I think you're missing my point, Dada. In Brazil your yoga audience is 80 percent women. We'd be fools to ignore that. And most Brazilian women will feel more comfortable with a female model, even if it's only at a subconscious level. I know I would."

Dada looked at her askance, then shrugged and threw up his hands. "Okay, if you really think it will make a difference, I won't argue. But redoing those photos is going to be a chore."

"Leave that to me. I'll organize the shoot. I've got a professional camera and I'm a pretty decent photographer. I'm sure one of our asana teachers will be happy to make the time. Oh, and in case you haven't noticed, apart from Rainjit they are all women."

"It has not escaped me."

"Okay then. We can shoot it in the upstairs hall over the weekend. If push comes to shove, I should be able to have them photoshopped and ready to go by the end of next week."

"Well, I guess I can't argue with that. Okay, go ahead, do it."

A Brazilian man could have argued with it and probably would have, if only out of habit. Certainly Fernando would have, entrenched as he was in the time-honored Brazilian tradition that men knew better than women. But Dada wasn't Brazilian and he had more than two decades of spiritual practice to soften whatever vestiges of male chauvinism he might have once had. Which made Priya feel more comfortable in some ways in his company, she realized, than she had ever felt around Fernando.

They spent the next forty-five minutes going over the text, until Maheshvari appeared in the doorway to say a quick hello before heading upstairs to prepare the hall for her four-thirty class. Priya suggested they take a short break and then move on to his Portuguese lesson, since she had a yoga class with Gunatiita at five-thirty. Dada was amenable but there was one thing he wanted to discuss before they switched over to Portuguese.

"You remember I mentioned doing another retreat for new people?"

"Sure."

"Well, I've been thinking and it seems to me we should develop a standardized program and take it on tour. Why limit it to Rio? It's a big country and as far as I know there's no other Dada or Didi doing this kind of work. I was thinking we could hold a public lecture in each stop to generate some buzz, make handouts for the classes. Once the new book's ready we could add a book launch to the program. Try to get some TV time. A whole campaign. Make a list of the key cities we should hit and do one weekend in each place. And that's phase one. If the tour is successful, we can follow it up with an advanced program. Say six months later? People are thirsty for spirituality, Priya. I see it everywhere I go. It's our job to give them what they're looking for. That's why Baba came to this planet. To raise a spiritual wave. So, what do you think?"

"I think it's a great idea. It could be really successful."

"Good. I'm glad you agree. Which brings me to my proposition. I need someone to help me organize it. That's where you come in—if you are willing. With your skill set you'd be the perfect person and I know you'd love it. So, why don't you consider working full-time for the mission? You can still do translation jobs in your spare time, but it seems a shame for you to be tied down to a day job when you could be doing so much more with your life. I mean, do you really want to spend your life teaching business English to Brazilian businessmen? Why not strike a blow against capitalism and come work full time for Baba? It would do wonders for your spiritual life."

Priya couldn't have been more surprised. "I'm not quite sure what you mean, Dada. Are you asking me to go on tour with you, be your official translator?"

"Translator, tour organizer, public-relations secretary, ghost writer. I can't do it by myself. That goes without saying. But if we did it together—now that would be something. I can already see Baba's smile. Just look."

Dada pointed toward the picture on the wall and Priya took a glance before she caught herself. "I … I don't know what to say, Dada. I mean, I have a job, responsibilities, bills to pay. I can't just drop everything. Do you know what you're asking me?"

"Oh, I know. Believe me. I went through the same thing myself, back in the day. It wasn't easy. But it was the best thing I ever did. By far. And I wouldn't ask it if I didn't think you were ready. Anyhow, all I'm asking is for you to think about it. For your own sake as well as for the mission. Just think about it. You owe it to yourself."

Did she? Well, maybe there was no harm in thinking about it, though she did warn him not to get his hopes up, citing once again her career and responsibilities — which was all true but then why did it sound like a ready-made excuse?

There was no more mention of it during their Portuguese lesson but that didn't mean that the elephant wasn't loitering in the room. Dada was diligent about his studies, helped along by the smattering of Spanish he had picked up while growing up in California, but whenever he looked up from the text they were using she could see the gleam of expectation in his eye that no amount of halting, thickly accented Portuguese could veil. For her part, she couldn't get it out of her mind. It wasn't a reasonable request in any way, shape, or form. She couldn't just drop her life to follow him around the country. But that didn't stop her from imagining herself traveling with him from city to city, turning the youth of Brazil on to meditation, yoga, and social change, wondering what it would be like and knowing the answer.

Those images were still in her mind when she unrolled her yoga mat in the upstairs hall and started following Gunatiita through a series of postures designed to bring her students to safe harbor in the calm waters of the heart. Guna was an elegant, soft-spoken Venezuelan in her midforties who had been living in Rio for more than a decade. Like many of the older women in the Rio satsang, she had separated from her husband when her growing spiritual pursuits had led their paths to diverge, and not long afterward she had given up a lucrative position at L'Oreal pursuing the chimera of outer beauty to dedicate herself to the pursuit of inner beauty as a full-time yoga teacher. Priya found her classes both soothing and challenging, and over the past weeks she had begun to understand that it was precisely the challenging nature of her practice that enabled Gunatiita to bring her students to such a profound sense of relaxation. Though they had never talked about it, she knew how difficult it must have been for Guna to give up the security of a successful career for the financial uncertainty that came with being a dedicated yoga instructor. And yet, the calm contentment and sense of purpose she radiated, not only during class but during all their interactions, seemed like more than sufficient recompense for whatever hardships or privations she had undergone. She had dedicated her life to her spiritual ideal and the results lit up any room she walked into.

By her best estimation, Guna had been nearing forty when she'd made the decision to radically transform her life, which made it all the more courageous. Priya could only imagine what her friends or relatives must have thought of such a decision. What she herself must have thought when the idea first dropped out of the blue and started tugging at her heart. Priya was only twenty-seven and she had a built-in safety net. With her work history and her contacts, she could take a few months off and her classes would be waiting for her; and in the meantime she could probably make enough money through freelance translating jobs to keep her apartment and pay her bills. It wasn't so far-fetched, now that she thought about it. And Dada was certainly right about one thing—it would be a lot more fulfilling than teaching English to people with money on their minds. Being in a spiritual environment all day long rather than spending the greater part of the day breathing the air of commercial ambition, teaching a skill to students whose principle and often only motive was to land a better job or move up the corporate ladder—there was no question how attractive that sounded. The real question was, did she have the courage to forgo her security blanket and devote herself to the one thing that made real sense to her: Baba's teachings and Baba's work? The more she thought about it, the more feasible the idea became, helped along by the soft sounds of the mantra serenading her from the yoga hall sound system and by the sense she felt of being more at home on her mat and in the yoga center than anywhere else in her life. She cautioned herself to be prudent, to give herself time to think it through. There would be consequences if she went down that road—her car payments for one, her family for another. She could just imagine how it would play with her parents if she told them she had given up her job to be an unpaid volunteer for some strange Eastern cult. But every time she looked up at Gunatiita and felt the grace and certainty that flowed from her as she guided them into the next posture, she knew that she wouldn't be able to achieve what she wanted to achieve if she was unwilling to accept the sacrifice and the challenges that the spiritual vocation demanded.

After an extended guided relaxation in corpse pose, Gunatiita had the class sit up and intone three long collective oms, followed by several minutes of silent meditation. As Priya let the sonorous echoes of the yogic incantation carry her into the silence of her interior self, she thought of Baba, sitting on the altar in his picture frame, and remembered that she was being guided by a power that knew far better what road she was meant to take. The thought brought an immediate sense of comfort. This wasn't her decision, it was his. She had signed over the power of attorney, and as intended, that simple act made everything infinitely easier. As it had been infinitely easier when she'd been a child and her parents had planned their vacations and took turns behind the wheel, leaving her free to enjoy the trip. She opened her eyes and laid a mental flower at his feet. Whatever you want, she told him. But I want it to come from you. I want it to be the voice of my own true Self guiding me through the next turning in the road. So if you could just manage some kind of sign, I would appreciate it. Just so long as I know who it's from.

7

$\mathcal{P}$RIYA HAD RECEIVED HER share of signs since she
first picked up *Siddhartha* and followed the address on
the flyleaf to The Bodhi Tree, and many, if not most of them, had been
connected with the books she had discovered in Maya's bookstore, part of
the shaman-like influence of Priya's favorite in-house astrologer. Hoping for
another well-timed apparition of the timeless, she headed directly for The
Bodhi Tree after her final class that week, determined not to give in to the
lure of going straight to the yoga center. Maya was alone at her desk in the
used-bookstore annex, and when Priya popped her head in to ask if she had
a minute, Maya rolled back her chair and asked her if she was up for a walk.

"I haven't been out of the store all day," she said. "I could use some
fresh air. What do you say? Should we head down to the beach?"

"That sounds perfect."

"Good. Let's go soak in some prana and you can tell me what's on
your mind."

Priya waited until they were walking on the sand with their sandals in
their hands before she brought up Dada's proposal, and as she talked,
she could hear the nervous energy in her voice, the difficult-to-conceal
excitement that kept bubbling up to the surface. Maya remained silent
while she talked, but there was an amused twinkle in her eye, as if she
were walking alongside a younger version of herself.

"It sounds like a dancing lesson from God to me," she said, when
Priya finally finished her narration and asked her what she thought.

"A dancing lesson from God?"

"Sorry. It's a quote from a book I used to love back in the sixties. *Cat's
Cradle*. By Kurt Vonnegut. Did you ever hear of it?"

"No," she said, her ears attuned now to the rumble of destiny. It was
just like Maya to steer her to a book, especially one she had never heard
of. Diving for pearls, as the older woman liked to put it.

"It's probably been forty years since I've opened one of his books but there are some things you never forget. *Cat's Cradle* was my favorite. The full quote was: 'Peculiar travel suggestions are dancing lessons from God.' The words of Bokonon."

"Who was Bokonon?"

"One of those great mysterious figures from literary history, even if no one remembers him anymore. He was a prophet and his words were collected in the Books of Bokonon. I have another quote for you: 'A good religion is a form of treason.' These were the sixties, remember. Turbulent times. So Bokonon deliberately arranged for his religion to be outlawed, because he knew it was the best way to get the people to accept it. Being a secret Bokonist became their way of getting back at the man, as we used to say in the day. It was a classic setup. A poor tropical island, an unscrupulous dictator, and a persecuted prophet. Ah, I tell you, that book was full of dancing lessons. Do you know what a cat's cradle is?"

"No."

"It's an ancient game. One person makes a figure called a cat's cradle with a length of string, the next person picks it up and alters the figure, then she passes it to the next person, who alters it again, and on you go, back and forth, depending on how many players you have and how long you want to play. And along the way the figure gets more and more complicated, until there is no longer any trace of the original design. And yet, it's still there, hidden in the web. It's symbolic of how our destinies are all intertwined. Each new figure is completely unpredictable and utterly unique, and yet they are all inextricably interconnected. Speaking of dancing lessons, did you ever see *The Wizard of Oz*?"

Priya was startled by the synchronicity. "God, it's funny you should mention that movie," she said. "I had a dream about *The Wizard of Oz* the morning I started reading *Siddhartha*, which is what brought me to The Bodhi Tree. In the dream I was wearing Dorothy's ruby slippers. I guess you could say I was Dorothy in the dream."

"Aren't you? Aren't we all?"

Priya laughed. "I guess maybe we are."

"Do you remember what Dorothy says, her most famous words?"

"There's no place like home."

"There's no place like home. That's our mantra. We're all trying to get back home, and sooner or later our inner guide points us down the yellow-brick road. Dancing lessons from God. Now why don't we get that coconut water and enjoy the sunset before you click your heels and disappear."

After she said goodbye to Maya at the entrance to The Bodhi Tree, Priya called Paco and asked him if he wanted a ride to the Zen satsang that coming Wednesday. She had seen him in class each week, but they hadn't had much of a chance to talk, and honoring their friendship despite the recent divergence in their respective paths seemed like exactly the kind of thing an enlightened being in the twenty-first century would do. After her conversation with Maya her mind was all but made up, but she was still hoping for one of his cards to seal the deal.

They met up outside his apartment as usual, and Priya wasted no time in filling him in on the latest developments in her life, a conversation that spanned both ends of their evening practice, first in her car on the way over and then during a leisurely stroll to a gelato cafe after the Ipanema satsang, where they sat and reminisced about the fruitful intersection in their respective roads. When she told him that something had finally clicked for her when she discovered Tantra yoga, leading up to it with the story of the letter she had launched over Guanabara Bay, Paco appeared genuinely pleased. "You're one of the lucky ones," he said. "It's not everybody who feels so strongly drawn to a spiritual path."

"So you won't abandon your friends, even after you start touring with this monk," he added a little later in the conversation, making it sound more like a statement than a question.

"You can count on it. And I'm counting on your cards to keep reminding me of what's real and what's not."

"Speaking of cards, I printed up a new one this week." Paco slipped a card out of the pocket of his daypack and leaned it against the napkin dispenser. "My latest painting."

She recognized the scene: Buddha meditating under the Bo tree amid a sea of stars, while above his head hovered a trio of horrendous, hair-raising demons, spitting venom at his imperturbable form, a frightening depiction of the obstacles the Enlightened One had to overcome before he entered nirvana. And yet, there was something strangely comforting about that solitary figure and the aura of tranquil determination that lay so lightly on his brow, as if by his meditation he were able to emanate a force field that kept the worst the world could throw at him at bay.

"It's beautiful, Paco. As always. Are those the three Maras?"

"The very same. Devaputtamara, Maccumara, and Kilesamara."

"And the inscription on the back?"

"Just four little words: *I see you, Mara!*"

"I see you, Mara?" she said, shaking her head.

"You haven't heard the story of the Buddha inviting Mara to tea? Well, according to the story, Mara never completely gave up after Buddha's enlightenment. He would still show up from time to time in one disguise or another, the ultimate tempter, going after the biggest prize of all, the Enlightened One. But the Buddha would always see through his disguise and say, 'I see you, Mara!' Then he would laugh and invite Mara to tea."

"Oh, I think I get it now. The battle never stops, even when you think you've won."

"Desire and attachment, Paula. They may change their disguise, but they're always going to be there, lying in wait. We have to be constantly on guard if we are going to see through the disguise."

"And then invite them to tea."

Paco flashed one of his rare smiles. "Something to keep in mind during your travels. Don't be fooled by the disguise."

Priya decided to file that one away. It may have been obvious, especially since she was so far from enlightenment she might as well be living in another galaxy, but it couldn't hurt to remember that desire and attachment wouldn't be taking a vacation anytime soon. There was something admirable about Paco's phlegmatic refusal to let himself get carried away by what he liked to call the "dance of deception." It wasn't her way of looking at the world, but she could see that there might come a time when it could come in handy. When those four little words might just be what she needed to tip the scales in her favor.

8

THE MORE THEY TRAVELED, the more Priya began to feel like a small-time promoter of a budding rock star. Nowhere more so than when they reached Campinas, halfway through a three-month tour that was gathering momentum with every stop. They had passed through Campinas a couple of weeks earlier, a brief stop for an on-campus lecture at the university that she had purposely failed to mention to her parents, and between the buzz generated by Dada's lecture and their contacts in the Mantra Center, the new-persons' retreat was filled to capacity—forty young Brazilians brimming over with anticipation, bundled into an old manor house just outside of town that belonged to the founders of the yoga center, husband and wife lawyers who were also co-owners of the city's premiere vegetarian restaurant, located two blocks from the campus. Some of the participants were already meditating regularly at the center, others were brand new, but all were looking forward to this chance to spend a weekend with the American yogi who had merited three and a half minutes of airtime on the local news two weeks earlier. If he wasn't quite a rock star in their eyes, he wasn't far from it.

Dada began the retreat with a Friday-evening yoga class, followed by a short guided meditation, dinner, and cooperative games designed to create a festive atmosphere and a sense of spiritual camaraderie. After the Saturday morning practices and a spectacular vegetarian breakfast ferried over from the restaurant, he gave his opening talk, "Meditation: the Art of Happiness," which Priya knew so well by now she could have given it on her own and barely skipped a beat. But rather than getting stale, she had appreciated it more and more each succeeding week, proof that well-chosen words, like good wine, mellowed with age.

"One of the characters I like most from spiritual literature," he began, "is Mullah Nasruddin. He was a thirteenth-century Sufi saint, and as you shall soon see, he was a very wise man. Now one evening a neighbor happened by and found him on his hands and knees beneath the lamppost outside his house. 'Mullah, have you lost something?' he asked. 'Yes,' the mullah replied, 'I have lost the key to my house and I can't find it.' 'Oh, what a shame. Here, let me help.' The man got down and started helping the mullah look for the key. Ten minutes went by, and then another ten minutes, and still no key. Finally the man asked, 'Mullah, are you sure you lost your key here? Where was the last place you remember having it?' 'In the shed.' 'In the shed? Then why are you looking for it here?' 'Because there is no light in the shed. I can't see anything in there.'"

The audience burst into laughter, right on cue, Priya included. Though she knew every nuance of the story, right down to the subtleties of Dada's well-timed delivery, she found it no less funny the seventh time around. In fact, she could feel the laughter bubbling up inside her the moment he mentioned Mullah Nasruddin, and it took a concerted effort not to let the laughter into her voice until she translated the punchline.

Dada waited for the merriment to subside and then broke into a playful smile. "Now, I think we all know the moral to this story, but it bears repeating. We have lost the key to happiness, and like the mullah we are looking for it in the wrong place. We are looking for it outside, in the external world, where it can't be found. If we want to find that key we have to look inside ourselves, in the darkness within. We have to open that shed door and install a light in there.

"Now it's only natural that we start looking for the key to happiness outside under the lamppost. It starts right at birth, when we find happiness in our mother's arms. She makes us feel safe and loved, and the other pleasures of the world soon follow. We discover a thousand and one delights as we are growing up, and eventually, when we get older, we meet the right someone and fall in love, we get that job we dreamed of, buy a new car, maybe have a child of our own. At least that's the blueprint. We may not win the lottery but life can sometimes feel like we did. And because we are able to achieve some measure of happiness in this way, we naturally think, on a subconscious level, 'okay, if I can just create the right conditions'—the right partner, the right job, enough money, a good reputation, good friends, a house with a view—'then I'll be happy.' Because we've seen all along how certain experiences make us happy. That is, they create conditions in which we feel happy. But there is one major problem with trying to find happiness in the external world: the world is mutative. It never stands still. In Sanskrit the word for 'world' is *jagat*, which means 'that which is constantly in motion, constantly changing.' Those conditions that led to your happiness are bound to disappear. The perfect partner starts to criticize you—'hey, what are you doing, watching TV all day, get your ass off the sofa and get a job!' Or she puts on twenty pounds. Or you do. We get a new boss we don't like and that perfect job is suddenly not so perfect anymore. We get sick, the neighborhood gets run down, a right-wing government gets elected, and on and on it goes. The conditions are constantly changing; they never stay the same. What was 'making' us happy no longer does, and again we have to try to create the right conditions so that we can feel the way we want to feel, and this ends up being a constant race for a carrot that is always just out of reach. It's like those dog races where the dogs chase after a stuffed rabbit. You don't have those in Brazil? Okay, well there is a stuffed rabbit going along the rail on the inside of the track just ahead of the dogs, and the lure of that rabbit is what makes them run. But they never quite get there, and neither do we. Or if we do, it is only for a few moments, and then we are off and running again after the next stuffed rabbit, the next carrot dangling from a stick. Thus the constant dissatisfaction of the human condition. Nothing is ever quite enough. And there is a simple litmus test to see if this applies to you: do you have any desire in your life? Is there anything you want? Okay then. True satisfaction means the absence of desire. Think about it. If you are truly fulfilled, then by definition you don't want anything, because you already have what you want. You are fulfilled, you are complete, you are full. But that, as we all know, is not our condition."

Dada had them now. They were leaning forward unconsciously, all eyes glued on the man in orange and his irrepressible smile.

"Now eventually a light goes on. 'Wait a second, even when I turn the key and open that door'—in other words, when I get the right conditions that make me happy—'isn't that happiness inside me?' Well, of course it is. That perfect girlfriend or boyfriend doesn't bring you a plate of happiness and set it on the table in front of you. That happiness was inside you all along—you just weren't able to access it until they showed up. It didn't come from outside, never did and never can. And if that's true—and in the end, nothing could be more obvious—then instead of trying to create the right conditions outside for the happiness inside to manifest, why don't I go directly to the source? It's in there somewhere. The fact that I can feel it under the right conditions is proof of that. So why not cut out the middle man? This external world is the middleman. Why not tap directly into that source inside me, so that I no longer have to depend on anything external? And *that's* when the game starts to get interesting—for as all the great sages throughout history have told us, there lies within us a fountain of unlimited happiness, and that fountain is our true being."

Priya loved the next part, as Dada returned to the Mullah Nasruddin story and invited his audience into the dark shed of the human mind, the unexplored lands within. They were barely inside when they began to notice something peculiar in there.

"Normally our minds are occupied with the outside world, hanging with our friends, trying to get something done, kicking back on the sofa and being entertained. But when we close our eyes and disconnect from the outside world, we begin to notice that there is a voice inside us narrating our experience, a voice that was there all along, even when we weren't aware of it, a constant dialogue we are having with ourselves or with any number of phantoms."

Dada began imitating that voice, eliciting howls of laughter as his students recognized themselves in his comic portrayal of the largely unnecessary and all-too-often obsessive ego-narrator. It was a masterful performance, not only because of his ability to make them laugh, but because of how obvious it soon became that all suffering could be traced back to the questionable sanity of that annoying and ultimately unwanted guest who never seemed to shut up—for in the substance of that inner monologue could be found all our complexes, fears, and anxieties, prompting Dada to point out that if we could read a transcript of this inner voice we might think that we were locked in a room with a crazy person. Which of course we were. The chattering ego had its good points as well, which he wove into his performance—the joys and accomplishments and little daily satisfactions that were also part of that incessant narration—but unfortunately you couldn't have one without the other. "Duality is the nature of the universe," he emphasized, when he was done with his comic monologue. "You can't have day without night, good without evil, foreground without background. You can't even conceive of it. There is no comedy without tragedy, no pleasure without pain, no happiness without suffering. Not at the level of mind, not if we are confined to the drama of our individual existence. Aaah ... but fortunately that is by no means all there is to us."

It was at this moment that Dada delivered the coup de gras, the key insight on which all spiritual endeavor turned.

"No matter what the peculiar and constantly mutating nature of our internal dialogue at any one moment, there is something behind our mind that is aware of what we are thinking, as if we were in a theater and our mind were on display on the screen in front of us—every thought, every feeling, every perception. What is there inside of us that is aware of that narrator's voice? What is that faculty that allows us to witness our thoughts, the one faculty that doesn't change with the weather? The yogis call it 'consciousness.' In the Western traditions it is more commonly called 'spirit' or 'soul,' but they are different words for the same thing. Consciousness is not our thoughts, not even the most subtle of all thoughts, the 'I am,' the pure feeling of existence. It is that by which we are conscious of our existence, the screen on which the drama of our individual lives plays out. If our thoughts and feelings are the text and images on the screen, then consciousness is the screen itself, without which they cannot be perceived, without which they cannot even exist. In Sanskrit it is sometimes called *satchidananda* — *sat*, immutable; *cit*, consciousness; *ananda*, bliss—the immutable blissful consciousness that is the witness of our thoughts."

There were a few blank stares while Dada paused and looked around the room, but one by one she saw the lights starting to go on behind their eyes.

"Think about it for a moment. We say we are conscious beings. What does that mean? What does it mean to be conscious? Think back a year, ten years, twenty years. None of the thoughts and feelings that are in our minds now were there ten years or twenty years ago. The content of our minds is completely different. Yet we know we are still the same person. How can that be? It is because who we really are hasn't changed, and who we really are is the consciousness that witnesses those thoughts. Our thoughts depend on consciousness for their existence. Not just our thoughts—our bodies and everything we see, the entire universe. Everything depends on consciousness for its existence. But consciousness doesn't depend on anything. One can claim, as materialists try to, that matter exists without consciousness, but that is just a thought, and that thought can't exist without consciousness. Take away consciousness and that idea disappears. Take away consciousness and everything disappears. When you realize that, your spiritual awakening has begun. All our fears and anxieties belong to the realm of our thoughts, to the theater of our individual drama, but we are not our thoughts. We are the immutable blissful consciousness that is the witness of those thoughts. Remove those thoughts and that consciousness remains in its pure state as the divine eternal Self. Descartes said, 'I think therefore I am,' but a yogi knows better. He knows that the deeper truth is, 'I think but I am not my thoughts.'"

Dada then had Priya read a long, scintillating passage from *A Search in Secret India* in which the great saint Ramana Maharsi describes the true self and what happens when a person discovers it for the first time. Priya could see the expressions on their faces as she read, running the gamut from bewildered fascination to something very close to rapture. If they hadn't been hooked before, they were now, and from previous experience she knew the spell would only grow stronger as the weekend progressed. For the next day and a half they would be hanging on Dada's every word—not only during programs, but during meals and free time as well, like groupies basking in the aura of a rock star. And like a good tour promoter, she would remain in the background, a nearly invisible shadow, despite being every bit as indispensable as the man on stage.

As far as she was concerned, it was the perfect arrangement. Apart from being Dada's full-time translator, she had selected the tour dates, booked the venues, written and mailed out the promotional material and press releases, set up the website and the Facebook event pages, collected inscriptions, answered queries, and organized volunteers in each locale to help with the logistics—in short, the tour depended on her for its existence, just as the mind depended on consciousness, depended on her seeing to the thousand-and-one little details that were indispensable to their success. But he was the one that all eyes turned to, and she preferred it that way. Had she her pick of superpowers, the one she would have chosen, the one she had most gravitated toward during her RPG days, would have been the power of invisibility, the power to affect the world sight unseen. And traveling with Dada, putting to use talents she hadn't known she had, made her feel at times that her childhood wish had been granted. "The best leaders lead in such a way that the people barely know they exist." She had read that in the *Tao Te Ching* and it seemed an ideal worth emulating, another chance to learn to act like an enlightened being. Dada couldn't have done it without her, but no one needed to know that.

With the possible exception of her parents.

They met up for dinner Sunday evening at Zen Roots, followed by a leisurely walk to her parents' favorite Italian ice cream parlor (they were politely appreciative of the restaurant's popular tofu lasagna but she assumed, quite correctly, that they would be happier with a more traditional, albeit less healthy dessert). She had debated over whether or not to invite Dada, knowing that the orange robes and turban would be a shock to their system, but in the end she decided that his natural charm might go a long way toward diffusing their cult-related fears. She knew of no better ambassador for Tantra yoga, and should the conversation turn in that direction, she hoped he would be able to explain what she was doing with her life better than she could.

It proved to be an uncomfortably prescient decision. Her parents were too polite to bring up her most recent lifestyle changes in front of the bearded, long-haired, orange-robed stranger whose improving but fragmented Portuguese still sounded jarring to her ears (she was thankful when they switched to English), but Dada had no such compunctions. They were barely into their meal when he began telling them how impressed he was with their eldest daughter. "How many people her age would give up a healthy paycheck and a comfortable career to go out and try to change the world by helping people to change themselves? You should be very proud of her." He said it with such conviction that she was almost glad he brought it up—except that she had been very careful to tell her parents that her voluntary hiatus from teaching was in essence a short sabbatical to shore up her spiritual life, rather than telling the unvarnished truth, in the words they might have used, that she had quit her job to go traipsing around the country selling Eastern esotericism to the young and the restless. But despite the familiar clenching in her stomach and the telltale narrowing of her father's eyes, Dada was so eloquent, so charming, so genuinely interested in what her parents had to say, in a conversation that ran the gamut from world literature to Brazilian politics (which he somehow managed to talk about intelligently without taking sides, despite being an American and new to the country), that by the end of the two hours they spent together, her mother was acting like a schoolgirl and her normally taciturn father had been practically glib.

It was a good beginning but the final results wouldn't be in until she completed her obligatory two-day visit to her parents' house that she had begrudgingly scheduled into the program—without Dada but with her two siblings, who were less worried than her parents over the unexpected direction her life had taken but infinitely more sarcastic. The one saving grace was that they would only be there for a few hours—they were driving down from São Paulo that Monday afternoon in her sister's brand-new BMW and had to drive back after dinner so Marina could go to work the next day and her brother could catch a flight to the capital.

Daniel was twenty and newly enrolled in the National Police Academy in Brasilia after having scored top-percentile marks in both the written and physical exams for the federal police force in a nationwide competition, one of only 180 successful applicants in a field of over ninety thousand. As expected, his ego had suffered the consequences, but even he couldn't compete with her sister Marina on that account. She was twenty-four now, with a masters in business administration from FGV-EAESP, Brazil's top-ranked business school (salutatorian in her graduating class), a prestigious position with PriceWaterhouseCoopers as a marketing consultant for the company's clients, and an unflagging need to prove herself better than her competition, which for the first fifteen years of her life meant continually butting heads with her older sister. Together she and Daniel made a formidable team, and Priya soon found herself sinking slowly into a morass of faux-capitalist ideology that appeared to have been imported directly from the weekly programming of TV Globo.

It was not what she had come prepared for. Her parents were staunch Roman Catholics, with two priests on her mother's side, and the initial sight of Dada's orange robes and turban the previous day had probably had them making the sign of the cross underneath the dinner table to ward off any possible evil. She had expected a polite but drawn-out battle in which she would have to defend the precepts of Tantra yoga in the light of Catholic doctrine, calling on their similarities to sound the virtues of a universal human spirituality that had found different expressions in different cultures and different ages, the denouement of a divine plan that could not be limited to a single faith if God's will was truly to be done. She had begun rehearsing her arguments before the tour began, even opening up the Bible and jotting down certain passages to support her thesis, along with some quotes from the writings of the Jesuit philosopher Teilhard de Chardin, a favorite of her Jesuit uncle, Alfredo. Had her uncles been there, the envisioned discussion would have lasted all afternoon and into the evening, covering everything from the dangers of succumbing to cultish thinking to the age-old debate between Western dualism and Eastern monism. And she would have welcomed the challenge, because it would have meant that they were taking her seriously, that life was a matter of the deepest thought and the utmost consequence, not merely a passage on a train to oblivion. But her uncles weren't there, and in the nine years she had been gone her siblings had staged a palace coup, taking center stage at the kitchen table. They had become adults in her absence, and their adult personalities seemed as foreign to her as she imagined hers must have seemed to them.

Not coincidentally, TV Globo was on in the background throughout the meal and the after-dinner conversation, Brazil's monolithic, ultra-conservative media giant and longtime supporter of the defunct military dictatorship, the world leader in moronic soap operas, platitude-filled talk shows, and formulaic news programming. A Globo anchorman had once compared the network's average viewer to Homer Simpson, and Priya had the disagreeable sensation that both her brother and sister had turned into more sophisticated, up-market versions of America's favorite cultural icon, more intelligent and less boorish but equally self-centered and materialistic, with the same unconscious parroting of capitalist dogma and an unconscionable fondness for the Brazilian right that had in Priya's opinion sold their country's soul to the devil (America's interests, Europe's interests, Brazilian billionaires' interests, take your pick). The tipping point came when Marina complained about handouts to the unemployed and the economic burden that SUS, the country's federally funded healthcare system, placed on taxpayers like herself, and then took advantage of a dramatic pause to add how disappointed she had been to learn that her own sister was content to add her name to the rolls of those who were dragging the country down. Her words and delivery seemed to have been lifted straight from a bad soap opera, which Priya was quick to point out after a contemptuous snort. "Just one question, Marina. Is that your best Adriana Esteves imitation? I would have thought you could do better. And to think, you made it all the way through business school on cliches like that. It just goes to show, miracles do happen."

Priya had left home before Adriana Esteves appeared in her most famous role as Carminha, Brazil's most unscrupulous and self-serving daytime femme fatale, but she knew the allusion would be enough to tip her self-righteous sister over the edge. Sure enough, things got testy after that, with her parents doing their best to sidestep the wreckage. Back and forth they went for the better part of the next two hours, with Daniel serving as Marina's aide-de-camp, right up until the moment they had to leave for São Paulo. There was no shouting, as there had been on occasion when they were young, but the lines between them were more clearly drawn than ever, and Priya did her best to give the lie to the conformist capitalist consumer machine and its insidious and nearly invisible ideology that her siblings had evidently swallowed whole and without choking. She found herself wishing she had invited Dada. He would have brought not only the gift of rhetoric and his habitual mental acuity, but a whole grab-bag of statistics and citations from contemporary thinkers that would have left her siblings with their bluster but little else. She had neither his gifts nor his experience, and so she had no recourse but to help herself to an assortment of anti-conformist cliches — fighting fire with fire, or in this case, mayonnaise with mayonnaise, which allowed her to more than keep up her side of the argument. Afterward, however, when she retired early for the night after helping her mom clean up and sharing a cup of coffee with her parents while they listened to Brahms on the stereo, she felt strangely disheartened, seeing how little mental effort was required to parrot someone else's views. It made her realize just what she and her companions were up against in their quest to change the world: it was one thing to have your heart in the right place; it was quite another to actually know what you were talking about.

Of course she didn't tell her parents any of that over breakfast when she apologized for her contentiousness the previous evening and assured them that she hadn't abandoned her career. "But there's no need to tell Daniel or Marina that," she added. "They might take it as an admission of guilt, like I secretly support a system that is fundamentally screwed up, which I don't." She reassured them about her career in part because she didn't want them to worry and in part because it was the truth — it was the premise on which she had accepted Dada's proposal — but as they made the welcome transition into light conversation she began to wonder just how true it was. Could she really see herself returning to a career that was nothing more than that? A way to support herself and occupy her time and talents, but not a calling, a vehicle to leave a mark on the world, to leave it a better place and herself a better human being. She could no longer imagine herself uttering the words "it pays the rent," as she would no doubt be forced to do if she could not put her talents to the service of a higher cause, as she was doing now.

Her father left for work after breakfast, and after arranging to meet up with him on-campus for lunch, she and her mother moved to the sofa for one of those long mother-daughter talks that had become all but extinct since she'd moved to Rio. It was the first time either of her parents had asked her about what her present life was actually like, other than a cursory outline, and she was surprised to see how curious her mother was about what life was like in an esoteric cult. Her mother didn't use that word, of course, but she didn't need to. She avoided the word and its connotations so scrupulously, so fastidiously, that it nearly made Priya laugh, and she soon realized that the best way to allay her mother's fears was by enticing her into her new world through the powers of narration. Fortunately, she had plenty of colorful stories and stock characters by now to keep her mother well entertained. At one point her mother shook her head with a bemused look on her face and lamented the fact that she had never run into any orange-robed monks when she had been young and ripe for adventure.

"Tell me one thing, Paula," she said, deliberately setting down the empty mug that she had been cradling in both hands as she listened to her daughter's tales, "is there anything going on between you two that you wouldn't want your fellow, well … what did you call them, disciples … to know about?"

"Mom, please! Why would you say something like that?"

"Well, let's just say there was something steaming at the dinner table in that restaurant, and it wasn't the lasagna. I'm just saying."

"Mom, he's a celibate monk. Okay."

"In my generation, that might have meant something. In your grandmother's generation, for sure. But things have changed, if you haven't noticed. Do you remember Father Morrel?"

"Yes, I remember Father Morrel."

"He's a father, all right, in more ways than one."

"Yes, I know, Mom. You told me all about it. More than once, as I recall. But this is not the Catholic Church. This is Tantra yoga. Maybe if Catholic priests did meditation and yoga and ate a vegetarian diet they'd be able to channel that kind of energy. Sublimate it instead of repressing it. Our monks and nuns aren't like that. They don't repress their desires, they channelize them into spiritual growth."

"Okay. If you say so. Forget I brought it up."

"As if I can."

Her mother didn't look convinced but Priya hoped the look of horror on her face would be enough to keep her from ever bringing it up again. Though she couldn't entirely blame her. The Father Morrels of the world had seen to that. Nor did she believe it had been any different in her grandmother's day, just less publicized. Either way, the travails of the Church's celibate priests had little to do with her or Dada, other than the sour taste in her mouth, which she hoped would disappear with a second cup of coffee.

By the time she met up with her dad for lunch at the administrative dining hall, which offered a regular vegetarian option, she had decided that both her parents deserved more credit than she had given them. They had had plenty of opportunity to let her know how much they disapproved of her most recent life choices and neither one had offered at the bait. There was no attempt to convince her to return to work or save herself from the "cult' she had joined. Other than some polite questions about her practices and her diet, they had left religion alone. Though she was sure she had caught flashes of disappointment and an underlying hope that she would return to her Catholic roots and her career, they had been far more tolerant than she had envisioned and decidedly more respectful than her brother and sister, who seemed to take her new lifestyle as a personal affront and an unspoken condemnation of their own way of life.

They were only a few minutes into their meal when her father surprised her just as much or more than her mother.

"Did I ever tell you that before I met your mother I dropped out of school for a time to be a rock musician?"

"No," Priya said, slightly incredulous. "I don't remember you ever telling me much of anything about your life."

This brought a smile from her father. "Well, it's true. Your grandparents weren't pleased, I can tell you that. I dropped out of college for eighteen months to play electric guitar in a rock n' roll band. We were going to be the next Mutants. And we might have been—if any of us were any good. But we weren't. At least I wasn't. Eventually I left the band and went back to school, and your grandparents cooled off after that. Though I will say, it took a while. Anyhow they figured I had got it out of my system and I had, but I'll tell you one thing: I wouldn't trade those eighteen months for anything. It was my chance to be a rebel and there's something to be said for that. It can do a person good to sow a few wild oats, get some experiences under their belt before they get married and settle down."

"Do you miss it, ever?"

"No, I don't. I've had a good life, a good family, knock on wood. If I had to go back I'd do it all over again and be thankful I did. Anyhow, there's nothing to miss, really. Those experiences are a part of me, just like everything I've been through is a part of me. It takes a lot of different pieces to make one whole."

"So does that mean you're okay with what I'm doing?"

"It was a shock, I'll admit. But if anyone had told me when I was twenty that I was making a big mistake I would have told them to shove it, and I would have been right. So yes, after giving it some thought I'm okay with it. That doesn't mean I won't worry. It's part of being a parent, which I didn't understand then, may my poor parents rest in peace, but hell, you're only twenty-seven and no kids. Enjoy yourself while you can, which you seem to be doing. And I imagine you're picking up some lessons you won't get anyplace else. I just hope they're the right ones. I like your friend, by the way. He may be full of shit with all this Eastern philosophy but I can see how he'd be fun to be around."

It was the longest conversation they had had in years, and it left her with the lasting impression that what she didn't know about people could have filled the Great Library of Alexandria. Which was probably a good thing to keep in mind the next time she was feeling judgmental.

9

THEY GOT BACK TO Rio at the beginning of December, and since Priya had already informed her landlady that she would be giving up her apartment at the end of the month—the day after Christmas, to be precise—she had a lot to do and little time to do it in. Nevertheless, she took a few days off for a much-needed vacation: no packing, no social media, no going to the yoga center to help Dada. She hadn't been alone in three months, and after having lived alone for the better part of the past three years she wanted to savor the solitude while she still could, before she began moving her stuff to Amarista's apartment three blocks from the yoga center where an extra room was waiting for her. Priya spent that time catching up on her reading from the comfort of her couch and taking long walks in her favorite haunts, including the trek up Sugarloaf to commemorate the six-month anniversary of the launching of her letter, those walks being her preferred means of processing what her father had referred to as lessons she wouldn't have picked up anyplace else.

Twelve weeks, twelve different cities spread over five states, and apart from the two days with her family in Campinas, the same routine each week. Loading their bags into the back of her two-year old Volkswagen Golf early Monday morning to drive to the next city, where they would stay in the local yoga center or else in the house of some welcoming family, the schedule planned out so that the longest drive would be no more than twelve hours. Getting to know the local Tantra yoga community over the next few days as they completed their retreat preparations, which usually included a public lecture and interviews with the local press. Then wrapping things up Sunday evening with collective meditation and a workshop for the local devotees. And yet every week was unique—different people, different places, different realities. How many people had she met over those twelve weeks? Too many to count.

A dizzying parade of faces, each of whom had touched her in some way, even if it were only an appreciative smile and a thank you for her translation. She had had intimate conversations with devotees from all walks of life: teachers, doctors, lawyers, secretaries, housewives, university professors, small-business owners, blue-collar workers, financial advisors, even two kindred souls who taught English and freelanced as translators—all bound together by their spiritual practices and their love for the tantric teachings. And countless more with the young people who attended their programs, searching for what she had found, their eyes lighting up just as hers had, with the recognition that they had happened on something extraordinary. She had also met other tantric monks and nuns, including one elderly Indian with a long gray beard who spent one unforgettable evening in Porto Alegre regaling a large gathering of disciples with firsthand stories of the guru that had them alternating between laughter and tears.

It had been a three-month journey through the pages of a spiritual text that she wouldn't have traded for any of the ones that were waiting to be boxed up for the move—*The Awakening of Priya Devi*, a book that was still in its early chapters but which thus far had her on the edge of her seat. But the best part had been her running conversation with Dada, who was apt at any moment to propel her mind into vistas that dazzled her with their beauty and challenged her with their unplumbed depths. Dada loved the spiritual teachings with a passion that made his eyes glow the moment any conversation began heading in that direction. And because he loved the teachings, she also began to love them with a similar passion, an infectious infection that she welcomed with her mind open as wide as it could go. They had six- and seven-hour drives where the moments of silence, all cobbled together, wouldn't have lasted the time it took to open the car door, and not a moment of that endless conversation was gratuitous or unproductive—not to Priya, whose soul seemed hungrier than it had ever been. The more they talked, the more she wanted to learn, to feel, to experience—as if the knowledge he was pouring into her was intent on washing away the barriers that stood between her soul and the ocean that beat at its walls.

When she thought of the people who had had the greatest impact on her life, her thoughts ran first to her parents: to her mother, who during those difficult adolescent years had been her closest and often only confidante, but even more so to her father, despite the fact that they rarely talked. She remembered one outing with her dad when

they took a boat out into the marshes of Goiás, a father-and-daughter
fishing trip that her mother reluctantly gave permission to (Priya was
sixteen at the time and more of a son to her father than his actual son).
For the better part of two days they drifted in a rowboat from one inlet
to another, always keeping close to the shore, while her father dangled
his fishing line in the water and smoked an occasional cigarette, his
daughter reading without pause from the assortment of books in her
satchel. Eight, nine, ten hours a day on the water, and they barely spoke.
"You hungry?" might have been the profoundest thing he said to her
that entire weekend, and yet she remembered those two days as among
the happiest of her adolescence. There was an unspoken sympathy
between them that didn't need to be acknowledged with words, and
real or imagined as it might have been, it gave her a sense of security
that provided a necessary bulwark against the vicissitudes of her teenage
years. He probably caught less fish in those two days than she had books
in her satchel, and she sometimes wondered, looking up from her pages,
what was passing through his mind as he sat staring off at the sky, his
fishing line hanging limply in the water. She could never tell. Yet most
of those books in her satchel he had either given her or suggested she
read—which was true for most of the books she had read since grade
school—and though they rarely discussed them, he had incontestably
shaped the direction of her thought, even more so than her mother,
with whom she had logged more hours of conversation than she had
with any other three people combined.

And then there was Fernando, her Fernandinho, all five foot eight of
him, who at first blush seemed to combine the best of both worlds—a
supremely confident young man who filled her with a similar sense of
security, but one she could actually talk to, like she had always been able
to talk to her mother. A true confidant who had seen something in her
that none of her friends or acquaintances had. He had been her mirror
to a better image of herself, a hand to pull her out of the quagmire of
her wounded self-esteem, but in the end the man who appeared beside
her in the mirror had turned out to be a phantom in the shape of her
own desires, glommed onto a human male whose one overriding virtue
was that he was interested in her.

But of all the people who had impacted her life, from her parents to
Lia Wyler—among her teachers, the one who came closest to being a
true mentor—Dada saw something in her that none of them had been
able to see: her destiny. The mission she had been born onto this planet to

fulfill. He saw not only the person she was but the person she was destined to become, and every lesson he passed on to her as they barnstormed their way across the urban wilderness of her homeland was designed to guide her toward the summit of who she was meant to be. She knew that the real teacher was Baba, that everything came from him and would one day return to him, that Dada was just a channel for that invisible presence that had been guiding her all along and which had started to acquire a visible form when she stepped into the Copacabana yoga center for the first time and saw the master's picture on the office wall, the same picture that graced the cover of the biography that had since become her favorite work of literature, a book she had begun reading for the third time after getting back from the tour. But for the time being, Dada was her conduit to the master's teachings. The invisible presence that peeped out from behind the photos that were everywhere she went these days, and whose miraculous and mysterious life had ended little more than a year after she had been born, was too ineffable for her to turn to with her real-time questions — at least for now, at least most of the time. Dada, on the other hand, was a living example of the teachings, one that she could reach out and touch (in theory, at any rate — as a celibate monk he wasn't allowed any physical contact with women, not even a chaste Brazilian hug, which still seemed unnecessarily severe to her, an unfortunate privation that clearly bothered her more than it did him). Maybe one day she would feel Baba's presence as palpably as she felt his, but for now he was her tangible link to an intangible world. Dada hadn't met the guru either — he had been sixteen when he died, a sun-burnished California teenager whose greatest love was his surfboard — but his dada had, and the way he talked about him, with such obvious reverence and love, she could almost see the light that Baba had lit in Krishnagitananda burning in Kamaleshvarananda, the same light that he was now passing on to her, as if it were a sacred lamp being handed down from one disciple to another.

The day after her commemorative climb of Sugarloaf, Priya got back to work, beginning with the arduous process of sorting through her things: deciding what to box up for storage, what to bring to Amarista's, and what was better off in the trash. She made several trips to the printers to check the galleys of Dada's book — his original goal of having it ready for the tour had proved overly optimistic, but they had stitched together enough time here and there during the past three months to finish proofing and laying out the text, designing the cover, and finding a printer who guaranteed to have it delivered before Christmas. She also had some important paperwork to complete for their next major event: a three-day meditation conference to be held the first week of March in the Riocentro Convention Center, the most highly anticipated alternative gathering in the city since Rio '92. Despite being on tour, she had been able to get Dada a booth and a favorable time slot for a one-hour lecture, thanks to one of her former English students, the personnel director at G2 Ocean, who was part of the organizing committee for the event. Her four-day vacation had been well spent and sorely needed, but she was glad to be back doing Baba's work, in her ongoing endeavor to become the person she was meant to become.

Early Christmas evening, before spending her last night in the apartment that had been the cradle of her newborn spirituality, Priya brought over the last of her boxes that were destined for storage. Dada's books had arrived two days earlier, one thousand copies in twenty cardboard boxes, fifteen of which they had stacked in the storage area below the yoga center, which was accessible only from the street (the other five boxes were in her car, to be sold at the retreat), but there was still room for some more of her things, and when they were safely stored, Dada mentioned that there was something he needed to talk to her about. It was an offhand remark, or so it seemed, a nonchalant aside as he reached into his pocket for the key to lock the roll-down door that abutted the sidewalk. Instead of going back inside, he suggested they walk down the hill to the nearest ice cream parlor, just around the corner. It had been a hot humid day and though it was finally starting to cool down, ice cream seemed like the perfect antidote to the aftereffects of some heavy lifting.

Dada waited until she finished her ice cream before he told her that he had gotten a call that morning from his supervising dada. "It seems some unnamed person wearing orange has brought a complaint against me for not setting a proper example before the local devotees."

Priya couldn't believe it. She had spent nearly every waking moment with him for the past three months; she knew better than anyone what kind of example he had set for the local devotees, and nothing could have been further from the truth.

"But that's just it," he said, when she expressed her indignation. "The complaint was about how much time I've been spending with an unmarried sister. I don't need to tell you who that is."

If Priya felt indignant before, she was practically livid now.

"Where do they get off! We've been doing *Baba's* work! I'd like to see them say that to my face, whoever they are!"

"You have every right to be mad. Neither of us has done anything we need to apologize for. Still, it is a delicate situation. There are rules, and sometimes a little diplomacy and a bit of circumspection is the best course of action."

"What rules?"

"Well, technically, dadas aren't supposed to have female assistants. Normally no one cares, as long as it's an informal arrangement and nothing gets out of hand, if you know what I mean. But it is a rule and this time someone complained. I suspect it was a didi, and I think I have a pretty good idea which one, but that's neither here nor there. My boss doesn't want any problems—which I understand—so he asked me to take care of it. That's the way things work in this organization. If someone lodges a complaint he's required to do something about it."

"Which means what, exactly?"

"Well, if it gets to that, they conduct an investigation, to see if there's been any impropriety, and if there has been, then that dada or didi becomes subject to discipline. Usually they get transferred, generally as far away as possible, like to the other side of the globe. Of course, that's not the case here, but still, this kind of complaint can make things uncomfortable for my boss, so what he'd really like is for me to make it go away."

"So am I a pariah now? Is it a crime that I'm sitting here eating ice cream with you?"

"No, of course not. It just means we need to be a little more circumspect, that's all. Like in the retreat, for example."

"So how is that going to work?" she said, somewhat sullenly.

"Well, for starters, I think we shouldn't be seen alone together during the retreat—sitting apart and talking, taking a walk, that sort of thing. All that would be fine in company, but not if it's just the two of us. Nothing that could be misconstrued. And maybe while we're there, it might be a good idea not to spend too much time together in general. That would certainly help to diffuse things."

"You mean we should put on a sham."

"No. I mean we should be diplomatic. Don't give anyone anything to talk about. It'll die down. People have short memories. We can't stop people from complaining; we can just make sure they have nothing to complain about. That's life in a spiritual organization. It's not all spiritual."

To Priya it smacked of Christian fundamentalism, self-righteous moralizing of the worst kind, and she liked it even less when he told her that in India the dadas used to call Brazil "the graveyard of acharyas," supposedly because Brazilian women were too free, too friendly, and all too often, too scantily clad. It was part of the culture, he knew, and nothing to be ashamed of—in many ways, that kind of freedom and friendliness was something to be celebrated—but the Indian monks in particular, and celibate monks in general, often had a hard time adjusting to so much freedom, as evidenced by the handful of monks who had ended up marrying Brazilian women. What he didn't say, and didn't need to, was that in their eyes it was the women who were to blame, the standard cop-out in a male-dominated society. As far as she was concerned, any monk who couldn't handle the company of women had unresolved issues that were to blame. But she wasn't about to make things difficult for Dada. She could be as circumspect as he wanted. After all, she'd had a lifetime of practice (so much for the stereotypical Brazilian woman). But that didn't mean she had to like it. Wasn't the whole point of the spiritual teachings to go beyond prejudice and mental complexes? To free the mind from any and all weaknesses that held it back?

To prove her point, she started telling a Zen story about a monk who pauses on his journey to carry a woman across a large puddle. Afterward, his companion criticizes him for touching a female. But Dada beat her to the punchline. "And the first monk says, 'I left her back at the puddle; it seems you are still carrying her.' Yes, I know the story. Let's just say there are some folks in orange who haven't put that woman down yet."

They left Christmas morning for the annual New Year's retreat at Ananda Kirtana, a Tantra yoga community in the hills of Minas Gerais, six hundred acres of rolling farmland and forested hills and valleys, boarded by one of Brazil's last unpolluted rivers and home to wildlife that had long since fled any of the places she had lived. It took her a while, however, before she was able to appreciate the idyllic setting and celebratory atmosphere. She was too conscious of who might be watching, of the unfounded suspicions that might be hidden behind any one of those smiling faces, especially the ones in orange. It didn't help that she and Dada pulled up together in her car, just the two of them, not fifty meters from the covered outdoor dining area where a small group of monks and nuns were eating lunch amid a smattering of devotees. The retreat would not start till the next day but the place was already getting crowded, and even from that distance she could feel the scrutiny heading her way.

Fortunately Didi Ananda Jaya had just sat down when Priya made it to the lunch line after depositing her backpack on a free bunk in the sisters' dorm. She served herself a plate and made straight for Didi's table, as if it were a safe haven where she could ride out the storm. Didi was sitting with a group of sisters who all seemed to be just as garrulous as she was, taking their cues from the cheerful, largehearted Filipina who had given Priya her next meditation lesson during the new persons' program in São Paulo. Priya knew most of the sisters at the table from the tour, and they greeted her with such unfeigned enthusiasm that she felt as if she had slipped into a warm cocoon. But no one made her feel more welcome than Didi Jaya, who reached out to squeeze her hand while she continued chatting with the other sisters and didn't let go for several minutes, turning her head from time to time to wink at her and give her hand another squeeze. Didi seemed to breathe the air of openness and friendliness, no matter whether it was a brother or a sister she was talking to, proof positive that orange robes were no impediment to a free spirit. She may not have had Dada's gift for spiritual philosophy, but never had Priya met a sunnier, more loving person, which was perhaps why she was able to work miracles with children in the slums of São Paulo.

After the meal and a dizzying whir of greetings and hugs from other devotees she had met on tour, Priya asked Didi if they could talk, just the two of them. They walked over to the shade of a spreading mango tree close to the dining area and sat down on the grass. When she told Didi about the complaint and how much it bothered her, the jovial yogic nun told her about the first time that a complaint had been lodged against her, when she had been a young didi struggling in Italy to start an alternative preschool. The circumstances were different—the complaint concerned her supposed "misuse" of project funds—but the sense of injustice and unfairness that seemed to have no place in a spiritual organization was the same.

"The problem, my dear, is that spiritual organizations are made up of human beings, and human beings can be very strange creatures sometimes. Even the ones who meditate. Sometimes I think Baba purposely gathered together all the spiritual crazies from around the globe and sent them to us. That's why I like to watch cartoons before I go to bed. The laughter helps me keep my sanity. You have to laugh; if you don't, you'll cry. And Baba doesn't want us to cry. He wants us to be happy. There's one dada in India, Bhaskarananda. When he was a new dada, back in the sixties, Baba gave a talk on ego, how ego was the greatest enemy in the life of a spiritualist, and Dada thought, 'oh my God, I have so much ego, what am I going to do?' So when he got a chance he went to Baba and asked him how to get rid of the ego. You know what Baba said? 'Get yourself insulted.' Those were Baba's exact words. 'Get yourself insulted.' Believe it or not, it works like a charm. Whether they're deserved or not, these kinds of criticisms chip away at the ego. And when they don't bother you anymore, then you'll know you've made real progress. Whatever happens, just remember, the guru's behind it. Sometimes the medicine tastes bitter, but it's all good if it gets us well. You're a good girl, I know it. Don't worry. Baba's going to have you shining like a freshly minted jewel sooner than you think. That's his job. Leave it up to him and you'll be fine. And if it ever gets too tough, or if you just need a change of scenery, you can always come stay with me in Peri Alto. The kids will make you forget all this nonsense in no time."

This was only the third time she had met Didi, but she always felt better after talking to her. The irritation didn't completely disappear, nor the uncomfortable feeling, real or imagined, that she was being observed and cataloged, but she relaxed enough that she was able to fully immerse herself in the retreat experience. She enjoyed the lectures and workshops, especially Dada's talk, entitled "The Spiritual Warrior," almost as much as she enjoyed the stimulating conversations with devotees and dadas and didis from around the country, and soon after the retreat began, Didi introduced her to Devashish, the author of *Tales of a Tantric Master*, who signed her copy with a beautiful poetic inscription and later sat for close to an hour after lunch with her and a group of other young devotees, narrating stories that hadn't made it into the book, including his own experiences with the master in the late seventies when he was barely into his twenties. But above all, the kirtans made her heartstrings sing, an empyrean intoxication that grew more and more intense with each succeeding day, culminating on New Year's Eve with a six-hour *akhanda* kirtan, danced in a circle around an improvised altar decorated with flowers, candles, and Baba pictures, in a hexagonal hilltop hall nicknamed the "temple," with glass walls and a magnificent view. Two hundred seekers combining their voices to lift the devotional fervor to heights no concert she had been to could have competed with. This "endless" kirtan ended with meditation and then more kirtan, arm in arm in a huge circle to welcome in the new year, and when it was over, it was obvious to her why Baba had given the place the name Ananda Kirtana, "the bliss of kirtan." The collective chanting was like a wave that lifted her higher than she could have ever hoped to go on her own, and she knew then and there that she would be coming back, year after year, drawn by mysterious beauty of this rustic ashram in the hills of Minas Gerais, where the residents told stories of hearing celestial strains of kirtan coming from the surrounding hills and forests at night when they were out walking under the stars, proof that the kirtan in that magical place was indeed endless.

10

ONE OF THE THINGS Priya had done while on tour was get as much video footage as she could with her well-traveled Canon Rebel and trusty tripod, including all of Dada's talks. By the time they got back to Rio she had scores of hours backed up onto an external hard drive, and somehow, along the way, she had managed to find enough free minutes here and there to slap together a twelve-minute promotional video that included clips from his classes, lectures, workshops, and television interviews, alongside other lighter, more informal moments. The video not only highlighted Dada's work and his persona, it also captured the spirit of the tantric teachings — at least that was her intention and she was proud of the finished product. Short videos had been a hobby of hers for some years now — she had made several videos of her teaching and translation work that had been instrumental in furthering her career, and she intended to do the same for Dada and the teachings. When she learned that her former student was on the organizing committee for the meditation conference she sent him the video, and it was on the strength of the video that he had agreed to give them not only a booth but a favorable time slot for a one-hour lecture. Two months later, and barely two weeks before the conference, he called her up and asked if she could drop by his office to talk about the program. The call released some butterflies in her stomach, but it turned out to be a stroke of unexpected good fortune. Not only was he excited to have Dada on the program and thankful to her that she had made it happen, one of the featured speakers had just canceled and he wanted to ask her in person if Dada would be able to take his slot. There was a hint of supplication in his voice, as if it went without saying that she would be doing him a favor, an old friend coming to the rescue, and he was confident from the video that Dada was just the kind of intelligent, charismatic speaker that would be perfect for the undercard. The slot was for Saturday evening from six to seven-thirty in the main auditorium, immediately preceding Monja Coen's keynote speech, and Priya accepted on the spot, without bothering to check with Dada. This was an opportunity that was simply to good to pass up.

As expected, Dada was happy to hear the news, though it did cost him a few deep breaths. He was already somewhat nervous about the talk, which he was determined to give in Portuguese, and the sudden promotion to featured speaker was enough to momentarily ratchet up his anxiety level. He had been making excellent progress in his language studies since she had begun tutoring him, and he had recently graduated to giving short talks in Portuguese after the Sunday collective meditation in the Rio center, but a public lecture was a challenge of a different order, one that had just gone up several degrees of difficulty, now that the venue had been changed to the main auditorium and considering that he would be going on right before the event's most celebrated speaker, with his poster soon to be plastered on the walls of the convention center, right beside Monja Coen's.

Priya allowed herself a few peals of laughter and a bit of chiding at his expense before she reminded him that she would be sitting onstage right behind him, giving him the option of switching to English whenever the need arose—though she was confident by now that he wouldn't need to. They had been working on his talk for the past several weeks, not only the content, which she had helped to polish by anticipating as best she could the audience's reaction to the logic of his ideas and the anecdotes and stories he had chosen to give those ideas their emotional impact, but also the language, which she had translated into Portuguese and then served as his audience while he practiced his delivery and committed the text to memory. There would be no teleprompter for him to lean on, as she had been told there would be for his TED Talk in May that she had secured for him with an updated version of the same video and whose text they had already begun crafting, but he wouldn't need one, not with another two weeks of practice to smooth out the rough edges. His accent was still pretty thick but that only added to his charm—for some reason, Brazilians loved the American accent. It sounded exotic to their ears, though not to hers, perhaps because she had grown too used to it. And even if he did stumble here and there over a word or phrase, his natural charisma would gloss over any mistakes and the orange robes and turban would blind them to the point that she doubted anyone would notice. He would be an authentic American yogi speaking Brazilian Portuguese in Brazil, and that would make him a tough act to follow, even for Monja Coen. Especially with an audience that was likely to be at least two-thirds women.

"Be ready to sign a lot of copies of your book," she warned him. "They're going to be lining up afterward, and trust me on this, you're going to need some pretty fancy footwork to get out of there without hugging any women. I'm looking forward to seeing you dance your way out of that. Personally, I've got my money on them."

She meant it in jest but they were words that proved to be prophetic.

The stir that she had foreseen began well before his Saturday-evening talk. His poster was everywhere when they arrived at the convention center for the three-day event, nearly as ubiquitous as Monja Coen's, a poster that Priya had designed around a photo she had taken of Dada meditating on a hill overlooking the magnificent Bragança Reservoir, on the way from Campinas to São José dos Campos. There were other spiritual teachers in exotic dress wandering the site, even a visiting Indian dada stationed in Europe who was making a short tour of South America, where he had worked for a few years some two decades earlier, but none so recognizable and none so striking as Dada Kamaleshvarananda, with his tailored robes and turban and his overflowing good humor. He took turns helping Priya and the other volunteers man the booth, which was stocked with books, pamphlets, incense, and yogic curios from India, and whenever he was there, a small crowd would inevitably gather to strike up a conversation or take a selfie. They had partitioned off a small area behind the booth with curtains and hung a sign above their table that read "Free Private Instruction in Tantric Meditation," and whenever Dada wasn't talking with visitors or signing books or perusing the other exhibits to network with the local spiritual community, he was usually behind those closed curtains performing initiations, nearly fifty all told, adding to a growing circle of admirers and acquaintances who helped to make it standing room only when it came time for his talk.

Whatever nervousness Dada had shown in the days leading up to the event, Priya knew she wouldn't see any trace of it once he stepped onstage. It was the showman in him that she was counting on (had he not become a monk, she was sure he would have been a bon vivant), and not once yet had he let her down. He loved an audience, any audience—it always seemed to bring out the best in him—especially an admiring audience, the bigger the better, and as soon as his passion started flowing, any audience she had ever seen him in front of soon became an admiring audience.

Saturday night was no exception. Priya was seated two meters away from him onstage, but other than a playful acknowledgment at the outset of the talk for his indispensable wordsmith, he never once looked her way. He even improvised his way through the written script at key moments when the emotion in the crowd was on the rise. Rather than let it dip again as he transitioned to the next part of his talk, he added analogies and exhortations, riding their emotion as far as it would take him. It wasn't planned and she would have bet that it wasn't even conscious. Even in Portuguese he had his finger on their pulse, and when he tripped over his words during those improvisational flights, he didn't seem to care, and perhaps for that reason neither did they. She couldn't call it masterful, not with his incomplete command of the language, but it was gripping, equal parts charisma and a well-honed ability to translate the power and profundity of the tantric teachings into the language of everyday experience. He even got some spontaneous yeses and bravos, which helped him measure the emotion, and when he was done, landing on the concluding words that they had sweated over to get just right, he got a resounding ovation that almost seemed out of place in that eclectic gathering of dedicated meditators and would-be saints.

"Meditation will indeed change the world," he told them, "because it will change you, and *you* will change the world."

Only eight minutes were left for questions, a full twelve minutes less than they had planned, but even that turned out to have been perfectly orchestrated. A short enough span to prevent the collective high from fully dissipating and avoid overtaxing his limited Portuguese. In fact, the two persons who stepped to the mic in that short period of time spent most of those eight minutes thanking him for sharing his wisdom with them.

There was a half hour break before Monja Coen's talk, and as Priya had predicted, the lines at the table outside the auditorium doors for the book signing were long and growing longer by the minute: one line for buying the book, with Priya as cashier, and another to get it signed, a task Dada took great relish in, joking with the people in line in a mix of Portuguese and English and pausing for pictures with his newly minted fans while letting them know that the world was counting on them. A continuation of his talk in miniature.

By then the doors to the auditorium had been closed and Monja Coen was being introduced, but there was a sizable crowd still milling about outside, most of them with a signed copy of Dada's book tucked underneath their arm or stowed away in their backpack, and most of them women, with the orange-robed monk and his flowing locks as the principal center of attraction. He had planned to attend Monja Coen's talk, but his "fans" came first, all of them prospective initiates in his eyes, and he was happy to continue chatting and answering their questions for as long as their interest lasted. Inevitably, some of them approached him for a parting hug, wearing huge smiles, women and men both, but mostly women, and Dada, as she had jokingly predicted, was undone by his success. After all that talk of love and inclusion, inner peace and human brotherhood, it would have made a poor last impression—the all-embracing, deeply empathetic monk who was too uptight to embrace a woman—and last impressions were the most lasting. She caught the telltale flicker in his eyes, the consternating realization that a night's work could be undone by a singular failure to understand the moment. And then the internal shrug as he stooped to embrace the first woman who extended her arms to put the finishing touch on an important moment in her life. No matter that she was a matronly senhora in her sixties, short and stout and beaming with appreciation. That opened the floodgates, and a couple of dozen women followed, none of them quite so old or quite so dowdy.

About halfway through the hugging line—which is exactly what it devolved into, a single-file line of people waiting for their hug with the charismatic young spiritual teacher in orange, 80 percent of them women—she noticed the door to the auditorium open and the visiting dada pop his head out, ostensibly to see if his brother monk was done signing books. His eyes widened in surprise and then his brow furrowed, accompanied by a frown. Whether it was a look of disgust or condemnation or both, Priya couldn't tell. But when he glanced her way, the look he gave her couldn't have been clearer: one way or another, it was her fault. Either working too closely with Dada had caused him to become lax in his morals, or else she had convinced him outright that this was a "necessary adjustment" if he wanted to be successful in Brazil. Either way, she could feel the blame crossing the space between them at light speed.

Priya had made a point these past couple of months to be extra circumspect whenever other dadas or didis were around—she had realized fairly quickly that the Brazilian devotees didn't care how much time they spent together or how free they were with each other, as long as certain proprieties were maintained. To them it was natural behavior—so natural, in fact, that it only increased their estimation of him. They used words like "authentic," "open," and "inspiring" when talking about Dada, and she was sure that part of the reason he was so popular was because they didn't feel any artificial barriers when he was around. Short of hugging the sisters, which everyone knew was against his monastic rules and thus didn't mind, he was a brother to everyone, men and women alike, and that closed the distance so rapidly you couldn't help but feel like family. But when other monks were around his behavior changed. It was subtle but she had learned to read the signs. A thin cloak of reserve settled softly across his shoulders the moment a flash of orange came within several hundred meters. She had learned to wear the same cloak as well, whenever the situation warranted, to the point that it was starting to become second nature—which was why the look the visiting Dada gave her felt so blatantly unjustified. It was an unwelcome reminder that certain prejudices were alive and well in a spiritual community pledged to the war against dogma.

They managed to make it in for the second half of Monja Coen's talk—the frowning dada had saved seats for them—and despite the uncomfortable though unspoken reminder, seated two seats away from her, that certain individuals saw her association with Dada as a "threat" to his monk's ideals, she was able to appreciate Sensei's talk even more than she had during the short time when she had been a follower of the popular Buddhist teacher. The fact that she was a strong woman who clearly didn't care what people said or thought about her—she was too mature and too wise for that—seemed even more important now than it had then. How great was it that the most popular Buddhist teacher in Brazil was a woman—a Brazilian woman! Of course, Coen Sensei had been married during the early days of her nun's life, to a Japanese Zen monk, no less, since Buddhist monks were allowed to marry. (How sensible that seemed!) Perhaps that had helped her to be so broadminded and sympathetic to the myriad struggles of the human kingdom. No doubt it had. But she knew that more than anything it was a result of her Buddhist practice, her long years of meditation dedicated to the enlightened ideal that any and all prejudices were barriers to the knowledge of the self and thus were nothing more than the shape one gave to one's own ignorance. So many years spent piercing the shadows raised by the ego that there was little she hadn't seen. Priya knew exactly what Coen Sensei would have told her had she seen that dada's look or heard the gossip that still made her feel at times that she was being watched by less than sympathetic eyes. "Ignorance has many faces, Paula. You have to recognize the disguise and see that it's all one face, Mara's face, putting you to the test. Don't let it fool you. Look past the shadows to the pure light of the Buddha mind." The same message that she was giving onstage, in different words and under different circumstances, and Priya was grateful for the reminder. And even more grateful that it was a woman who was reminding her.

The Indian dada rode back with them. He didn't say anything about the hugging line but she was sure he would give Dada a dressing-down once she dropped them off at the yoga center. She could only hope that he would be able to placate the senior monk by offering a humble version of the truth: he was taken by surprise and couldn't gracefully get out of it without creating a bad impression and undoing all the good work he had done, but rest assured, in the future he would take precautions. And if he needed a fall guy, he was welcome to lay the blame on her for not stepping in and explaining to the crowd that his monk's vows didn't allow him to embrace women or kiss them on the cheek in the traditional Brazilian greeting, allowing him to save face by taking the rap as the inattentive, unthinking bodyguard (maybe she should have stepped in but she had been enjoying it too much).

Whatever the Indian monk may have thought about that prophetically heralded and preordained transgression, he was certainly impressed by Dada's talk and the excitement it generated. "We could use a dada like you in Europe," he said emphatically, with his thick Indian accent, as she eased the car onto Nossa Senhora. "You would be very successful there." As if he weren't already successful in Brazil. Or was it that success in Brazil didn't really count? The graveyard of acharyas, indeed! Anyhow, he was theirs now and they weren't about to let him get away. Europe was the past and Brazil was the future, as she had told him more than once while she was getting him up to speed on the intricacies of Brazilian culture and the guiding spirit of its people. It wasn't pride in her eyes but a true reckoning of where the world was headed. He was where he belonged, the place destiny had chosen for him, and she hoped he had realized this by now, no matter what the other dada thought.

11

THREE WEEKS LATER, PRIYA was sitting behind her desk in the office when Dada came downstairs to tell her about the idea for a new project that had come to him the night before. She had received his text just before going to bed, but he had been deliberately mysterious about it—*tell u when u get here*—and those few little words had been enough for her to suspect that their three weeks of relative calm were about to come to an end.

"It came to me in a flash during my evening meditation," he said, pulling up a chair. "It dropped out of the Cosmic Mind and landed right in my lap."

"Well, don't keep me in suspense. I've been wondering all morning what it is we're going to be doing for the next I don't know how long."

"Okay, tell me what you think of this: two professional trademarked courses, one for the general public and the younger crowd, one for the corporate world. The first we call 'Change Yourself, Change the World.' The second, for the corporate world, 'The Enlightened Leader.' Much of the material will be the same, but we tailor it to two different audiences. And in case you are wondering, I reserved the domain names last night, just before I texted you. You see where I'm going with this, right?"

"I think so. Relaxation, meditation, yoga, positive thinking—lifestyle change for health and happiness—coupled with learning how to use your new skills to positively affect the world around you, from family to friends to the workplace. Am I getting warm?"

"Positively scalding. The packaging and overall slant will change according to the audience, but the basic principles will be the same. Let's start with the business side. You were part of that world. What are the biggest buzzwords in the business sector these days?"

Priya shook her head.

"Productivity and creativity, especially creativity. Most jobs being lost these days are being lost to machines. The grunt work at Amazon is being taken over by robots, computer algorithms are phasing people out in the financial sector, but the one thing machines can't do is think creatively. That's what every business is looking for these days: creative thinkers. It's where the future's at. The more creative your company, the more successful you'll be, the better chance you'll have to survive. What sets Apple and Google apart? Why are they the most successful companies in the world? Because they're the most creative. Their real edge is that they are able to hire the most creative minds on the planet. Not necessarily the smartest, in traditional terms, but the most creative. The ones who have the ability to think outside the box. Innovation, that's the key. If your company is not innovative, it's going to be left behind. Do you know how much money goes into funding studies on creativity these days? Hundreds of millions of dollars a year."

"Really?"

"Absolutely. Although it should come as no surprise, since creativity is what drives marketing and advertising."

"Ah, of course. The joys of capitalism."

"Let's call it one of the few positive side effects. And what is the one exercise that has been conclusively shown to enhance creativity?"

"Meditation."

"Right you are. There are others—yoga's been shown to increase happiness by stimulating the pleasure centers in the brain, and there is a direct correlation between happiness and creativity—but the real story is meditation because regular meditation is the one activity that has been scientifically proven to stimulate the growth of the neocortex, including those brain centers directly associated with creativity and well-being, *and* to decrease the volume of the amygdala, which is responsible for fear, anxiety, and stress—all factors that reduce productivity. And what is the single biggest cause of lost revenue in the business world?"

"Employee turnover."

"Right again. The more complex the business, the more time and money goes into training your employees. Obviously, I don't need to tell you that, since that was what you were doing for a living. The biggest investment in any modern business is in human capital. And what is the biggest single cause of employee turnover?"

Priya was pretty sure she knew but she shook her head and smiled, not wanting to break Dada's flow, not when he was on a roll.

"Conflict in the workplace, especially with one's bosses, and especially due to unenlightened decisions made by those same bosses. Now—and here's the kicker, what's going to make our course different than other meditation-in-the-workplace courses—we are going to use the science of Tantra yoga to show exactly where creativity, wisdom, love, compassion, and empathy come from, the higher layers of the mind, and what practices develop each of those layers. The *atimanas kosha* to stimulate creativity, the *vijinanamaya* for wisdom and enlightened decision-making, and the *hiranamaya* to develop love, compassion, and empathy, all essential qualities for cutting-edge management. We are going to train them to create a harmonious, empathetic environment in the workplace, the kind of environment in which their employees will flourish, the kind that will have them looking forward to coming to work each day, that will have them coming in early and leaving late—in short, the kind of environment that leads to maximum productivity. And we'll package it together with research that shows conclusively that these are the exact qualities that foster maximum growth and productivity in any company or institution. You want your company to succeed? People it with enlightened leaders."

"And in the process make gobs of money."

"Unstated but implied. And ultimately true."

"Isn't that just a little perverse? Helping the capitalists be more successful capitalists?"

"Not at all. It's the next and perhaps final step in the undermining of capitalism. Like Baba says, capitalism is a mental disease. You cure the disease, you solve the problem. If there are no capitalists, there is no capitalism. What does Baba say in *Problem of the Day*? 'If the infinite longing of the human mind does not find the proper path leading to psychic and spiritual fulfillment, it becomes engaged in accumulating excessive physical wealth by depriving others.' We are going to help them to fulfill that longing. And that, my dear, is a game changer."

"Okay, I'm convinced. By the way, I don't know that there are any meditation-in-the-workplace courses in Brazil. I know there are in the States, especially in California, but as far as I know, that hasn't caught on here yet."

"Even better. We'll be the first. We'll set the standard for everyone else. The first and the best."

"And the other course?"

"Change Yourself; Change the World. The same practices but a different slant, different packaging. Here the focus is on personal growth, but we'll show how the development of those same qualities will, by themselves, automatically transform your relationships and in the process make the world a better place. I'm thinking of calling it the force-field effect. You develop a force field around yourself of enlightened energy—wisdom, harmony, creativity, empathy, happiness, peace of mind—and that force field not only protects you, it affects the vibration of everyone you come in contact with. Friends, family, colleagues. I've already started getting some quotes and studies together.

"So, what do you think?"

"I think it's going to be a lot of work."

"Just the way Baba likes it."

Dada was positively glowing, and behind that glow she could see his vision taking shape in his mind: a parade of students and managing directors filling her video camera with glowing testimonials of how the course had changed their lives and their companies; the growing cracks in the foundation of capitalism widening into gaping chasms, causing whole buildings to sway—thirty-story high-rises housing the managing boards of banks and think tanks and diverse corporations, the shakers and movers of the capitalist world holding onto their chairs as the walls oscillate and their coffee mugs slide down the conference table, a cataclysm set in motion by the mere fact of having learned to close their eyes and look within. Meanwhile, on the streets below, the rat race slows to a languid, gentle pace, a once-fragmented society finally blending its discordant flows into a single, glorious river moving steadily toward the ocean of divine realization.

His vision was so compelling and so attractive, she could practically see it reflected in the pupils of his eyes, but what painted itself on the canvas of her mind was all the work that would be involved in pulling it off. Especially for her, since he was the visionary in their relationship, the man up front, while she was the one behind the scenes who was going to have to find the ways and means to materialize that vision. The lion's share of the work and none of the glory.

"Have you ever heard of EST?" he asked. "Well, that was in the seventies; now they call it Landmark."

"No, I don't think so."

"Maybe it hasn't made it to Brazil, but I'm surprised you didn't come across it while you were at Berkeley. Anyhow, it's a personal development course that caught on big in the seventies. The founder, Werner Erhard, studied Zen in the sixties with Alan Watts, and he adapted some of the Zen teachings when he designed the course. It had a huge impact on the counterculture, even to a certain extent on mainstream culture, until it ran into some scandals, partially over some of Erhard's more controversial techniques and partially over the fortune he made from the course. No one knows how much, although the IRS did go after him. That was in the early eighties. It disbanded for a few years after that and then resurfaced with a facelift. A new name and new management—less actionable but still very, very successful, to this day."

Dada reached into his pocket and handed her a CD.

"This is a documentary about EST. It will give you an idea of just how successful this kind of thing can become if you are able to tap into the collective psychology. No sense reinventing the wheel, right? If we are going to do this, why not study as many successful models as we can. And Landmark is as good a place as any to start. Their material is nothing like ours, but still, there's a lot we can learn from them. From how they package and market their product to the dynamics of their course. Then we can see what other relevant models are out there, get the lay of the land, so to speak, see what you think might work for Brazil. Not the content so much as the packaging, the organizing, the marketing. The content is all ours, and that's why we're going to be successful. Because we have something to offer that no one else has."

Dada leaned back with a satisfied smile and interlaced his hands behind his head. He had finished his pitch and he was confident that he had sold the script. It was good to see him like this. As always, his confidence was infectious, even if it was only a vision at this stage. Since the meditation conference, he had seemed a little distracted, as if he weren't quite sure what to do with himself without a serious challenge to occupy his talents. They had a local retreat coming up in a few weeks, the TED Talk in May, some other small activities here and there, plus a yoga center to run and local devotees to guide, but being the leader of the Rio Tantra yoga chapter wasn't enough to contain the kind of surging energy that coursed through a man like Kamaleshvarananda. She had begun to realize just how ambitious he was—if ambition was the right word for a yogic monk hellbent on changing the world for the better—and this was exactly the kind of challenge he needed to put his energy and ambitions to the service of the world. And if this was what he needed, then it was probably what she needed as well, considering how intertwined their destinies had become.

"Okay. Then we might as well get to work," she said, tapping the CD. "I'll give this a watch and start doing some research. If we are going to pull this off, there is no sense in wasting time."

"That's the spirit, Priya. Baba may have given me the vision, but he meant it for both of us."

It was the beginning of April now, a little over a week into what would prove to be a typically mild Rio winter, and by mutual agreement they decided to launch the Change Yourself; Change the World course first, setting a target date of June 1 for the pilot program. Two months was an inordinately short time in which to put such a program together, but the idea was to do a trial run while they were still developing the material, so they could get a feel for what worked and what didn't. A couple of trial runs, maybe three, spaced out over a few months' time, and if things went well they should be able to trademark the course and officially launch it at the end of the year. By that time the students would be beginning their summer vacation and looking for something to do. In the meantime, they would also be working on The Enlightened Leader, which would require a higher level of sophistication and more lead time if they were to gain a foothold in the marketplace, and whatever success they had with the first course would give them added credentials for the latter. They needed a brand, built around Dada and his charismatic talents, and the more they were able to develop that brand, the easier it would be to break into the corporate world and begin their quest to undermine capitalism from within.

As expected, developing the courses meant a huge amount of work for Priya, but a lot of those hours were spent with Dada as they worked through his ideas and fashioned them into a concrete shape that she could begin turning into course materials, and the trade-off was well worth it. Most of their time together was spent on the work, including attending other programs to learn what made them tick, but Dada was getting more Brazilian by the day, and they managed to find time for other, more relaxing pursuits as part of his ongoing education in Brazilian culture (as long as there were no other dadas or didis in town): going out to listen to Brazilian music; visiting some of the other local satsangs, including the Zen satsang in Ipanema one balmy evening in early May that featured a long, enjoyable conversation with Paco; turning Dada on to some of Rio's hidden treasures that gringos rarely discovered on their own, including the hike up Sugarloaf and the one up Corcovado; and even making the occasional obligatory trip to the beach—his favorite was the surfer's beach at Arpoador, where they would typically do a short meditation on the outcropping, which reminded him of Point Dume in Malibu, before he would go off to rent a shortboard while she lay on her *canga* with a book and watched the surfers riding in on their waves of glory.

On one of those outings, they ran into a small group of devotees camped out on the sand near Arpoador, and Dada spend the next couple of hours in the slanting sunlight telling stories of his beginnings on the spiritual path, foregoing his usual dalliance with the waves to submerge himself in his memories of another surfing Mecca where he had had his first and second births—the first when he emerged from his mother's womb, and the second when he emerged from the womb of ignorance to take initiation from Krishnagitananda, bewitched by the sound of a flute so otherworldly it soon made him exchange one ocean for another.

He had been surfing that afternoon at the north end of Zuma Beach in Malibu, on a clear day in early spring with the wind whipping up to fifteen knots, as it often did that time of day, the incoming waves forming perfect A-frame peaks with a slow-rolling break, the closest thing to paradise on earth in his twenty-year-old surfer's mind. He rode his last wave with the sun hovering at the edge of the horizon, bathing his body in incandescent shades of orange and red as he rode into shore and packed his shortboard into the back of his mother's SUV. Instead of going straight home to hit the books, however, he returned to the beach and sat down on the sand to watch the sun flame out over the water. While he was sitting there he heard the distant sound of a bamboo flute serenading the dying of the day. The faint music was so beautiful, so profoundly melancholy, so inseparably fused with the scene in front of him, that he started tearing up with the onset of a longing so large, so bittersweet, that he began to feel as if his chest might burst from the joy and pain of being alive under the immense cathedral of the western sky. The sun had just sunk below the waves, suffusing the beach in shadow, when he began to feel a sense of time slipping through his fingers, the sobering recognition that if he didn't do something truly worthwhile with his life, then the miracle of his being alive in that moment and on that beach would turn to ashes, like a diamond incinerated in Odin's furnace.

The distant music had grown graver by then, more in keeping with the twilit shadows and the solemn turn his mind had taken. As he started walking toward his car, he noticed that the music seemed to be coming from the low cliffs behind Pacific Coast Highway, just beyond where he was parked. He saw what looked to be a trail, and instead of getting in his car he started clambering up the steep incline toward the houses above, a thin scattering of million-dollar Malibu mansions overlooking one of the world's most celebrated vistas. He knew he shouldn't be doing this—these were private villas, there were trespassing laws and guard dogs. At the very least they would have state of the art security systems—this was Southern California, after all—but he wasn't going to be doing anything more than apologizing for having been bewitched by a flute that few sane men could resist and begging to be allowed to listen from a distance, with a promise not to disturb whatever guests might be there for what he assumed was a private outdoor concert.

But when he reached the top, honing in on the flute as he climbed, there were no guests, no dogs, not even a fence, just a border of thick ornamental hedges at the edge of a spare but meticulously cared-for garden of flowerbeds, desert shrubs, and sculpted patches of lawn at the back of a somewhat modest but elegant mansion, where a couple of muted clear-sky lamps flanked a pair of French patio doors in whose glass he could see reflected the first stars in the soon-to-be-night sky. It took a moment before he saw him, sitting cross-legged on the grass: a tall, dark figure in orange robes with a bamboo flute pressed to his lips, arising out of the gloaming like an ancient genie or a medieval sorcerer holding the world in thrall. The flautist's eyes were closed, but after a few moments he opened them and put down his flute, a flash of white in obsidian skin that startled his uninvited guest.

"What took you so long?" he said. "Didn't you realize I was calling you?" Very nearly the same words, he would come to find out later, that the master had said to Krishnagitananda when he first met him in India nearly three decades earlier after a long and eventful search.

Confused but relieved by what he took to be some kind of cryptic welcome, he apologized for the unwarranted and illegal intrusion. "It's just that the music was so beautiful," he said, "I couldn't help myself."

"Well now that you're here, it's time you learned how to meditate. Come, sit here, in front of me. We can talk about the music later."

Not wishing to be rude, he sat down in front of the dark-skinned yogi, and half an hour later he had been initiated into tantric meditation. This was followed by a long conversation on the nature of consciousness and the true purpose of human life, during which the moon gradually rose over their heads, suffusing the garden in its growing radiance. He couldn't remember having had a single spiritual thought in his life before that night—his parents were lifelong atheists who were proud of never having seen the inside of a church (except while sightseeing in Europe when they stopped in to admire the artwork), and they had passed on to him their proud disregard of spiritual mummery—but from the time Krishnagitananda gave him his mantra to the time their conversation ended over three hours later, everything he heard and experienced that night made sense in a way that life itself never had. None of what he heard seemed strange or esoteric or even difficult to grasp. It was his own experience of the world explained in a way that made him finally understand what that experience meant, the true nature and purpose of the longing that had driven him forward since the time of his earliest memories. The quintessential "aha" from which there was no turning back, as if everything in his life had been pointing him toward that cliff in Malibu.

"I still remember everything he told me that night, practically word for word," Dada said, shaking his head in wonder before the silent, rapt audience stretched out on the sand. "That was twenty-two years ago and it could just as well have been yesterday. That's how deeply engraved it is in my mind. Baba says that when a person receives tantric initiation he becomes *dvija*, twice-born. The first birth is the physical birth and the second is the spiritual birth. I don't remember my first birth, but I'll never forget my second."

That first night on the cliff was followed by two more, this time entering by the front door from the street above, during which he received his second meditation lesson and the answers to a thousand questions he didn't know he had. The house belonged to a well-known LA music producer who had asked Krishnagitananda to house-sit for him while he and his family were on vacation, knowing how much the elderly yogic monk would appreciate meditating and playing his flute on that breathtaking promontory, but his official residence was a sprawling old two-story yoga center in a seedy section of Koreatown in the gang-infested redoubt of South Central Los Angeles. The contrast couldn't have been more striking: crackheads selling their wares at either end of the block, garbage on the streets, bars across the windows of local businesses, even the remains of charred buildings from the LA riots a couple of years earlier when the neighborhood had been smack in the middle of ground zero. And yet Krishnagitananda was just as much at home there as he was on the cliffs of Malibu. "The Divine Consciousness is everywhere," he told his young initiate as he pulled his car up to the gate for the first time, understandably nervous about leaving a late-model SUV parked on the street in that questionable neighborhood, even in broad daylight, "but sometimes it doesn't hurt to have to dig a little deeper to see it." It was also, as he soon learned, an ideal place to do service, stranded on an island with the people who needed it most. Krishnagitananda had numerous friends and admirers in the upper echelons of the LA music scene, even some actors and politicians, including many who considered him their spiritual guide, but he had just as many friends in the neighborhood, most of whom had fallen through the cracks in one way or another, and he was there for them in equal or greater measure, to pick them up in whatever way he could, if that meant a handout to get them through the month, a meeting with a local councilman on their behalf, or a good scolding when a good scolding was called for.

Dada didn't know enough about yogis or the yogic lifestyle to register any shock during those first visits to the LA yoga center, other than the shock of being in a part of town he would have never thought to visit (for good reason), but whatever images he had stored in his mind of smiling meditators from magazines and movies, they were quickly dispelled in the company of this former jazz musician turned yogic monk. The first Sunday after their meeting in Malibu he accompanied him to the soup kitchen the local satsang ran downtown, in the middle of the biggest congregation of homeless people in the city, handing out plates of rice and beans and vegetables to several hundred grateful souls. Afterward, Krishnagitananda sat on the steps of the boarded-up warehouse where they served the meal, surrounded by a disheveled but happy crowd, talking about everything under the sun and recounting his many adventures across several continents. When he joined him again the next Sunday, and the Sunday after that, and recognized many of the same faces waiting for Krishnagitananda to join them on the steps after everyone had their food, it dawned on him that most of the down-and-outers that came every week for their plate of rice and beans were more interested in hanging out with the hippest yogic monk ever born than they were in the food.

Soon he was tagging along for city council meetings where Krishnagitananda was a source of both smiles and chagrin, a yogi with right on his side and an admonishing tongue reminiscent of a black Clarence

Darrow; or helping him with the food bank that he ran out of the yoga center's garage. He began teaching English literacy classes in the living room and helping him with the local neighborhood watch — in short, whenever he had free time and Krishnagitananda could use a hand, he made his way to South Central, and once he graduated from UCLA, he started making that crosstown trip nearly every day of the week, until it didn't make any sense anymore for him not to move in. By then his unformed image of a yogi had coalesced into that of a social activist spreading consciousness as he set out each day to change a little bit of the world, even when that world included spiritual get-togethers in Hollywood's most exclusive mansions or recording sessions in LA's best studios (Krishnagitananda didn't accept many gigs, just the ones that interested him and just enough to give him the money he needed to fund his many activities). When he first met Krishnagitananda, Dada was a second-year university student with no conscious interest in either spirituality or social activism, attached by a seemingly unbreakable surf leash to his shortboard and the pursuit of an all-around good time, but by some kind of divine alchemy, a catalytic reaction began inside his skull within minutes of meeting his dada, and soon he wasn't interested in anything else.

"My parents were pretty cool about it," he mused, "when I look back on it. They didn't like it that I was hanging out in the seediest part of the city, but I was doing good things and it wasn't hurting my studies, so they didn't try all that hard to talk me out of it. If they were afraid I had gotten involved in some sort of cult, they didn't show it, and anyhow I invited Dada to the house about a month after I got initiated and he charmed them right out of any prejudices they might have had. My parents are both into jazz, big time, and once he started telling stories about playing with all these famous jazz musicians in the fifties, he had them eating out of his hand. Then he started talking about Indian classical music and some of the Indian musicians he'd played with and studied with — he even gave an impromptu concert for them on his flute — and after that I think they actually envied me. They were kind of shocked when I told them I was going to move into the yoga center, but that was because of the location. It wasn't quite like moving into a favela in Rio — nothing in LA can compete with the favelas here — but it was about as close as you could get. I remember, I told them that it was an opportunity to live and work with a real live saint, and how many people can you say will ever have that kind of opportunity. It wasn't the most psychological thing to say, given their views on God and religion, but I think they actually got it. They had only met him once, but once was enough to know that they had never met anyone like him in their life and probably never would.

"And that was the thing: he *was* a saint. Maybe not the typical saint you read about in books. I mean, what kind of a saint plays jazz saxophone, right? But he was, no question about it, and you didn't have to be all that perceptive to realize it. I didn't have a chance to meet Baba physically, but being around Dada was the next best thing. He was so tuned into Baba, it was like having a live channel to the master. You could see it in his eyes, he was so connected to the guru. You know that picture of Baba, the one where he is looking directly into the camera, so that whatever angle you look from, Baba is looking directly at you? It was uncanny, but whenever Dada looked at me it was like I was looking into that picture, looking directly into a fountain of compassion so deep you could get lost in it. He was my direct channel to Baba. And that's why I never looked back. Not once. I was with him for seven years, until he passed away, and he was the one person, the *only* person, I've ever met, before or since, who was exactly the same with everyone, whether it was a wino on the street in South Central or a famous music producer like Quincy Jones — whom he took me to meet, by the way. The same respect, the same sense of presence, the same being there in the moment with that person and giving them his full self, without reservation. With everyone else I've always seen some variation in their eyes, some ripple of emotion, a moment of distraction, a flicker or two of self-consciousness, even people who are highly spiritually developed. But Dada was the one person I've met in this life that every time you looked into his eyes they were always the same: the same calm, the same presence, the same compassion. That's the real satsang, spending time with someone that when you look into their eyes you see pure consciousness looking back at you. Because they are looking into pure consciousness."

"And you never thought about becoming a monk before he died?" someone asked, after a suitable pause.

"Sure I did. By the time I moved into the yoga center, I already knew I was going to be a monk one day. We talked about it. He was ready to pay my ticket to the training center anytime I wanted. But as long as he was there, I wasn't leaving. I figured I could always do that later, and it was the right decision. He had seven years left when I met him, and

I got to be with him right up until the moment he left his body. That's one decision I'll never regret."

Someone asked about how Krishnagitananda died and several more stories followed, but Priya's mind began to wander, flitting back and forth between the past and the future. As she lay prostrate on the sand, looking up at Dada as he talked, his eyes shining with memory, she could feel herself drinking in his brio, his passion for life, his contagious enthusiasm for the spiritual quest, and that set her to wondering what their life would be like in seven years. Would they be sitting on this same beach together, perhaps, talking to another rapt group of young devotees, taking a few hours off from the workshops and courses that had made Dada a household name in the spiritual community of Rio and beyond? Would she be nearly as recognizable as him by then, stepping out of his shadow as she worked alongside him to spread the tantric teachings to a new generation of spiritual seekers? Dada was no Krishnagitananda, not yet at any rate, but he was still young and there was no doubt that the spiritual spark that she saw in him was a glowing ember of the same fire that had burned in the older monk, needing only the passage of the years to fan it into flame. The spiritual transmission in its purest form, from guru to disciple to the disciple's disciple, the real royal lineage. She would love to see what Kamaleshvarananda would be in seven years. What she would be if they both kept to the same trajectory. She could see now where he got his idealism, his conviction, his spiritual fervor, his passion for social change. He had someone behind him that had made it all possible, as she had someone behind her, and she couldn't help but think back to the letter she had lofted over Guanabara Bay and the poster she had seen the next morning with Dada's rugged but charismatic face. Calling her as Krishnagitananda had once called him from the cliffs of Malibu?

The trial run of the Change Yourself; Change the World course took place in a small second-floor hall in Botafogo with a view of Sugarloaf through the plate-glass windows. Dada had argued for a larger venue but Priya had convinced him to think small for the time being, and the wisdom of that decision was borne out when only sixteen people ended up enrolling, barely enough to cover the cost of the hall and materials. Dada had been counting on a much larger audience, and he found it difficult not to see this as a setback, but Priya considered it a blessing. Until they were sure they had a course that really worked, a professionally designed and psychologically and spiritually impactful weekend program that would have its participants hounding their friends to do the course as well—the one marketing strategy, if it could be called a strategy, that had withstood the test of time—they were better off with a small group that would barely raise a ripple. "You want a modern-day, Tantra-yoga-style EST," she told him. "Then let's refine it to the point that it blows people away before we start pushing it for real. We get to that point and then we'll rent a big hall in a prime location. Because then we'll need it."

It wasn't EST or Landmark yet, but despite his reservations and the low turnout, it was pretty good. Nearly everyone left there that Sunday afternoon on some kind of natural high, with tools for living that they were convinced would make their lives better. Its biggest flaw, as she saw it, was that the course depended too much on Dada's personal charisma. That was fine at the start, as a way to get the ball rolling, but she wanted a course that anyone could teach and enjoy the same success. And for that they had to refine the logic and the simplicity of what they were teaching until it bowled people over the way Krishnagitananda had bowled him over that night in Malibu when he took apart life in this universe and showed his new initiate what made it tick, as clear and as precise as a Swiss watch—an analogy that brought Dada over to her way of thinking. They had another retreat coming up at Ananda Kirtana the third week in July, one that she felt far less apprehensive about this time around, and after that they should be ready for a second trial run. It might take more time than he had envisioned to get it off the ground, she told him, but the mere fact that the first of their two programs had begun to materialize was a major landmark for them both. "Landmark with a small l," she said, "but soon to be followed by a big F for a big future." It barely qualified as a joke but it was enough to elicit a smile. The course needed a lot of improvement, no doubt, but that was just a matter of time, and time was stretched out in front of them.

What was more important to her was that they were doing it together. He had had his seven years with Krishnagitananda, and now she was coming up on her one-year anniversary with him. She had no way of knowing how long it would last, but if the sages were right, then the present moment was eternal, and eternity would be just long enough.

12

RIYA WAS LOOKING FORWARD to the retreat as she used
to look forward to her vacations back before she had
become a yogi. After the long hours she had put in these past couple
of months and the investment of so much emotional capital, she could
use a break, and these days she could think of nothing more enjoyable
than attending a spiritual retreat. It was how she used to think about her
vacations in the old days, but perhaps there was no more telltale sign
of how far removed those old days had become than the familiar surge
of excitement she felt when a dada who had been recently transferred
to Brazil from Australia asked her if she could translate his workshop
on the opening afternoon of the program. It was the same sense of
anticipation she felt each morning when she left Amarista's apartment
and headed for the yoga center. Or when she opened her computer
after evening meditation to start revising the latest material they had
been working on for the course. The satisfaction of putting her talents
to use for the best possible cause: Baba's work, as she had come to think
of it, a chance to do something truly meaningful with her life, to throw
herself into the sacred mission of spreading the tantric teachings as an
instrument in the designs of the Cosmic Mind. It was a thrill to see so
many kindred souls whom she hadn't seen since the New Year's retreat,
but it was when she sat beside this dada in the hall and picked up a mic
that she felt most truly in her element. Doing Baba's work and thankful
for the opportunity.

His talk was on service and spirituality, and it sparked so many ideas
that were begging to be added to the course that on more than one occasion she lost track of the translation, something she couldn't remember
ever having done before. The dada found it amusing, as did the audience. Fortunately, a few attentive souls were kind enough to fill in the
missing phrases so Dada wouldn't have to repeat himself, and despite

her embarrassment she ended up joining in the laughter. Afterward she corralled him and he spent the free hour before evening practices elaborating his ideas and answering her questions, a conversation in the outdoor dining area that drew other participants who were glad to see the seminar continue. It was a chance for all of them to go even deeper into the teachings, and it was while one of her compatriots was asking a question that she realized that the retreat was not a vacation but a chance to go deeper into the one work they all shared: the work of becoming a vehicle through which the teachings could spread. The deeper they went, the deeper they became, and *they* were the real work.

Two things especially stood out from Dada's talk. One was his demonstration of how altruism, not egoism, was the more authentic expression of human nature, a finding that ran against the grain of contemporary social science but which became patently obvious to everyone in the audience as Dada laid out his arguments, amply supported by studies and statistics, all veering toward the simple conclusion that the practice of altruism overcame the shackles of egoism and thus enabled the human being to achieve profound and lasting happiness, the goal of every human life, a fact demonstrated over and over again by people from all over the globe who had made a habit of helping others because of how good it made them feel.

"Imagine a world," he said, "in which everyone was motivated by altruism, not egoism. I think anyone in their right mind would agree what a wonderful world that would be. But I'm going to take it one step further: what a wonderful world that *will* be. Because that is where we are headed. It is where every one of us is headed, turning egoism into altruism through the power of spiritual meditation, and the world is right behind us. You may not think so, looking at the politicians who run this country, or the corporate executives who pay them to run it the way they want it run, but take a closer look. They may be the world's most powerful minority, but they *are* a minority, a very small minority, and they are getting smaller every day. Eventually they are going to go the way of the dinosaurs. Dinosaurs are still around but we call them birds now. Sixty-five million years ago there was a massive extinction event that killed off all the dinosaurs except for a single group of feathered reptiles that got smaller and smaller over time until they became what we now call birds. Far too small to make the earth shake, as their predecessors had. That extinction event is coming for the world's most powerful minority."

Though Priya was translating, it didn't stop her from joining in the clapping and adding a whoop of her own to the other whoops and hollers that were cascading through the hall. The other point that really caught her attention was something Baba had said in a discourse about the future of the spiritual path, which she translated for the audience from one of the PowerPoint slides (all in English) that Dada was kind enough to pass on to her later during their post-seminar detente.

"In order to be established in perfect spirituality, a person must fully embody the spirit of service to the creation, even if it is only right at the end of their spiritual journey. Otherwise spiritual realization is not possible. Those who accepted this truth only at the end of their journey might not have lost anything personally but humanity lost out on their service, as did the whole of life, the plants and animals and even inanimate matter. In the future more and more people will realize this and make service to the creation an integral part of the spiritual path right from the outset."

The quote was new to her but it went right to the top of her list of inspiring Baba quotes. Many of the spiritual stories she had admired over the past year and a half were of yogis and saints who had gone into seclusion to perform their spiritual practices, isolating themselves from society so they would have less roadblocks to navigate on their way to the supreme beatitude. She couldn't call them selfish—she was sure they had helped the world in some way during their years of seclusion, even if their only service was the harmonious waves they emanated—but how much greater would have been their impact had they lived their lives among their fellow human beings, working alongside them to make the world a better place. She thought about people like Che Guevara and Nelson Mandela, how much they had done for the world, and she was sure that those sages who had lived out their days in forests and caves would have done far more than Che or Mandela, had they been living in places like South Central Los Angeles, sending waves into the world that no one could sidestep, waves that would rock the boats of those whose boats needed rocking. Or in Rio or Paris or Peking. If that was the profile of the yogis and saints of the future, then Dada was right. That wonderful world of altruism was coming, and quite possibly a whole lot faster than anybody could foresee.

The retreat would have been perfect had it ended in similar fashion, on the high-breaking wave that she rode into the akhanda kirtan on the final night like a surfer riding the perfect big kahuna, but it turned out that the master had other plans for his beloved daughter. Having danced all night, she took a nap after breakfast with the mantra still pulsing in her blood vessels and capillaries. When she sat down to lunch after packing her things and stowing them in the car, she overheard a conversation that reminded her of the old adage that heaven and hell can be found on opposite sides of the same street. A couple of Indian dadas were sitting one table over, talking in English, when she heard them mention Kamaleshvarananda. She was involved in her own conversation with a group from Campinas, but her ears had a volition of their own, and moments later she heard them say that if Kamaleshvarananda's transfer went through, then they were going to have to think carefully about who should take over for him in Rio—the dada who was coming over from Europe to take his place would be the logical choice, but Rio was too important not to consider other options.

Her first reaction was disbelief. If it were true, Dada would have told her. But as her ears strained to pick up the rest of the conversation, the sinking feeling in the pit of her stomach seemed a far more reliable barometer than any of the objections her mind could raise. There were no more life-shattering revelations from the next table over, but she continued to feel as if she were wading through molasses as she finished her meal and helped Amarista and another Rio devotee load their bags into the car, wondering where Dada could have gotten to and when she would be able to get him alone for a private talk.

Her chance didn't come until the following day. The thought that it might be a Black Monday was impossible to avoid as she opened the office at 6:45 and did her best to stay busy until Dada came down for breakfast at his customary hour. Once they were alone in the office, Priya didn't waste any time. She told him what she had overheard and then slumped deeper and deeper into her chair as he began telling her how the dada who had been visiting during the meditation conference in March had started lobbying the central authorities for his transfer as soon as he got back to Europe. His own boss had to agree to a swap for it to even become a possibility, something he didn't think would ever happen, but he had been wrong. One week before the retreat his supervising dada had called to tell him that after a long and difficult deliberation he had decided to agree to the swap that would be sending him to Portugal. All that was left now was for the central authorities to officially authorize the transfer and set a date.

Priya, who only one day earlier, at the end of the akhanda kirtan, was sure she had never been so high, was equally sure now that she had never been so low.

"Why didn't you tell me?" she asked, unable to keep the tremor out of her voice.

"And ruin your retreat? No thank you. Today was plenty soon enough."

"So what are we going to do?" she said, her eyes as clouded as her future.

"I think what we should do right now is get some fresh air and find someplace more private to talk."

They left the office open and walked the four blocks to the beach, where they took off their sandals and skirted the water until they found a good place to sit, a patch of smooth, dry sand with no one else within ten meters. It was a mild, sunny day, in stark contrast to her mood, and they were silent for some time before she realized that Dada was waiting for her to speak. She could see the concern in his face, and it troubled her to think that he might be suffering as much as she.

"What I don't understand," she said, making a belated effort to get her mind in gear, "is why he would agree to such a thing. There's no better dada than you in all of Brazil. He must know that. After the new persons' retreats, the meditation conference, the TED Talk, now the courses? It just doesn't make sense that he would let you go."

"Oh, you're quite right. He didn't want to let me go. That's why it took him so long to decide. But in the end he thought it would be best for me, and by extension, for the mission."

"Why? Because Europe is more important than Brazil? He's supposed to be thinking for Brazil. What is there that you can do in Portugal that you can't do here?"

Dada had a pained expression on his face. "That's not it, Priya. I didn't want to tell you this, for your sake, but you're probably going to hear about it anyway, sooner or later. He thinks it's best I go because he thinks it's the best way to protect me."

"Protect you? Protect you from what?"

"From what could be misconstrued as an unhealthy attachment. Or more to the point, what he is afraid could or would develop into an unhealthy attachment."

She shook her head in disbelief. "That again! I thought we had put that behind us?"

"So did I."

"God, these Indian monks! I think he's so worried about one of his dadas getting involved with a woman, he's the one with his mind in the gutter. Sorry for being so blunt about it, but it's the same old story. He's still carrying the woman in his mind after you helped her across the puddle. Why can't they see that a monk can have a perfectly healthy relationship with a woman without sexual attraction being involved?"

"To be fair, Priya, I don't think it's that simple. His heart is in the right place. He's a senior monk looking out for a junior monk, trying to protect him and protect the reputation of the organization."

"Why are you defending him? You know he's wrong."

"I'm just trying to be fair, that's all. He's a good man. He's just trying to do the right thing. I may not agree with him, but I have to try to see things from his point of view also, not just mine. Remember, he comes from a very different culture."

Priya felt like she was trying to keep the lid on a pot that was about to boil over. "Are things really that different in India? It's hard to believe that women and men don't have platonic friendships there, including dadas and didis. I mean, come on."

"Actually, in his generation I don't think they do, outside of the family. The younger generation, sure, but I think his generation sees that as a degeneration. In fact, I've heard them say it. The way they look at it, the easiest and best way not to fall into temptation is to keep your distance. I know it sounds strange but that's the way they do it in India. Then they come to Brazil and it's like entering an alternate universe. It's not an easy adjustment. He just thinks I'm playing with fire and the best and safest thing is to get me far enough away that I don't get burnt."

"So you don't get burnt?" Priya let out a sarcastic snort. "Come on. And he honestly thinks Europe is going to be any different? They don't have fire in Europe? If that's what he wants, he's going to have to send you to a place without human nature."

That made Dada laugh, the first bit of levity in a difficult conversation.

"I take it you mean a place without human beings?"

"That's the place."

"Yeah, well, I don't think they are going to transfer me there."

Priya shook her head. "These guys, they're like dinosaurs. How can they expect to have any success in Brazil if they can't adapt to the culture? People aren't blind, you know. They see what's going on, and I tell you, it doesn't go down well. Sooner or later, they are going to have to stop trying to impose Indian culture in Brazil; otherwise they are never going to get anywhere. Well, that settles it. If they transfer you, they might as well transfer me too. I've got some money saved up. Not much but it'll be enough to get us started. The same course we're doing here, we can do there. I've got news for them: they can't stop me from going too. I'm not wearing orange."

Priya wasn't looking at Dada anymore. She was staring out at the ocean, riding a rising wave of indignation.

"I don't think that's a good idea, Priya," he said, after a few moments silence.

His voice had dropped in tone and when she turned her head his eyes were impossible to read. "Why not?" she said, suddenly afraid of what she might hear. "We're doing Baba's work. Why should we let them stop us? We're a team."

"Priya, think for a moment. What would it look like if you went chasing after me to Portugal?"

"That's their problem, not ours."

"No, Priya, that would be our problem. People would see it as proof that we had a romantic attachment."

"So what? Where is it written that we have to lead our lives by what other people think? Two people can love each other without having a physical relationship. What's the harm in that? You wouldn't be breaking any rules."

The defiance in her voice started to falter the moment she saw his reaction—the sudden, unconscious drawing back, followed by a rictus of strained self-control, as if she had placed a hex on him. But by then it was too late and the thought had her teetering on the edge of mortification.

His words, when they materialized, were slow and measured, as if he were negotiating a dangerous minefield that required all his sangfroid. "I appreciate your sentiment, Priya, I really do. And we do make a great team. But I don't have the same feelings you do. I'm a monk, Priya. The world is my mistress. I hope you can understand that."

"I do," she said, the tears clouding her eyes as she somehow, foolishly, soldiered on. "Of course I do. I just mean that we have something beautiful together, something pure and spiritual. We're doing Baba's work. Why should we let them ruin that? You're not breaking any vows and I'm not asking you to. Here or Portugal, it doesn't matter. We have Baba's blessing, I know we do."

Dada picked up a small shell and threw it into the water.

"Be that as it may, Priya, if you followed me to Portugal it wouldn't be good—for either one of us. People would talk and it would get very uncomfortable for me with the organization, and I don't want that. And sooner or later you would be frustrated with the situation. Trust me. It just wouldn't work. I'm sorry."

He waited for her to say something but she couldn't. Her chest felt like it was caught in a vice, and no matter how often she blinked, her eyes remained covered by a thick film of tears.

"You know, you may not want to hear this now, but I think you would make a great didi. What's more, I think you'd be happy in orange. One day you're going to be in love with God the way I am. The world will be your lover then, and this will all make perfect sense."

It literally hurt to hear him say that, but he didn't go on and she was grateful for the silence. Eventually she got her voice back. "So what now?" she said. "We can't just go on like nothing's happened."

"I don't see why not. What was said on the beach stays on the beach, and when the tide comes in, it gets washed away."

"Really? After what I said?"

"It's human nature, like you said. Attraction is the law of the universe. Some things needed to be said, we said them, and we move on. Nobody needs to know; it's just the two of us here."

"And Baba."

"And Baba. But he's on our side. Anyhow, that transfer is still months away—if it comes through at all. In the meantime we have his work to do. He wanted us to talk, we talked, and now he wants us to work. It's all good. You'll see."

But it wasn't all good, though Priya did her best to pretend it was. When Dada suggested they head back, she told him she would catch up a little later and instead went for a solitary walk along the beach to give her emotions time to settle down. Half an hour later she was still hurting, still embarrassed, still angry at herself for having misjudged things so badly and letting her emotions—or rather, her illusions—get the better of her, but she had managed to gain enough distance to be able to parse through the wreckage of their conversation. She hadn't come right out and said that she was in love with him, but it amounted to the same thing, as his reaction had made painfully clear. The strange thing was that she couldn't remember having ever thought about their relationship in romantic terms before. Not really. He was her mentor and theirs was a spiritual relationship. That was what she had fumbled to explain after her true feelings had sabotaged the conversation by escaping from captivity. She had never admitted to herself — not openly at least — that she was in love with him, and in a curious twist of fate, he had known it before she did, if only a split second earlier. But now that she was honest about it, helped along by the anguish and the embarrassment, she knew that she had been in love with him for a long time now and it amazed her that she hadn't seen her feelings for what they were.

As she walked up and down, a few paces from the waterline where the tide was slowly coming in, she went back and forth over what they had said, trying to pair up her real feelings with her words. It made her wonder what other aspects of her inner life she had failed to understand, and it occurred to her that maybe Dada suffered from the same malady. He was wiser and more experienced than she was, but he had been living like a monk since his early twenties, since well before he became one, and maybe there were feelings in there that he wasn't aware of because he didn't know where to look. She had been so sure that whatever she felt, he felt it too, so cognizant of the crackling energy that seemed to leap back and forth between them that she found it difficult to believe that it had only been crackling in her imagination. Could it be that he wasn't fully aware of his feelings, as she hadn't been fully aware of hers? Or if he was, that he wouldn't admit them, even to himself, because they didn't fit with his ideal of what it meant to be a monk, and perhaps for that reason was secretly glad for the transfer? That he wanted to get away — not from her but from his feelings for her? She thought about this for several minutes and decided it didn't matter. He was a monk and the world was his mistress. Sooner or later he would be leaving for Portugal and she wouldn't be going with him. Whatever tears lay in wait for her, she would cry them on her own and let sleeping feelings lie. After all, no one ever died of a broken heart (she doubted this was true but in her case it was).

Priya was a few paces from the sidewalk, ready to head back, when she noticed that she was coming up on station four, a few short steps from the kiosk where Fernando had told her about his infidelity. What is it with my karma and Copacabana? she thought. Each time I find out that the man I love has a mistress it's right here on this godforsaken stretch of sand. The thought made her smile, a weak smile but she was grateful nonetheless. She hoped it was a sign that this time she wouldn't be so long getting over what she could only think of for the moment as a cosmic infidelity.

13

THE TRANSFER ORDER WENT through ten days later, three weeks before their next—and final—trial run of the course they had such high hopes for (unless he decided to pursue the course in Portugal, which undoubtedly he would, but then it wouldn't be *their* course anymore). In the meantime, what had happened on the beach hadn't been entirely washed out by the tide. The memory was too strong, too conflated in her mind with other disappointments, and unfortunately—or fortunately, she couldn't quite decide—she saw less of Dada in those first few days than she normally did. He let on that he was being sensitive to her "need for space," but she got the feeling that he was counting on the tide and a little extra distance to eliminate any possibility of an addendum to their dialogue on the sand. She would have rather'd the opposite—the same gut-wrenching discussion jolting forward through the difficult terrain of being totally open and honest with each other until it eventually reached stable ground. It would have made it easier for her to work through her feelings, which were still too jumbled for her to completely sort out. But either he didn't want to heap any more fuel on the fire (a jealous mistress, perhaps?) or else he had feelings of his own that the distance would help keep at a distance.

After those first few days, things more or less settled down into the old routine. No mention was made of what was better left unsaid, and gradually they returned to a reasonable facsimile of their old camaraderie. Priya still had a nagging feeling that Dada hadn't been entirely honest, either with her or with himself, but if that was the price of being a monk then so be it. Who was she to tell him how to live his life? That's when the call came.

By then they were back to working long hours getting version two of the course ready for the coming test run. They had both come up with new ideas during the retreat and it was proving a challenge to incorporate them in such a short span of time. She was the one who answered the phone, and when she recognized Dada's boss on the other end of the line, she immediately regretted having reached for the receiver before he did, given that it was after nine in the evening and she was alone with him in the office, which in his boss's mind probably nudged her several steps closer to the category of wanton female, hell-bent on undermining the morals of her saintly mentor.

"Oh, is that Priya?" he said, sounding only mildly surprised after the initial hesitation, but she could practically see the wince on his face.

"Oh, Dada, how nice to hear your voice. I was just leaving. Here, let me pass the phone to Dada Kamaleshvarananda."

The "I was just leaving" came out sounding reasonably spontaneous, but of course she had no such intention. She handed the phone to Dada, crossed her arms, and leaned back in her chair, trying to make her exaggerated smile appear as wicked as possible. Though she only heard one half of the fifteen-minute conversation, gleaning what she could of the other half from the mutating expressions on Dada's face, it quickly became evident that the transfer had been approved and that he was expected in Europe by the end of September, enough time to teach his course and wrap up his affairs, which she assumed meant ending his nonexistent affair with his female assistant. What irked her, though, was the brief look of elation that swept across his face when he got the news, leaving no doubt that he was looking forward to leaving, despite the deliberately pensive look on his face during the rest of the call. Maybe it was just the thought of working and living in Europe, but she couldn't help but think that at least in part he was relieved to be able to disembarrass himself of an awkward situation.

It was after eleven when she finally left, but they didn't get any more work accomplished that night. They spent those couple of hours reminiscing about his time in Brazil, talking about Europe (neither of them had ever been but both had always wanted to go), what plans the organization had for him there, what the dada was like who was coming to take his place (they had done their monastic training together and he had nothing but nice things to say about him), what her role would be in the Rio center after he was gone. They danced around the prospect of not seeing each other anymore by leaning on those modern incantations: Skype, Whatsapp, Facebook Messenger. As if nothing substantive was really going to change, when they both knew otherwise.

"It's just another bend in the river of karma," he said, when she was heading out the door. "The goal is to get to the point that you are always in the same place, no matter where you are. Who knows, you might even get there before I do. I wouldn't be surprised."

She flashed a deliberately weak smile and headed off down the hill to Amarista's apartment, marveling at how spiritual philosophy was tailor-made to get you off the hook.

The course was a qualified success. The material was stronger the second time around and they had nearly thirty students, enough to turn a small profit, but the fact that Dada was leaving made it seem like an empty gesture, a shout into the wind that no one would hear. One week later he booked a one-way flight to Lisboa for the end of the month, where he would spend a couple of weeks with the local dada getting up to speed before that dada caught his own flight to São Paulo. They had not yet decided if he would be assigned to Rio, but according to Dada the longer they took to decide, the less likely it was. There was growing talk of a senior Indian dada coming over from Buenos Aires, and Priya couldn't help but think that they didn't want to expose another young Western dada to the kiss of the spider woman, trusting instead that a more seasoned Indian monk would be able to shake off her silken threads.

Priya didn't really care who replaced Dada—or rather, she knew that there was no replacing him. Her life would be moving in a different direction once he left, and his absence would be a permanent feature of whatever the new landscape looked like. Despite the sporadic early onset of separation pangs, and as sensitive as she was to every sign that he was looking forward to boarding that plane, she contrived to spend every possible waking moment she could in his company in the three weeks he had left, and though he was certainly aware of her determination, he didn't put up any resistance. In a way, it seemed not only unwise but borderline masochistic. Each morning before leaving for the yoga center she would mark off the day with a red pen on the monthly calendar that hung on the wall beside her bed—most often with an *om* symbol but sometimes with a flower and sometimes with a heart, depending on her mood—and then count the days she had left until the bright blue 25 that marked the day of his departure, knowing that a parade of empty days would follow, five until she discarded September, thirty-one in October, thirty in November. There were times when she questioned what she was doing. Wasn't she just making it worse, exacerbating the heartache that was sure to follow? But the opposing voice was stronger. She was saving up the memories of her mentor, savoring these last moments with the man who had irrevocably changed her life before placing them in the cryogenic vault of her remembrance, where she would be able to resuscitate them in the days and years to come. The fact that each day was bringing her one day closer to his leaving gave their time together a poignancy that made her feel more alive than ever, as if sadness were an elixir that heightened her senses and illumined her soul. And she was sure that he felt it also, because he was gentler and more attentive than she had been accustomed to, which only made the poignancy even stronger.

When the twenty-fifth arrived and her calendar received its final red stain—an *om* symbol, to remind her of the unseen hand that had brought them together—she had a good long cry that felt like a blessing when it was over, a necessary cleansing that seemed to lighten her load. Then she washed her face, dried her eyes, and got ready to go pick up Dada for some last-minute shopping before she brought him to the airport. She had been hoping to have him to herself for those last few hours but she knew it was a vain hope, one of those secret wishes that you hope the other person can see in your eyes, even though it can't be acknowledged. There was a small crowd in the office when she arrived, and it took two cars to ferry them around town, including a boisterous farewell luncheon at a vegetarian restaurant in Leblon before going on to the airport. The festive atmosphere helped her to stay in the moment, instead of in her thoughts, and afterward she was glad at how it played out. There were a few tears when they crowded around Dada in front of the security checkpoint, but it had been a day full of smiles and laughter, and there was no question that it had been the best way to say goodbye.

And then there was the hug, one last luminous moment that she hoped he would never forget.

There were nine of them altogether who had come to see Dada off, and one by one they each gave him a parting hug before he showed the attendant his ticket and passed through to immigration, first the brothers, and then, surprisingly, the sisters. But perhaps she shouldn't have been surprised. This was Brazil, Dada's last taste of what he would be missing once he took off for the frozen tundras of Western Europe, and he wasn't about to stand on ceremony at such a moment, monk or no monk. Especially with no other dadas or didis around. She made sure she was the last in line, and she made her hug last as long as she possibly could, wrapping him up so tight she wouldn't have been surprised if he had trouble breathing. She wanted to make sure that that was how he remembered Brazil, the last, indelible impression, so that he would feel in his body what he had left behind. So that he would know that before he was a monk, he was a man, and in case he had forgotten, this was what it felt like.

PART THREE

A WORTHY ADVERSARY

1

ALL THINGS MUST PASS. It was a comforting refrain in the weeks that followed, a musical solace in the form of the George Harrison record she would put on each morning after Amarista went to work, a timely discovery to go along with the books that were once again piling up alongside her bed—mostly novels this time, on the pretext that in trying times escape could be good for the soul. Unfortunately those timeless words of rock-and-roll wisdom applied equally to that glorious hug that was grudgingly starting to fade, despite her remembering it nearly as much as she remembered her mantra, leaving a lingering veneer of resentment. Resentment of what, exactly? That she couldn't quite pin down. There were moments when she thought she knew and even considered the resentment justified. He had been using her, unwittingly or not—her time, her energy, her enthusiasm, even her money, which she had given freely without his ever asking. But she knew full well that he had given her so much more than she had given him. Or else it was the organization she blamed, because it had sent him away and made her the bad guy, the spider woman weaving her deadly web. But this was the same organization that was spreading the teachings that had captured her heart and lit her imagination, that had given her a new home and a new family, that had introduced her to the guru whose picture graced the cover of the book she loved above all others, the formerly unseen hand that had guided her out of the darkness and helped her awaken to her true purpose in life. Even resentment of Baba for having put her in this predicament in the first place. But that was like shaking your fist at God: so full of useless hubris you couldn't help but laugh. Never mind the philosophical explanation, that it was her own karma that had gotten her here; or the devotional explanation, that suffering brought her closer to the Divine; or the tantric explanation, that this was the guru's test, designed to make her stronger. That was precisely what she didn't want to hear, not from her own mind, which was supposed to be her friend but which kept informing her in her more honest moments that the real reason she felt this way was simply because she hadn't gotten what she wanted.

The calendar was getting ready to flip over into November when Priya decided that whatever excuse she had for wallowing, she had exhausted its validity weeks ago. At this point her idleness was pure indulgence. She was lying on the sofa with her head propped up on a pillow and a book cradled in her arms, staring up at the ceiling in what had become her favorite morning asana once Amarista left for work—modified corpse pose. Her body was idle but something was stirring inside her. On impulse, she sprang from the sofa and went to her room to rummage through her box of CDs. It took a minute but she found it—her favorite album of Sufi music, the one she had often danced to in the privacy of her apartment in Jardim Botânico, turning circles in celebration of the Divine. She returned to the living room, slipped it into the CD player, and started dancing freeform over the tiled floor—circles, ovals, parabolas, wherever her body wanted to go, her eyes closed and her heart gradually starting to feel as if it were coming out of a long hibernation. She remembered something Sara had told her in the hospice, when she had opened up to her about Fernando and the heartache she had been feeling since his betrayal. The Sufis sometimes referred to the Sufi path of love as the "path of the bloody heart," Sara had said, because opening one's heart to love also meant opening oneself to heartache. How had she described it? Yes, that it was like the pain of childbirth, the feeling that your insides are being ripped out, but at the same time knowing that the pain presages the miracle of birth—in this case, the birth of a newborn love for God, for what was the heart's pain in essence but the anguish of being separated from the Divine. Then she remembered Harimayi Devi's refrain from that weekend seminar: "love is service and service is love." It had been the guiding spirit behind her volunteer work at the hospice, and her time there among the terminally ill had enabled her to cut through her self-misery and heal her heart of what had ailed it. Suddenly she realized that she knew exactly what she needed to do. It had been gestating inside her all along, and it had taken this spin across the living-room floor to birth it into the visible world.

Priya showed up at the restaurant that night shortly after closing. She would have called first, if only to make sure he would be there, but she wanted it to be a surprise, and the thought of showing up there after hours, her face framed in the plate-glass window just beside an open menu and the baskets of fresh fruits and vegetables, seemed somehow fitting. A sudden apparition in the dark, a ghost from the past on a ghostly Rio night.

She knocked on the display window several times, as loudly as she dared, and after a couple of attempts she saw Paco emerge from the kitchen with a mop in his hand. He had an annoyed look on his face, but as soon as he recognized her he broke out into one of his infrequent smiles. A couple of minutes later they were seated at one of the tables, each with a cup of the green tea in their hands that Paco brewed for himself each night when he arrived for work.

"So how long has it been exactly?"

"Since Ipanema?" Priya counted off the months on her fingers. "That was the beginning of May, as I remember. Six months. Wow, I hadn't thought it was that long."

"Well, you've been busy, judging from what I remember of our conversation that night. Bringing Tantra yoga to the masses. How's that going?"

"It's been eventful."

"And that monk you were working with? What was his name?"

"Kamaleshvarananda."

"Ah yes, the lord of the lotus. Are you still working with him?"

"Not any longer. He was transferred to Portugal about a month ago."

"Ah, too bad. I liked him. Very enthusiastic."

"Yeah, so did I."

They made light conversation for a while, which with Paco was never very light, since he never strayed very far from the Buddhist doctrine that informed how he saw even the most trivial matters. Priya was reminded of their talks when they used to attend the Zen satsang together, how Paco could turn a short chat into a dialectician's debate, and she found it more agreeable now than she had then, now that her appetite for small talk had gone the way of hamburgers and nights out at one of Rio's fashionable bars.

They had been talking about mindfulness and mopping when Paco asked her if there was anything she needed from him other than a cup of green tea and some janitorial satsang.

"Not really," she said, shaking her head and smiling, "though I *was* hoping for another card. The main reason I stopped by is that I'm going to be moving to São Paulo after Christmas and I wanted to see you before I left."

There was a brief flash of disappointment in his face but he shrugged it off, undoubtedly chalking it up to karma. "Is this a permanent move?" he asked. "As far as anything can be permanent in a temporal world."

"That remains to be seen. If I had to guess, I'd say no. I still love Rio but I'll leave that up to my inner guide. Desire and attachment. Weren't those the two things you warned me about before I went on tour with Dada?"

"Ah, so you haven't forgotten."

"No, I haven't forgotten. I couldn't, even if I wanted to. I've had more than my share of lessons in that department since the last time I saw you. Let's just say that Mara has kept me on my toes."

"Well said. So what are you going to be doing in São Paulo?"

"I'm going to be working as a volunteer in a service project in a favela, Peri Alto."

"A favela? Really? Now that is a surprise. What kind of project?"

"There's a yogic nun there who has two big preschools right in the middle of the favela and another after-hours project for adolescents. She's basically the Mother Teresa of the São Paulo slums. I don't know if I told you about her. She was the one who initiated me into Tantra yoga. I talked to her today and it's all set. I'm going to start off in one of the schools but I'll probably end up splitting my time between the different projects, whatever she needs me to do."

"That's a big change, after what you've been doing."

"It is, but I'm looking forward to it. Teaching Tantra yoga to the middle class was a great experience, I wouldn't have traded it for any-thing, but what I feel like I need to work on at the moment is opening my heart, and I can't imagine a better way to do that than working with kids in a favela. I think working with kids anywhere is good for opening your heart but especially these kids. These are the ones society has left behind. I stopped in to see Didi's project while I was on tour and I was totally blown away. I don't know if I've ever felt as much love as I felt being around those kids. I was there for two hours and the entire time I was there I never saw a kid without a smile on her face. I don't know how Didi does it, in the middle of all that misery and violence, but I plan on finding out. It's the next step in the journey."

"I don't know what to say, except that you're a brave woman, Paula."

"Oh, I wouldn't say that."

"I would. A brave woman with a big heart. That's quite a combination."

Priya felt embarrassed by the compliment—embarrassed and pleased at the same time. It crossed her mind, for the first time, that perhaps Paco had feelings for her that went beyond that of fellow travelers on the spiritual path. Or maybe he once had, and this was a residue of something that had completely passed her by because she had been too myopic back then to notice. Well, if he did, there was nothing wrong with that, as her own recent experience had taught her. Attraction *was* the law of the universe, and she was glad it was, because it was attraction that held the planets in their course. And human beings as well.

"Well," she said, hoping her thoughts weren't too transparent, "is there any chance you have a new card with you that I haven't seen?"

"It just so happens I do. A new painting, a new card. Only the Buddha knows if it's what you need right now, but that's his domain."

Paco threw up his hands as he said this, but the smile on his face was a dead giveaway. He reached into his shirt pocket and drew a card from what appeared to be a small stack. Surprisingly, it was a painting of Guanabara Bay at dusk, lights glimmering from the top of Sugarloaf, slanting down faintly to the water. In the lower right-hand corner a cable car of happy visitors was about to dock at Urca, and she was startled to see a tiny sliver of white in the upper left that might have well been a paper airplane. His usual impressionistic style, as if Renoir or Monet had survived into the twenty-first century, but not his usual subject. She flipped it around to the quote on the back: "A generous heart, kind speech, and a life of service and compassion are the things that renew humanity." Exactly what she had come to expect from Paco: the right quote at the right time.

"Thanks, Paco," she said, blinking back a tear. "I wish I could tell you how much this means to me."

"Did it come at the right time?" he asked softly.

"Oh, I think you know it did. By the way, I need to apologize for not keeping in touch all this time. It wasn't very thoughtful of me. It wasn't very compassionate. I've got a long way to go on that count."

"We all do. No need to apologize."

"Yes, I do. I should have been a better friend. You forgive me?"

"That goes without saying. What kind of a friend would I be if I didn't? So are you going to see Maya before you leave?"

"Tomorrow."

"Good. She was asking about you the last time I saw her."

"Like I said, I have a long way to go."

"And like I said, we all do."

They chatted for a while longer, mostly about Paco's art, Coen Sensei, and the vagaries of the spiritual path. Before leaving she scribbled her new address on a piece of paper and asked Paco to come visit if he was ever in São Paulo. He walked her to her car, not a bad idea at that time of night, and when she eased it out into the smattering of late-night traffic she was glad she had gone to see him. It had been the right thing to do, and that was what she wanted from here on out: to string one right action after another and let compassion be her guide.

2

Hᴇ ꜰᴏʟʟᴏᴡɪɴɢ ᴅᴀʏ Pʀɪʏᴀ stopped at The Bodhi Tree to see Maya and then walked over to the yoga center to see if the new Dada could use her help in any way during the two months she had left in Rio. She found him laboring over the accounts and far happier to see her than she had expected. They chatted for the better part of two hours, mostly about his plans for the Rio chapter, for which he was thankful to get her input, and after that she not only resumed her usual hours in the office, much to his delight, and translated his talks after the Sunday collective meditation, he even asked her if she would be interested in teaching the introductory philosophy course on Tantra yoga Saturday evenings, intended for students from the daily yoga classes who were interested in the philosophy behind their practice.

Their relationship remained rather formal by Brazilian standards, but it was polite and respectful, and she ended up regretting the prejudice she had harbored. He was Indian, the very culture that had coined the phrase "an unhealthy attachment," but the more she was around him, the more she started to open her mind to the idea that there were different ways to look at the world and one wasn't necessarily better than the other, even if the two were polar opposites. She was still an outspoken advocate for the ubiquitous openness and freedom she had grown up with, but there was also something to be said for the careful observance of social propriety and well-defined social roles that seemed to be a hallmark of Indian culture. Indeed, there were even times, albeit brief moments, when the latter appeared more conducive to the spiritual life, a thought that would have seemed blasphemous a few short months earlier, and she soon found herself picking up certain habits from Dada, including a quieter, more respectful way of dealing with the people around her that resonated with some part of herself that she was still getting to know. On a couple of occasions she even found herself subconsciously cataloging Brazilians as being *too* open and *too* free, an inner observation that startled her so much she started questioning her own sense of identity. It was as if for a few incongruous moments she wasn't Brazilian at all but a free-floating eye that saw everything from a vantage point one step removed from her habitual sense of individuality. In the end, she decided that her mind was expanding, encompassing more of humanity within its boundaries and in the process edging a few millimeters closer to the universal vision that was the goal of her yogic practice. Either that or Dada's Indian-ness was rubbing off and she would do well to get away.

Leaving Rio, however, wasn't as easy as she thought it would be. It had been her home for essentially all of her adult life, and her strongest relationships had been forged there, giving it a sense of home that Campinas had never had. She used the week before Christmas to say her goodbyes, both to the people and to the places that had figured so strongly in her journey into adulthood, including a surprising invitation to Lia Wyler's home in Leme for dinner and an evening of literary reminiscences; and the many visits, including the cable car to Sugarloaf for a nighttime concert, were enough to cloud her vision of the city with a thick mist of nostalgia. But Rio had also been the site of some of her greatest disappointments and the emotional turmoil they had left in their wake, and once the chartered van she had hired to ferry a group of Rio devotees to the New Year's retreat broke free of the city limits, motoring up the Linha Vermelha, she turned her head from the back window where she had been watching the city skyline gradually recede into the distance, convinced that some portion of her most difficult karma had been released somewhere back among the densely packed buildings with their canopy of smog, as if it were a balloon that she had set free to meander in the atmosphere. She knew it would come back to earth one day, but she wasn't planning on being there when it did.

That feeling was even stronger six days later when she climbed into Didi's crowded van a few hours after the closing *akhanda* kirtan to make the eight-hour trip to São Paulo. True, the philosophy did not entirely support her in this respect. Karma could not be left behind. You carried it with you wherever you went, even if that involved changing bodies, waking up in a new culture and a new century. But you could get a respite, come back and deal with certain things later on, when you were better equipped, and that was what she was banking on. A stronger Priya the next time the winds of karma blew, thrusting her into the tempest of a romantic relationship—something she had no doubt was coming, just as she knew that the future was something that could not be fathomed from the uncertain staging grounds of the present.

Didi Ananda Jaya lived in a quiet street in the hills of Santana, one of the oldest and most historic neighborhoods in São Paulo, site of the composition of the Paulista manifesto in January 1821 that led a few months later to Brazil's independence from Portugal. In those days Santana was a sprawling rural hacienda given over to the cultivation of grapes and the making of wine. Now it was the heart of the city's North Zone and one of the most densely populated districts in the New World. But you couldn't tell it by walking down her street. Traffic was minimal, the sidewalk was lined with shade trees, and the houses seemed to rest tranquilly behind their stone and concrete walls.

The projects were still closed for the New Year's holiday, which gave Priya a few days to get her bearings. Didi installed her in the spare room and showed her the neighborhood the day after their arrival, stopping for lunch at the dadas' place, a fifteen-minute walk from the house. When they got back late in the afternoon after a great deal of walking and a spirited conversation with the dadas, they went out to the second-floor balcony with a pitcher of fresh lemonade to enjoy the relative coolness that was beginning to set in after a hot summer's day. Didi had yet to ask her about her reasons for leaving Rio, but the cushioned recliners and the reclusive atmosphere of the shaded balcony seemed to be made for just that kind of conversation.

"So, Priya, was it your heart that made you decide to leave Rio or was it your head?"

"My heart, Didi, definitely my heart," she answered, as her heart began to thump louder and more quickly than it had while walking the streets of Santana on a sunny summer day. Fortunately Didi didn't pry the door open any further.

"I thought so," she said. "I could hear it in your voice when you called. Anyhow, you're young. A change of scenery usually works wonders at your age."

"That's what I'm hoping for—a fresh start. And I can't imagine a better place for it. This is a great chance for me to do some real service."

"Baba says that social service is the best remedy for depression. Not that you're depressed, but you know what I mean. Whatever ails you, working with these kids will cure you of it. They have a way of keeping you grounded and taking your mind off your troubles. You have to set aside your ego so much, it ends up becoming a habit, and anything that lessens the ego is good medicine. Did I tell you that my first posting was running a preschool in Italy?"

"I think you mentioned it."

"Between Italy and Brazil I've been doing this a very long time, but before I came to the mission I was a supervisor in an upscale firm in Manila. You wouldn't think it, would you, looking at me now? But I was. I wore a suit to work, pulled down a good salary, dealt with important people, went on business trips, the whole shebang. I was good at it, too. My bosses loved me because I got things done and the people who worked for me loved me because I took care of them. Then I came to this mission with all its mishmash, never any money, running around like a chicken with its head cut off to keep the projects going. It's not easy, I tell you. Seventy-seven employees and I am alone running this whole show. Just so you know, hardly any of the money comes from the organization or the local devotees. No, no, no. If I had to count on them I would have folded up shop years ago. Most of it I collect from the public. The municipality helps a little. I have one friend, her husband is a vice president of Banco do Brasil. You should see her house. Vila Magdalena. Five stars, the best of everything. She has her own driver, a house full of servants, you name it. I stayed there for a few days once. She insisted. 'Didi, you have to stay here so you can get your health back.' That was when I was having heart problems. She paid for my treatment. When she saw the projects, she had tears in her eyes. 'Didi, whatever you need, just tell me.' That's the way she is. Now she brings her friends and asks them to help. Last month she gave me thirty thousand reals for the third-floor construction. I didn't know how I was going to get it done. Then she called me, out of the blue. 'Didi, what do you need?' Just like that. It's people like her that keep the projects afloat. Baba is always sending me the right person at the right time. I tell him, 'Baba, it's your project. I'll work until I drop, do or die, but what comes of it is in your hands.'

"I'll tell you a secret. Whenever things get to be more than I can handle, no money to pay the teachers or whatever it is, you know what I do? I cry in front of Baba's photo. That's my last resort. I sit in front of Baba's picture and have a good cry. And it works, every time, one way or another. It's like a magic charm. Whatever problems I might be having, he solves them. That's the beauty of devotion. You surrender and he takes you on his lap. That's his job. The cosmic father is duty bound to take care of his child. Did you bring a Baba photo with you?"

"Yes, Didi."

"Good. Whatever photo you like best, put it on your altar in your room, and whenever you feel the need, just sit there and pour out your heart to him. It doesn't matter if you're able to meditate or not. Let him know how you feel. Ask him to take care of you and he will. You'll see."

Didi's smile was so charming and her good cheer so abundant, Priya didn't doubt for a second that she was talking from experience. For her part, she still felt far away from developing such a deeply personal connection to a disembodied master, but she felt a kind of subterranean thrill listening to Didi talk about him in that way. The balcony was like a small oasis in a sea of urban life, and sitting there with Didi made everything seem so simple. God is in your heart, seated there in the form of the guru; make your way there and never again can a sea of troubles swamp you with its waves.

"Of course, he'll test you," she warned, with a mischievous twinkle in her eye. "I suspect you've already found that out. But that's just another proof that he's looking out for us. The teacher gives the students tests because he knows they need the challenge. Otherwise they won't do the work. But he doesn't give us any tests we can't handle. Once you realize that, you'll have the confidence to take on whatever comes. He won't test you on Euclidean geometry while you're still working on your ABCs."

"That's good to know, Didi."

"Do you like cartoons?"

"Cartoons?"

"I love cartoons. They relax me. They make me laugh. That's also medicine. I come back after a long day's work, I put on some cartoons and I forget everything. My favorite is Tom and Jerry. They are sooo funny! Do you know Tom and Jerry?"

"I don't think so, Didi. I haven't watched cartoons since I was a kid."

"Then you're in for a treat. We can watch some tonight after dinner. Tom and Jerry. It will make you feel like a kid again, and we can all use a little of that."

Cartoons and crying in front of Baba's photo? *I have a feeling we're not in Rio anymore, Toto.* She could see the scene in her head: Dorothy being swept away by a tornado and waking up to find herself in a Technicolor world of futuristic plants and singing munchkins. A balcony in São Paulo wasn't quite Oz but she hoped she was at the beginning of an adventure that would prove every bit as transformative as Dorothy's. Dorothy had a Wicked Witch of the West to deal with and other serious tests before she could make it to the Emerald City and find her way back home, but it had brought out the best in her, and Priya hoped the same would prove true in her case. And if ever things got rough she had her very own orange-robed Glinda, her personal Good Witch of the North, to protect her and guide her as she clicked her heels and made her way down the yellow-brick road.

The analogies with *The Wizard of Oz* continued after the vacation ended and Didi assigned her to the larger of the two schools, a daily sojourn in the land of the munchkins. Priya hadn't been around little people since she had been one, not that she had much more than vague impressions of those times, and she soon began to realize that many of the stereotypes she carried in her head bore only a superficial resemblance to the incarnate life of two- and three- and four-year-olds. They were indeed little *people*, tiny in stature but bearing all the marks in miniature of full-blown human beings. Somewhere along the way she had come to assume that young children were something close to a pure slate who gradually became imprinted with the best and worse of the world around them, until they eventually found themselves in a lifelong struggle to come to grips with the planet on which they had landed. But as Didi schooled her in the interior lives of the little, it didn't take long for her to realize that her simplistic notion, no doubt imprinted in her brain by society along with other simplistic notions, couldn't have been further from the truth. Even the youngest children, barely into their twos, had such unique and resonant personalities that they would have been equally at home in the bodies of senior citizens, even if they lacked the ability to articulate their equally fecund interior life. Perhaps what perpetuated the illusion was their natural ability to remain in the moment, unlike their adult counterparts who were troubled by past regrets and future apprehensions, an ability that was noticeably more present in the two-year-olds than in the four-year-olds. That by itself was enough to imbue them with a certain innate happiness that could almost immediately be undermined by the presence of bad vibes. It was with this in mind that Didi had created in both of her schools (situated a few blocks from each other) an environment that Priya considered to be little short of miraculous. Rarely did she see a child in a state of discontent, and even before she talked to Didi about it she had figured out why. It was because the teachers and other staff members wandered through the halls and classrooms with a perpetual smile on their face that was rooted in their hearts and thus facile to maintain. This by itself was a minor miracle. Never once did she see a teacher or staff member be short with a child or react to their antics with anything but good humor, affection, and a ready hug. It wasn't as if the staff didn't have their challenges at home, their anxieties and frustrations. She knew this for a fact because they talked about it during meals and during breaks, when the children were taking one of their several daily naps. But right down to the janitorial staff they had a surprising ability to set their personal lives aside when they were interacting with the children and be the matronly (and in one case, the fatherly) figure that the children relied on to feel secure and unencumbered. The result was a school full of happy children. They didn't always arrive in that state, and petty squabbles sometimes flared up among them, but any youngsters who entered the gate in tears or in a tantrum seemed to shed their problems like a burdensome coat, and any momentary squabbles were invariably diffused in short order by a generous blanket of affectionate attention proffered by an attentive staff member.

When Priya finally asked Didi about it, wondering if there were any kind of particular magic involved, Didi laughed.

"I'm surprised it took you so long to ask. Actually, it *is* a kind of magic, but like any good magic act it takes a lot of hard work and practice to pull it off. First of all, I only hire people who already have that native ability. It's easy to spot, if you know what you are looking for. You have it, for example. And then I train them so it becomes a conscious skill. It's part of the very first seminar on neohumanist education, which everyone has to take before they can start working here. Not just the teachers but everyone on staff. We call it 'leaving our troubles at the door, no exceptions.' The school belongs to the kids, it's their kingdom, and anyone who wants to work here has to be able to put their welfare first for the eight hours or however long they are here. It's a contract I make with every employee. And they love it, because the school becomes not only a sanctuary for the kids but a sanctuary for them also. The kids help them stay grounded in the here and now because it comes natural to them, and that's a boon to adults who have lost that ability. So I tell them, these kids are going to teach you far more than you will ever teach them. And they do."

Priya hadn't had the opportunity to take the seminar before she began working in the school (she took it during the next school break), and the fact that she had come to that discovery on her own made it take root even deeper. Whenever she was with the kids, she found it far easier to remain present, and sometimes, when the kids napped after their lunch and the staff sat down to whatever wonderful vegetarian food was on the menu that day, she lamented the kind of instantaneous loss of innocence she felt the moment the conversation leapt the school's boundary walls and began meandering among the deceptions and challenges of the outside world, both past and future. This was the first and biggest lesson the kids taught her, but there were others, and she soon understood why Didi had been so emphatic when she told her that the kids were going to teach her far more than she would teach them.

One day back at the house, Didi pulled her aside and began explaining that little children, up until the age of four or five, retained impressions from their previous life that surfaced as disconnected images for which they had no context and thus paid no more attention to than they did to any of the other jumbled impressions that filled their dreams and daytime fantasies. But if you knew what you were looking for, you could decipher those past-life memories and understand them in a way a young child could not.

Priya was fascinated by Didi's revelation, and even more fascinated by an article of Baba's that Didi gave her on extracerebral memory in which Baba talked about how an unborn child's dreams are almost entirely composed of impressions from the past life—proof that the mind exists apart from the brain. After birth those memories gradually start mixing with impressions from the new life, until by the age of four or five the memories from the past life get so completely overlaid they can no longer be retrieved. She soon had a chance to put this theory to the test and the results completely altered the way she looked at children.

It began with a seemingly innocuous remark by Rafael, a precocious two-and-a-half-year-old who loved to talk and was better at it than some adults, forever trying out new words and endeavoring to fit them into his constantly expanding syntax. The other two-year-olds were still submerged in their midmorning nap, no doubt navigating an ocean of past-life memories, when Rafael sat up, still rubbing the sleep from his eyes, and toddled over to where Priya was reading a book in a corner of the room.

"Grammy," he said, using the word with which he addressed any woman over the age of twenty, "Hermes is very sick. He needs medicine."

"Who is Hermes?" she asked, thinking that it must be a playmate or relative, since there were no children in the school with that name.

"My son."

It was the kind of remark Priya would have smiled at a few days earlier, laughing it off as the kind of fantasy-born non sequitur that made young children so adorable. But this time her ears were alerted to a possible glimpse of a previous lifetime.

"Is he awake?" she asked.

"No, he is sleeping. I'm afraid he don't wake up this time." Then Rafael grabbed Priya's hand. "Let's play blocks," he said, guiding her gently to the corner where the building blocks were kept, the sleepiness now gone from his eyes.

Priya got no more out of him that day, despite several subtle but apparently ill-timed questions, but in the weeks to come she started piecing together a story that she was sure was not a child's fantasy but the product of long-ago memories that Rafael could not differentiate from his memories of the day before. It was not like any narrative she was used to—there was no linear connection to go by, no obvious context to mine for clues—but as the weeks went by, she was able to connect the dots in a way that Rafael could not, latching on to chance remarks and bits of dreams immediately after his naps that felt rooted in another place and time.

He'd had a son, a middle-aged son, it seemed, since his son also had grown children of his own, and it was in his son's home that he lived, though this was interwoven with images from an earlier time when his son was young. But the memory that surfaced most seemed to be connected to his son's death, from some kind of wasting disease the doctors had no name for. Priya could see the sadness on Rafa's face at these times—not the sadness of a young child, but a kind of ancient sadness that made him seem ancient in those moments, despite his child's body and infantile voice. In one particularly lucid moment, when she was helping him through a juvenile word game, the word "bed" came up and she asked him about his son's bed, if it was hard or soft, big or small, and suddenly he started describing the room, the furniture and colors and even the layout, but especially the smells. "Smells like bath-room," he said, turning up his nose. And then a few moments later, "like bad food." He was talking about the smell of urine and putrefaction, she realized—the scent of death, she would have called it, with words taken from a book. She wanted to ask more questions but she could see the anguish creeping into his face, with no effort to disguise it, as an adult might have done, and thanks to his transparency she was quick to divert his mind to the present with the help of a new game and a couple of playmates.

She soon discovered that with the right words she could often bring up memories from that life when his mind was not otherwise engaged—jumbled together with impressions from the present, no doubt, but easy enough to sort through once she had gotten sufficiently familiar with his inner landscape. A couple of months in, she brought what she was doing to the attention of Didi, unsure how she would take it and hoping that she had been sensitive enough and gentle enough not to raise any warning flags. It was, after all, their kingdom, Rafa's and the rest of the young children's, and she was apprehensive that her experiments in transmigration might not fit into Didi's credo, even though it had been Didi who had taught her what to look for.

Didi smiled and nodded when she told her, flashing her typical big-sisterly smile that irrupted whenever their conversations turned toward spiritual topics, a smile like a warm embrace that invariably put Priya at ease. It was evening and they were sitting on the second-floor balcony after dinner, as they often did to take advantage of the cool nightly breezes while the weather was still warm. Didi loved to talk and Priya was happy to keep her company, usually more audience than interlocutor. She had learned to appreciate Didi's taste for cartoons but she still preferred a good conversation or a good book, and Didi was an accomplished conversationalist who didn't need much input to keep a conversation going.

"Don't worry about it," she said. "These kids are more resilient than you think. They have to deal with these memories whether you coax it out of them or not." Didi patted Priya on the back of her hand and leaned toward her with a conspiratorial whisper. "But I probably wouldn't ask him any more questions, if I were you. I think that would make Baba happy. Baba says it's an act of Providence that we forget our past lives, and it's not hard to see why. We have enough to deal with in this life. Just imagine if we had to bear the burden of all the problems and attachments from the last one. Or the ones before that. Didn't you say that Rafa gets sad every time he remembers what happened to his son?"

"Yes, Didi."

"Wouldn't it be better then if he didn't remember?"

"Yes, Didi, I suppose it would."

"So let's help nature do its work and not remind them of what they are gratefully destined to forget."

"Okay, Didi. No more questions."

"Good. If this kind of thing comes up again, be aware of it — that's why I told you about it in the first place, so you can have some insight into what they're going through inside those little heads of theirs — and then steer them away from any memories that might upset them or take them away from the present life. Help nature take its course."

Priya nodded, perusing her thoughts for the next couple of minutes while Didi leaned back in her recliner and sipped from her customary glass of sweet lemonade. Priya was convinced — there was an eminent logic behind Didi's words — but her curiosity wasn't entirely satisfied.

"Didi, can there be times when it might actually be helpful to remember things from our past life? For example, spiritual memories, spiritual experiences? If we were on the spiritual path in our past life, it seems like a shame that we can't remember the lessons we learned."

Didi raised her eyebrows. "If we really learned those lessons then we don't need to remember them. They're already part of our makeup. If you learned the importance of patience in your last life then you don't need to remember how you learned it. You're born a patient person and that's what matters. Of course, there are some memories it might be nice to have. I wonder sometimes if I was with Baba in a past life. I like to think so. And if I was, then sure, I would love to be able to remember it. But the thing is, you can't just have the good memories. It's a package deal. They come together with the bad ones, with all the mistakes we made, all the attachments and desires and whatnot. So it's much better just to wipe it clean, a clean slate. Spiritually speaking, you start out in this life from wherever you left off in the last one. You're starting over in a new body but it's the same you. You see these kids and if you look close enough it's clear as day who they were in their last life. Not what they looked like or what they did or where they lived, but *who* they were. That's what they're working with this time around. Our job is to help them move forward and not look back. What is it that Baba says?"

Didi left a pregnant pause, and Priya knew exactly what she was referring to, since she had heard her say it a thousand times.

"God gave us two eyes in the front of our head so that we look forward, not behind."

"Yes indeed, and that's the best advice there is. You know, I have a friend in Taiwan. She has two sons. One's about eighteen now and the other must be twenty or twenty-one. One day, when the younger boy was about the same age as Rafael, maybe a bit older, his mom took him to the market and they walked past a butcher's shop. Like the ones they have here, you know, with the carcasses hanging down and that terrible smell—no door to keep the smell in."

"An *açougue*, yeah, I can't stand them. There ought to be a law."

"One day there will be. Anyhow, she was carrying her son, as I remember, and when they passed the shop, he said, 'Mommy, the people on this planet are so primitive, they eat meat. Where I came from no one eats meat. It smells so bad. I don't like it.' Talk about a precocious kid, right?"

Didi was laughing and Priya laughed alongside her.

"My friend didn't know what to say, it was so totally out of the blue, but she went with it. 'You're right, son. They are very primitive. But we're not like that. We don't eat meat, do we?' Then he started talking about the planet where he came from, how it was so much better than this one, how everyone meditated there, that sort of thing. Now she knew about extracerebral memory and all that—she's a serious yogi, she and her husband both—but she wasn't really sure until she got home and brought him into the meditation room and showed him Baba's photo.

"'Do you know who that is?' she said.

"'Yes, Mommy, he sent me here.'

"That's when she knew for sure. She told me this story in India a few years ago. Then I stopped in Taiwan on the way back. Delhi, Manila, Taipei, San Francisco, São Paulo. I took that route so I could visit my mom in the Philippines and my sister in the States. When I got to Taiwan I stayed at her place for a couple of days, and I asked her son about that story. He just laughed. 'My mom tells that story all the time, but I don't remember any of that.' And you could see, it didn't mean anything to him. It was just a story his mom tells sometimes, like the stories that all mothers tell about their children when they were young. Except that his mom's a yogi, so her story is a little more exotic, that's all. But the thing is, this kid is so sentient. So calm and quiet and sure of himself. And he meditates like a statue. His older brother is completely different. He's a good kid, does his meditation, but next to the younger brother he seems so ordinary. You can't say that about the younger boy. There's nothing ordinary about him."

"Like somebody from another planet?"

"Exactly, like somebody from a planet where everyone meditates."

For the next few weeks, forgetfulness was the one thing Priya could not forget — the soothing mantle it laid over the human mind, which might otherwise be too weighed down by its memories to make any significant progress. Everyday she was a little more sensitive to the jetsam and flotsam that floated up from previous lives in the mental waters of her kids, sometimes forcing them to alter their course slightly as they navigated the unexplored byways of their new lives, and each time it happened, she steered their minds clear of its debris and back into the present. And the more adept she became at this subtle and satisfying exercise, the more it shed light on the often murky waters of her own psyche.

She had gone through the same process of forgetting that these children were going through, a process she had been totally unaware of, just as they were, and it made her realize just how tenuous the footing was that her own anxieties and preoccupations, attachments and desires, stood on. It would all be gone in a few decades, a half dozen if she was fortunate, washed away as it had been washed away at the end of her previous life, and the one before that, and only the Lord knew how many times before that. When seen in this light it was hard to take it all so seriously. She knew she still had some resentment over Dada's transfer, layered on top of the resentment she still harbored against Fernando, like the uppermost layer of a cake whose bottom disappeared below the table on which it was displayed, the cake rising up from underneath through a hole in the table to wow the guests without ever revealing how many layers were hidden from sight, each with its tiny manikins in their miniature tuxes and wedding gowns. Why harbor resentment against anyone if it was just another layer on a cake that could probably feed a multitude, like a modern repetition of the loaves and fishes? Why harbor any resentment at all, when it did nothing more than stand in your way, both in this life and the next, even if it was forgotten by then? Eventually she would be right back where the kids in her classroom were, housed in a two-year-old body, getting on with her journey, albeit with a radical change in scenery.

Forgetting was a blessing. She was more and more sure of that with every passing day — not just the memories she had carried into this life and thankfully forgotten, but also the memories she had stored up during this one, the ones that came back to wreak havoc at the most inopportune moments. Forget them and they lost their power to derail you. The thought burst in her mind like a cannon shot. So what if Dada had unwittingly led her on? Or if Fernando had torn out her heart in dramatic fashion like a character from a Puccini opera? They were just minor incidents in an epic saga, ones that could just as well be a source of amusement. More grist for the mill as she made her way down the path. More texture, more color, in the mise-en-scène of her life.

The more time Priya spent with the children, gazing at them in fondness while they took their nap, fast asleep in a jumble of mixed-life memories, the more she felt a growing sense of gratitude for what they were teaching her. This one particular lesson, one among many that the munchkins were passing on, was slowly but surely beginning to relieve her mind of some of its burden, helping to anchor her more firmly in the present. She knew that forgetting was not enough, that the tendencies that had taken root from those forgotten experiences were still there, conditioning the present moment, the past- and present-life karma that would determine in which direction the winds of her life would blow. She would have to work with the residue of those hidden layers until she could make it vanish, but the forgetfulness made it so much easier. A fresh start, each and every day, with the clay she had been given, molding it into the image of the Priya she held in her mind, the divine sculpture that she hoped to one day become.

3

WHEN PRIYA SAW THE poster for the yoga teacher training on the bulletin board outside the dadas' downstairs hall, she felt a sudden flash of synchronicity, followed by a humbling awareness of karma bearing down on her. Just two days earlier she had approached Didi about giving some yoga classes for the adolescents in the afternoon activities center, which had art and capoeira but no yoga, and maybe down the road some classes for the parents and families of their students. She had never given an asana class before, but she had taken plenty of them, and she felt confident that she could teach a simple class until they could find a more competent teacher. Didi not only loved the idea, she proposed adding an evening yoga class for senior citizens, a first step toward her dream of eventually opening an alternative lifestyle home for the elderly, and when Priya showed Didi the poster before the Sunday collective meditation she had no trouble divining Priya's thoughts.

They talked about it on the way back from the meditation, a leisurely evening walk from one Santana neighborhood to another. The first two weeks of the training coincided with the school's two-week winter recess in late July, so she would only need to take ten days off from her school duties to complete the twenty-four-day course, which was fine with Didi. She would also have to miss the July retreat at Ananda Kirtana, which she had been looking forward to since the New Year's retreat, but this was in the service of a greater cause and there would always be more retreats in the future. Her teacher's certificate, sanctioned by the Brazilian chapter of the Yoga Alliance, would give her classes an added level of credibility, and the additional exposure for the school was something Didi was quick to appreciate.

The fact that they had been talking just two days earlier about teaching yoga classes in Peri Alto, however (almost certainly a first for that neglected favela), was not the karmic red flag that had caught Priya's attention. It went deeper than that oblique flutter of synchronicity that she would have likely tossed off as mere coincidence a few years earlier. Something had been stirring in her for a couple of weeks now, the first sprouting of a seed that was just pushing its way to the surface. In the five months that she had been working with Didi, Priya had learned firsthand how much a life of social service could open up a person's heart and enrich their spiritual journey, especially when it involved working with disadvantaged children barely into their new lives. She had learned and grown more than she could have thought possible in that short span of time, and she was eager to see what experiences the coming months would bring. Nevertheless, she woke up one morning with a vague sense of nostalgia for the days when she and Dada had dreamed of changing the world one initiation at a time. She couldn't remember what she had dreamed that night, but the itch to be spreading the teachings in the wide world beyond stayed with her throughout that week and into the next, an involuntary scratching in her subconscious that her work with the children drove from her conscious mind—until she got home in the evening and started wondering again what it would be like to be back out there, challenging the minds of her compatriots to look beyond their daily concerns and into the heart of the universe. She had no intention of leaving Didi or the children, but the idea of giving yoga classes seemed like the perfect way to calm that itch. And wasn't it just like Baba to second that motion by pointing out exactly how she could go about doing that (especially seeing as how he had planted the desire in her in the first place).

The morning after school let out for the two-week recess, Priya changed into her yoga tights and walked over to the dadas' place along with five other sisters who would be staying with Didi for the duration of the training. The course was demanding—twelve hours of classwork a day, not only learning how to teach the postures but also anatomy, alignment, methodology, yoga history and philosophy, and the basics of yoga therapy—but after two years of tantric practice, Priya found the long hours and detailed instruction both invigorating and enjoyable. She had become far more flexible over these past two years, and her stamina, both mental and physical, had increased by leaps and bounds. During the final week of the course each of the fourteen participants had to design and teach a yoga class, which was then graded by the other students, and Priya came away with the first prize (a kirtan CD), which she attributed to her year of regular classes with Gunatiita, who had taught her through osmosis that the practice of asanas was in essence a cultivation of inner peace and harmony that began with the breath and ended with a sense of surrender to the Divine Architect who had fashioned her body and set it in motion. It was the kind of yoga class she had envisioned during the time that she had been Dada's aide-de-camp. In her ideological training, two years earlier, Dada had mentioned that the best way to assimilate the teachings was to teach, and that was foremost in her mind while she was designing her class. She wanted it to be spiritual to the core, treating body, mind, and spirit as one indivisible whole, and she was both surprised and gratified when her fellow students gave her the highest marks and talked about how transformative her class had been.

She was even more surprised when their trainer, Visheshvar, brought it up during his evening seminar on yoga history and philosophy as an example of what they should be striving for. Yoga was in fashion, he began by saying, not only among young people but among people of all ages, even senior citizens. It was a stressful time to be alive, and yoga had become famous in Brazil for promoting inner peace and optimum health. Movie stars and artists made a point of letting their fans know they practiced it, and doctors were prescribing yoga and meditation for their stressed-out patients. Multinationals were even using it to sell their products, a sure sign that yoga had gone mainstream (Priya's favorite was a Volkswagen ad with a beautiful model meditating on the hood of a Volkswagen Jetta, her hands on her knees, thumbs and index fingers curled into a circle, a classic meditator's pose that let a prospective buyer know that one route to inner peace was through the right choice of car). But most importantly, Brazil was filled with people in search of spiritual connection, especially young people, and yoga had taken on a kind of magical aura in the youth culture. Unfortunately, most of the classes offered in gyms and spas and even yoga centers were bound to disappoint, since they were only concerned with the physical benefits of the practice—not a bad thing, in and of itself, since taking better care of their bodies became for some people a stepping stone to taking better care of their minds and eventually their spirit, but it was so much less than yoga was meant to be.

"Which was why Priya's class was so instructive," he said, startling her into a heated flush that made her chide herself for being so easily embarrassed. "We all felt it. She used the postures and the breathing to bring us into a meditative state. If you can do that for your students then you will have realized the true import of what it means to be a yoga teacher."

She was uncomfortable with the praise and thus was glad when he segued into a discussion of how the modern schools of yoga had adapted these ancient practices to changing times, but her mind remained caught up in the aftereffects of his approbation. Yoga was the widest, most inclusive, and most sought after of the many doors open to people looking to better their lives. If she could give them a taste of the inner calm that could be achieved through the right postures, deep-breathing exercises, and guided visualizations, and use that to entice them into meditation and an exploration of yoga philosophy, then maybe one day she would be able to give the kind of public seminars in Brazil that Kamaleshvarananda had wanted to give before he had been waylaid by the puritanical mindset of his monastic order. The thought was exhilarating, filling her with a pulsating, hopeful energy that she hadn't felt since the day Dada sat with her on the beach at Copacabana and let her down far less gently than he thought he was doing, and she was still riding that natural high the next morning when Visheshvar took a seat at the breakfast table directly across from her and complimented her on her class.

She had seen him at Sunday meditation at the dadas' place, but she had never actually talked to him before the training. He was a few years older than her, lithe and athletically built, with a face full of freckles, something akin to a crew cut, and the serious, determined air of a man whose goal in life was never out of sight; and after nearly three weeks of classes she had no doubt that his goal was nothing less than spiritual illumination through the intuitional science of Tantra yoga. His classes were detailed and precise, the step-by-step instructions of a technician in love with his craft, but his conversation at the breakfast table that morning couldn't have been more different. It traveled over such diverse terrain as spiritual philosophy, Brazilian politics, and the future of civilization, and like Didi he didn't need much help to keep the conversation going. At one point he latched onto an old discourse by Baba in which the master had said that as the human brain continued to develop, the head would gradually grow larger and the limbs smaller and weaker; that the humans of those future days would look back at the humans of today and consider them ugly and boorish by comparison, much as we look at the Neanderthals. Visheshvar made a point of saying that psychic and spiritual beauty will be much more highly regarded than physical beauty by the humans of the future, just as it is nowadays by yogic adepts, and at that moment he gave her a complicit look that she interpreted as a sign that he was talking about himself. It was only when he sat next to her again at lunch that it occurred to her that he might have also been talking about her.

Her suspicions were confirmed over the next few days, when Visheshvar made a point of sitting next to her at mealtimes and catching up with her during their infrequent breaks—when he wasn't deluged with questions by the other students (usually female, though Priya couldn't fault him or them for that, since there were only three males in the course). He was casual about it. There was no visible eagerness on his part, nothing out of the ordinary in any way, but the sight of him sidling up alongside her at the dining table made her feel like one of those high school girls where the confirmation that they had a beau was the sight of a boy sitting next to them each day at meals (no, she had never been one of those girls). She was flattered by the attention, and at first it seemed almost conceited on her part to imagine that he might be interested in her in any kind of romantic way. There was no such vibe in his demeanor that she could detect (in that respect, he hardly seemed Brazilian at all, not that her filters had ever been that well refined, ostensibly for lack of practice). He was simply too focused on the spiritual path to be interested in her in that way. But that was just it. Of the five initiated sisters in the course, Priya was the only one who was working for the mission, and when he asked about Didi Jaya and the project and her time working with Dada he made it clear that her dedication to the mission had a very real cachet.

When the training ended and they got their certificates, signed by Visheshvar and the dada who had organized the course, Priya still wasn't entirely sure what to make of his attentions. She didn't even know if she was attracted to him—or rather, she knew she was attracted to him but to what extent? It had been much the same with Fernando. His attentions had been so unexpected that she found herself glancing over her shoulder in the university cafeteria, unsure if he were really looking at her as they talked or through her to the burnished blond at the table behind them. His interest had been so flattering, and the void inside her so deep, that looking back she wasn't sure she hadn't willed herself to fall in love with him, mesmerized by his storybook apparition and scared that she might never get another chance. She didn't want to make that same mistake with Visheshvar. She had come to São Paulo to distance herself from the wreckage of her last two relationships, the one that was and the one that wasn't, and she was wary, to say the least, of stepping back behind the wheel of a car that she hadn't learned how to drive. She no longer felt the menace of getting left behind in the romantic race to fulfillment, and that instinctively made her want to pump the breaks. For both their sakes. Any trip with her at this point in her life was sure to be a bumpy ride, and if he didn't realize it already, then it was her responsibility to raise the proceed-with-caution sign. Whatever wisdom she had gained thus far, she might as well put it to good use, rather than rushing headlong over a karmic cliff. Visheshvar was no Fernando, not by a long shot, but she was still a sucker for the illusions thrown up by her mind and she mustn't lose sight of that. Now that the training was over, they would go back to living worlds apart, and maybe it would be best if they left it that way. They would see each other at the Sunday meditation and perhaps reprise their entertaining conversations, but the walk back to Didi's place afterward and her daily sequestration by the children seemed like a ready-made panacea for any possible love-related ailments—out of sight, out of mind.

On that particular point, however, she couldn't have been more wrong.

The Sunday following the conclusion of the teacher training, Visheshvar came up to her before dinner and asked if she were going to attend the public meditation in Ibirapuera Park that coming Saturday to protest the mounting corruption inside the two-year-old right-wing government that had taken over after the president's impeachment for similar but less flagrant offenses. If so, he would be happy to pick her up at Didi's place on the way. It was an innocuous-enough invitation, tailor-made to avoid any raised eyebrows from the men and women in orange. Many devotees were going, along with several dadas, and all he was really doing was offering her a ride. She told him she had to ask Didi, but in principle yes, she was planning on going (a plan that was thirty seconds old, since she hadn't even heard about the meditation). They exchanged phone numbers and she mentioned the public meditation to Didi in a casual way during school hours the following day, asking her if she were planning on going. She wasn't, she had to do some fundraising with some of her wealthy contacts, but she encouraged Priya to attend, and when it came time for Visheshvar to pick her up on Saturday, Didi had already been gone for a couple of hours.

She felt a little nervous at first—in some circles, being picked up in a car by an eligible bachelor couldn't be construed as anything but a date—but a few minutes conversation was enough to set her at ease. Visheshvar was so self-contained, so self-possessed, that she might have been conversing with a talking mirror. Apart from an occasional glance, he kept his eyes on the road, attentive to the never-ending challenges of São Paulo traffic, and surprisingly he let Priya do most of the talking. When they got to the park and made their way to the lawn outside the Oca exposition hall (a ten-thousand-square-meter low dome that resembled a flying saucer, right down to the round, ground-level windows obviously intended to appear like portals), it was already filling up with indignant meditators wanting to do their part to bring the country to its senses. The last few years had been as turbulent as any in living memory, the years of dictatorship and disappearing citizens notwithstanding. The endemic corruption of the country's politicians had become less obvious and less brutal in the past three decades, as Brazil strove to take its place among the world's leading powers, but it was no less brazen or disheartening. It was as if centuries of exploitation by the nation's leaders had bred it into their blood—you got away with whatever you could get away with; that was the Brazilian way. They had a word for it in Brazilian Portuguese, *malandro*, scoundrel, a word that inspired both disgust and admiration, for there was something profoundly appealing about the idea of a rogue who could get away with murder and maintain his roguish smile. The Workers Party had pulled up the country's poor by their bootstraps, for which they had been rightly applauded (and reviled in some quarters), but being true to their culture they had lined their pockets while doing so, and the biggest difference between them and the right-wing elements that had taken their place, apart from the fact that the right-wingers were in no way beholden to the poor, was that the new regime was far less subtle about their equally voracious appetites.

It took a few minutes in a crowd that was approaching one thousand souls, but Priya and Visheshvar soon found the other members of the local satsang who had come, homing in on a pair of dadas whose orange robes and turbans seemed perfectly at home among the eclectic assortment of Hindu swamis, Buddhist monks, Sufi mystics, and Christian divines that were circulating in the larger sea of the Greater Paulista spiritual counterculture. The meditation was organized and led by Monja Coen, her shaved head and brown robes serving as a beacon for the crowd. She began with a chorus of drawn-out *oms* in her gravelly voice that spread over the square like rising water as everyone joined in, followed by a twenty-five-minute silent meditation in front of a sizable contingent of curious onlookers. Afterward she gave a talk about spirituality, ethics, and public life that made Priya wish that Coen had been elected president instead of the career politician her fellow citizens had voted for. It was the only way, she thought, to fix what ailed the country, and indeed the world: hand over the reins to the most spiritually elevated, ethically rooted, and worldly accomplished elders you can find. Put competent people at the wheel whose sole interest was the welfare of all living beings, and then this world would really have a chance—if not at paradise, then at least at getting its act together. In her lifetime? Difficult to imagine but not beyond the realm of possibility, not if the people-in-the-park's numbers continued to swell. It could happen. The world would have to wake up at some point, wouldn't it, if enough of its residents were hellbent on waking up themselves?

It was the first thing she said to Visheshvar after they said goodbye to the other devotees and started heading for his car.

"Oh, it's coming, Priya," he said, "and sooner than you think. Most people don't see it, but the old order is crumbling in front of our eyes. You've heard of the death rattle, right? Well if you listen closely, you can hear materialism, capitalism, and all those other isms rattling their way to extinction. They just don't know it yet."

He said it with such calm assurance that Priya found herself automatically revising her previous assessment.

"So are you hungry?" he said. "What do you say we drop by Govinda's on the way back, have some lunch?"

"Isn't Govinda's in the opposite direction?"

"Not if we take the parabolic route."

So he did have a sense of humor.

It was just after one when they got to Govinda's, and as was usual at that hour they had a long wait before they could get a table. Priya had gone there once with Didi and a small group of teachers, and it had taken a good forty-five minutes to get inside the door—a surprise given the nondescript exterior—but once inside, the esoteric decor and the gourmet vegetarian Indian cuisine soon made it obvious why the place was in such demand. This time the wait was half an hour, which they spent watching the other people in line and stamping up and down in place to keep warm after the sun disappeared behind a thick bank of winter clouds. When they finally got their table, Priya was reminded why she had liked the restaurant so much. The food was excellent but the background music and the paintings on the walls were even better: Sanskrit mantras and scenes from Krishna's life, reminding her and everyone else that the food they were enjoying was an offering to God.

They had just ordered dessert, in the midst of what, as usual, had been an enjoyable and stimulating conversation, when Visheshvar caught her completely off guard.

"I heard some talk that you're thinking about becoming a didi. Is it true?"

"Me? A didi?" After the momentary shock, Priya felt her blood starting to heat. "And who exactly has been saying this?"

"I overheard a couple of dadas talking about it, but I wasn't part of the conversation so I'd rather not name names."

"Well they didn't hear it from me, and if they're mind-readers then they are pretty poor ones, since I've never so much as entertained the possibility. I do know one or two dadas who would like it if I became a didi. It might ease their conscience."

"I thought so. It would have been a shame were it true."

"And why is that?"

Visheshvar hesitated for several moments and Priya felt some small measure of satisfaction to see that she had been able to ruffle his customary self-composure. But he recovered quickly and with visible aplomb.

"Well ... the obvious for one. We need people like you in Brazil if the mission's going to grow. We need good didis too, don't get me wrong, but if you became a didi, you wouldn't be working in South America. Call me selfish, but I'm focused on Brazil. When I see someone with your potential, I don't want to let her get away."

Priya didn't know quite how to answer that, conscious as she was of the possible double entendre, so she did the next best thing: she changed the subject. She started telling him how important the yoga teacher training had been for her. Working with Didi was a blessing and she loved what she was doing, but eventually she wanted to start teaching classes and courses to spread the tantric teachings, and the training had been an important step in that direction.

"From what I've seen, that's exactly what you're meant to be doing, Priya. We all have a calling and that seems to be yours. It's mine also, by the way. Which is why I think we would make a great team. It's not easy to find the right partner."

"And by partner, you mean?"

"Whatever you want it to mean."

Visheshvar's smile widened to the point that Priya felt an impulse to shield her eyes from the glare. He had spoken these words with an air of such serene confidence that she felt her own will beginning to waver. Fortunately the unmercifully tardy waitress chose that moment to arrive with their desserts: strawberry cheesecake for her, black forest cake for him, both specialties of the house. Priya welcomed the reprieve with something close to undying gratitude, a chance for her to repeat her momentary mantra: *not so fast, girl*. She was hoping to extend the reprieve to the end of her cheesecake, which she intended to savor as long as she could, but Visheshvar was more punctual with his black forest.

"So what do you think?" he said, after polishing off the last of his dessert.

"I think this is a very special cheesecake. But I guess that's not what you're asking."

"No, it's not." Said once again with the same unflappable self-assurance.

"I never did tell you why I came to São Paulo, did I?"

"Not in so many words."

"Are you in a hurry?"

On Visheshvar's suggestion, they left the car in its street-side parking spot and walked the long city block to Acclimation Park, where they found an unoccupied bench under a shady copaíba tree. After extracting a promise from Visheshvar that everything she was about to tell him was sealed to the public by judicial order, she spent the next hour and change narrating her experiences with Fernando and Kamaleshvarananda, the sum total of her two principal romantic adventures in this life, and the emotional eddies they had left behind.

When she was done, ending with a subdued and somewhat shaky affirmation that she wasn't yet ready for another romantic relationship and couldn't promise how long it would be before she was, Visheshvar didn't skip a beat.

"Okay. I'll wait."

"Come again?"

Visheshvar tilted his head and smiled, as if he were just stating the obvious. "You're special, Priya. I don't know if everyone sees it, but I do. So I'll wait. I'm thirty-three years old. I've got time. I don't need to jump into a relationship—unless it's the right relationship. I've done that before and it wasn't pretty, but I like to think I've learned my lesson. As a friend of mine once said, it's better to be alone than to wish you were alone. I think that's true for anyone but especially for a yogi. Being alone is good for the soul. Being with the right companion is even better, but it has to be the right companion. The spiritual connection has to be there. I think we're kindred souls, and if that's true, then it's worth waiting."

"So you're not disappointed?"

"No. I think 'hopeful' is a better word."

"Are you sure? It might be a long wait, and like I said, I can't make any promises."

Visheshvar laughed. "The Chinese have a saying: when eternity is the goal, what's the hurry? Anyhow, these things are all a matter of samskara. Best just to let the winds of karma blow. No hurry. We'll get there when we get there."

There was that phrase again: the winds of karma. Those winds had been quiet for a while, a good long while, but it sure looked now as if a storm were brewing.

4

I

T WAS THE "I'LL wait," she decided, that had done her in. It had been so unexpected and so subliminally gratifying that she had fallen for it without so much as a casual inspection. What woman doesn't want to hear one time in her life that a man will wait for her, no matter how long it takes, because she's worth the wait? Had someone asked her that question in a vacuum, her answer might have been "her kind of woman," but life wasn't lived in a vacuum. Life was lived in a maze of karmic entanglements, and in that tangled maze she was just as susceptible to a well-timed line as the next girl. Even if the price for her all-too-human susceptibility was that sooner or later she was going to have to give him an answer. She had bought herself some time, but that was little more than a temporary reprieve. And wasn't that just like the tantric path. Just when she thought she was making some real progress, listing toward an almost even keel, the universe throws in a well-timed complication: in this case, a well-timed "I'll wait."

This time she blamed it on Baba. The conversation in front of his photo that evening began as a referendum on why he had chosen to complicate her life just when she was finally starting to get the upper hand on her inner demons, and it ended with her feeling markedly better—as if she had just had a long conversation with her own soul (which she had) and found it the best of all possible companions (which it was). If ever two eyes were smiling, they were Baba's in this particular photo, her favorite, and they were smiling at her, the eternal accomplice holding steady in his affection while she slipped and slid and forever lost her balance. She supplied the words, but behind her complaints and her confusion she had an unmistakable sense that someone was listening—listening with an absolute attention that was all the stronger and steadier for its absence of words, a calming, guiding force emanating not only from the photo but from deep within her, as if the image in the picture frame were in both places at once, steering her unerringly down a path that disappeared into the gloaming. An absolute knowing that was waiting patiently for her to look its way.

Just what is it, she asked him, with me and romantic relationships? Why do they have to be so complicated, so much like a trip to the dentist? Or how a trip to the dentist used to be in the years before Novocain. Was it because she was complicated and thus had given him no other choice? Just then an image flashed in her mind: Visheshvar sitting next to her on the bench at Acclimation Park, smiling, steady in his conviction. "No hurry. We'll get there when we get there." She heard the words again, but instead of sounding like a sudden fall in the barometer that presages the coming of a storm, they seemed to resonate with an aura of wise counsel, the words a friend would say if that friend could know exactly what she needed to hear. She looked again at the photo and Baba's eyes smiled back at her in recognition. Suddenly she caught a glimpse of the road opening out in front of her, reflected for a single instant in the pupils that held sway at the center of her soul, as if illumined by a flash of lightning on a new-moon night. "So that's how it is," she said out loud after a ruminative pause, in something between a whisper and a friendly growl. "Your choice, no matter what I choose." So be it, she thought. She couldn't run away from this one (as if she could run away from anything), and so she reached for her phone and texted Visheshvar: *let the winds of karma blow.*

It was not their first official text — he had sent her one that morning to let her know he was on his way — but it was like the official cutting of a ribbon to inaugurate their unofficial and unacknowledged courtship. After that, the text thread began to fill up with comments on how the week was going, mixed with spiritual observations, and toward the end of the week the inevitable invitation to do something over the weekend, always innocuous and informal, just a couple of friends hanging out without a hint of romance and with just enough frequency that before long the whole São Paulo satsang assumed they were a couple — or if not yet a consummated couple, then certainly heading in that direction, and wasn't it adorable that they were taking it so slow and proper, like good little yogis. There were times when Priya felt backed into a corner. Not so much by Visheshvar and his "I'll wait," lounging on its comfortable recliner in the back of her mind, prodding her at random intervals with a lazy stick — in truth, he couldn't have been more cool about it, a spiritual brother if ever there was one—but by the glare of public opinion. Not only was she uncomfortably aware of the glances that came their way whenever they sat together after the Sunday meditation, she had begun to catch subtle intimations of a campaign by the men and women in orange to convince her to join their ranks. And eventually not so subtle.

It began with casual remarks by the different dadas that passed through the São Paulo center about how much the mission needed talented young didis who could become the leaders of the future. These comments were usually embedded in a general summing up of the state of the organization that made no mention of her particular future, but the subtext was obvious: they were sounding her out as they sounded out all the young devotees who fit a certain profile, combing through the fields for that one diamond in the rough whose ears would perk up at the mere mention of the subject, ready to cross her off their list if she didn't betray at least a modicum of interest. But as she gradually discovered, it wasn't quite that simple.

One of the many duties of the monastic order was to create more monastics—the vision Baba had given for the mission was both electrifying and daunting, and they needed to uncover as many monastics-in-waiting as they possibly could if they were going to succeed in bringing his vision to fruition. And once they had what they thought was a viable candidate in their sights, they were not about to let her go until they had exhausted all the stratagems in their arsenal. Especially when that viable candidate had a prospective beau to lend their efforts an added sense of urgency. These stratagems included appeals to her innermost aspirations (tales of how becoming a monk had speeded up their spiritual growth, their reward for a life of service to the guru); the promise of adventure (a chance to travel the world and do fascinating work that would be impossible were she to remain in her native country, bound to a conventional life); the pride-and-prestige gambit (the opportunity it afforded to become one of the true architects of the future, a spiritual revolutionary whose name would be writ large in the annals of recorded history when all was said and done and a new spiritual society emerged from the wreckage of the present); and a touch of guilt when all else failed, since the mission depended on noble souls like her who were willing to sacrifice their personal lives to be the master's direct representatives in the world. She got all of these and more at different times as the months passed, and while she didn't go so far as to assume an overt conspiracy, she was sure they talked among themselves about possible candidates and that her name had vaulted to the top of the list, a feather in the cap of anyone who could convince her to take the leap.

The alternative, should she decide not to trade in her wardrobe for a single shade of orange, was to get married and become a pillar of society. Apparently, Baba had encouraged everyone to choose one of two paths: either become a renunciant and dedicate one's life to the service of humanity, or else get married and raise a healthy spiritual family that would become one of the foundation blocks of the future spiritual society. Serial monogamy was not a recognized option, much less casual relationships, and she thought she could detect a sense of urgency among the dadas and didis to enlist her before Visheshvar got her to the altar and put a garland around her neck in the tantric wedding ceremony. No matter that she and Visheshvar weren't actually a couple. "Just friends" in their eyes was merely a euphemism for a dig-nified courtship, a trial period to give her time to choose between one path or the other (they had given up on Visheshvar long ago). And this extended beyond the dadas and didis. She soon got the feeling that her fellow devotees were laying bets on which way she would go, become a didi or marry Visheshvar. She could see it in their smiles and hear it in their jokes. It was just public opinion, she told herself, an ephemeral abstract entity with no real substance, but there were times when it felt like an actual corner whose walls she could feel pressing against her back.

Even Didi Jaya, who was constitutionally opposed to meddling, got into the act one Monday morning on the bus to Peri Alto, when Priya mentioned a visiting dada who had called her aside two days earlier to talk about her future (she had begun teaching a Saturday-morning yoga class at the dadas' center) and told her point blank that there was no higher calling than to become a didi.

"Be careful," Didi said, dropping her voice to a conspiratorial rum-ble, just loud enough to be heard above the rattling of the bus and the jumble of voices from the nearby seats. "He's a very persuasive dada. If you don't watch out, he'll have you bundled off to the training center before you even realize you're on a plane."

"Don't worry, Didi, I'm not so easily persuaded. But what do *you* think? About what he said."

"It doesn't matter what I think. What matters is what you think. It may even be true, but unless it's true for you then that's neither here nor there. But I will tell you this: that dada has no idea what's best for you. Trust me, I know his history. He's sent a lot of people to the training center and most of them have come back. He got the credit for sending them, but they weren't ready. And there's no point in going to training unless you're ready. But try telling him that. It goes in one ear and right out the other. Believe me, I've tried. He just wants to send as many people as he can. What happens to them after that is their problem. People in South America are very emotional. They're like Filipinos in that respect. They get inspired easily, and that's all well and good, but then they get to the training center and they clash out. You can't become a didi or a dada on emotion. That's not enough. Emotion doesn't last. You have to have determination, you have to have dedication. That's why I don't encourage anyone to go unless they're really truly prepared. It's not an easy life, I tell you. It's not easy at all."

"I can see that, Didi."

"So if you ever do decide to go, make sure you're ready."

"And how do you know if you're ready?"

"You'll know. How do you know if you're in love? You just know. And no one can tell you otherwise. If you really have that level of determination and dedication, then nothing can stop you from going. It's still going to be hard, but if it's what you really want to do with your life, then you'll get through the difficulties. It's like marriage. It's not going to be a bed of roses, no matter how nice a guy you marry, but if it's what you really want, then you work it out."

"Or you give up, which is what most people seem to do when it gets hard."

"That may be true for some people, but it's not true for me and it's not true for you. When you do decide what you want to do, whether you decide to get married or become a didi, go into it with the idea that this is for life. Either way it's a calling. You've been called by Baba to do his work—either as a didi or as a family person. So no matter how hard it gets, surrender and see it through."

Priya told Didi about the subtle pressure she was feeling to get married—sooner rather than later—if she didn't want to become a didi. With all eyes on Visheshvar, naturally, as if it were written into the stars by universal decree. She had no desire to become a didi, but she didn't want to feel any pressure to get married either. It felt like a kind of prim morality that belonged to the past rather than the future, a stifling of individual freedom that went against the grain of society's onward motion.

Didi was more accommodating on this point than many of the other dadas and didis, but only to a certain extent. "This is Brazil," she said.

"Time, place, and person. You have to adjust with the culture. But if you ask me if it's better—yes, it's better. If you are not going to be a didi then you *should* get married. To the right person, at the right time, of course, but in the meantime don't play around. That's my advice, if you ask me. Fortunately most people don't ask me."

Priya chewed on this for a minute or two while didi patted her on the hand and glanced out the window at the traffic piling up at a particularly intransigent intersection.

"Did Baba ever say anything about what age a person should make a decision by?" Priya asked after the bus lurched into motion, curious but still uneasy about the idea.

"Not that I know of. But we're not supposed to send people to the training center without special permission if they are over thirty. So if you ask me, I would say thirty, give or take."

Priya was twenty-nine. Though she wasn't about to subscribe to an idea she didn't believe in, she did breathe a half-conscious sigh of relief, knowing she had at least one more year of latitude before the wolves of propriety came howling at her door.

That Saturday after her morning yoga class, she and Visheshvar caught a matinee at the Santana Cine Teatro multiplex. Afterward, over a late lunch, he entertained her with a string of mildly amusing stories of the dadas trying to get him to sign up with them several years earlier. "Eventually they give up," he said, an observation she found comforting. "Brazil hasn't been particularly kind to them." He counted out on the fingers of one hand the number of Brazilian dadas and didis left standing. "Stand tough, Priya. They'll get over their disappointment."

It occurred to her just then that he had never even considered the possibility that after living with Didi and listening to the dadas she might have begun to feel some attraction to the life of a renunciant. She hadn't, but she felt a quick flush of annoyance that he had taken that for granted. She remembered a conversation in which he had said that celibate monks were an endangered species, a dying animal on the slow road to extinction as the human race threw off the shackles of religious dogma and embraced the fullness of the human incarnation. She hadn't been fully convinced, even after he laid out his rationale, but she liked the idea prima facie. It felt provocative and somehow progressive, almost visionary in a way, adding to the luster in his aura that she imagined radiating from his shoulders and head while they talked.

But the implied assumption that she would never consider becoming a celibate renunciant, since that would be going backward according to his vision of the unfolding of human spirituality, triggered a latent spike of indignation. She should be free to make up her own mind, she thought, without anybody trying to sway her thinking with their two cents—neither the dadas nor the didis nor the would-be boyfriend. Especially the would-be boyfriend, who was by definition supposed to have her best interests at heart and enough respect to allow her to decide what those were.

Right on cue, he brought up his theory about the endangered nature of celibate monks and nuns, and as she watched his self-satisfied glow light up their table, she thought that maybe she should become a didi—at least for a day or two, just to put him in his place. It was well back in her subconscious, a brief authorial intrusion in the background narrative while she was dutifully listening to his exposition, struggling once again to piece together the logic in his argument, but she was surprised to find that the idea held a kind of odd attraction. Not merely the imagined pleasure of bringing him down a peg but an actual subliminal attraction to an image of herself in orange, becoming a pure channel for the teachings.

It was a startling observation, though she didn't have time to turn it over in her mind until she got home that evening, where it unfortunately ended up commandeering the major part of her attention during her evening meditation, and she went to bed that night with the well-founded suspicion that Baba had a vested interest in making her life more difficult—as she let him know in what was starting to turn into a private nightly ritual: her bedtime conversation with the guru.

Why close her life to the future, she told him, lying supine on her sleeping mat with her hands clasped behind her head and her unfocused eyes staring at the ceiling, if the future was an unknown integer of indeterminate duration? No matter how laudatory the dadas' motives for wanting her to become a didi, that didn't mean it was in her best interests. And the same held true for those in the Visheshvar camp, including the prospective beau. Doing either without feeling a true calling seemed a sure way of closing herself off to life's possibilities, and up until now that call had yet to come.

Priya unclasped her hands and reached out for the photo on the altar. She balanced it on her chest with her head propped on the pillow and stared into those magnetic, enigmatic eyes from point-blank range. It was comforting to feel this close to a realized master, even if that master's principal mode of communication was silence. It was enough that she could feel his guidance, even if she could not yet hear his voice. A smile crossed her lips as she wondered what her former students and colleagues back in the day would make of her talking to a picture, especially this picture. She had a pretty good idea and she couldn't blame them. Even now it still ran contrary to her instincts to hand over power of attorney to an unseen force peering out at her through a pair of disembodied eyes lodged in a fourteen-real aluminum picture frame. But she had gotten acclimated to the idea, and those old instincts were starting to appear atavistic. Especially since she knew that if left to her own devices she was practically guaranteed to lose her way, goaded as she was by so many contradictory impulses whose origins and salubrity she couldn't trust. If a realized master could somehow communicate with her across an abyss of time and space, she had no doubt that his guidance would be a far more reliable astrolabe to help her navigate the heavens than any modern star chart she could pull up on her phone. The infinite intelligence that had created the universe was directing her footsteps, and it was comforting to give that infinite intelligence a face, in the hope that in time it would also become a voice as recognizable as her own.

And if that voice told her that her destiny was to become a didi?

The thought produced an involuntary shudder, and this in turn made her laugh. The key to her destiny was somewhere in those eyes, but for the time being she had too many warring thoughts to be able to tune in to that invisible homing signal. What would her kids in the school make of her if they could see into the spinning top of her mind at this moment? Blinking incomprehension? A compassionate shake of the head at an adult who had obviously lost the plot? She could just see one of them grabbing her hand and asking her to come and play. Which was precisely what she needed to alleviate her chronic condition of mortgaging her life to an imaginary future. She placed the photo back on the altar and curled up beneath the sheets, already looking forward to Monday morning and the bracing challenge of life in the kingdom of the two- and three- and four-year-olds.

5

School was letting out a week before Christmas for the two-month summer vacation and the staff was in high gear, getting ready for the graduation ceremony for the four-year-olds. Didi, in particular, was squeezing every spare minute from her already overloaded schedule to see to every major and minor detail so that the program would be its usual roaring success, right down to the choice of Santa Claus, for whom she interviewed no less than seven candidates from among the families of the children and the patrons of the school (being chosen as this year's Santa was a singular honor in Peri Alto). Priya was as busy as anyone, and she didn't want to bother Didi at such a hectic time, but she knew Didi wouldn't be happy if she kept her in the dark any longer than necessary, so she pulled her away from her cartoons one night after a particularly long day and told her that she had decided to spend a month in Rio after the New Year's retreat to make a determination about her future. Teaching yoga had been a profoundly gratifying experience, and it was getting hard for her to ignore her desire to spread the teachings that had wrought such a remarkable transformation in her life in a mere two and a half years. Didi listened patiently to her hesitant explanation, despite her obvious tiredness. She even winced when Priya told her how much she would miss the kids, should she decide after that month that she wasn't coming back. But when Priya finished unburdening her heart, Didi gave a resigned nod and took her hand.

"I can't say I'm surprised," she said. "But sometimes you can't help but wish that the inevitable would take its own sweet time."

Somehow the poignancy of the occasion gave them both extra energy, and they ended up talking well into the night: about the kids, about her year in São Paulo, about the future of the mission and what role she might be destined to play in its unfolding. They were both bleary-eyed when the school van showed up the next morning to pick them up, but afterward Priya looked back at that night as perhaps the most satisfying lack of a night's sleep she had ever known.

There were tears in her eyes when she said goodbye to the kids and the staff after the graduation ceremony, not knowing if she would be back, and traces of those tears were still there when she arrived at Ananda Kirtana one week later, but they were quickly erased by the onrush of spiritual energy she felt the moment she stepped down from the school van. It had been a year since her last retreat, and though it had been a fairytale year in many ways, the year of a magical growth spurt, as if she were one of Jack's enchanted beans, there was something about the unmistakable hum of two hundred minds tuned to the same spiritual frequency that eclipsed anything she had experienced during that time. She felt an upsurge of emotion as she saw the familiar faces milling about, including a bevy of monks and nuns, and it only took a couple of deep breaths for the intoxication to enter her lungs and send her careening from one welcome conversation to another, until it was time for evening practices and a resounding kirtan that reminded her how powerful the kirtans in that magical place could be.

The succeeding days passed in a whirl of spiritual satsang that made her feel at times as if she were barely anchored to her body. Not that she hadn't had ample satsang in São Paulo—living and working with Didi had been full of its daily inspirations—but there was strength in numbers, and it was an inescapable fact that the more spiritualists there were in a single venue, the easier it became to ride that collective wave to heights few could attain on their own. The experiences she had during those six days, both in and out of meditation, were incontrovertible proof of how far she had come since her last retreat, and among them was one particularly memorable conversation with Devashish on the veranda of his house at the far end of Ananda Kirtana.

She had met him briefly during her first New Year's retreat, when he signed her copy of Baba's biography and told stories from his time with the master, but she hadn't had the opportunity for an actual conversation, or else she had been too shy to make it happen. This time she made it one of her goals to correct that error, and she didn't have long to wait. Prashanti was revising the translation of another of his books, *When the Time Comes*, and when she told Priya the morning after her arrival that she and Devashish were going to meet over lunch to discuss some questions she had about the translation, Priya volunteered to lend a second set of eyes, those of a professional translator. Prashanti, in her normal upbeat manner, declared it the best idea she had ever heard, and true to her word, Priya uncovered some nuances that had been left out of the Portuguese text, as well as a couple of outright errors.

When the lunchtime summit was over, Prashanti excused herself to go see what mischief her son was up to, and Priya took advantage of the opportunity to ask Devashish some questions about *Tales of a Tantric Master* that had been on her mind for quite some time. Like most authors, he had endless patience when it came to discussing his work, and when he mentioned that he had to go up to the house to get his computer, he asked her if she wanted to tag along and continue their conversation, promising to have her back in time for the afternoon program.

They made the two-kilometer trip in a pale-green, 1972 Volkswagen Beetle, climbing up past the temple and into a pristine valley surrounded by forested hills. His car reminded her of the beat-up Beetle her father had bought when she was a toddler, which he sold a few years later for a hatchback better suited to their growing family. She only had vague memories of that car, but there was a framed picture of it in the living room of her parents' house, and it had come to take on mythic overtones in family lore, an aura she immediately attributed to the rattling oval that navigated the intermittent mud between the retreat center and Devashish's house better than any 4x4 on the market.

Minutes later they were sitting on his veranda, switching over to English as they looked out at the valley, a magnificent panorama with no visible sign of human interference, other than the house and a couple of barely visible wires that snuck through the trees to an electric post at the back. It was, as he told her when he handed her a glass of mineral water piped in by gravity from a natural spring, the perfect place for spiritual meditation.

"And the perfect place to write, I imagine."

"That too, although it pretty much comes to the same thing. Quiet the mind, direct it toward Consciousness, and let the Supreme will his words into the world, if you'll forgive the heavy-handed alliteration."

Priya had fallen in love with the philosophy right around the time she had fallen in love with Dada, and for many of the same reasons. There was something so attractive, seductive even, in the vistas it opened up within her, in its subtle power to respond to the longing that fueled her search, adding ever-expanding pieces to the puzzle that she was slowly piecing together on the table of her awareness. As Devashish began describing his artistic and meditative efforts to gain access to the higher layers of the superconscious mind, Priya felt a tingling in her body and a sense of heightened awareness that she recognized as the thrill of the chase — the hunt for knowledge of the Self. The ideas weren't new to her — she had read about the layers of the mind in Baba's books and discussed them with Dada; they had even integrated them into their course — but hearing about them firsthand from someone who had made the effort to reach those higher layers the touchstone of his artistic endeavors made it seem as if they were right there in front of her, just on the other side of an inner door — an infinitely creative, infinitely knowing sky waiting only for her to develop the requisite strength to crack that door open.

"There are these moments — I think every serious artist has them — when you touch something ineffable and become a conduit for it to clothe itself in language or color or sound." As his words reached her from a distance that was infinitely greater than the single meter of finite space that lay between their chairs, she knew exactly what he was talking about, as if she were the artist at the moment of creation, catching a glimpse of heaven as her kundalini rose, and then clothing it in the poverty of words as her kundalini made its descent. These were the kinds of moments that had drawn her to Dada, the source of the attraction and admiration that had gradually inundated her heart. He had been her principal conduit into the esoteric regions of the tantric path, and his absence had left a void that she had covered over without actually filling. It occurred to her then that what she had felt for Dada she had never felt for anyone. Certainly not for Fernando, who had ignited her passions but left her deepest aspirations untouched, or for Visheshvar, a good companion whose biggest fault was that he failed to inspire in her the feelings that Dada had (he was in Hawaii at the moment for a one-month yoga therapy course and it was telling that Priya didn't miss him). Suddenly, she was waylaid by the same sense of loss that had waylaid her when Dada had passed through immigration and out of her life, a helpless plummeting sensation that she hadn't felt for close to a year, as if the cure she had been working toward had merely been a temporary remission. It had taken her until that conversation on the beach before she had been ready to call it love. Until then she had thought of it as what her uncles would have called "being filled with the holy ghost." But whatever label she gave it, she missed that feeling terribly, as she couldn't help but miss the man who had lit her up from within, and perhaps she would go on missing both until she learned how to get there on her own.

Her mind was spinning now, fleeing further and further into the past, but a sliver of her attention was still on the veranda, just enough to keep the sadness confined to her chest and out of her face while her interlocutor explored the similarities between meditative practice and the sadhana of the arts. But perhaps she wasn't quite as successful as she thought, for somehow the conversation segued into romantic attachments and their role in the spiritual journey. She wasn't sure at all how they had gotten there. Had she given herself away, let her sadness and pain find their way into words, given him some subtle or not-so-subtle hint of what she was feeling? Or had he simply divined her thoughts, caught a glimpse of the empty space in her heart and turned to the philosophy as a sure remedy for what ailed her? Either way, his words caught her attention and soon she was back with her host, body and soul, struggling to understand just how they had gotten to this point in the conversation.

"You may feel like it's holding you back," he was saying, "like you're living with a ghost you can't get rid of, but that ghost is there for a reason. You just have to turn it to your advantage."

"Turn it to your advantage?" she said, still disoriented.

"Exactly. When two combatants enter the ring for a martial arts match or a boxing match, what is the first thing they do?"

Priya shook her head.

"In the martial arts the contestants bow to each other. Boxers touch gloves. Then they come out fighting. And why do they bow or touch gloves before the fight begins? So that they remember that this is sport. A test of skill being staged for entertainment, both theirs and the audience's. They are not enemies in real life; they are only combatants from the time the opening bell rings until the time the match ends. It is the same with the fight against our internal demons. We call them enemies and fetters, *ashtas* and *pashas*, but it is in this same spirit of sport that we do so. You need two contestants for a match to take place. God created the *ashtas* and *pashas*, just as he created your desire for spiritual liberation. So whatever you are going through, always remember that it's been arranged for cosmic entertainment. He gets to enjoy the match through your eyes as your individual consciousness, as well as through his cosmic eyes. What the philosophy calls *ota* and *prota* yoga.

"Now if you are going to take part in a martial arts contest, you need some training, right? Otherwise it won't be a fair fight and there's no fun in that. It takes all the drama out of it. The cosmic promoter wants a fair fight, so he arranges for us to get some training, to prepare us for what we are going to face, and that gives us the confidence we need when we enter the ring, the confidence that we can win—if we can just stay the course. That's the spirit of Tantra. You go to battle with your inner demons so that one day you can come out victorious and earn the gold belt of spiritual liberation. Not the best of analogies, perhaps, but it will do. And an essential part of that training is how to deal with love—or more to the point, how to deal with attachment. Since that's what we're really talking about here. Do you agree?"

"I do. Although I'm not sure where one ends and the other begins."

"That's a hard one for all of us, but there is a simple litmus test: where there is suffering there is attachment. That doesn't mean that love is absent; it just means it's a mixed bag. Pure love in its natural state is as rare as pure iron. It almost always comes mixed in nature, in some kind of ore, like iron oxide. You have to smelt out the impurities, and one of the ways you can do that is by turning the attachment to your advantage. It's the same principle in the martial arts: you use your opponent's force against them. Maya created the attachment, it's one of her best moves, but you can learn to use it against her. You can use the attachment to throw her to the mat."

"Okay. So how do I do that?"

"Simple. Just remember that the object of your attachment is a manifestation of Divine Consciousness. If you take the shelter of spiritual ideation, Maya becomes powerless to stop you. Once a disciple asked Ramana Maharsi how to realize that everything is God. His answer was, 'Call everything God.' Suppose you can't stop thinking about a certain someone. If you can remember that that certain someone is Divine Consciousness in a particular finite form—in this case, a particularly attractive finite form—then every time you remember that person, you remember God."

"I understand the principle, but I have actually been trying and it's a whole lot harder than it sounds."

"Simple doesn't mean easy. It is hard. Very hard. You have to practice. But if you practice long enough and hard enough, it eventually becomes second nature. And in the meantime the attachment is your sparring partner. To extend the analogy, you can't become really skilled in the martial arts unless you have a chance to hone your skills under match conditions against a worthy adversary. The better your opponent, the better it forces you to become. You can practice all you want on your own, but without a worthy adversary you will never become good enough to earn that belt. And attachment is a truly worthy adversary. Do you remember how Baba defines devotion?"

Priya shook her head, now fully invested in the moment.

"Bhaktir bhagavad bhavana. Devotion is thinking of God, directing your mind toward Consciousness. And one of the meanings of the noun *bhava,* from which the verb *bhavana,* 'thinking,' is derived, is 'attachment' or 'sentiment.' If you think about it, it makes perfect sense. It is next to impossible to keep your mind fixed on a single object for any length of time if you don't feel a strong attraction to that object. Eventually your mind will run away. It will go looking for something it likes. Better yet, something it loves. A mathematician can think about numbers and formulas for hours on end because he loves math, but most of us will get bored within minutes. Before we know it we'll be daydreaming about our favorite TV series or a certain someone or whatever it is we are attracted to. Literally, meditation, dhyana, means directing your mind in an unbroken flow toward a single object. And that is not possible without sentiment, without attraction. So you start with attachment for this person or that story or this valley here with its beautiful scenery—for the world itself—and eventually, through constant practice, that attachment turns into attraction to God. And once that happens, meditation is easy. Ramakrishna used to say that doing spiritual practices without devotion is like trying to cross the ocean in a sailboat with no wind. You have to row, and rowing is incredibly hard work. How long can you keep it up? But when the winds of devotion rise they fill the sails and your boat starts speeding across the water. Then you can drop your oars, kick back, and enjoy the wind in your face. What could be better than that?"

Priya could feel the wind rising, though she suspected she wouldn't be letting go of those oars anytime soon. "So would you say that getting your heart broken and putting it back together again is a kind of training for developing devotion?"

"Absolutely. It's practice for the main event. Call it the undercard. It's a chance to go mano a mano with attachment, so we can work our way toward that gold belt. In the end, the only real difference is who we are in love with. But of course, that makes all the difference. You love books. I'm sure you've come across novels where the partners in a romantic relationship become so close it's almost as if they were one person. They take on each other's characteristics, know their partner's thoughts before they speak, complete their sentences. It's rare in real life but there is a reason why it gets idealized in fictional stories: the closer the relationship, the more fulfilling it is. But there is a limit to how close you can get in any worldly relationship, romantic or otherwise. You can get very close, it can be very fulfilling, but there will always be some separation. What we really want is oneness—that's what's really behind our longing for relationship—and that can't be found in the mundane world. It can only be found when we fall in love with the soul of the universe, which is our very own Self. That's why kirtan is the ultimate love song. We start out singing that everything is God. *Baba nam kevalam.* We look out on the universe and we see the Beloved, but there is some distance between us, just as there is in the beginning of any relationship. But the more we sing, the closer we get, until the mantra takes on new meaning: 'O my Beloved, your name is the only name on my lips.' And that flowering of love reaches its culmination when we become so close we forget ourselves entirely. The *we* becomes *he.*"

They fell silent after that, turning their attention to the valley in front of them, and Priya welcomed the opportunity to let her mind steep in its reflections. There was something so still, so serene, so subtly alluring about the valley in that moment that it seemed the perfect backdrop for the soul's search for itself. The eyes of the world returning her gaze, measuring her thoughts, waiting for her to pierce its veil and leave her small self behind.

After a few minutes of quiet contemplation, Devashish glanced at his watch and mentioned that they should be heading back if they were going to catch the afternoon program. As they were getting up to leave, she took the opportunity to tell him how much his book had meant to her.

"I feel much the same," he said. "Having the chance to write it was pure grace from beginning to end. It was like being in constant meditation: thinking of Baba for hours at a stretch, day after day, totally immersed in the drama of his incarnation. That was a magical time in my life. Of course, it ended once I finished the book, but as the saying goes, 'I'll always have Jamalpur.'"

So would she. The Jamalpur of her heart, where the master sat and smiled upon his favorite daughter as he led her on the journey from separateness to oneness.

6

HE HIGH POINT OF the retreat was the New Year's Eve akhanda kirtan: six hours of chanting in the temple, with its magnificent vista, led by a series of excellent musicians. This was followed by meditation and a short talk by one of the dadas, after which everyone linked arms in concentric circles and sang kirtan, swaying side to side as they waited for the clock to strike twelve. When the countdown reached midnight, the hall erupted with shouts of *Parampita Baba ki, jai,* "victory to the Supreme Father," and everyone started looking for someone to embrace, prompting a hug-fest that went on for nearly half an hour. Then everyone trooped down the hill to the dining area where a feast had been laid out for the two hundred devotees still walking on air from their kirtan high.

This was Priya's third New Year's retreat, and she couldn't think of a better way to end the year: great kirtan, great food, great company. But this kirtan was especially meaningful, for she somehow made the leap from singing God's name to singing *to* God. Apart from a short medita-tion break, she spent the entire six hours dancing in a circle around the improvised altar, pouring out her heart in Sanskrit to the Lord of her dreams. He was no longer the abstract, formless consciousness he had once been, hidden behind the veil of her ignorance. He was a living presence now, who loved nothing more than to spend his time playing hide and seek with his erstwhile devotee, smiling at her from within her mind as she courted him and he her, a sometimes tearful, sometimes joyful, but always playful dance that continued even after the music stopped, a going-round-and-round in her heart that she knew could only lead to the center of her soul.

She was still trailing clouds of glory the next morning when she reached the dining area before breakfast for a short closing ceremony, bleary-eyed but buzzing with energy (it had been after two when she went to bed and not yet five when her alarm sounded so she could straggle into the main hall, one of the few kirtan revelers who actually made it to the five a.m. meditation). The closing ceremony was a chance for people to share their experiences, and Priya was glad that no one asked her to speak, for she was sure she would have choked up the moment she started talking (as it was, there was no shortage of tears during the sharing). When it was over, Kamaleshvarananda's old boss stood up and invited those who weren't leaving that morning to attend a meeting after lunch to discuss the World Social Forum that would be taking place in Porto Alegre just after the carnival retreat. The Porto Alegre satsang had managed to secure a large booth and a half-dozen time slots for lectures and workshops for the five-day global conference, which was expecting several hundred thousand participants and fifteen thousand official delegates, including many if not most of the world's leading activists. Dada was looking for volunteers, and Priya knew this was an opportunity she couldn't pass up. She hadn't been involved in anything remotely like this since Kamaleshvarananda's departure, and even if she hadn't been staying for sadhana camp, the annual seven-day meditation intensive that followed the New Year's retreat, she would have delayed her departure, ready to roll up her sleeves.

The first hour of the meeting was spent in a collective debate over possible themes for the workshops and lectures. The dadas and didis had come up with a list of suggested topics, but narrowing that list down proved to be a somewhat chaotic experience, given the Brazilian penchant for letting everyone get a chance to express themselves, no matter how far off the topic they veered or how loud they got in support of their opinions. It wasn't unusual to hear two or three people speaking at once, but it was all in good spirit and everyone was satisfied with the outcome, no matter how long it had taken them to get there.

It was only after the topics had been agreed upon, and people had volunteered for different duties, that Dada mentioned the two guest speakers who would be coming from overseas, and it was the second of these that registered as a significant seismic event in Priya's consciousness: Dada Kamaleshvarananda, who by organizational fiat had been given the most prestigious time slot—high noon on the final day of the program in the UFRGS campus theater, the second largest of the fifteen venues where the forum's events would be held. By then she had already agreed to be in charge of publicity and logistics—in essence, the principal organizer—and to serve as translator wherever needed (the main event halls would have simultaneous translation in various languages and receivers and headsets for the audience). Her initial impulse was to renege on her commitment and skip the retreat and forum altogether, but she discarded that option the moment it reached her internal censor. This was a momentous opportunity, both for the organization and for her, and she wasn't going to let a ghost from the past frighten her away. Or rather, the unresolved feelings that ghost might resuscitate. That would be like admitting defeat before she even stepped in the ring. Barely eighteen hours earlier, as the year of her magical growth spurt was drawing to a close, she had told Baba during the kirtan that she was ready to welcome whatever challenges he sent her way—*let Maya do her worst,* was how she put it in the sanctuary of her mind, *just so long as you don't let go of me.* She'd had no idea that his answer would be so immediate or so literal, but if this was his response to her surge of inspiration then she would take it on faith that it was just what she needed, a worthy adversary to accelerate her training.

After the meeting broke up, Dada asked if he could have a word. They walked over to a couple of vacant wooden benches beneath a shady loquat tree, full of succulent yellow fruits.

"So are you okay with this?" he said. "This is a really unique opportunity for us, and as far as possible I want everything to go off smoothly."

"No need to worry on my account, Dada. What's past is past. Ancient history."

"Good. I'm glad to hear it."

"You might want to check with Dada, though, just in case, make sure he's okay with my being involved."

"Actually, he asked specifically for you. He said that if he's going to come all the way from Europe, he wants everything to be as professional as possible, and he considers you the best person for the job. I agree. As long as there won't be any problems."

"Not from my side. My only focus is Baba's mission. Like you said, this is a great opportunity for us, and if I can help, then I can't think of a better use of my time. And I appreciate your confidence in me. I promise you, I won't leave any stone unturned. I'll make sure we're as well organized and as well publicized as possible. Just out of curiosity, you didn't mention which topic Dada Kamaleshvarananda would be taking."

"Meditation and Social Change."

"I thought so. That's his bread and butter. I don't know anyone who can do it better. Maybe I can set up a couple of talks for him in town beforehand, to help generate some buzz so that we get a good turnout. Contact some of the local community leaders, get them on board, that sort of thing. I need to get things organized in my head first and get it all down on paper, but once I do I'll run my ideas past you to get your feedback."

"Excellent. I'm leaving for São Paulo in the morning and I heard you're staying for sadhana camp, but once you get to Rio send me an email and we'll take it from there. I take it you're not going back to São Paulo?"

"Not for the time being at least. I still have to decide what I'm going to do with my life, but for now I've got the forum to keep me busy. After that we'll see."

"Well, now that you're on board, I must say, I feel a lot more relaxed about the whole thing. As soon as Sudama informed me that he had gotten us those time slots I thought of you. You really are the best person for the job."

Priya was gratified by Dada's words. They had had their differences in the past—it had taken her a long time to make peace with his reasons for agreeing to Kamaleshvarananda's transfer—but she was glad those differences were behind them. She was also glad that he hadn't perceived how much the news of his participation in the forum had destabilized her internal gyroscope. She had dissimulated well, mostly because she had fully (or almost fully) believed what she'd said. The past *was* the past. The present, however, was thick with her feelings for a man she had thought was out of her life forever, only to discover that he was on his way back in. It would only be for a couple of weeks, but empires had been felled in less time. There was one thing, however, that she knew for certain now that she hadn't known back then: Kamaleshvarananda was neither the saint she had once idealized him to be, nor the ogre that she had grappled with in her darkest hours during the weeks that followed his departure: he was just a flawed human being draped in a cloak of glory handed him by the guru. Her fight wasn't with him, or with whatever unfinished karma they had together, and never had been. It was with her own internal demons—with her attachment, her anger, her disappointment, and on down the list of the mind's reactive chains that stood between her and freedom. She knew what Devashish would say, that this was a priceless opportunity to throw sand in the demon's eyes. To step into the ring and do battle with those aspects of herself that kept her from her Self, while the Lord looked on from his ringside seat and enjoyed the show. The conceit didn't make it any easier, but nowhere was it written that the spiritual path was meant to be easy. Especially once you signed on with the tantric guru. She remembered Baba saying in one of his discourses that peace was the result of fight. So be it. She had a worthy opponent in the opposite corner and the best of trainers in hers. She would wait on the bell, and when it rang they would touch gloves and come out fighting.

7

*P*RIYA COULDN'T HAVE ASKED for better conditions under which to begin her training than the sadhana camp that began the following morning: seven days of silence with eight hours a day of kirtan and meditation. In short, no distractions to keep her from a full-on tilt with her unbridled emotions. It amazed her how often she caught herself daydreaming about Dada during her meditation, as if an internal switch flipped on the moment she closed her eyes. At times they were simply shards of memory rising to the surface that she was able to shunt aside with a few repetitions of her mantra, but all too often she was caught in a web of long, elaborate fantasies that would keep her completely spellbound, redoing scenes from their past and altering them to her advantage, or inventing new ones from their future, her mantra long forgotten—until the sound of a guitar signaled the next round of practice. It had been a long time since he had dominated her thoughts like that, not since the first month or two after his departure, which was part of why she had thought she had gotten over him, but obviously those feelings had simply gone under-ground, waiting for the right opportunity to spring from hiding. It was a sobering reckoning, to see her mind backsliding this way after more than a year of what had seemed like steady progress, but she realized early on during that week that while her mind was still awash in con-tradictory emotions she was looking at them from an entirely different vantage point—and that made all the difference. Back then she had been trapped in her feelings, as if she had fallen into a whirlpool and had to fight for her survival. Now she seemed to be watching them from the shoreline—getting sprayed, no doubt, her clothes soaked, her hair dripping water into her eyes, but her feet holding steady in the mud and silt, safely out of the current's reach. She could see her attachment, her attraction, her anxieties and her fears, just as clearly as if they were opponents standing across from her on the canvas, leaning forward and flexing their muscles as they got ready to counter her next move. And because she was so much more conscious than she had been then, she was able to marshal every stratagem she had learned since the day she had picked up *Siddhartha* and taken her first hesitant steps on the spiritual path: trying to anchor her attention in the here and now; ascribing Godhood to Dada whenever he popped into her mind; repeating her mantra, both in and out of meditation, to bring herself back to the real and cut off the power of those feelings to derail her; dusting off Dada's old suggestion and raising the opposite wave to counteract her darker emotions (the occasional puffs of anger seemed to respond well to this technique); above all, remembering that she was in the midst of a dramatic reenactment of the soul's search for itself, a story that had been told in an infinite variety of ways, each of them entirely unique and endlessly creative, knowing that the challenges she was facing had been expressly designed by the Lord of her heart to lead her down the sure path to enlightenment. It was all a drama now, while then it had seemed like life and death. And even life and death were not what they had been, having been magically transformed through the power of tantric alchemy into way stations on a long and miraculous journey.

After Ananda Kirtana, Priya stopped in Rio for a few days, using her time at Amarista's desk while her friend was at work to draw up a plan for the World Social Forum and embarking on what would become a litany of regular phone calls. That was followed by four days in São Paulo to keep her relationship with Visheshvar on life support and then a flight to Porto Alegre, where she took up residence in the didis' house near Redemption Park. The weeks that followed were both hectic and stimulating—designing the posters and flyers, sending out promotional material, organizing the ancillary programs and securing venues for them, including a workshop for government employees in the Porto Alegre town hall drawn directly from Dada's never-realized course, The Enlightened Leader—but her focus remained on her interior work, trying to deal with the turbulence of her romantic desires as skillfully as she could until the day that the object of those desires came back into view, shifting the stage of the contest from the sheltered precincts of her mind to the world of flesh-and-blood human beings.

The summer retreat began on the Friday morning before carnival with a twenty-four hour kirtan in the Viamão retreat center, a fifty-acre property forty minutes from Porto Alegre with a huge meditation hall and dormitory space for three hundred people. The center was presided over by the same elderly Indian dada who had spent one memorable night regaling her and a group of local devotees with stories from his days with the master during her one previous visit to Porto Alegre, an old-fashioned yogi whose favorite pastime, when he wasn't riding his tractor, was sitting in yogic trance during meditation. Dada's flight was due in from Lisboa on Saturday, and Priya took advantage of the short reprieve to spend most of those twenty-four hours in the meditation hall, either dancing or meditating or sitting and singing, leaving the hall only for meals and a four-hour reclusion in her room before returning at five a.m. to dance the final two hours, the best and most boisterous, ending with a one-hour Indian-style call-and-response kirtan led by the same Indian dada, a kirtan that was more shouting than singing, and more jumping than dancing, but which nevertheless filled the hall with manna from the gods.

Dada arrived in the afternoon but Priya didn't see him until evening practices, when she got a glimpse of him dancing kirtan in the front of the hall alongside the other dadas. Her heart raced a little, even at that distance, and it raced a little faster when she entered the dining hall after meditation and saw him seated with some of the other monks at one of the tables, but she was prepared for it and that little touch of tachycardia registered as no more than a little minor turbulence en route to her final destination.

The thought crossed her mind that it might be best to avoid him while she could, under the pretext of not disturbing the unruly beast, but that would have been contrary to the spirit of her last two months of training, so she purposely lay in wait for him before the beginning of the evening program and then made it look as if they were crossing paths by accident when he finally made his way into the hall. It was a short conversation (touching gloves was how she thought of it): a namaskar, a somewhat shaky smile, a few well-rehearsed platitudes, and a polite inquiry about his work in Portugal that was cut short by the beginning of the program, about as close to the script she had in mind as could have been reasonably expected. She knew full well that she couldn't let either of them escape without an actual conversation—the past was the past, but that didn't mean it could be safely ignored—however, she wanted that conversation to be on her own terms, and it seemed prudent not to force the issue. They had two weeks in which to get there, and she was in no particular hurry.

As karma would have it, that conversation took place just after the retreat ended, during an interval of buoyant clarity that couldn't have been better chosen—sure proof in her eyes of the benevolent nature of the Creator. She had danced until one-thirty in the morning during the closing akhanda kirtan, and when her tiredness got the better of her she lay down in a corner of the hall on a blanket that she had brought expressly for that purpose, trying to be as inconspicuous as possible in case some marauding dada or didi objected on the grounds that she was violating the sanctity of the kirtan. But there were no dadas or didis left in the hall at that hour and likely wouldn't be until four or five, just a raucous contingent of kirtan-crazed devotees who favored those late-night hours to shed their inhibitions in the spiritual version of the carnival madness that was taking place during those same hours in cities all over Brazil, most famously in Rio. Those who weren't dancing were seated in a semi-circle around the guitar player, banging away at percussion instruments, and when she curled up on the blanket with her bunched-up shawl as an improvised pillow, the decibel level seemed to go up ten-fold, passing through the concrete floor as if it were a superconductor and straight into her body.

Ordinarily, trying to sleep in a hall with music blaring over the loudspeakers and a chaotic jumble of percussion instruments pushing the decibel level as high as it could go would have been an exercise in futility and frustration, but this wasn't ordinary music. This was kirtan, and the power of the mantra soon had her suspended in a state somewhere between dreaming and waking. She found herself shuttling from one disconnected dream fragment to another while never losing touch with the mantra, which seemed not only to fill her ears with its resonance but her blood and breath and bones. It was the one constant in the almost psychedelic parade of images that swept her along just beyond the edge of waking (there was something about the rhythmic intensity of the music that made her dreams appear more colorful than normal, as if the music were stirring up her internal pigments as its vibrations passed through her body)—until a curtain of calm fell and she found herself in a quiet room with Baba and a handful of devotees, the kirtan still faintly audible in the background.

The master was seated on a wooden cot covered by a satiny white sheet with a hand-embroidered border, while she and the other devotees were seated on the floor in front of him, all eyes fixed on his smiling figure. Out of the corner of her eye she caught a glimpse of Dada to her left, but his presence barely registered in her consciousness, for like him she could not take her eyes off the master. Baba was telling humorous stories that had them all beaming in appreciation, but that wasn't the reason she couldn't keep her eyes off him. He was so attractive that she could not bear to look away, even for a moment. The soft sheen of his olive skin, almost golden in its radiance; the sweet, soothing fragrance of sandalwood that seemed to emanate from his body; the elegant figures he traced with his hands to add color to his stories, every gesture redolent with a dulcet grace that she had never seen in any human being; the way his eyes danced and sparkled like two bright sapphires; the lilting sound of his voice, more music than any music she had ever heard. She had never seen anyone so beautiful, never felt a human presence so perilously close to rapture, and it was all she could do to keep from leaping up and embracing him. He is the sun, she thought, and we are all satellites moving round him, shining with his reflected light. That very moment Baba turned his head and smiled at her, a smile so huge she felt as if it were about to engulf her. "Yes," his eyes seemed to be saying.

Suddenly the scene shifted. She was alone in his room now, her head resting in his lap. The master was stroking her hair with an infinite tenderness that surpassed anything she could imagine. "Now do you understand the attraction?" she heard him say. She did, but when she looked up all she could think about was how beautiful his eyes were, how nothing else in that moment mattered, and as she drank in the sweetness of his gaze she saw stars appear in the black of his pupils, and behind them a vast shining expanse of celestial space. The whole universe is radiant with his light, she thought, and as if in answer she could hear his laughter ringing in the far reaches of the cosmos. And that was the last thing she remembered from her dream when she woke up moments later, still curled on her blanket, kirtan reverberating all around her in the darkened hall.

As she sat up she felt a thrill in her body and mind, a feeling of lightness so pronounced it seemed as if she might float up from her blanket at any moment. She could hear his laughter in the music now, a joyous cadence that propelled her to her feet and into the circle of kirtan-maddened souls. Within moments she was jumping and shouting the Lord's name as she skipped in circles around the altar, running and dancing at the same time, her arms flung upward in an unseen embrace as she threw herself into the *hari pari mandal*, the great circle of devotees dancing around the Lord—in love not only with him but with the world, because the world was the dress in which her Beloved had clothed himself.

The retreat ended a few hours later but Priya barely marked the transition from one scene to another. She said goodbye to her friends who were leaving, as they piled their luggage into cars and taxis and vans and turned back for a last obligatory hug, but her body seemed to be acting on its own, playing its role, reciting its lines, while her thoughts remained in Baba's room, still engrossed in her fascination for the master's radiant form.

When all the goodbyes had been said, Priya walked over to the spreading banyan tree in front of the main dormitory building and sat on her folded blanket, the same blanket that had been the site of her Baba dream, leaning against the huge gnarled trunk and staring off into an impossibly blue sky. She had heard devotees recount their Baba dreams time and again during the past two-and-a-half years, beginning with that very first ideological training in Araruama, and while their stories had never failed to move her, she had at times felt a tinge of envy or a sliver of regret that she did not have any Baba dreams of her own. She had met one older devotee at Ananda Kirtana who dreamed of Baba practically every night and had for years, her compensation for not having had the means to make the trip to India to see the master while he was still living. Priya had heard that Baba dreams were unlike other dreams, that they were not really dreams in the ordinary sense of the word, recompilations of past experiences swirled together in the mixing bowl of the imagination, but actual visitations from the master in subtle form; that no one could dream of a realized master or hear his voice in the dream state unless the master willed it so, and when he did, it meant that he was truly there, for this was the most visible of the chosen ways that the sadguru employed to communicate with his disciples once he had left his body. But she had never been so fortunate, despite trying to induce one by homemade methods—meditating on his image right before going to sleep, asking him formally to pay her a visit, even tucking his picture under her pillow in the hope it would be an added inducement—and she had been left wondering how much longer she would have to wait before the master revealed himself to her in his subtle form. Now that it had happened, it had been everything the older devotees had claimed and more. So very much more.

Priya was still deep in her reverie when she saw Dada approaching. This time her heart continued in its same placid motion as she took in the mischievous slant of his smile and invited him to sit, motioning to an unoccupied patch of grass a decorous meter or so away.

"I thought it might be a good time to talk," he said, as he sat and laid his turban down beside him. "Things were too hectic during the retreat to catch up, but we have a little calm now before the storm picks up again."

He was referring to the three o'clock meeting for the World Social Forum organizing committee that Priya would be chairing, the start of what promised to be a whirlwind of activity with the forum opening its doors in two days' time. In the meantime, however, she was just as happy not to think about it; and so apparently was he, for when she brought up his schedule during the coming week, he deflected any talk of the forum with his usual self-assurance that she remembered so well.

"There's plenty of time for that," he said. "Let's leave it for the meeting. I'm more interested in finding out how you've been. It's been a long time, a lot of water under the bridge. I know we talked about staying in touch, but I had a lot on my plate, getting things going in Portugal, and anyhow it was probably for the best. So I heard you were in São Paulo for most of that time? Working with Didi Jaya?"

"Working with the kids, yeah, in Peri Alto. I still have to decide if I'm going back, although to be honest it's looking less and less likely."

"I was kind of surprised when I heard that. I wouldn't think it was the best use of your talents. What inspired you to go there?"

"A broken heart."

Dada winced and Priya had to stifle a laugh. She was both audience and actor now, and as a member of the audience she enjoyed seeing him squirm.

"Were you expecting a different answer?" she said.

"I … ah … I don't know what I was expecting," he said, looking more and more uncomfortable. "I was just asking."

"You asked a question. I gave you an honest answer."

"Well … I am sorry to hear that," he said, clearly scrambling to regain his balance. "I wish I could have done something to make it easier for you, but Baba knows, I did the best I could. I *am* sorry, for what it's worth."

She was enjoying his discomfort, but she figured it was time to let him off the hook, and anyway her mood was too buoyant to keep up the pretense.

"I was just joshing you, Dada," she said, permitting herself a quick laugh. "Well, half joshing. You did break my heart, in your own well-meaning way, but like you said, that was a long time ago, and things couldn't have worked out any better. What can I say? We have an amazing guru. He has a way of erasing the past with one wave of his magic wand."

Dada let out an audible sigh. "I'm glad to hear that. I was a little worried there for a moment."

"Worried that I might be after you again? Or worried that your samskara might come back to bite you?"

Dada waved his hand gently, in a gesture of negation. "I don't think I'm going to go there."

"It was a joke, Dada. I was just joshing you."

"I got that. But I'm still not going there."

She laughed, a good bit louder this time, and he laughed with her. They spent the next forty-five minutes swapping stories from their seventeen months on opposite sides of the ocean. She enjoyed hearing about his successes in Europe, where their Change Yourself, Change the World course had really taken off, knowing that it sat well with his samskara (what she would have called his ambition back in the day), and she shared a few anecdotes from her time with Didi as a kind of counterpoint to keep the conversation lively. It wasn't exactly like old times, but near enough for her to keep a close watch on her emotions. When the bell sounded to call everyone to noon meditation, they looked at each other and knew immediately what the other was thinking: *I don't want to miss this kirtan.*

"There is one thing I wanted to ask you," Priya said, as they were walking toward the meditation hall.

"Yeah, what's that?"

"Is the world still your mistress?"

Her question drew a blank stare, but this was followed a few moments later by a gleam of recognition and a somewhat sheepish smile. "Oh, I did say that, didn't I? I see you haven't forgotten."

"You know how it is. Some things you never forget. So I take it there's nothing—or no one—for her to be jealous of?"

This drew a laugh that was thick with sarcasm. "I guess I deserved that," he said. "But yes, she's still my mistress, and no, she has nothing to be jealous of."

She had been holding on to that one for a few weeks now, wondering if she would ever get the chance to use it. She was glad she had, for it seemed to bring the wheel full circle—even if his words on the beach had taken on an entirely new meaning for her in the last eight hours.

"Good, I'm glad to hear it," she said. "It is one of my favorite lines, you know. I'm thinking of holding on to it in case I need to use it one day."

This time there was no hint of sarcasm in Dada's laugh.

8

As the hall started steadily filling up, Priya detected an energy in the air markedly different than that of any of the other programs she had been to during the last five days, even the most eagerly anticipated and well attended. It might have been her own projection—this was, after all, the most relaxed she had felt since before the forum began, now that her duties were all but over—but she was convinced otherwise. Perhaps it was the sight of an orange-robed monk on the dais, his long hair and turban drawing the eyes of everyone who entered; or the rich fragrance of incense wafting from the four large incense burners she had stationed in the four corners of the hall; or the music coming from the loudspeakers, the sonorous tones of Sanskrit mantras floating above a tambura-and-tabla accompaniment, lulling the listener into a subliminal awareness of the sacred hiding within the mundane. Or maybe it was the title of the talk—Change Yourself, Change the World—a reminder that the real reason they wanted to make the world a better place was because they wanted to be better, happier people and were convinced of how difficult that was in a world that had gone off the rails. Whatever the reasons, she could sense it, and she knew they did as well. She could tell by the hushed conversations, the way no one dared raise their voice, as if they had entered a temple and had been overcome by a sense of solemnity that was mostly missing from their lives.

She breathed a sigh and pulled herself away from her reflections to make one last round before she settled into her seat in the second row. She started on stage with a quick tap on the lectern mic, which answered her back with a loud thud, and then a brief word with Dada to make sure he was ready and had everything he needed, though she had no worries on that account—his confidence had grown since he'd left Brazil and he hadn't been short on confidence then. That was followed by a trip to the translators' table, where she tested one of the headsets that were being handed out to anyone in the audience who needed simultaneous translation—French, German, Spanish, and Portuguese—a table laden with memories from earlier days and earlier aspirations. From there she made a last circuit of the hall to check on the incense burners and the ushers, and to offer a final prayer to the gods that the air conditioning wouldn't cut out as it had the day before during a panel discussion with Vandana Shiva and Arundhati Roy in a hall so crowded that those seven or eight minutes before the AC came back on sparked jokes from the two panelists about how it made them feel like they were back in India.

At two minutes to twelve there were no free seats left and those who arrived afterward had to sit or stand in the aisles. Three minutes later the surprisingly punctual municipal minister of culture, in a gray suit and tie that seemed out of place in that sea of counterculture, stepped to the lectern to introduce Dada, delivering a seven-minute peroration that highlighted his meeting with Dada earlier that week in the town hall and the importance of self-discovery and personal growth in the context of social betterment. When Dada thanked him and stepped to the lectern there was a sedate round of applause, more expectant than celebratory, followed by a far more boisterous round of applause when he addressed the audience in accented but flawless Portuguese to thank them for coming and to apologize beforehand for giving a talk in English when any forward-thinking individual knew that Brazil was the real country of the future.

Priya knew the content of his talk almost as well as Dada did. It was based on a prototype they had written together nearly two years earlier, though he had revised and expanded it since going to Europe, and they had sat together in Viamão and gone through it line by line, like in the old days, right down to the dramatic pauses and exclamatory gestures. She had assumed that she would pass the hour relaxing in her cushioned seat and catching the pulse of the audience, but she was mistaken. Within minutes she was so caught up in those familiar words and well-rehearsed cadences that she lost all touch with the audience, entering a kind of kaleidoscopic stratosphere filled with fragments of her life and visions of what the world could and should be, if only enough human beings awakened to the infinite potential that lay sleeping inside them. She could feel that potential inside herself coming into greater and greater clarity with each succeeding sentence, opening into a future that was greater than her imaginings, reaching out until it enveloped the entire living world and beyond, swallowing planets and constellations in its ever-widening vortex. This was why she was here, she thought, her heart swelling with a sense of triumph. This was why they were all here. To remake the world in the image of their remade self. The one challenge beyond all others that gave incarnate life its meaning.

At some point during his talk her mind flashed back to that morning at Cabo Frio, when she had emerged from a dreamless slumber into a rolling premonition that carried her back into the land of the waking with an overwhelming sense that something portentous was about to make itself felt, the irruption of an old aspiration that had been forced into the darkness by twenty-six years of fretful somnambulism. The same music that accompanied those final moments before she broke her pact with sleep was sounding now: the wash of an unseen ocean against an unseen shore—only now it was not the Atlantic, though perhaps it hadn't been even then, but the crashing of a far greater ocean against the shores of her life, the sound of the universe calling her from slumber. The three years between then and now stood suspended as a kind of lucid dream, and though she might still be dreaming, she could feel the clear light of day on the other side of that divide, pressing upon her with its dazzling clarity, just as she had felt the newly risen sun pressing on her eyelids that morning through the closed shade of the bedroom window, making it impossible for her to remain asleep.

When Dada finished his talk the applause was so thunderous it caught Priya by surprise. It dawned on her then that everyone in that hall had been waiting for his talk, just as she had been waiting for the sun to rouse her from her bed in Cabo Frio. They might not know it consciously but somewhere inside they felt that call, as she had felt it, and there was something so miraculous about that, it nearly brought her to the verge of tears. The world *was* changing—it was not a myth or a hope or a belief, but a reality that was already upon them. The world was changing because they were changing, growing slowly but surely toward the light.

She soaked up the feeling for as long as she could, until well after the applause died down and the forum organizers began clearing the stage for the next event. She was one of the last devotees to congratulate Dada, and when they left the hall she was at the end of a cortège that had swelled since they'd arrived. At least twenty unknown members of the audience walked out of the hall in Dada's company, alongside the devotees and the other dadas and didis, as if they instinctively knew that here was a carriage they could hitch their fortunes to. She veered off once they were out in the punishing sun that was skirting forty degrees Celsius without a single cloud to dampen its glare. The cortège was headed to the cafeteria for a celebratory lunch, while it was her turn to man the booth, but despite the lack of cloud cover she stopped in the middle of the walkway with her hand shading her eyes to watch Dada recede into the distance. The man and his mistress, and not a jealous bone in her body. She smiled and continued down the path that led to the NGO pavilion, ready for the next worthy adversary to put her to the test.

Acknowledgments

The Richard Bach quotes are taken from:

Bach, Richard. *Jonathan Livingston Seagull*. New York. Macmillan, 1970.

Bach, Richard. *Illusions: The Adventures of a Reluctant Messiah*. New York. Delacorte Press, 1977.

The Javier Cercas quote is from:

Cercas, Javier. *El vientre de la ballena*. Barcelona. Tusquets Editores, S. A., 2003.

The Hermann Hesse quotes are from:

Hesse, Hermann. *Steppenwolf*. New York: Holt, Rinehart and Winston, Inc., 1957.

Gonzaguinha's "O Que É, O Que É?" (What is it, what is it?) © 1982 Luiz Gonzaga do Nascimento, Jr.

The Baba quotes are taken from:

The Electronic Edition of the Works of P. R. Sarkar. Calcutta. Ananda Marga Publications, 2009.

About The Author

Devashish holds an MFA in fiction from San Diego State University. He divides his time between Ananda Kirtana, a spiritual community in the Brazilian countryside, and his farm in Puerto Rico, where he has a yoga center and a tropical-fruit plantation. You can reach him at:
www.devashishdonaldacosta.com